2024 CLUB ANTHOLOGY

2024 Club Anthology

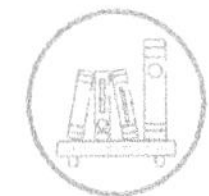

The Creative Writer's Guild at UCR

CONTENTS

OCTOBER: ANALOG

Winner: Sophia Breeze

WE WENT DOWN TO ROTHERSHAW

SOPHIA BREEZE

I always told you I hated this stupid camera the moment you got it, with the slow and sputtering way it snapped its photos and its impossibly ugly rust-colored coating that made it look as though you already weathered and worn it from the moment you opened its package. It's grimy, I said, it's too loud and cheap and I hate the clicks it makes and I hate when you bring it up to me and shove it in my face.

Now I cradle it in my lap like a lifeline. I thumb the cracked lens and keep it free of film. Like a tumor it sticks to my person; jacket pocket, backpack, pants pocket, crook of an elbow, palm of my hand. It's always there.

Even still I know why it took years for me to develop your photos. That fall trip we went down to Rothershaw, New York, captured in these rotten shots of memories I can't help but carry. The thought made me sick; the idea of you and where you are makes me nauseous. But the thought that those photos sat there, hidden and unseen, waiting and watching me for the longest time made me feel even worse until the brunt of it sharpened into something that could seize my body and split me apart. The idea of them: it was enough to kill me.

They're real now, pasted so lovingly in a cheap scrapbook I had as if they're something worth being sentimental about. The saddest thing? A part of me sort of is.

1. You snapped this first photo in the backseat of our moving car. The blurred beauty of Rothershaw woods countryside and the grainy, faraway first look at the house we'd all be staying in: homely, picketed, and carved into the heart of rural nothingness. It was Autumn; you can see it in the sky. Nice and gray.

The picture couldn't show someone how cold it was, but I remember the utter briskness of everything. Two months back Dad's car sputtered and broke its heating and, in his insistence we only travel with the beat-up pickup truck of his, we piled together on a long stretch of road with chattering teeth and jackets that could never be shed. "I'll fix the car," he'd say, and when the trip came into view and nothing had been done, Dad said, "I don't need to fix anything. The car's just fine! It can't be that cold in Rothershaw. You can all handle a little chill."

In the corner you can see the pleated, gray backing of the driver's seat and I know Dad is sitting just out of sight. He was freezing, too. We all were.

2. You made Mom pose for this one because no one else wanted to. She's halfway through turning the door key and looks at you over her shoulder with a small smile that says, "Why are you taking a photo now? Of this?"

The large doors to the Rothershaw house are white and cracked with peeling paint, surrounded by rigid blue siding and shut-tight windows with empty flower beds. To the right of Mom is the gaudiest doorbell I have ever seen, with a plethora of flowery decor twining around it, coated in sun-faded shades of paint colors unlike the entire rest of the house. At the end of the doorsteps you can see me, close-up on the back of my head as I walked towards the entrance at the same time you took the shot. I'm blurry, because I'm not the focus of this photo: Mom is.

Her slightly cocked head, mouth wilting its worth of a smile and her eyes not playing along. It was a long drive and, looking back, I don't think she was ever really for this trip at all. Maybe

I enjoyed being as willfully ignorant as I was then more than I'd like to admit.

3. This is a nice picture. The first night at that house in Rothershaw the power had decided not to work, and the early-setting Autumn sun quickly put us into a cavernously dark and equally empty-feeling vacation home to struggle settling down in. Dad said he'd see the fusebox in the morning and Mom, the charitable, found us some candles to light.

I'm sitting at the far end of the stained oak dining table, a long-wicked candle inches from my face and illuminating the whole of it. I'm smiling, I look in the midst of a laugh. The golden flame brightens my teeth and sets sparks in my pupils. In limited light the fire cast harsh shadows around the both of us and I remember feeling as though we'd been encased in entirely our own world; the candles our home, the rest in unknowable night. Somehow, it felt safe.

4. You took a photo of our pumpkin's face and let its orange bigness be the entire frame. We were both in the backseat of the pickup again when you took it and I was watching you pull the camera in close, closer to the smooth gourd skin that I spent the rest of the car ride rubbing my palms against. That morning Mom suggested a pumpkin patch and, of course, we clamored to go.

Dad drove and stopped us at the first available spot, which was some off-shoot on the side of the road helmed by an old man who'd brought up his own harvest and hay bales to hawk at passing cars. The hay made me itch and a majority of the pumpkins were too bumpy for my liking, but we were pumpkin-picking, and for me that was enough. "Only one pumpkin," they'd told us. "Only one." Did I ever tell you how shocked I was when you let me have the final say? It felt like an extension of kindness, an open palm, but I'm not stupid enough to keep thinking that's true. You must've just wanted the same big round, smooth, orange beauty I set my sights on.

On our way back to the house, you took it from its seat in the car and cradled it to the front door. When I went to rub it one last time you freed a hand and smacked me away.

5. My ratty, worn cat stuffed animal is sitting on the window-sill of your room. I can see the outstretch of trees on the horizon and, unknowingly cropped at the bottom of your photo, I stand just underneath your window. The fact that you took the time to prop him up and pose him pretty for this shot almost makes me cry, because it reminds me of every screaming why and reason I've ever hated you.

Some time after pumpkin-picking it seemed clear you'd have your way with the carving and it deflated me. Being a child, I chose to sulk, and when asked by Mom how much fun I'd had, I said "It would've been a lot *more* fun if we could get *two* pump-kins." Then Dad, the driver, the payment-maker, sighed the earth-shattering sigh that when you're young you recognize as meaning everything is ruined now, and you were the one to ruin it. I couldn't take it back, I coiled inwards. I left the two to start on the conversation I'd heard plenty of times prior to the trip before I could hear them devolve into shouting; the kind about money, Dad's job, what they're doing, why they're doing it.

My room was downstairs, yours was upstairs and away from everything and everyone. I knocked on that ever-shut old oak door and willed for you to open up. Did you ever care to think that I was lonely? That I, a child, took everything I ever heard and let it hurt worse than it should? No: you thought me too desperate. You opened that door to kick me away, and when push came to shove you stole that cat plush I so deeply loved and solely carried so I could accompany it with you. You posed him and made him picture perfect while I begged at the base of your window outside, weeping tears you never cared to see. I called your name. I cried all night.

6. It's just a photo of tree branches. They're black and they stretch over the sky like veins, obscuring the billow of dim clouds behind them. I was avoiding you then. I think you went off and spent your time alone in the woods.

7. In this shot I stand next to a pile of rocks I'd stacked, in the foreground an equal pile of your own stands tall. Besides the country house was less-of-a-river and more of a water run-off I liked to drop leaves in to watch float, and the two of us stepped out to gather there, together, following the mess that was that day's breakfast.

Remnants of the fire that is a parental spat still had itself linger and stifle us all uncomfortably until Mom decided she'd spark it up again, as she would and as she had always done before, with breakfast time seeming her time to do it. A small comment here, a jab there, and Dad soon gathered himself in a huff to leave the table, stomp away, and slip on the hallway rug that promptly sent him bashing his head into the staircase banister. We rushed to see him and I was beyond shocked. *Was he hurt? Is he going to be okay?* You stood quiet on the sidelines as Mom came to his aid, wash-cloth for the blood and some mustered-up passion for the playact that the resentment wasn't still there. I left to clear my head and you followed me out the door.

In the photo you can see I wrapped myself in a scarf and throw blanket before making the journey outside, too lazy to properly put on a jacket. We dropped pebbles in the water in silence until you turned to me and told me that Dad's fall would leave a scar. Then, you pointed at your own forehead blemish from an age ago you jumped off the bed and fell to the floor and told me I no longer matched the family. You were a pair, you and Dad, and now I stood the outsider without a facial scar.

You handed me a rock. You told me we could change that, that I could join them.

"Do you know what you have to do?" you asked, "Do you know what you have to do? Are you willing to go and do it?"

In my hesitance I stacked rocks and you did the same. In the photo I tentatively hold the top of the rock stack in my hand, its rough edges making dents in my palm from where I clutched it. The rock will never leave its tower. You will never hear an answer.

8. A crow bashed itself against the dining room window and this photo shows the angelic pose of its dazed self, soon corpse. We were both present when it happened and we both ran outside to see the carnage, the grab of your stupid camera on the way out imperative to you.

The crow (or is it a raven? I could never tell) landed on its back with its wings splayed above its dead-eyed head and cracked beak, black plumage spread far outwards like a splash of water spilled across the ground. I reached to touch the body but you stopped me; bird diseases and flesh-eating bugs and such living in feathers.

9. Living room picture. It soon became much too drizzly and miserable for either of us to stand exploring the Rothershaw woods so we were resigned to the house's quiet and contained insides instead. Mom was feeling ill that morning and spent it resting upstairs, outside the camera lens.

The rare thing about this photo is that you are actually in it. In this you see Dad in the dusty, red pleated recliner that points towards bay windows, your body melded into his side. His stare is blank and a bandage covers a spot on his forehead with its white hand. Your head is whipped towards the photo-taker, a second-made split of anger beginning to break apart your previous sense of placidness. Who could be the one touching *your* camera?

Of course, it was me. In part, I wanted to know what it was like to snap a picture, and, in truth, I wanted to see you pissed. How dare I!

10. Dad stands poised, brandishing a shovel far from his body. His face is turned away and hidden from the camera scene, but his grimace is shown in the way the rest of himself is tensed up. At the end of the shovel you can see a blurry, furry mass limply hanging one of its hands off the side of the blade. Something dead. Your thumb is clumsily in the corner of the shot.

That next day we awoke to continued dreary skies, muddy ground, and more dead animals littering the base of the Rother-shaw house. Gophers, I think. They dug themselves out from under the porch before dying in the open air, free to sink life-lessly into wet grass and gather some flies before morning. You and Dad spent the time shoveling up those that died and dump-ing them a place farther than our problem. I watched from the window. Staring at massive, wet lumps of fur you know once had beating hearts and breathing lungs terrified me far worse than the crow, in a sinking way someone as young as I could never have had the words to properly express. Honestly, would you blame me if I said that, even now, they would still scare me?

11. Everything about this photo is hard for me to look at. It is the only photo of this album where all of us stand together, posed and packed as a family. The typical shot you'd see in any scrapbook where everyone huddles close, holds one another, and scrunches up their face into a smile before it's snapped and captured. It depresses me.

Mom's mood and illness lightened enough for us to dress up and get out on her insistence we treat this vacation like a vacation. We drove down to the small cluster of shops and restaurants to eat a family dinner, something we'd neglected to do since showing up, and Dad chose the first dive he saw:

something rustic and furnished entirely in wooden furniture. You brought your camera and kept it in a jacket pocket. I almost brought my stuffed cat, but I worried too heavily you'd find a way to steal it again. We sat down, we smiled, we went through the motions. We ate a family dinner. I remember a ceiling fan above our table spun so fast I worried it'd break free and crash its blades down onto our heads.

On the way out, Dad shoved your camera into the hands of a stranger and asked us all to pose. He huddled us outside the mouth of the rustic restaurant, modeled like the obvious tourist and insisting we pack closer and closer together. Turn up your head, and smile!

In the photo we are posed like this: Dad, Mom, you, me. The smiles we shared were weak and pressed too hard into our faces as we were forced to wait an indeterminate amount of time on the stranger figuring out which button he had to hold. Dad's hand is grabbing Mom's shoulder, her clothes bunched in his grasp as he leans her towards his body. Her arms stay at her side.

It's odd to look back and know I ever thought either of them were old, because even looking at them here, faces wrinkled up and creased with folds of fat, I know that, at that very moment, we were all the youngest we could ever be.

12. The pumpkin again, but this time you didn't dare get as close to it as you once did. Pumpkins rot fast, isn't that what they say? But it shouldn't have rotted as fast as this; the thing hadn't even seen itself gutted of its seeds yet and you never even had a chance to see it light up our front porch. A sickness had seized your pumpkin with the frenzy of a ravenous cancer.

We inspected a terribly rotten gourd with a wince and deep frowns. Decay covered what was once a big, orange beauty. The molding pumpkin had sagging sides akin to pus-filled skin, its flesh folded over and wrinkled under the weight of its own putrid self. A great blackness was eating away at it, the innards pregnant with maggots.

You can see me hovering over the carnage, brow furrowed intensely and you a good distance from the scene. What purpose did you have to capture this moment? For posterity? Memory?

You kept the worst of it outside of your album, but I remember. Morbid curiosity caused me to extend a finger towards the pumpkin's walls, and in that movement you encouraged me to keep going. You only wanted me to touch it because you knew that doing so would cause the rest of what stood to collapse like a popped balloon, but I didn't want to go any closer. Your egging turned into a whine until you were right besides me, grasping my hand in your own and, in a struggle reminiscent of a playful grapple, you drove me directly into the flesh.

The warm ooze of rot squeezed through my fingers. It had the sharp, sweet smell of wet leaf litter mixed with that of liquid shit. I saw your face when you did it; you weren't smiling or laughing. You did it just to do it. When I broke away, I watched you stare at the remains with a blank-eyed expression of being less than impressed. The pumpkin was utterly destroyed. Desecrated.

13. Another shot taken by me, but this time you insisted it done. Taken lower to the ground, the photo stares up at you smiling and sitting in the bed of Dad's pickup truck. If you squint hard enough, you can see the back of Dad's baseball cap and his squared shoulders in the dusty rear view window of his car, preparing to drive off. He let you ride in the back because he knew you liked it, that you got to feel the wind in your hair and have the thrill of no seatbelt, no safety.

You were going to the store for some light painkillers. I had followed you two out of the house and watched as you loaded in, clicking into place and preparing for a crisp Autumn cruise through wooded roads. "Can I come?" I'd asked Dad. With Mom hidden away on her own again, the house would've felt its absolute emptiest, and I feared how that would make me feel. My hand still stank with sticky pumpkin mold.

Dad lumbered a response. He grumbled something inaudible and soft in my denial, but I understood his answer most in the way he eyed me before swinging open his truck door and thumping it behind him. He was never a man who kept his feelings close to his chest. I wasn't stupid, I knew I was never the favorite. Dad and me had a way of standing beside each other like there were several panes of glass separating us, always.

How could he have time for someone like me? I was the one who complained, the one who always found a way to whine and cry about something, and I was the one who caught him getting his dick sucked by a coworker in the back of my bathroom during his own home-hosted work party. Who could I be to him, then? His petulant child that might one day not help but tell the truth, the child that didn't listen and stay put where the grownups told them to stay put. The only thing he could do was keep us apart, close the truck door on me and let me stay behind.

I never told, but I don't think it mattered. I'm sure Mom knew. Why else would he have gotten fired so fast, so out of the blue?

You demanded the camera back once the shot was taken. On the way out of the driveway, you waved.

14. Broken glass sits on a tree stump, presented for a rare ray of sunlight to catch and show off a multicolored sparkle.

I didn't hear what you and Mom were fighting about once you returned home, though I heard a warbled voice through the walls demanding respect, asking the other to shut up and to shut up now. I didn't see who had thrown the glass and shattered the shouting into utter silence. I don't know where Dad was when this happened.

In the end, I guess you gathered up the glittering pieces and used them for an art project. Whatever you did with it all, afterwards, I don't know, either.

15. The camera peers down a hole in the wall, the photo capturing less than just darkness, dust, and installation.

We'd been at Rothershaw for a while when this was taken. The fresh air would be good for us, Dad stressed, and where else would we rather be, anyway? A boring little house sat in some simple suburbia with barely any room or woods for us to disappear into? Each day was getting shorter, every night colder and closer to being miserable.

Mom's sickness came back with a fight and often she would shiver and cough and spit up into the sink. If I compare her to the earlier photos, I swear you can see the shades of her skin draining away with each instance of existing for the camera. She woke up that day in a frenzy.

"Something must've died in the walls," she said. "Something must've died. I swear to God, something must've died. I can barely think straight. I can't even eat."

Her voice became shrill. She repeated herself, louder and louder, and she grappled herself to Dad's lapels in desperation that someone, her husband, might hear her. The walls! The walls!

"The walls?" Dad was shouting too. "You think something died in the fucking walls? Okay, let's see what's died in the fucking walls, then." He stomped downstairs, grabbed a hammer, and rammed a hole into the living room's side. The wall burst open, splintering wood and skinning apart wallpaper where the hammer punctured its body.

Mom started crying. I think we both cried, too. Us hovering in the doorway and watching everything unfold.

"We need to leave," Mom said.

"To where?" Dad was inches from her face, spit dripping into his stubble from where he was screaming. "To where?"

Would anything be any different?

16. I can't tell if you meant to take this photo or not. The angle is odd, almost upside down, and the focus is blurry.

Mom sits alone at the dining room table. The room around her is dark, and the bright kitchen bulbs illuminating her side darken the half of her in shapeless shadow. Her head is in her palms, her body curled inwards.

If you look closely at the wooden plank floors that point themselves to Mom, specks of mold are blossoming. Black pockmarks sprouting from the dirt beneath.

17. The night sky of our last night in Rothershaw. I'd seen you climb onto the roof before, fearless and brave in a way that almost makes me miss you. I could never scale the rickety side of the Rothershaw house like you did when you wanted to get away, and as I know from your photos, you must've done it that night.

You aimed the shot at the stars, pools of them sparkling in the black of night. The moon is large and blinding, a bright mass that sits in the corner of the photo and whose beauty could never be captured by so rickety a camera. How long did you sit up there, I wonder? Would you have slept up there if you could?

That night, I heard the beams of the house creak, the walls sighing. Every time I tossed and turned, the house bent under my weight, and I would feel myself shiver at the thought that, with another rollover, everything might crumple down and fold over on top of me, of everyone. Everything was as weak as pumpkin pulp, and I, the one in the middle of it, was nothing but useless and scared.

18. The last photo. It captures almost nothing, but I know exactly what it means; what happened and where.

It shows simply the blurry photo of the wooden floor, the photo taken when you were moving. I'd avoided the house like the plague the next day, from the moment of early dawn to sometime I thought the sun looked close to setting. What you all talked about in the morning, whether you all fought or screamed or punched more holes, I didn't know, and I still don't know or care to know. I'd returned to those white, paint-flaking doors and gaudy doorbell, and I swear to God, the place was bending inwards. My feet were sinking into the wooden steps like something soft and wet.

When I opened the door, you were already running out. I looked over your shoulder and saw what you were running from.

Black mold, scarring the insides of our rustic, rural home with growth unlike anything I'd ever seen. The sharp smell of something chemical stabbing at the inside of my nose and immediately throwing my stomach into a violent lurch, the smashed pumpkin spewing into my palm but everywhere and on everything, all at the same time.

Mom and Dad were in the living room. They were sunk halfway into the wooden floors, wood warped by something wet and oozing. Mom's hand was reached towards the open front door, her skin so pale it throbbed with bright veins. On Dad's lips gushed black spit that already started attracting its worth of flies, looking to eat and lay eggs. They were both still moving. Their eyes still darted around the room, their mouths still wanting to move.

You threw yourself outwards, and even as we stumbled down the steps together you still ended up collapsing at the foot of the house. It grabbed you by the foot, you sunk into the worms and dirt. You were reaching out just like Mom had, begging someone to grab you from being swallowed. What did I do? I grabbed the camera you dropped. My hand did not extend, I did not look back.

Now I'm here. I've poured myself over these photos a hundred times, a thousand. I always thought it would be the best to forget, to move on, to live my life when I had so graciously been given it in favor of everyone else's. But why? It means nothing to survive if this is what surviving feels like. I've never been anything more than a scared child, always looking for an excuse to cry.

I feel it: the great, black mold is living in my chest and everyday it eats another bit of me away. I've wasted my entire life trying to pretend it wasn't there. We all did. In every wrinkle, in every shot of us smiling, I know the truth of what lay dormant in us: the rot, the spoiled meat held up by bags of presentable human skin and its happy family of four.

I don't want to ignore anything anymore. I don't want to carry your stupid, ugly, weathered camera anymore. I'm sitting in my parked car, the night is deep and the only light is from my dying flashlight a few more flickers from blinking out. The scrapbook is spread out on my lap. In the back, a shovel is laid across the seats like a corpse.

I never thought I'd see the Rothershaw house again, but that was always a naive way of thinking; of closing my eyes and looking the other way. In shadow it stands tall, perfectly upright and tidy like any other house living in the countryside. You are all my family, the house another member. Where else can I be, but with you?

The scrapbook finally gets closed. The camera is slid into my jacket pocket and I feel the car keys snug beside it. I sit here now, in the quiet of my own breath and steady heart, and I hear you ask the question.

Do you know what you have to do? Are you willing to go and do it?

NOVEMBER: SHUFFLE

Winner: Charles Swanepoel

THE SUBLIME OF TIME

11/8/23 - 11/15/23

CHARLES SWANEPOEL

A nameless face, the man lays in debris
A wretched wasteland from which he tried to run but could not flee
Life ebbs from his ails of body and brain
His last thoughts are of a life in a tangent plane

Another life, another time
Ponder the sublime

A man, perhaps the same, finds a life with his kin
A simple peace should fill his time, complacency his mind
A wife, a son, a daughter who plays the violin
A mundane life bordering on banal, ill-defined

Another life, another time
Indulge the sublime

The endless night, filled with smog
The seriatim of life's exams fill his mind
Inspiration strikes the soul, purpose does not
As he finds himself in the eternal slog

In this life, another time
Embrace the sublime
Lest it passes you by

CROSSROADS OF FORTUNE

SAMANTHA PACINI-CARLIN

Fernis leaned forward, hands laid on the polished wood of the bar – victims of unkind years, riddled with scars on scars. The stool underneath him creaked, muffled by his old coat. His mussed black hair shaded his eyes, though Maire could easily spot the mischievous glimmer that lurked underneath. Normally, she'd dread scheming vagrants like him; they drank her stock dry, swore their heads off, and fought patrons ten times their size. But Fernis wasn't any usual scheming vagrant.

"So, how's about it?" he drawled.

Maire pursed her lips. She stifled the urge to polish a glass by folding her arms over her white button shirt. Loose strands of black curls tried to wriggle into her eyes. Bastards. She'd shave them off her head someday.

"Aw, that ain't an answer. Just think of what you could do with it all!" He swept an arm across her tavern, the Leering Snake, for emphasis. The stool creaked with encouragement. "This is all real nice, don't get me wrong, but you could build bigger! Better! C'mon, Mar, trust me on this. You can't be satisfied with a tavern hanging on by a thread."

He had a point. The walls, striped to boards, were layered with stains upon stains from years of bar fights. Cracks laced the windows like spiderwebs. All the tables and chairs wobbled on three or less legs – or one, in the case of a resilient little chair. The ones splintered beyond repair crackled in the fireplace. It at least saved her some coin, given the costs of good firewood nowadays.

"It's damn risky," she stated.

He shrugged. "So's taking out one of those loans; damn bankers'll drain you with interest before you get a gold to climb outta that hole. But I'm looking out for you." He gave her a wide smile – the same he wore as a child.

"Appreciate it, Fernis." She grinned back at him. "Good to see time hasn't driven you that far away."

Fernis clapped her on the shoulder. "I'd never let it. Well, why don't you think it over, and I'll swing by tomorrow to hear your decision? I know you'll make the right one."

"Sure. Swing on by in the afternoon while the drunks aren't hounding me."

He spun from his seat and waved over his shoulder. A gust of wind slipped past him as he opened the door, heralding the dying light of the evening. The bells over the door clanged a farewell.

Maire sighed. She pulled her personal wineskin out from under the bar, then slipped into his stool. Its creak rang in her ears. Gods, she wanted to rip that thing out from the floor to hurl it at someone. Unfortunately, the rowdy drunkards would not arrive for a while. She popped the cork off her wineskin and mulled over his offer in the meantime. A little bit always helped sharpen her thoughts.

She took a swig. Heaven, rich in age and flavor, poured down her gullet. The conflicts between her emotions dulled, letting thoughts come into focus. She closed her eyes. But before she could embrace it, a shrill, nasally voice disrupted her clarity.

"Oh, I do not like this, mistress!" it cried.

Maire let out a deeper sigh. "I can't remember a time when you liked anything, Delkah."

"I like things. Your friend, however, I dislike greatly. Can't you see the danger? The danger is oh-so terrible, mistress. Stay away!"

"Last time I checked, you listened to me – not the other way 'round."

His voice dropped to a whimper. "Apologies. I just fear for your safety. I can't imagine what I'd do if you…if something happened to you."

"Find some stuffy scholar, probably." The stool groaned as she adjusted her weight on it and took another sip.

"Only if the Lady of Sights wills it. I'd mourn you quite a bit, though – more than the others who have held me. You're surprisingly likable."

Surprisingly? Though slighted, she barked out a laugh. "Appreciate it. But could you settle back down there, Delkah? Your worried voice is gonna deafen me if you keep at it."

"I speak in your mind, though."

Maire took a longer swig of the wine, and let its flavor simmer in her mouth. "Shush. Think I can already hear the world fading."

That afforded her three sips of silence before Delkah broke it again. "Why not do a reading?"

"Hm."

"Just 'hm'? Mistress, surely you can see the wisdom in it. It'll certainly quiet me as well."

She bit her lip. "Dunno. It'd feel like me saying I don't trust Fernis, I guess. He earned it a while ago; doesn't feel right to go behind his back and do this outta paranoia."

"Well, why not read it to protect him – see what you might miss in the moment?"

Gods, he made a good point. "Can't even get a damn moment to think for myself," she muttered. "Fine, you annoying little bundle of paper cuts. You win."

"Excellent!" He fluttered in her pocket like a bird. "To the back?"

Maire restrained herself from a third sigh. Her mama shared a lot of wisdom with her on the streets, but never mentioned how much adulthood she'd spend exhausted from other people. Then again, Delkah was not a person. "To the back. Doubt I'll see anything useful, though you're being a pain about it. An annoying one."

"A pain worried for your well-being, mistress."

She tucked the wine away, then locked the front door. Maire wove back through the tables and reached a plain door behind the bar, where she produced a key from her shirt. The worn silver shined, inconspicuous yet well-kept. It slid into the lock without a fuss. After it clicked open, she turned the knob and slipped into the dim room beyond it.

Faint incense twisted through boxes of spirits. Parchment lists spilled out between the lids, the contents' age marked in crimson ink. Dust lingered on the crates pushed to the back wall. In front of it, a star-speckled cloth pushed itself against their bottoms, desperate for space this room barely provided. Tankards with candles pinned the corners down. Their wicks sagged like wilted plants in the pool of wax. She had wanted to replace the shoddy things for months, but the candlemakers charged a fortune for a single wax droplet. Damn pricks.

Maire snapped her fingers, which sent sparks flying to the wicks. Blue flames erupted on them. They lapped hungrily towards her – their countenance similar to the rowdy patrons at night.

"Ready?" she asked.

Delkah rustled. "I am always ready, mistress! May the Lady grant us a sliver of her fortune."

"May she not fuck me over." She knelt on the cloth, and plucked Delkah out of her pocket. His cards shifted into one unified deck. The blue reflection of the candlelight washed over the violet, silver-swirled backs.

Maire placed him in front of her. She then leaned over to trace her finger through the stars – the stroke trailed by a silver glow. Each star she touched burst into motes of the same light. Something zapped through her veins, which she'd come to call "magic". Gods, magic. Of all the paths she thought she'd walk, life sure led her down a strange one.

Maire completed the circle. She held her fingers in the air between her eyes, and spoke to the incense. "Lady, I need your aid."

She pulled her eyelids shut, slowly exhaled, then grasped the deck. The cards flew between her fingers, and soared through the air with the grace of birds. Another pair of hands sprang from them. They fell into the shuffle's rhythm, catching cards where she would've dropped them. Soft skin brushed over her calluses where their hands collided.

Her lungs began to burn, desperate for a gasp of air. She ignored it until a sliver remained on her lips, at which point she cut the deck into five.

"Words," she whispered.

Delkah's voice echoed in her ears. "One is now five. My eyes..."

"One's now five. My eyes are yours 'till the cards go blind."

Maire drew in a deep breath, air sharp with incense. She opened her eyes. The room looked about the same, but a weight loomed over it like a bouncer; the Lady enjoyed the mystique. Though ominous, that suited her just fine. She'd seen too many things than a person ought to have seen in these last few years.

"I am honored, my Lady," Delkah trilled.

She drew cards from four of the decks, and placed them face-down in a diamond pattern. Gods, her fingers quivered. She already knew what the deck would tell her, so why did nerves cling to her?

Delkah flipped the first card up. On it, crimson spilled from a heart punctured by a dagger. The blade's silver was lost in the glisten of red that licked down to the protruding blade. Yet in the silver light, it still beat on with an impossible, admirable stubbornness. The Wounded Heart's kindness could not easily be killed. Although kindness would not be the first word she'd use to describe herself, let alone the tenth, the Lady knew best. Besides, worse cards to represent her lurked in the deck.

The next depicted a cup frozen in a toast to the sky – the aptly named Wine Cup, an old friend whose companionship aged well. Reunion brought about merriment and memories revived, but too much led to trouble. She knew those consequences firsthand, unfortunately. No card could fit Fernis better than this.

A mound of king's gold flooded the image of the third card. It almost distracted the eye from the dragon perched on top, its mouth drawn in a snarl. Flames licked at the corners of its mouth. Well, that was blunt. Fernis sought the steal of a lifetime, though it lay in the clutches of something powerful. Fools would be scorched to ash. The most clever, however, could avoid its flames to claim their reward. With a little luck, he'd be the latter.

Criss-crossed paths littered the final card – dream-like in the endless choices presented to the tiny figure. Maire didn't need the Crossroads to know her conflicted feelings. Fate loved its drama, though, she supposed.

"What'll Fernis's offer grant me, Lady?" she called.

She drew a card from the fifth deck and placed it in the center of the circle. The sparkling Chalice greeted her – fortune gained or lost. From it, a pulse coursed through the room. The walls blurred, then spun like she had too much to drink. Wood gave way to metal. Crates burst into chests choked with golden coins, from which Fernis shoveled by the armful into sacks. He looked strange in his elegant violet coat. A future version of her, dressed in green silks, piled gold into her own sack alongside him. Sweat clung to their brows.

"See? It'll all be fine, you whiner."

"Hm. You asked a leading question, mistress," Delkah responded. "Let us keep reading. We do not want to waste our Lady's time, yes?"

She rolled her eyes. "Fine. Just quit yappin', or you'll muss up the cards."

Maire flung the next card diagonal to the Chalice. It seemed garish in comparison to the Wheel's plain wood and four spokes. She had never been sure if the artist drew four to save time or to drive in its meaning: a team united by a single goal, doomed to fail should one falter. Success relied on their togetherness.

The vault's gold melted into deep burgundy stone walls and polished tile floors. A group of people huddled by a door. Two surveyed the hall that led to them with dagger-sharp focus, hands clutching elegant spears and bodies draped in blue coats. Maire's eyes glazed over the bald man in favor of the woman. Gods, she *recognized* her from the tavern. The red curls that flew when she twirled around the floor were bound in a ponytail. Stoicism drained the usual joy from her face.

"Next one," Fernis hissed. He bent over a metal panel emblazoned with green squiggles – runes, the fancy language mages used for magic.

Future-her shuffled the deck, then drew a card. "Doves – three."

"Right." He tapped a squiggle, which resembled a dog more than a number. "Read for the guards after I'm done."

"Coin. One-"

The woman grew alert, bracing herself like a predator ready to pounce. "Someone's coming." Her lilted voice had been grinded down by the tension.

Future-Maire cocked her head. Footsteps stomped down the hall, and echoed off the vast walls. "Shit. Uh, next one's the Spire. One again."

"Thieving One aid me," Fernis muttered. He jabbed the final rune in, then flew to the door handle. It hissed. But with a click, it relented to his pulls. He flashed a grin at them all, and his eyes glittered. "Good work, Maire. She's all unlocked for us."

A man in gold painted armor rounded the hallway. Red plumes bobbed on his helmet like a child hitting their parent to demand something. Gods, his spear was twice his size, too. She'd laugh at him in less intense circumstances.

"HEY!" he shouted.

Fernis threw the door open. The group piled in behind him, and sprinted into whatever lay beyond.

"Can't believe he got her involved," present-Maire said, shaking her head.

Delkah bent one of the cards upwards. "'Her'? Oh, you mean *her* her! Yes, I caught a glimpse of her past that guard's very sharp spear. I think it craves her blood. All the more reason to avoid this, I'd say."

"Shut it." Maire laid the next card down – the Coin, its polished dulled by the dozens of hands that passed it along. Some rich folk took a singular one for granted; others would fight each other for it, and see the value in something easily discarded.

The stone crumbled into gray pebble walls. Decrepit buildings leaned over a narrow alleyway, the sky above them cloudy. Laundry flapped on taut ropes. A hint of their original colors clung to the fabric, yet no amount of washing could rid them of their stains. The same applied to the cracked streets. Grime burrowed into them, and smothered anything nice that could've grown underneath. Maire wrinkled her nose at the odor, but shame crashed into her immediately after. She wasn't a fancy-pants noble. She would not turn up her nose on the streets that raised her.

Two children raced down the alleyway. The skirts of a young Maire's tattered dress brushed against the young Fernis she pulled behind her. His shirt fared no better than her clothes. The apples they clutched in their free hands sparkled like jewels in contrast. Though, in a way, both were reserved for hands far cleaner than theirs.

"Think they're gone, Mar," Fernis squeaked.

Maire stumbled to a halt. "Bastards're harder to shake than I thought – lot harder. Don't they got anything better to do?"

"You said it. But now we get to enjoy our score, yeah?" He bit into his apple. Juice dribbled over the red skin and splashed onto the ground. "C'mon."

She shook her head. "Yours is yours, but this one ain't for me."

"What?"

Maire walked up to a door farther down the alleyway. She stretched her hand up to rap her knuckles against the old wood. "Hello? Miss Vala?"

A woman appeared in the doorway. Dark circles ringed her eyes like a raccoon, and a cloth bundle sagged off of her chest. Maire almost expected her to pass out on the spot. Instead, she mustered up a friendly smile for the children. "Mornin', Maire."

"I got something fresh for you, miss." She held up the apple.

The cloth bundle whimpered, draining the smile from Miss Vala. She cooed to it. Once it settled down, she accepted the apple.

"I know it ain't much," little Maire said. "Figured you'd want something fresh and full of the good stuff, though."

"Oh, child." The smile returned to her face. "You're real kind. It's nice to see something good grow 'round here. Sorry I don't have anything to pay you back, but I will someday. Maybe a nice meal when I have something?"

She nodded eagerly.

"Alright, then. Take care of yourself." Miss Vala closed the door, which muffled the lulluby she offered to the bundle.

Little Maire skipped down the street. Fernis stalked behind her – his glare unregistered.

"'The hells, Mar?!" he shouted. "We were chased halfway across this damn town for *this*? To give your score away? I sure ain't giving you a piece of mine after that! Find something else."

She turned to him, frowning. "Miss Vala needed it. She has a baby, Fenris, and less slickness than us."

"And you're gonna starve without that apple!" He shook his head. "Damn it, we can't let our hearts bleed if we're gonna survive. It's us or them. Gotta keep your eyes on yourself, Mar."

"Horse's ass," she shot back.

Present-day Maire grinned and nodded in agreement. Her mama hated that swear, but it packed a punch in an argument.

Fenris spat at her feet. "Go eat some, then. I'll find us some more scores – ones we *won't* give away. 'Cause I actually care if we live or not, unlike you."

He ran off before little-her could squeeze in another swear.

It had taken a long time for Maire to understand why the Lady included readings of past events. The reason behind this one, however, eluded her for the moment. It would reveal itself once she delved further into this session, and the way forward lay in the next card. She tossed it down.

Waves crashed against the Cliff – the end of a road, or escape at a high cost. Ripples washed out from the card. Pillars the size of old redwoods crashed through the street, slamming against sky-high burgundy stone. Sunlight sputtered into dim lanterns. Glints of gold paint crawled over gates, which chomped on the vaults locked behind them like dogs with treasured bones. The alley's odor faded into the incense that lingered in the backroom.

Footsteps thudded on the tiles. A moment later, Fernis pulled Maire behind a pillar – one arm clasped over her opposite, and the other at her waist. Both dropped the sacks next to them.

"This way!" a man's voice called. Six guards stomped through the hall, their manacles a chorus of clangs as they swung from their hips. The commotion added a hundred more men to their ranks. But for all their intimidation and focus, none thought to look behind the pillars in their rush.

Once they passed, Maire shoved Fernis off her. "We have to go back," she pleaded.

"Can't." He nodded in the guard's direction. "They'll 'round those vaults long before we get there. 'Sides, it'll take some heat off us. Us or-"

"You knew." Her voice grew hoarse, and her fists curled at her sides. "Bastard, you *knew!*"

Fernis sighed. "'Course. I only needed you for this job; the rest were handy, but weights need to be cut when you've gotta run. It's how it works. Guess you left this life too early to learn."

"Bastard."

He clasped her shoulder – her hands unable to pry it off. "The money'll help."

"I...We'll deal with this later." She wilted like a flower deprived of water, eyes to the ground. "I'm given' my cut to something good. Do whatever you damn well please with yours."

"Aw, don't be sour."

She yanked the sack over her shoulder, and shoved past him. He sauntered behind her. Gods, he had the audacity to keep a smile on his lips while hers bore a troubled frown.

A chill seeped through Maire as they exited the scene. That wasn't the Fernis she knew in her youth. Was it? Sure, he looked out for few things outside of them, but this betrayal was a mismatched piece in the puzzle of him. Maybe not, though. He saw the apple as a waste when it brought someone else its benefits, regardless of Miss Vala's situation.

"Gods, Fernis," she whispered.

She reached for the next card, but a wave of dread froze her fingers. The woman – did she get caught? No. No, she had to be alright.

Delkah lifted a corner of the Cliff up. "Mistress?"

"Lady, what the hells happens to the woman?! Tell me she's gonna be fine." Her voice quivered, then surged with desperation. "You owe me that much. Now *show me.*"

Delkah gasped. "Mistress! My lady, I apologize for-"

"Shut it."

The incense thickened, and formed violet clouds around the ring of light. A weight pressed against her. Eyes, though unseen, pierced her flesh to gaze into her soul. The visage of a white-masked woman, cheek stamped with a diamond, flashed in her mind.

"Please."

Delkah stammered out more apologies. She'd smack him if he had a body, though the slight shift of judgment to include him froze her thoughts. Sweat crawled onto her brow. The Lady wouldn't smite her favorite acolyte for a little favor, would she? She needed her worship. Spirits loved that stuff like a rich lady loved pearl necklaces.

"Oh! Oh, goodness, thank you, my lady."

Maire cocked her head. "That's a 'yes' from her, yeah? Spit it out 'fore you choke on her skirts."

"That is indeed a yes." He paused. "I sense a weight behind whatever you draw next, though, mistress. A terrible one. Are you certain you want to see it?"

She nodded, and grabbed her hand to stop its quiver.

"Very well. I just pray it is a burden you can bear."

Maire slammed the next card down, heart pounding like the gallop of a horse. Delkah raised it up slowly in response. But with a glare from her, he hurled it onto its back.

The image on the other side choked her breath. No. No, no, no – anything but the Skull. Its bleached teeth stretched into a sneer, glee-ful in reaction to her horror. Maggots crawled in its sockets. Though the void filled the space past those nasty creatures, an air of contempt lingered within it.

The golden gates dulled and shrank to fit the holes punched into giant walls. An iron scent suffused itself into the dirt courtyard. The sun overhead cast a single shadow within it: wooden beams stabbed into a platform, flanked by black-garbed guards. Ropes swung from it.

No.

Chains rattled. Maire turned, heart plummeting into her stomach at the red haired prisoner marched to the shadow. Her coat was shredded to rags – the cuffs bound by manacles. More chains swung in the guards' hands. Gods, the woman tried to keep a stiff lip, but the red blotches around her eyes and tears on her cheeks exposed her terror. Whenever she dug her feet in, the bastards shoved her forward. They treated her like a rebellious pig forced to its slaughter, not the person who lit up the Snake every night she appeared.

"I am truly sorry, mistress," Delkah whispered.

Her stomach rocked. She turned away from the horrid scene, but her eyes fell upon the Skull again. "'Us or them'. We ain't children running through the market anymore." She gritted her teeth. "All horse's ass."

"If you are convinced enough this is a terrible route to go down, perhaps we can end the reading here? There is one more card, though-"

She snatched the next card off of the deck. "I'm seein' this through. Besides, he ain't able to do much worse than gut me like this."

"Oh, mistress."

The final card fluttered into place, and completed the trail that snaked through the circle-diamond: the Dagger. Its wielder held it behind his back. The man's grin, directed at a group of people, was wide across his face. Betrayal. Gods, Fernis; of course he wouldn't be satisfied with the daggers he already buried in their compatriots.

Darkness swallowed the execution site, accompanied by a stab of cold wind. The walls shedded their bars. Grass and bushes sprouted over dirt, which smothered the scent of iron. Spots of light flew over the scene. Underneath it, Fernis pulled Maire through the green – their off-hands wrapped around sacks of gold.

"Lady help us," future-her choked out. "Oh gods, don't let us down, Lady."

Fernis tackled her into the bushes before the light could swoop onto them. "Don't lose your nerve now, Mar; we're almost there."

She scrambled to her feet, and ripped a sack off the branches it caught on. A flash of light illuminated her glare, softened by wide-eyed terror. "Damn you. Next time I see you, you're a dead man. Dead."

"Sure, but let's get outta here first."

They ran through the darkness, guided by the same light that searched for them. But they did not go for a gate. Instead, Fernis led her to a wall. Present-Maire frowned, searching for clues to his plan on the flat surface.

Fernis dropped to his knees, and pulled a glove out from his coat – the texture marbled, as though ripped out of a rich person's floor. He held it over the dirt at the wall's edge. "C'mon. C'mon, please…"

The dirt shifted. An invisible shovel pushed mounds aside to form a cup-sized hole.

"Can't that go any faster?" Maire snapped.

His eyes bore into the hole, willing it to dig itself deeper. "'Least it goes faster than yours. The amount of times we almost got caught 'cause of your shuffling took a year off me. Probably two."

"Horse's ass. Just shut it and dig while I ask the Lady something." She took out her cards. They flew between her fingers – too smooth for her hands alone – then settled into a stack. Maire plucked one from the top. Though the darkness obscured the image from present-day her, it drained the color from the future version's face. "Lady have mercy."

A spotlight drove away the shadows, and burned them in light. Guards shouted. The ground rumbled with the approach of a hundred men, all eager to claim the prey they sought.

"Hurry!" she shouted.

Metal rattled towards them, loud as a giant. Fernis glanced between her and the guards, his eyes pained. A frown tore at the corners of his mouth. "Sorry, Maire." Dirt crawled up his form and enveloped the gold. "I'm real sorry."

Maire leapt for him, but the dirt-bastard collapsed between her arms. "NO!"

The guards swarmed her. She snarled, leaping onto her feet. Light glinted across her teeth – carved into fangs by the shadow of her lips. She swung her fists at any who approached. Their faces crunched against them, and toppled bastard after bastard.

Unfortunately, they persisted. Several piled on her, and locked her wrists into shackles. More clamped on her legs. She thrashed against her restraints, though the iron held strong against her unbridled fury. All she could do was scream Fernis's name. Bloodlust choked her voice, powered by waves of agony that crashed through her veins. It distorted her screams into shrieks for his death. He had killed whatever tenderness remained with this betrayal, and it would see him punished in the most painful ways possible.

The light that circled her cards illuminated a dainty finger. It wound its way along the line, and erased what it touched. Maire, numb, forced herself to bow to it.

"Thank you, my Lady," Delkah said, reverent.

Once the finger smothered the last bit of silver, it pressed into the candles' flames. Smoke streamed from the wicks. The scent tickled her nose. She raised her arm to wipe it, though it moved like it had been dipped in molasses. The incense faded long before her sleeve touched skin.

Her future self's screams faded. The scene writhed, then warped back into the backroom's wooden walls and crates. Gods, an age had passed since she last saw them. That tiny bit of comfort unstuck Maire enough for her to wobble to her feet.

The cards flew back into a pile, pressing into her hand. "Are you alright, mistress?"

"He abandoned me."

Delkah shuffled in her hand – a clunky attempt at comfort. "I am deeply sorry. On the brighter side, you can say 'no' without much more turmoil. Perhaps you can save the woman as well?"

"The bastard…" She shook her head, and forced herself to breathe. He didn't want to. Gods, conflict had danced in his eyes in the moments that led to his betrayal. But he still betrayed her. Well, he would betray her if she agreed to this job. Not by choice, though. She had to remember that; he would not leave her behind if those bastards did not charge them.

"What now, mistress?"

Maire combed a hand through her hair, raking the strands out of her eyes. "First, a drink. My damn head's spinning from all this."

"And then? Surely you cannot-"

"Shut it. A drink, then I'll give this some thought. 'Sides, it's almost time to open the Snake for the evening. Gods, she'll probably show up – another thing to get a handle on." She sighed. "Really wish you could bartend for me tonight, Delkah."

He chuckled. "If the patrons are anything like you, they would throw my cards into the hearth before I could ask them what drink they want. Perhaps sooner."

"Well, you ain't wrong about that."

The cards fluttered back into her pocket, and nestled in a perfect stack. "Have your drink. I will await your request to contribute my insights on how to proceed, mistress. Rest assured, I have plenty."

"'Course you do." Maire rubbed the blur from her eyes, then gripped the doorknob. What an hour. She'd have to sort out the present from the future before speaking to the lady. Hells, she might finally get her name tonight. Could she face all the nonsense that awaited her on the other side, though? "Hey, Delkah?"

"Yes, mistress?"

The words lagged between her mind and mouth. "Thanks."

"Of course." He couldn't smile without a face. Still, the impression of one wove itself through his tone – brighter and more annoying than sunlight in the eyes.

Maire turned the doorknob, and headed for her wine.

A LIFE'S WORTH

OLIVER VU-DE LEON

"Have you or a loved one suffered some serious bad luck in the past? Have the strings of fate bent out of shape and out of your hands? Then call me, the Cardmaster! I will change your fate at the twist of my fingers! Call today to book an appointment at..."

Joan's eyes glazed over the television screen. The same commercial that she would see everyday at the same time is playing again. She's sick of it. She's sick of thinking. She's sick of existing.

Joan takes a long drag from her cigarette as she leans back in her reclining chair. The TV is covered in old laundry that she has yet to fold up. In front of the TV, her dirty clothes litter around the room. Food containers she had delivered overlap the dirty clothes and the negative spaces between to finish the portrait of a broken soul.

'I hate that I live like this,' Joan thought to herself. 'If only I had energy to fix everything.'

Earlier that year, Joan's aunt had passed away. She became the last of her family. As the last of kin, Joan inherited from her family one final blow to the stomach: an exuberant debt that was hers to pay off. Her dead end job at a hat store could never pay off this debt in her lifetime. She had wished she could make a better life for herself. Joan saw herself raising kids, starting a family, moving to a new city and finishing her education. But through all of the pain wond the hardships, she learned only one bludgeoning truth: It was hopeless to be hopeful in her life.

The alarm clock she had bought from Dollar Store started to ring in the corner of her apartment. It was time to get ready for work.

Joan put out her cigarette on her coffee table and threw it onto the pile of cigs that laid there. She got up and stretched. Her bones and muscles were tense and ached from a long life of misery. But she swallowed that feeling up. She needed cash to pay off this month's rent. She walked over to her bathroom. Her work clothes laid in the corner after she threw them there the other night. Joan quickly put them on over the underwear that she had been wearing for the past few days.

Her emerald colored eyes came with heavy eye bags. Her skin was auburn and ashy. Her skin was sun-freckled and flaked at the crevices of her face. Her lips looked like cracked pavement, felt like it too. Her hair was a great red beast that dared not to be tamed. She used a lint roller in place of a washing machine to pick off the gunk and hair that laid on her sky blue uniform. On the uniform, was a logo depicting a smiley face with a red baseball cap on. A cruel reflection of what she could be. It took about 13 minutes but she was ready. She made a mental note: '30 minutes until work starts.'

After microwaving a bagel she found in one of the food containers, she ran onto her bike to get to work. She threw her bagel and her string backpack into the basket of her bike. Then she was off.

The street was more packed than usual. Cars sat in long lines separated by cones. Police officers were called by the city to direct traffic. People yelled at each other to move faster and the mall parking lot that began at the mall and reached her apartment was packed to the brim. She had never seen the mall get this busy. It might interfere with her bike route.

As Joan biked down the busy street, she was glad that the sidewalk remained empty so she could bike the long way with ease. She lifted her hands off the handlebars to do her hair on the road. She took a brush from her pocket and removed the loose hairs and dander from her hair. Joan then molded it into an acceptable shape while using the breeze to finalize her look. She pointed the rear view mirror on her bike towards her face to see if she was presentable. It could have been done a little better if she cared more. But then she would be even more late for work so it was just good enough. She finished off her look with a headband that barely held her thick hair in place.

After 10 minutes on her bike, Joan had arrived at her workplace: the Gaping Maw Mall. This mall was built into the mouth of a beast that lay dormant for hundreds upon hundreds of years. It had buried its body into the ground dynasties ago, leaving only its mouth and nostrils above ground to breathe. Its exterior was a gray cracked mess of dry skin. It towered over Joan, not in the way a monstrous horror typically would; It was just stationary and large. It was dormant and waiting. For what? I don't know and Joan doesn't know nor does she care to find out. The nostrils were great holes that protruded from the mass of solidified flesh that became the main mall building. The mouth laid below the nostrils, eternally gaped open to the public. The calcified teeth were yellowed and sedimented together. The front two lower teeth were removed to insert a convenient sliding door. Cheesy ads on the doors beckoned for patrons to enter.

Joan parked and locked her bike on a rack that was fashioned from the spiral, spiny claws of the beast that poked out from the ground. She checked her watch.

'Damn I got here with 20 minutes left to spare,' she thought, barely excited. She picked up her bag and ran into the mall. The teeth of the beast were stalactites, intimidatingly piercing down over her head. The glass doors automatically opened and Joan was hit with the humid air that the beast produced. The muggy fumes that emitted out smelled of eternal morning breath and floral air fresheners. This smell was definitely new. She stumbled back, overwhelmed by the stench. It took her a second to acclimate and she took a deep breath to recollect herself. This was precious time that could be spent heading to work so she could get an early work bonus for the day. Once she came back to her senses, she looked towards her workplace, a cheap, crummy hat store for people who are embarrassed about their hair or balding.

The store was barely visible over the crowd of people. The mass of humans stretched to cover all of the squishy, budded tongue of the beast. With barely any space to squeeze through, Joan was definitely going to be late.

The mall was structured around the interior of the beast's mouth. The bright red tongue, littered with taste buds, became the mall's main floor. The wide expanse came with a scattering of concession carts selling their wares and benches for husbands to wait for their partners to finish shopping as they played games on their phone. The scarred walls of the cheeks had concrete-built stores with bright neon signs integrated in to denote which store was which. A multitude of displays of signs were scattered all over the mall, begging for customers to enter: "Hat Store," "Chair Store," "Clothing Store." Located in the back left molars of the beast was the food court. It was detailed with many large signs imploring the mall's guests to feast: "Meat store," "Plant store," "Hot Dog on a Stick." Several large metal tubes stabbed out from the cheeks and mazed around the ceiling of the mall to provide breathable air for its visitors. The uvula had an electronic advertising billboard chained and hung around it with supporting cables strung against the walls of its throat. The hat store where Joan worked was located in the very back of the mall right under the uvula right behind the massive crowd.

Joan hopped onto a bench to scan the mall grounds looking for an opening in the massive pile of people to reach her workplace. Just then, she heard a booming voice in the distance.

"Come one Come all! For you are now about to be in the presence of The Twister of Fates! The Changer of Futures! The Mystic Emissary from Beyond! Please put your hands together for..."

The crowd roared. Joan could barely hear the announcer over their exhilarated cheers. The sound reverberated around the maw and rumbled the main floor. Joan nearly lost her footing on the bench and jumped down. She took a deep sigh and began to push through the crowd to get to her work.

As moved past every man, woman, and child, she began to tune out the crowd and the announcer. She just needed to clock in before it's too late. After several minutes of pushing and shoving people out of her way, Joan checked her watch.

"Only three minutes left, crap," She tracked. "I better hurry."

Just then, Joan began to notice that people were staring at her in shock. Every face in the audience had turned in her direction. Had she done something wrong? Did she mess something up again? Or had the announcer said something about her? She began to tune back into what the booming voice was saying.

"Yes you!" The announcer shouted and pointed in her direction. "You're the lucky guest who's going to have their fate changed. Why don't you come on stage, young one!"

Suddenly the crowd began to part away from each other to reveal a path to the stage. They began to clap and cheer for her. For Joan, it felt as if she was chosen to be sacrificed in front of this population.

Joan thought to herself, 'If I'm gonna have to do this demonstration just to squeeze through, then I'm gonna do it cuz some of these people are stinky and smell like cheese sticks.'

Joan approached the stage and hopped on. And there he was. The source of the booming voice. The announcer was an odd looking bald fellow with a button nose, pale skin, and short squinting eyes. His mouth was contorted to always produce a smile for show. He wore a deep blue suit with a tacky red patterned tie. Of course, because he was bald, he had a black top hat on. His outfit was gross to look at but it really did shine and tell Joan that he was a man who was utterly confident in himself. Whatever this man had in store for her it could not be good.

"I'm so glad you can make it!" the odd looking man grinned. "Now approach my table and let the fate reading commence!"

"Yeah sure, whatever. I'm down for anything," Joan sighed as she approached the table. The table had a gaudy mess of magician's symbols. Yellow Stars, slightly more yellow moons, red hearts, black clovers and the other symbols that are typically on cards littered its surface along with the words in a bolded font: **The Cardmaster.**

"So, Cardmaster," Joan sarcastically smiled. "How do you wanna read my fate?"

The Cardmaster chuckled to himself: "It's quite simple actually." He flamboyantly lifts his hand to show her the back of his palm. "I already have all that I need right HERE." He turns his hand around. A card deck appeared, seemingly out of thin air. The audience roars like monkeys seeing an alien monolith for the first time.

'Dang this dude's got tricks,' even Joan was impressed. He placed the deck on the table. Its design was very plain and simple like one you might find in a casino. There had to be something more interesting than simple cards. With a rapid hand movement, even faster than Joan could process, the Cardmaster waved his hand over the table and placed down all of the 52 cards face up. Joan was shocked. The last time she'd seen a magician this smooth was during her 6th birthday. At this point in the story, Joan was 23.

On each card were single words. Joan quickly scanned through the words. One read, "hero." Another displayed "Martyr." Most of the others flat out said, "deadbeat" or "coward" or similar undignified terms.

"These cards display the type of person that you will be at the end of your life," the Cardmaster boasted. "I will shuffle this deck and whatever card you pull will become your fate!"

Joan was confused at the system he had. He was a weird magician. "Like if I pick the deadbeat card, then I will be fated to die as a deadbeat?"

"Yes exactly! If you pull the thief card, you will end your life as a thief. If you pull the coward card, you will be no more than a coward. Although my cards are vague in description, they have been known to change fates 100% of the time! Really looks like you haven't read my job description." Chuckles emerge from the crowd.

"Okay. But I'm still skeptical. Is there a catch here?"

"NO CATCH!" The Cardmaster shouted towards the crowd and was met with screams. In the distance, a deep lowly rumbling that had always been there had become more audible. "Your fate will change if you pick according to which card you pull from my shuffled deck."

He moved his slick supple fingers to signal that she could look at each card closer.

"But what if I don't wanna die as a deadbeat or a villain or..." Another card's text surprised her: "sustenance?" Joan was fully invested in this bit and had suspended her disbelief. "What If I just wanna be happy? Why aren't there any cards that say that I will be a happy woman when I die?"

"Well the cards just appear like this. If I could, I would have all of my clients pull the happy card every time. But, it seems that these cards are determined by different potential paths that you are pre-determined to follow in life."

Joan was bummed out. She had hoped this guy could just make her happy again so she didn't have to trudge through the dirty sad parts of her already miserable life.

"But I do have a new system that I'm willing to try that could place the odds more in your favor. Would you like to hear it?"

"Yes sure, please go on with it. But make it fast I'm already late for wor..."

"Excellent! Look here." He somehow produced an entire trash bin from nothing and now carried it in his hands. "This is my Cosmic Trash Compactor. You may place cards that are not to your liking into here. If you do, you will completely remove the chances of ever pulling that fate!"

"Sure that sounds fun. Let me just get rid of..." Joan began to scan the cards for fates that she didn't like.

"HOLD IT!" The Cardmaster for the first time jumped out to block her from touching the cards. It was the first time he seemed nervous or frightened. "THIS TRASH COMPACTOR HAS A CATCH!"

"I thought you said there was no catch?"

"Well you see, the trash compactor has a catch but not the cards. No, the cards are just fates you have. Easy as that. But you see the trash compactor takes your life away."

Joan was now scared. Exactly what did this mean for her? Was she gonna die before her debt was paid? Would she die sooner with even more regrets? Will it kill her on the spot? The mixture of fear and anticipation made the pause between sentences feel like they were a millennium apart.

"For each card you throw into this trash compactor, depending on how unfavorable the fate is to you, the trash compactor will take a portion of your life span away. Let's say you're pre-determined to live until you're 80. For you, that's like what? 40 more years?"

"Dude, I'm like 23."

The cardmaster seemed to do a double take. "Goddamn! Are you being for real with me? Then you need to take better care of yourself. 23 year olds don't look so… rugged." Joan caught the Cardmaster off guard but only for a moment. "Well, if you were meant to live to 80 and you throw away a particularly unfavorable card. Then that means that you will also lose an amount of your life proportionate to how unfavorable that card is to you. It might take 4 years making your life-span go down to 76. Or it could take 30 years away, making you live to 50. We can never really tell with the fates. But that's just a brief rundown of it."

For Joan, this was great. Less life meant less sadness right? She didn't care if she lived or died the next day anyway. She didn't know or care if her debts carried on with her in the afterlife and she most certainly did not have anyone that she could pass them onto. Joan just wanted to have a favorable fate and death. Without a word, she had already begun to mentally pick out the cards to throw away in the trash. Scoundrel. Rat. Creature. Villain. Deadbeat. Elderly. Beneficiary. Coward. All the words that came with a vaguely negative connotation went into the trash. She had focused so hard on the words she would throw away that she zoned out. Joan threw away the cards with reckless abandon.

Everyone in the audience was stunned. All of the trashing she was doing was being televised on the uvula billboard for the entire mall to see. People in the crowd were shocked and horrified. How could someone as young as her care so little about their life? She was just making herself die younger. This was too much to watch for the younger children in the crowd who had begun to cry at the unfathomable display of self hate at hand. In the deafening silence left by Joan's sad display of self-worth, a deep sigh erupting from the beast's throat became barely audible.

Once Joan discarded her final card, she was left with two cards from the 52 she started with. The words on both cards were as follows: Martyr and Sage. They were the only ones that were vaguely positive out of everything.

"Okay. I'm done with discarding my deck. Now what happens next?" She turned to look at the Cardmaster. He was stunned. For the first time throughout this entire act, his smile dropped into a more sullen expression. Never before had he seen something so depressing. He needed to bring up the energy in the room before she ruins the demonstration.

"Well done Joan! You've successfully discarded your deck!" Claps came out haphazardly from the audience. "Now allow me to shuffle your two fates together!" His hands quickly swiped the cards and over-lapped them on top of each other so the fates were not seen. He continued to shuffle them until Joan's naked eye lost track of where the two cards were in the stack. The Cardmaster's shuffle had bested Joan's astute card tracking skills she obtained from her years of following her family into casinos. He then places both cards face down.

"Now Joan." the Cardmaster settled down. "Choose wisely. What will your fate be?"

Joan had always been a right handed person so she chose the card on the right. As she flipped the card over, a white smoke emerged from it. It enveloped her faster than she could process it. Then in an instant, the smoke was gone. She was standing in the same spot in front of the same crowd inside the same mall inside the same beast. Joan was dis-oriented but she had not moved from her spot. 'What a weird feeling,' she pondered. Joan quickly shook it off and looked at her card.

Martyr.

"EVERYBODY SHE WILL BE A MARTYR!"

The Cardmaster has effortlessly hyped the crowd up once again. The cheers and screams towards his wonderful acts got louder and louder. Suddenly, from the deep recesses in the back of Joan's mind, a voice rang out.

"JOAN! GET EVERYONE OUT OF HERE NOW!"

"Who is this?" questioned Joan. "What are you? Are you my fate? Manifested from the cards of the Cardmaster?"

"What are you talking about?! NO! I am your Fight or Flight response and I'm telling you that y'all need to leave this mall right now!" Joan hadn't had her fight or flight triggered in years. She had forgotten what it felt like to feel scared. She was skeptical of her mental processes.

"Okay... why do we need to dip though?" Joan questioned further.

"Haven't you noticed something different about our mall? The humid air stenched with morning breath. The deep rumbling of these buildings. The enormous crowd of people. Joan. This mall has sat inside this beast for so long, that it's starting to make the beast uncomfortable. And with this crowd making the beast even more uncomfortable, the beast will..."

Joan came to a conclusion: the beast is about to wake up and swallow up the mall with everyone in it. Her fight or flight response was right. The deep rumbling that she once heard became a light crackling. The cracks that were on each concrete store since the beginning began to elongate across each other. The advertisement on the uvula began to sway back and forth. The humid air became even more humid and smelled so much worse. Everyone was in danger.

Joan ran to the Cardmaster and ripped the microphone that was attached to his suit. Her movements wrenched the Cardmaster's suit all the way until the collar was completely torn off. Her adrenaline had kicked in.

"EVERYBODY HERE!" The mall's speaker boomed. The sound was so sudden that she could see the crowd wince in surprise. "THE BEAST WILL AWAKEN IN THE NEXT SEVERAL MINUTES AND CON-SUME ALL OF US! WE ALL NEED TO LEAVE RIGHT NOW!" The audience was more shocked than anything. They began to talk among themselves. Has she gone crazy? Did the fate of "martyr" mean that she would talk nonsense? They had not noticed the beast waking up from under their feet.

Before conversations could get more complex on this, Joan's voice erupted from the speakers. "I'VE WORKED AT THIS MALL SINCE I WAS 10. I KNOW WHEN SOMETHING IS WRONG HERE. YOU ALL NEED TO MOVE OUT OF HERE AS SOON AS POSSIBLE. NOW!" Abruptly, the building that housed "Hot Dog on a Stick" in the food court collapsed for everyone to see. The general manager of that fast food stop along with one teenage employee were buried under the rubble. After this incident, they were never seen again.

Suddenly everyone broke out in a panic. They looked at themselves and found that they're in the worst position to evacuate. Some of the individuals were packed in so tightly that they could not move their arms or legs. The crowd began to scream in horror at the prospect of being eaten by an eldritch being of an incomprehensible. Panic ensued and a crush was about to happen. People were about to kill themselves out of panic. Joan had to do something. She had been working in this mall for so long. She had to know how to help calm the crowd and guide them out of this disaster. That's when the one thought that could potentially save so many lives hit her. She knew where all of the exits were.

From her position, underneath the uvula, there were 5 exits in the mall. There were 2 located to her direct left and right with concrete corridors leading to the outside. These corridors could collapse, burying individuals to be rescued. They were not efficient enough to move this many people either. There were two more exits about 40 meters away; it was located closer to the front entrance. These exits were reinforced with steel rebar and metal beams. Her bloodline built this mall. This was her family's only surviving property. Joan had to know its architecture to a tee. About 10 seconds had passed since Joan had last said something into the microphone. Her brain is working the hardest it has in her entire life.

"EVERYONE! THERE ARE TWO EXITS WAY OVER THERE!" Joan pointed towards the safe exits "THEY ARE MARKED WITH BATHROOM SIGNS!" A subtle sound of crackling concrete reverberated across the entire mall. Then everyone, in a panic, began rushing to those exits. "PLEASE HELP ANYONE WHO HAS FALLEN OVER AND PLEASE DON'T SHOVE! WE NEED TO SAVE AS MANY PEOPLE AS POSSIBLE."

The back of the massive crowd began to run towards the exits and the main entrance. The panic was palpable. Screams poured out from the crowd. Their footsteps and sheer terror that they felt made a cacophony so intense that the sound alone could put you in therapy for life. A conglomerate fear washed over each and every adult and child. But it worked. A good amount of the crowd had dissipated and exited the beast to the outside where they breathed a communal sigh of relief. The escaped fled on foot or drove out in cars, ignoring every traffic law for the safety of themselves and their loved ones.

There still was, however, a little less than 50% of the crowd still trapped in the beast. The crackling quickly turned to crashing. The buildings which all housed the stores simultaneously crumbled. The work and artistry built over the years by Joan's family had been demolished in an instant. The beast has begun moving its jaw.

"You, Cardmaster. Get off the stage right now," Joan grimly demanded of the Cardmaster who had frozen in place with a permanent look of shock in his face. He shook off his emotions and hobbled off the stage in fear that it would collapse from under his feet.

She looked up and realized that the advertisement attached to the uvula had been swaying this entire time. 'It's about to fall onto the stage.' Her legs, after years worth of biking, sprung into action. She grabbed the Cardmaster before he could even realize what's happening and threw themselves off the stage onto the tongue below. Suddenly, the support cables snapped and whipped against the throat of the beast. The beast can now feel the full weight of the billboard on its uvula.

The beast opens its mouth wider, shaking around most of the rubble to reveal most of the clothing, toys and technology that lay underneath.

There were a few bodies as well. Suddenly, the lowliest sound played from behind her workplace. It sounded like a gurgle, as if someone was clearing their throat… She knew what was coming and didn't know anything better to do than shout…

"EVERYBODY GET DOWN! DUCK NOW!"

Joan and the crowd crouched in near perfect unison. Suddenly, the hat store that Joan had to clock into had burst. Horrified screams poured out. A volcanic eruption of the mall emerged from the back of the beast's throat. The sound was ear-piercingly wet and visceral. The billboard flew off the uvula and over Joan. Bits of buildings clattered against each other as they soared. Electricity surged as their wires were exposed. The smell was worse than death. The beast had coughed. Everyone was shaking in absolute and utter fear, including the Cardmaster. Joan, however, was completely steady. This was what she was made for. All of her years parasitically attached to this mall had led up to this. She had to save everyone.

The material that was destroyed by the cough of the beast flew over their heads through the mouth and outside of the building. They crashed into several different cars, littering the parking lot in bits of broken pieces. There were so many casualties caught in their flight path. They were the bare remnants of Joan's past and they killed people. She couldn't let her grief get to her. She needed to save everyone else.

"EVERYONE TO THE EXITS NOW!"

Suddenly the power was cut. In an instant, the lights shut off and the mall became a pitch black abyss. The humid environment was lit only by the light from the outside barely piercing through the beast's opened maw.

A twinkle emerges from the crowd: a single LED from a father's phone. He had just lost his wife in this disaster in the most terrible of ways. But he was not about to lose his children too. The light coming from the phone was barely enough to make the mall visible but it was enough to illuminate the heads in the crowd. There were still so many trapped within the maw of the beast. Then another phone light turns on. Then another. Then another. All of the phones' lights powered on to illuminate the interior of the beast. The true horror of this situation had finally been revealed to the crowd like a spotlight on the worst tragedy they have ever seen. Screams shoot out from the crowd. The concrete of the buildings had melted and conglomerated together. The products sold in these ghosts of the mall had been mixed together with the remains of humans by the beast's acidic saliva. It was the beast's unconscious artistic rendition of human greed and its genocidal effects.

This cruddy dilapidated mall ruined Joan's life. Her family had built this place several years before she was born. They believed that it would create a financial boom that would help bring the family's social status to a whole new level. They thought it would attract people from all over to see the "Mall within one of those beasts that have been here for a millenia!" They were even thinking of franchising the mall into the other beasts that lay dormant around the planet. They even planned to open amusement parks within them. Their blind optimism was their biggest flaw.

Every year, government representatives and auditors forced the family to pay fees and fines for safety failures throughout the facility. Faulty wiring, lack of solid air flow, ramps that were not wheelchair accessible, and no solid assurances that the beast wouldn't wake were among the few flaws that obliterated her family's fragile wealth. Joan's grandma died hoping the mall would find success. Then her grandpa. Then her mom. Then her dad. Then her uncle. Then her aunt. Then it was just Joan. Within a blink of her eye, all of her family passed and she had become the sole inheritor of the mall. Because she owned it before she was qualified to do so, Joan brought in a co-owner to see if she could get someone to potentially spruce up the mall and bring in more people while she worked at its understaffed establishments. This idea backfired. The co-owner believed that a fun demonstration of the Cardmaster's skills could bring in a massive crowd that would shop around and amass enough cash to have all her debts paid off in a day. But in the end, 27 people had died already with one hundred more still in danger. Her vast knowledge on the inner workings of the mall had failed her then . But she can't let it fail her now.

She needed to save everyone.

She could feel a breeze coming in from the outside of the beast's mouth. 'The beast inhales once again,' Joan understood the sensations clearly. 'Another cough or something worse beckons from the beast and could kill all the living still here. We need to make an exodus right now and fast.'

Through the dim lights from the crowd, Joan could barely see that all four exits on the sides of the beast had collapsed and melted. There was one sole exit at the front of the beast through its mouth. But knowing that the beast had just coughed, Joan was unsure if the front entrance was covered in acidic saliva or not. There had to be another route out. There must be another route out.

Suddenly, it clicked. There was a shipping depot that had massive freight doors that opened to the outside. However she could not confirm if the bridge over the throat was still intact and sound for more than 100 people to cross. It probably collapsed after the cough. Crap.

Joan was running out of time. She couldn't panic now. A lot of people depended on her now. She quickly checked her watch to reorient herself. Only two minutes had passed since this tragedy had started. Her mind had been thinking and moving at light speed. This was good. Joan's mind shifted to figuring out where the best exit to the outside. A mental map of the mall manifested in Joan's mind. She used her own phone to shine a light into the different potential exits in the mall, a majority of which lay in the back of the collapsed stores. She checked off each exit as she heard the sizzle of acid or saw the melted mess coming from their direction. Unfortunately for them, every single exit was wasted. They were trapped in this sea of waste and muck.

No. She couldn't accept this as fact. These people depended on her. Like a firefly in the night, the people's voices flicked into her ears. Everything was overwhelming her. Everything was coming down. Everything was so complex. She needed to reach into the deepest recesses of her mind to find that one potential exit that could save everyone.

Suddenly, a memory appeared. Joan was in the back left corner of the mall. There was a dense, plastic, blue ladder that was lodged into the right cheek wall. Her father and uncle climbed down the ladder wearing hazmat suits holding buckets of slime.

"Papa! Uncle Jared," she cried. "What did you two see up there? Was it scary?" Joan's voice sounded higher than it was now. She couldn't have been more than 8 years old.

"Don't worry my sweetheart," her father smiled through that alien spacesuit. She could barely see his face through the clear polyethylene face shield. Hearing his voice again after so many years calmed her so much that it could lull her to sleep. "Luckily there was nothing scary up there. Just a whole lot of boogers."

"Boogers."

"Boogers."

The word, Boogers in her head echoed louder than anything. But why? What did it have to do with the escape?

"Oh my farts. The nose is an exit."

"The huh is a what now?" the Cardmaster uttered, taken aback. He was curled up in a ball at Joan's feet. His once perfect performance outfit was now muddied and wet from the loose mucous on the tongue. His grandiose stage presence was now reduced to a sniffling, tear-ridden husk. It was only natural. The blatant horror of the situation had mentally destroyed all trapped in the gaping maw of the beast. Prayers were muttered. Foreh

"Joan! Save us!"

"Joan! We're nearly out of time! Hurry!"

"Our children are scared! What's going on?"

eads were kissed. But Joan was calm. She had to stay strong for everyone.

Joan cupped her hands together and shouted toward the crowd: "EVERYONE FOLLOW ME! WE'LL ESCAPE THROUGH THE NOSE!" Joan pulled out her flashlight and waved it in the air as she ran in the direction of the plastic blue ladder.

A voice rang from the crowd: "But, what if we get melted by the acid in the nose?"

"That's the thing," Joan smiled. She was feeling very confident in herself. "The beast's nose is the delicate tissue of the body. If there's anywhere that will be safe it would be the..."

Joan thought to herself:

Oh no. Wait. But... Oh Crinsten. Oh Cranston. We're dead meat for the beast. I might be wrong about all this. What if this nose isn't the exit anymore?

Now I'm extremely certain that the nose is the safest part of the beast to traverse. My papa and Uncle Jared went into the nostrils and kicked ass and came down talking about boogers and whatnot. I think I know what's up around those parts. But the big cough must've thrown the beast's acid into the nose. There could still be acid all around! Cranit! Cranit! Cranit! I dunno if I should even risk it. Shoot shoot shoot! Someone could get hurt real bad.

But if we don't even try then we'll all get hurt real bad. Shoot alright. I guess we'll try the nose then.

Joan cupped her hands once again: "EVERYONE! JUST FOLLOW ME! I WILL LEAD YOU ALL TO SAFETY!"

Without a doubt in their collective minds, the crowd immediately ran to catch up with Joan. She remembered the location of the plastic blue ladder to a tee: lodged into the right cheek wall next to "The Clothing Store." Hopefully, it was still intact after all these years.

She arrived at the melted mess of concrete that was "The Clothing Store" to find the ladder still upright. It rose 50 feet into the ceiling and led into nostrils. It seems like the acidic saliva had no effect on this extremely strong ladder.

"Everyone stay here for 20 seconds!" Joan shouted. "I'm going to survey the nose to see if it's safe to exit this way." Without a moment to lose Joan had hopped on the ladder and climbed all the way to the nostril without breaking a sweat. Once she got to the top she hopped off the ladder and saw the light from the outside shining into her eyes. The path out was unblocked and available for herself and the crowd to escape. She needed to make sure the path was clear for the rest so she ran the short distance to the end of the nose. Because her shoes were not melting during that run, that meant there was no acidic saliva in the nose; It was safe to escape through. When she reached the end of the nose, she caught a glimpse of chaos that laid outside the beast.

Concrete pieces of the mall were scattered across the parking lot. Cars were thrown and thrashed together. The sheer pressure of the cough created utter catastrophe outside. Luckily there was a military helicopter along with troops already on the scene, ensuring that survivors are safe and taken care of. A voice spouts from the helicopter: "HEY YOU! HOW MANY MORE SURVIVORS ARE INSIDE THE BEAST?!" Joan squints her eyes. A man from inside the helicopter is shouting into its intercom, looking directly at Joan as if waiting for her words.

"THERE'S ABOUT 100 PEOPLE STILL LEFT INSIDE. THEY WILL EXIT OUT OF THIS NOSTRIL. CAN YOU ARRANGE FOR A RESCUE DRONE TO HELP ALL OF THESE PEOPLE OUT?!"

"WE CAN ARRANGE FOR THAT! JUST BRING THESE PEOPLE OUT AND THE RESCUE DRONE WILL CARRY THEM TO SAFETY!"

Joan gave him a thumbs up. It looks like things were looking up from here. She checked her watch; 25 seconds had passed. Shoot. She needs to make sure the survivors are safe. She ran back to the ladder and looked down. Everyone was dead silent and watching in fearful anticipation to see if Joan survived her scouting mission. When they noticed that she was back, everyone cheered for her. People clapped. Children jumped for joy. The elderly danced. They were saved.

Joan had never had such recognition before. She usually would be in the background of other's lives, waiting to help someone with their shopping experience or just reorganizing another store for the 1000th time. But this recognition was overwhelmingly positive. A tear falls off her cheek onto the ground of the beast. She's finally happy with her life and what she's done for people. She needs to just be strong and brave just for a little longer before she can revel in these positive emotions: "Everyone starts climbing! You got this!"

Within 30 seconds, the first guest of the mall had reached the top of the ladder. The man was looking shaken and nervous as ever. Joan gently guided him to the other end of the nostril to where a rescue drone was waiting to pick him up. Once the man got to the end, he found a 4-bladed drone hovering in the air. It was carrying a large metallic box open on the top. It was big enough to hold 5 cars and had the words "Human Rescue Team" on its side. He then heard a voice: "Please jump in!" The man mentally prepared himself and he hopped down 5 feet onto the box. The drone had stabilized itself and the box so that the man felt zero impact when he fell onto the box. He was finally safe here.

Joan continued to carefully guide each person that climbed to the top of the ladder. Each survivor jumped into the rescue box with ease. From the outside, the people in the box shouted words of true encouragement towards Joan. She was their savior.

After about 10 minutes of providing support for everyone climbing the ladder, Joan looked down to see who was left from the crowd. She expected to see people who were scared of heights, small children or the elderly. But no. The Cardmaster was just sitting there. His back was to the wall and he had a completely different look on his face: one of somber sadness. Joan quickly slid down the ladder and approached the final survivor.

"Yo, Cardmaster! Come climb this ladder. I'm going to rescue you."

"It's too late for that, Joan. I did this."

Joan was confused. "I have literally no idea what you're talking about."

"Joan. Can't you see? I hurt all of these people. I meant to have all of these people watch my acts and have fun and be happy. But look at this mess."

The mall was nothing more than a melted wet bolus. The slimy concrete mass traveled past the two of them slowly towards the back of the beast's throat.

"Joan, I'm not even qualified to be a fate changer. I used to be a child's magician and I had perfected my craft of card tricks. But one day, I just found this pack of cards on the ground that could change fate. And it all went wrong from there. I don't even truly control people's fate. I just helped them shuffle their fate up so they can have a different one. And the fate that you picked after I shuffled those cards just massacred this mall and the people in it. I'm useless and I've killed people with these unthinkable powers. Please let me just die here. I think I deserve that much."

"Cardmaster..."

"Call me Eugene"

"Okay Eugene. Listen man. I think I'm qualified to talk about this being the granddaughter of the owners of this mall..."

"Your grandparents conceptualized this mall within a beast and actually built it without a care for safety concerns? And they built it out of concrete knowing that the acidic saliva here can melt through it? Are they stupid or something?"

"Yeah I don't know probably." Out of the blue, a thought popped up in Joan's mind. The low grumbling of the beast grew louder. "Hey, Eugene. I can recognize someone who is overexploited and tired. You have a talent that should not be exploited, man. Why don't you climb that ladder and make some good in the world?"

"But my power to change fate has created futures where tragedies such as these exist. How can I not do that in the outside world?"
Joan smirked. "Well I think this tragedy with the beast was a long time coming. No changing of fates would have stopped any of this from happening. Here, just pass me the deck of cards and I will show you something. I think I understand how they work now."

Eugene reached into his pockets and felt the deck of the cards on his fingertip. With one single brush, he could feel immense power seep from between each card. It was too much power to wield but he had it. He pulled out the deck and handed it to Joan.

"Thank you, Eugene," She puts the deck into her back pocket

"Okay uh, what are you going to do with the deck? Is it a magic trick or something?"

"No tricks man. I'm holding onto it."

"Huh?! Does this mean that you're going to use it on yourself again? You might lower your lifespan by an unknowable amount by accident or something!"

Joan interrupts Eugene's worrying and overthinking. "I have come to realize that no matter what card I drew, it would never help me escape this life. I can't escape this mall. I can't escape my family. I can't escape their debts. I can't ever escape from the conditions I was born into. The cards themselves don't generate new fates based on pure luck. These fates are based on your past and future: essentially the position you're born into and the choices that you make afterwards. If I were born into a better family, I would have better cards to pull like: Queen or CEO or happy or whatever. But because I was born in such filth, I got cards like: villain or coward or loner and all that negative stuff. This tragedy with the beast and all was always going to happen. Each card just represented the person that I would be afterwards. There's no way a different pull at those cards would have fixed this." A metal tube detaches and falls from the ceiling, crashing into the melted rubble of the mall.

"You didn't make the fates or cause this tragedy. These cards just plant a seed into people's minds that would eventually lead them to become what's written on the card. If I pulled the coward card, I would have thought that this tragedy was too scary and I would have just run for the exits when I noticed something was wrong with the beast. I would have just let all of these people die and live the rest of my life knowing that I was a coward. If I pulled the deadbeat card, I would have escaped this tragedy and be sad for the rest of my life because I didn't save enough people. I would live out the rest of my days wallowing as a deadbeat. These fates that I was given to pull from are utterly tragic just as my past determined it to be. But with that said, I pulled the martyr card and look at me now. I have saved so many people from a fate worse than death. I am a hero to these people and I have you to thank for it."

Eugene teared up. He has never had someone so eloquently talk about his fate changing services. The fate business had always troubled him. He had always thought that he just ruined people and made a profit from it. But after hearing this, he feels that he can finally forgive himself for the tragedies that he thought he caused.

"But Eugene, I'm going to keep it 100 with you. I'm going to die in this mall holding these cards and I'm gonna make sure no one can shuffle these cards ever again."

"But why Joan? We could do so much good out there. We could change so many fates for the better. If what you say does come true, we could even prevent entire conflicts and horrific events from happening."

"To change someone's fate in this way just forces them to become a version of themselves that they can't derive from. It does not remove the past. It does not stop tragedies. It doesn't just let someone be forgiven for all their past mistakes and even if it did, that's a pathetic life to live. A life of forgetting and moving on. I can never move on from my life because my past is so deeply integrated into my identity."

"But I noticed too, Eugene, that the beauty of life doesn't come from the fact that things are always going to be perfect in the end or that we know the person we'll be when we die. The beauty in life comes from the fact that anything can change. Flowers aren't beautiful because they're all the same. They all have different colors and shapes and when you arrange them together they can create an image that is so awe-inspiring. And then they die with gorgeous memories of their appearance lingering in the witnesses of their beauty. Life is absolutely amazing but removing the unpredictability of it removes a lot of the potential for change. Because I pulled one of your cards, I will never be more than a martyr. I can never do more than what I am doing right now. And I guess I have to accept that since I'm dying with this stupid mall."

Eugene snapped out of it. Since Joan had pulled so many cards from the deck before she changed her fate, that meant that she could die in this mall today.

"I always figured that when I die, it was always gonna be with this crap place. I want to make sure the bad decisions that my family made don't hurt more people. And there's still a lot of people trapped here, Eugene. They all still need rescuing and I'm the only one here who's qualified to help them. After meeting you, I realized something. We're all prisoners to our past. Although my past and your cards inform the person I'm fated to be, you haven't picked up a card from the deck yourself, have you?"

Eugene gulped. "No, I haven't but what are you saying? I don't want you to die just yet, you're so special to people and you're so brave in the face of danger and people could really use you outside of the beast. Maybe you can still live after this tragedy and inspire even more people."

Joan gave a warm smile. "I'm saying that you are not a prisoner to any fate or any crappy past. If you can survive in this economy as a child's magician for this long, then surely you came from a good family."

Eugene looks down and chuckles. "I love my family so much. They treated me so well and made me so happy all throughout my childhood and they continue to support my job into adulthood too. I just took this job because I want to make other people happy like my parents did for me."

Joan clears his throat. "Once you pick up any one of these cards, you said that you would become the person on the card. Well, if you haven't picked up your card that means your fate is probably not set in stone yet. You can do anything you want with yourself. You can go on to do good and continue making people happy. You're an incredible performer and you have a talent to make people smile. You're absolutely special in a way you can't even comprehend."

Eugene teared up. No one had ever said something so meaningful to him before. All of the years of performing for people has paid off. Someone has finally recognized him for being a person who is special.

"Thank you for recognizing me, Joan. You're making me feel so confident in myself in a way that I've never felt before."

"Me too Eugene. Thank you so much for letting me choose my fate. Because of you, my life now has worth. My vast knowledge of the mall's layout has saved so many people from horrifying death and I will continue saving people till my last breath. If you and I are this special, just imagine the worth of your audience. The people who showed up to the mall today. Each individual that I have saved has lived their life in such complex and different ways that it would be incredibly difficult to even put it into words right now. It's unfathomable how special and important every individual is and has the potential to be. And that's why I have to say this to you." Joan stands up with a look on her face that tells of a calm content feeling that now moves her to say these next few words.

"I'm going to sacrifice myself," Joan says slowly and confidently. "I'm going to go out helping all the people that are still trapped here. But I want you to go out there and live your best life. You have so much potential and I may have it too but if I leave the beast, then..." Joan shudders and looks down. "I'll have to answer to the world and explain why this tragedy happened and I'm just tired of having to answer for the sins of my family." Joan looks back up at Eugene, her emerald eyes pierce into his soul. "Eugene, please go out there. Make a new life for yourself. Keep making people happy. And, please make sure everyone you come across fully knows that they're special."

Eugene wanted to refute everything that Joan was saying. She was amazing and smart and brilliant and she's just as special as him. She deserved to live a different life away from the beast and away from everything that her family was. But her expression said otherwise. Her face was absolutely still, smiling warmly towards him. Not one thing about her showed any fear in the face of cosmic horror. Nor did it show that she's envious of him for his good childhood or anything else. Not one part of her wants to continue living in such a cruel life. She has made up her mind to become a martyr.

"I understand, Joan." Eugene nodded and he stood up and began to climb the ladder. Before he reached the ladder's halfway point, he turned to her. "Joan, i know what i want to do with my life now. I want to be an oratory. I will narrate your story to great audiences near and far. You'll inspire millions."

"I am very grateful for that. Thank you. Take good care of yourself and enjoy the rest of your life, Eugene. I'll enjoy the rest of mine. Just know that your life's worth is entirely determined by you despite the circumstances you're born into."

Eugene teared up again. But suddenly, a grumble erupted from the beast, shaking the ladder vigorously. He had to hurry up right now or he'll be its next meal. He looked back down at Joan to wave to her but she's gone. She had already jumped back into action, trying to look for people who needed help.

Eugene had reached the rescue drone and jumped into the box. The crowd of people cheered for him. He started to tune out the sound and just looked at every individual's face. A tall man with burgundy skin and boisterous laugh. Two twins danced and chased each other through the crowd. A now widowed husband holds his kids tightly as tears rush down his face. Everyone looks so relieved that they survived and that their beloved Cardmaster survived as well. He smiled to himself.

"Come one! Come all! And hear the tale of Joan, our savior and our martyr! It all started about 23 years ago. Her family bought out space in..."

As the crowd gathered around Eugene, the drone took off towards a safe location while transporting all of the survivors.

Eugene, as he narrated Joan's story, looked back towards the beast. More survivors waited at the end of its nostril while a different drone fashioned itself in place for survivors to hop into the rescue box it carried. The massive wreck in the parking lot caused by the beast looked like it would take eons to clean up. The beast's mouth and by extension,

the Gaping Maw Mall, was now eternally closed to the public. And
Joan was never seen again.

DECEMBER: CONVERGENCE

Winner: Lindsey Simmons

BETTER LUCK NEXT TIME

LINDSEY SIMMONS

She wasn't who he thought she'd be.

The club was packed to the rim, sound waves of electronic music reverberating through his rib cage. Kai had only a limited description of her: *female, iseijin, white hair.* The agency was vague like that. She could be anyone here.

He casually surveyed the crowd. With so many people here, it was hard to discern faces. Shafts of cool toned light illuminated go-go dancers on raised platforms. One in particular quickly caught his attention.

A blue-haired dancer swayed to the beat, her movements as fluid as the neon lights that illuminated the warehouse. Her hair, styled short, sharp, and angular, glowed like sapphires from beyond the bars of her cage, reflecting a halo of white. Her body was clad in an pearlescent latex outfit that hugged her curves as she moved to the pulsating beat of the synth. Her makeup was heavy and striking, her eyes lined with a thick, black liner, and her lips painted a deep metallic blue, fine glitter accentuating her cheekbones.

She was entirely and utterly captivating, and Kai couldn't help but fall victim to magnetic pull.

Kai flicked his visor glasses over his eyes and activated them with a simple touch. His vision darked, and lines of cyan etchings raced across the silhouettes of everyone around him. But he wasn't focused on just anyone. He was looking at her.

"White hair," he scoffed, and pushed them back onto the top of his head. His eyes tracked the rhythmic swing of her hips for the next five beats before he decided to make his approach. Standing at eye level to the platform sole of her vinyl white boots, he seized the opportunity of momentary silence to flash a bright grin up at her.

"Can I buy you a break? Or a drink?" He leaned against the cement of the platform. "Or both?"

She crouched and her perfume washed over him, fresh and clean with notes of coconut and sea salt. Her voice dripped with sarcasm and intrigue. "I'm always up for a good time."

The air outside was crisp. Mirrored advertisements reflected in the slickened streets as thick clouds hung low in the atmosphere, shrouding the towering skyscrapers in mist. Kai let out a breath, watching the cigarette smoke curl towards the gray skies.

The dancer found him quickly. An ivory, synthetic fur jacket rested loosely on her shoulders. Her dark, almond shaped eyes roved over him, up and down, before a smile crept across her lips. "You're exactly as described," she noted.

"You're not."

She pulled off the bobbed, blue wig and allowed cascades of diamond bright hair to fall free. Kai felt a jolt of surprise, even though white hair was what he was expecting. He couldn't help but stare. He had never seen hair that color before, not beyond digital magazines or holo ads. It was nearly translucent, and caught the surrounding light like a prism.

"I didn't catch your name, stranger."

"Call me Kai," he said, forcing himself to tear his gaze away.

"Call me Keiko," she purred in response.

Both names were fake, Kai knew that much. But to be an agent is to own a couple hundred names and know a thousand more, yet not have a single one matter to you.

"Kiki," he snuffed out his cigarette, "I like it."

The apartment was small and simple, but it had everything they needed for this mission. A kitchen, a couch, a bedroom and bathroom. The walls were a plain white, and the furniture was minimalist, though functional. A large window looked out to the cityscape, casting a dim glow over the room. The air was clean and fresh, thanks to the building's advanced filtration system. The only sound was the soft hum of the city outside. The agency was generous, this time. It would be easy to adjust to.

Kai dropped his backpack at the table to begin a cursory inspection.

"That's it?" Keiko glanced at his bag.

"I travel light," he said simply. Besides, it was all that would fit on his motorbike. "Keys?"

Keiko flashed her keycard. "Check."

"One each," he noted, as per usual. "Guns?"

"I don't have mine yet. I'm still a recruit."

That was fine. Kai has his and that's what mattered. He asked this next question as casually as the last.

"What do you know about Vitae?"

She froze, halfway unpacking a box of medical supply. "That's a blunt approach."

Kai leaned against the bedroom's doorway. He noted only one bed but that would be a problem for later. "I waste no time."

"Vitae," Keiko shoved the box under the nightstand right of the bed, "is a new substance appearing in black market exchanges."

A drug, no doubt. Only recently has it been circulating the city and in sparse amounts. It was expensive and the demand was only growing.

"The agency hasn't been able to secure a sample and identify exactly what it's made of," she continued. "It's an opaque blue fluid that is denser and more viscous than water. That's all I know."

"They put us right in the highest traffic point," Kai added with a nod. Across from an amusement park and below a net of criss-crossing freeway bridges, it was a prime location for illicit exchange.

Keiko studied him for a moment. "Come here."

He obliged, sitting a respectable distance away from her on the comforter. She took his wrist and fastened a thin band around it.

"Heart rate monitors. You have mine and I have yours. We'll know if the other needs assistance."

He glanced at the wristband then back at her. She was inhumanly pretty, but something was off about her. He couldn't help but notice how much smaller she was than he, especially without the added height of her boots. Maybe it was the white hair, the dark eyes, or the perfect complexion, but he couldn't quite place it.

Kai thought of himself plainly. He was the perfect agent, mundane and uninteresting, the ideal face to blend into crowds. He was tall, fit, as the agency would have him, with dark brown hair and pale blue eyes–contacts, of course, cybernetics that paired with his visor glasses and motorbike helmet. Removable, but intended for long term wear. It was the only work he had done. He was a nearly intact human, a rarity to come by these days. He could only imagine the amount of work Keiko had gotten done to perfect her flawless appearance.

"You have medical imports," he observed and watched her heart rate spike on the slim black screen of his wristband.

"I have aplastic anemia," she stated. "Nothing serious."

That sounded serious, but Kai decided to press her about it another time.

Within a few days Kai had already adjusted to life with Keiko. He appreciated the monotony of a simple routine: wake up before sunrise, go for a morning run, eat a light breakfast, then check surveillance and gather data with Keiko. Sometimes she would join him for dinner, but she never ate much. She would leave in the evening in athleisure wear with her hair pulled into a high ponytail and a pair of rollerskates slung over her shoulders. She would return late and shower before climbing into bed with him.

Kai slept on his side, facing the window, deciding to politely ignore her nightly infusions. He often slipped into sleep watching coaster trains climb and fall over the sleek metal tracks, dreaming of sandy beaches and temperate waters.

He slowed his motorbike. With the magnetic wheel attachment and electric motor, the NovaStar model was silent even at high velocities, and even a seasoned agent wouldn't detect it. Keiko wouldn't see him coming.

His modular helmet's interior screen activated and zeroed in on her instantaneously.

The wheels glided over the smooth floor of the open-air rink. The checkerboard floors were backlit with continuously changing lights, the roller skaters atop becoming a kaleidoscope of color and motion. Rhythm and blues music encompassed the wide expanse, palm trees bordering the cirque. Kai pushed on slowly, careful to weave between wheels and to remain on the outermost ring. He knew he was getting glares and odd looks but he disregarded them. A motorcyclist on a roller rink wasn't the weirdest thing out there.

He caught the sheen of white hair first and lifted the visor of his helmet. Keiko was an image of precision and poise, executing each movement with discipline. Her skates, a powder blue with clear wheels, rolled smoothly over the floor. She made it look easy.

"Kiki!" Kai called and snapped her out of her trance. She swung her body around and leaned her weight on her toes, the friction pulling her to an urgent stop. She stared at him incredulously.

He grinned lazily at her shock. "I brought takeout."

Hues of orange, rose, and mauve painted the sky before it darkened into a deeper shade of indigo. Holographic advertisement dominated the night, betwixt the tall structures, roller coaster tracks, and freeway bridges, washing the cityscape in an ethereal glow. They sat together on a set of stairs, enjoying their fried rice and chow mein packed in tiny white boxes, when Kai got the first alert.

"There's an exchange," he reported quickly, under his breath, transcribing the message as it crossed his vision. "Palm Court."

"That's in the center of the rink," said Keiko, pulling her laces tight. "I'm on it."

She raced off without waiting for a response, her roller skates carrying her quicker than Kai's mind could keep up. He let out a frustrated growl and threw on his helmet, slamming down the shield.

I'll beat ya to it, Keiko's taunting message blinked across his visor screen. Adrenaline flashed hot through his chest as he mounted his bike and squeezed the clutch.

Reality warped around him, distorting in a haze of lights and color. He sped through the district, weaving in and out of traffic with ease. He narrowed his eyes at the cyan etchings, directing him towards a cluster of palm trees. Keiko's form was nearing.

He relented to flip up his visor and flash her a teasing smile. "Try to keep up!"

She bumped his bike with her hip, momentarily throwing it off balance before it auto-corrected. He flailed, she laughed, and the checkerboard flooring rushed to meet them. Wind whipped through his hair and he closed his visor and clenched his jaw.

Kai pressed himself low against his motorbike. He skirted around the ring of palm trees, turning so fast the side of his leg scraped against the slick ground.

His visor screen identified the suspect. An etching outlined a hooded figure's silhouette as biometric data was retrieved in a matter of milliseconds. The visor identified a vial in his pocket. Bingo.

Kai locked in his target. He reached for the stun gun tucked in his belt, as his vehicle skidded to an abrupt stop.

"Freeze!" he shouted through his helmet. The suspect panicked and dashed leftward. His shoes slipped on the roller rink flooring and the vial of incandescent blue fluid went skittering across.

It would be crushed in minutes if he didn't do something. The sample would be useless full of shattered glass and scraped from the ground.

The suspect seized Kai's moment of distraction and fled. Kai shoved the gun back in his belt and Keiko broke through the skaters, darting for the vial. She dove, and just before her fingers closed around it, a hooded figure swiped it and hastened upstream.

But instead of chasing after him, Keiko rolled over to Kai. "I need you to accelerate as fast as possible and slam the brakes when I say when!"

She fixed her hands on the back of his bike.

"Are you crazy?!"

"Are you really asking me that now?!"

He didn't have time to argue, already picking up speed. The rink was cleared out as mass panic rippled through. The hooded man scrambled towards the nearest building. He was about to get away when Keiko shouted, "Now!"

Kai squeezed the brake lever and sent Keiko flying ahead at in-human speeds. His bike groaned in protest, failing to grip the polished floor. There was nothing he could do to stop his bike from slamming into the window.

Glass showered down from every direction. Kai saw Keiko's wheel hit a shard and sent her tumbling out of control.

Security cameras flashed like lightning.

Keiko stared wide eyed.

The suspect and the sample had gotten away.

And they were in *big* trouble.

He couldn't go anywhere without seeing her face. It was plastered on every billboard, illuminated on every holograph, and ribboned across newscasts. Keiko was a wanted woman.

"This can't be happening," she groaned dramatically from the bathroom counter.

"Oh, it's happening, sweetheart." Kai couldn't help but to find humor in the irony. An agent with a bounty on her head. For *disrupting the peace* no less. He could only imagine how much worse it would have been if she had gotten that vial and had been caught red (or blue) handed. Saved by the veil of his helmet, Kai's identity remained masked.

A thick liquid splattered onto the bathroom tiles.

Kai stifled a laugh. "Isn't there a pigment pill or something for that?"

"Just wait for me downstairs," Keiko grumbled.

The cafe below their apartment was small. Kai waited, boredly sipping his iced green tea with coconut water. It had brown, squishy tapioca pearls in it, as per Keiko's recommendation. Strange, he thought, but not unenjoyable.

The sound of heels striking cement stairs descended first, and he snapped his attention up. Nothing could have prepared him for this moment. She was unrecognizable. Keiko became a vision of dark beauty. Jagged black bangs with sharp layers of electric purple now framed her tan, angular features. Smokey eyeshadow and thick, winged eyeliner darkened her eyes, while the bold, metallic violet added a stark pop of color to her face. Her dress clung to her body like a second skin, highlighting her every curve and contour.

Something changed in him. A new feeling pitted in his chest, something strange and unfamiliar and warmer than the allure of desire. It frightened him.

"Well?" Keiko gave him a spin.

"Kiki, you look…" he couldn't drink in enough of her, "dangerous."

"Do you think it will work?" she clarified. "Heavy makeup minimizes the effectiveness of facial recognition software, and the hair, well," she shrugged, "it's different."

"It's beautiful," he said all too quickly. "You look beautiful."

He prayed Keiko didn't glance down at her flashing wristband.

He waited in silence. Hours passed, and he remained pressed against his bike. His vantage point was decent, hidden on the second story of an unfinished parking structure, though his sight was muddled by rain. It fell in sleets, warping the holographic signs and darkening the light polluted skies.

It was cold. But Kai clutched the grip of his gun with his gloved hand, watching carefully through the lens of his visor glasses.

He was only here with a tip and a hunch.

A cyan etching blinked into his vision as a figure strode towards a parked car. Kai didn't even think twice and pulled the trigger.

He lowered himself from the ledge and dropped into the street below. His boots landed in a puddle, the thick rubbery tread silencing the sound, in front of the unconscious body of his target.

Kai rolled the man over on his back. He checked his pulse. Steady. He peeled back the man's coat and rifled through his pockets. Met with a luminescent blue glow, he knew exactly what he beheld. Kai stowed three vials of Vitae.

The apartment was dark and empty when he returned. Keiko was probably at the roller rink, despite the rain. He shucked off his drenched jacket, resting it on the coathang before he kicked off his boots. He padded over to the bedroom and pulled a silver briefcase from the depths of the closet.

The spectrometer was compact, and quick to power up. Since his visor screens could tell him nothing about the chemical makeup of Vitae, he had low hopes.

Skilled hands extracted a small sample of the blue liquid. All it took was one drop of Vitae on the clear disk and a strong beam of radiation before the spectrometer's screen started listing elements of the chemical composition.

Kai identified iron, carbon, nitrogen, oxygen, hydrogen, and furrowed his brow. This was eerily similar to the chemical makeup of *blood.*

His head swam. A million questions pounded in his mind. He had no possible idea what this could mean. Was Vitae made from human blood? Was this a form of trafficking? Or a biological weapon?

He shut the briefcase with a shaking hand and pocketed the vial.

Kai deliberated informing the agency, forwarding his sample analysis and his suspicions. He had a feeling that this was much, much greater than a simple interception of illegal goods, and he couldn't shake the feeling that something was deeply and irrevocably wrong.

He woke up in a cold sweat. The bed was empty. There was a spike of light on his wristband monitor before it went dark. Kai's blood went cold. Keiko was in trouble.

He groped for his glasses and threw on his boots, bolting for the door.

"Come on, come on," he breathed as the cyan lines in his vision failed to pinpoint her precise location. He pulled his NovaStar bike down from the rack and pushed into the haze of the night.

One ping and she appeared on the map, a faint scratch.

Kai broke every traffic law to exist, heedless of his own safety. The route drew him deeper and deeper into the heart of the city, through intersections, under monorail tracks, and through narrow alleys. The night air whipped around him, moisture accumulating on the shield of his helmet.

Panic rose as her light dimmed. He swerved into the subway track, desperate for any way to reach her quicker. Flashes of orange beat past him and he veered back out and onto the street. He was near.

Gunfire bounced off the cement edifices. Kai ditched his bike and ran towards it, clicking off the safety on his handgun. His training screamed at him to move with caution, but in this moment, he disregarded everything that he had been taught.

He didn't even give his first opponent any acknowledgement before he swung his fist. The back of the handgun made contact with his head first with a sickening thud, and his legs collapsed beneath him. Kai leapt over the crumpled body and trained his gun on his next victim.

Kai's voice was low and threatening. "Get. Away."

He only counted to three before he pulled the trigger. The bullet burned through the shoulder of Keiko's attacker. He screamed and recoiled into the shadows.

Kai's stomach dropped when he saw her.

Keiko lay on her side, clutching a hand to her chest. Her hair veiled her face, but a consistent *drip* fell beneath her. The metallic tang of blood hung heavily in the air.

He dropped to his knees. "Kiki–"

He took her by the shoulders and gingerly eased her onto her back. A dark wetness seeped through her shirt. His hands trembled as he drew a knife from his boot and took a handful of fabric.

"Don't–" she warned, panic rising in her voice. He shrugged off her half-hearted attempt to shove his hands away.

"You're bleeding," he breathed. "Let me help you."

Years of medical training flashed before his eyes as he ripped open her shirt, revealing not warm flesh and blood, but a cold, transparent surface.

He froze, his eyes widening as he took in the sight of her artificial heart, encased in a protective titanium rib cage. Organic bone melded to carbon, ivory vertebrae turning silver the further down he drew his gaze. The glass-clad polycarbonate paneling of her chest was shattered, viscous blue fluid spurting from a tear in her tubing every time the synthetic heart contracted, exactly where the left pulmonary artery would be. Her circulatory system was entirely artificial, and it was defective.

He blinked as his cybernetic contacts attempted to analyze the problem and locate a solution, but only the loading wheel flickered in the corner of his sight.

"I'm losing Vitae," she said quietly.

It wasn't a drug. No, not at all. And with a chemical makeup similar to blood, it was exactly that: *artificial blood.* Kai's head pounded with a million questions.

The empty space of her glass chest was filling quickly with the blue fluid. The beats of the heart-like device were slowing down. She was dying.

"Kai."

"Right, right." He drew a shaky breath. "What do you need me to do?"

Her answer was a hopeless whisper. "You need to repair the conduit."

He fixed his gloved hand under the broken polycarbonate and pulled upward. The left panel lifted and Vitae trickled from the cracks. Shit, shit, *shit.*

He carefully extracted the bullet lodged between the first and second titanium rib, and with slight pressure, it came loose, releasing a fresh surge of warm Vitae that spilled over his hand. He grasped at the recesses of his mind to find a solution, something, anything, to stop the bleeding.

A vague memory rippled to the surface. When the hydraulic system of his motorbike was struck by crossfire, the hose was cut and hydraulic fluid leaked. In a pinch he melted the tubing back to itself with an open flame–

Kai fumbled for his lighter. He held his breath, patting down his pockets. There. It failed to ignite.

One spark.

Two. Nothing.

Then it lit.

A trembling hand held the flame within her chest.

Vitae congealed on contact. The flame flickered and the clear plastic tubing adhered to itself. Kai shoved it back into the valve and looked up.

Keiko was fading and fading fast. She had lost enough blood to puddle beneath her. Her dark eyes gazed distantly into the sky as she fought to keep them open, eyes once so full of life and brightness.

"Stay with me, Kiki," he mumbled.

"It doesn't replenish," she gasped. "The Vitae."

Her medical imports. Her nightly infusions.

Kai drew the three vials from the innermost pocket of his jacket and looked at her. "Let's get you home."

She was in and out of consciousness. The drive back was a blur. One moment he was scooping her up in his arms, and the next he was setting her down in the plush sterile whiteness of their bed. He had never witnessed her initiate an infusion, but that wasn't going to stop him from trying to figure it out.

It was just intravenous infusion therapy, he assured himself.

Her stash of Vitae was small, equipped with latex gloves, a catheter, and hospital tubing. It was easy enough to administer.

Deep blue liquid flowed steadily through the clear tubing, reminiscent of the ocean's depths enchanted by bioluminescence. Two extra vials were seemingly enough to supplement two bags and replenish the liter lost.

He waited. And he waited. And while he waited he studied her closer than ever before. She lay reclined against the softness of pillows, her purple hair fanned out around her. He noted the steaks of silver that shined through. Her eyes were shut, her brows knit, an expression of pain written across her face. Even near death, she was beautiful.

A symmetric line, thin and fine and nearly undetectable, ran from her ears to the corner of her lips. With her makeup washed away, the difference in texture was visible.

Silicon, he thought. *Prosthetics.*

His gaze fell to her chest. Her body blurred the boundary of human and machine, blending organic and synthetic. Everything from her lower jaw to her neck and collarbones, ribcage and spine was gutted. Flesh, blood, and bones replaced with silicon, chemicals, and titanium.

He had never seen anything like her. And he could only imagine the horrors of what a being like her could entail– what horrible things had happened to her to leave her like this.

Kai had just finished washing his clothes, changing Keiko's, and burning the evidence when the light of dawn glowed at the horizon. Keiko roused as the morning light crept over her face and began to glisten on the vibrancy of her hair.

"Answers," Kai demanded. "Answers now or I forward the footage to the agency."

"Footage?" she echoed, hazy.

Kai pointed to his eyes, the intensity of them pinning her down.

She opened her mouth to respond, faltering, before resorting to, "I never wanted you to see me like this."

He crossed his arms. "*What* are you?"

Keiko's black eyes waivered. "A person who has undergone severe amounts of trauma and reconstruction."

"Does the agency know?"

She shook her head.

Kai was suspended between his feelings and his orders. He was tasked with understanding the emergence of this new substance, and the answer right about fell into his lap. But to complete his mission, he would have to expose her. That wasn't something he wanted to do. If the agency knew the extent of her modifications, he could only imagine what jobs they would task her with.

His next question would determine his plan of action.

"Tell me what Vitae is."

It took her a full minute to find the words. Eventually she took a breath and said, "Kai, I lost my heart, my lungs, even my bones have been replaced. I cannot create or process blood. Vitae gives me life."

He went for the jugular. "Then why is there demand for it on the black market?"

"I don't know," she said and he almost believed her. "I don't know."

He dropped his weight at the foot of the bed and pinched the bridge of his nose. "I want to trust you, Kiki."

She gently pulled his hands away from his face.

"Then trust me, Kai."

She had never touched him before. Nothing more than a casual brush or a cursory tap on the shoulder. She took his hand and pressed his palm to her chest. Through her silk pajamas, and with the warmth of the blankets, the beat of her artificial heart felt convincing, real, *human*. And when he closed his eyes, he could pretend it was.

Keiko guided his hand up, along the curve of her neck and to the edge of her jaw. Soft, smooth, textured silicon. Almost skin-like. It was impressive. Her eyes drew him in, big and black like the wonders of the galaxy. He wanted nothing more than to lose himself in them.

He drew her into his arms and immersed himself in the essence of plumeria, hibiscus, pineapple, seawater and sunshine. He savored the gentle touch of her finger tip on his back, her head on his shoulder.

The world melted away for just a moment, leaving only the two of them, lost in their own little paradise.

This alert was unusual. Suspicious activity reported in the flooded district.

Keiko paused while lacing her roller skates. She shared a long glance with Kai.

"There's only a location," he pointed out. A pinpoint on the map, flashing urgently. No other information was given. Kai flicked his visor glasses over his eyes, but their screens supplied nothing more.

"I have a bad feeling about this," he muttered. No suspects, no descriptions, no names. Just a location.

Keiko, having ditched her skates in favor of boots, stood and straightened. She gave his arm a squeeze. "Let's go investigate."

An old abandoned industrial building stood silent and still before them, its walls and floors submerged beneath the murky waters. The air inside was thick with the dampness and decay, the scent of rust and rot permeating every inch of the space. Machinery loomed out of the darkness like skeletal fingers reaching up from the depths. Water lapped at the crumbling concrete, casting eerie refractions on the walls. Once a symbol of industry and progress, it was drowned by the relentless march of time and the unstoppable force of nature.

Keiko waded silently ahead. Kai scanned for movement, but the cyan etchings in his vision glitched the deeper they pushed on. The water deepened, slowly climbing towards his waist.

Kai's heart raced, his palms slick with sweat. He scanned his surroundings, searching for the source of his unease. The air was heavy with an unspoken dread, like the calm before a storm. He felt watched, the eyes of an unseen threat locked on him. The world around seemed to close in, the cold cement walls seeming to press into him. Kai felt trapped, unable to escape the sinking feeling that he was a lamb being led to slaughter.

"Kiki, wait–" he hissed, but she ignored him, hastening her pace towards the clearing ahead.

"Kiki!" Kai was struck with a bad realization at the worst of times. He caught up to her, the echoes of splashing water bouncing off the walls and returning thrice. "Kiki, why *were* you attacked?"

She ignored him. He grabbed her shoulder and she whipped around and something cold pressed against his abdomen. He didn't need to glance down to know it was the barrel of a gun.

He raised his own in surrender.

Two figures emerged from the shadow. Though Kai's contacts failed to identify either of them, he noted the agency's emblems embroidered on their bullet-proof vests. His eyes flicked from one to the other and back to Keiko.

"I'm sorry," she whispered, refusing to meet his gaze.

Kai tried to ignore the flashing of his own heart rate on her wristband. "I don't understand–"

"You completed your mission."

"I didn't–"

She stood awash in moonlight. A silent tear struck the water below.

"The Vitae..." he trailed off, his mind a tempest of thoughts that refused to settle.

"You don't get it, do you? The agency knows I'm *bion*, Kai. *They* did this to me."

The world swayed around him.

"You were hired to intercept stolen vials and return them to the company that produced them, the company sponsored by the agency. Vitae is modified human blood meant to sustain *freaks* like me." Keiko's voice broke. "They picked you because you do your job, no questions asked. They picked you knowing you would discover me."

"Kiki," he said firmly, "*why were you attacked?*"

Tears streamed down her face. "I'm the one distributing Vitae."

He stood there, stunned. Her words echoed in his mind. He couldn't process it, couldn't make sense of it. *Why?*

She looked up at him through her bangs, trembling. "They can no longer control me if Vitae is replicated and mass produced."

"You *let* him get away on purpose," Kai mumbled, staggering back. Keiko let distance lapse but she kept her gun trained on him. "You *let* yourself be caught." She wanted the Vitae to escape. The bounty placed on her head was a strong message sent to the agency. Keiko was desperate for freedom.

And they attacked her.

Color drained from her complexation. Her next words were hardly audible. "I traded my life for yours."

"Kiki, no…"

She stifled a cough, but blue trickled down her silicon chin. She raised the gun to his head, unable to hold it straight. It wasn't her emotion preventing her from squeezing that trigger.

She stumbled back, slumping upright against a support beam.

The two men seized Kai before he could rush to her aid. They slammed Kai against the wall and something shattered in his pocket. Shards of glass stabbed him through his clothes, but that was the least of his problems.

He thrashed, throwing a punch with his occupied hand. It landed with a satisfying *crack*, metal against bone. One down, one to go.

A deft kick sent his next opponent reeling back, but he regained his composure quickly. Kai dodged a series of punches, but pain spiked through his body when a fist connected with his face. He saw stars and fell back into the water. He rolled, avoiding the boot bearing down inches away from his face.

Kai gasped for breath, scrambling to his feet. One solid swing sent his attacker onto his back. He hit the cement before he hit the water.

Standing over him, Kai wasted no time. He raised his gun and fired.

And the bullet struck Keiko right in the chest.

Her eyes widened before they rolled back into her head.

He threw down his weapon and ran for her. Keiko fell into his arms, grasping for handfuls of his shirt.

"You– you shot me," she murmured, numbly. "And… you poisoned me–"

Kai wiped away the Vitae dribbling from her lips. "I'm sorry, Kiki," was all he could muster.

"How..?"

"I swapped out your last infusion." With coconut water, substitute for intravenous fluid. But not Vitae. And the vial he swapped had just shattered mere moments before.

Inky blue darkened the water around them, spreading in swirling tendrils as all life ebbed away from her. Kai couldn't save her. Not this time.

A gentle hand reached up to cup the side of his face. Keiko smiled sadly at Kai. "Better luck next time."

She pushed through the cracks in her polycarbonate chest, and her fingers closed around her heart. With the remaining strength in her body, she tore it out. Blue ran in streams down her arm. She put it against Kai's chest.

And his wristband flatlined.

Kai combed his hair back before a mirror. He straightened his suit jacket and squared his shoulders. He took a steadying breath before he exited the bathroom.

"I'm ready," he said and meant it.

He was led down a darkened hallway and brought to the showroom. It felt like he was waiting an eternity before he was finally let in.

He held his breath, staring intently down at his wristband. He hadn't taken it off since the day she–

He didn't want to think about it. That was months ago.

What mattered was that he was here now, and–

A rhythmic beat appeared on the slim black screen.

His attention shot up

The android blinked open her black, almond shaped eyes for the first time. Her perfect face framed by silky waves of diamond bright hair, beamed up at him.

"Kiki," he breathed.

"Kai," she sighed and cold silicon lips pressed against his.

JUDGMENT

JASON NGUYEN

In the cold and pitch black darkness of the night, the wind howls, pushing in and giving way to a big object. Slowly, the gusts push in on a smaller object,the size and general shape of a rodent.

Bing

A box flashes, revealing its contents as a yellow and blue screen depicting three letters and a horrifying mascot suit akin to a rat committing emesis: UCLA.

Noise slowly pours in as small noises such as a chatter, scratching, and the-

"Yeah yeah. Honey? Honey? Honey please let me answer your question, if you were going on a rave about it why ask it? I know look I'm just busy OK, I'm not doing nothing I swear, I'll be there. Trying to foster the future, every decision counts. Mmmhmmm, mmhmm OK OK *i love you yeah* bye"

Andy hangs up the phone, walking in with his keys and several small objects, greasy and repugnant enough for the gases emitting from it to be visible and stink up the room like a lit- up cigarette. As Andy approaches the computer, Andy mutters,

"OK, let's see what we have today."

He pulls up an email attachment from what looks like a committee, as he clicks the entire screen is eclipsed with sheet filled with information. Andy goes quickly left to right with his eyes, skimming the starting information, which says

About you
Elaine
Buffy
Yang

February 14, 2001

Long Beach, CA, United States

Home address

Contact information
Home address (permanent)
Address line 1
7248 Plainview Cir.

In a rather ordinary high school, drabbed with gray architecture side-to-side, many students pass by back and forth. Mostly out of the school as a loudspeaker squeaks a sound unpleasant to the ears. Among them is an Asian American girl, with very broad Asian American traits, black hair, brown eyes, with a flowery patterned shirt as well as a skirt and tight pants. With her is a similar looking girl, but slightly bigger, with curly hair, and a black cardigan.

"Come on Elaine, I really thought you would've hit it off with Journalism."

"Elaine" darts a look,

"Uh, 'COME ON' Anna! You do remember when I brought Laurie an interview with Sharon Quirk-Silva right?"

Anna is bewildered but beams with remembrance.

"Oh yeah! Man, we had the craziest stories! How did you manage to sneak in like that?

An awkward air is brought as this introduces some deadly silence.

"I dunno, I just thought it would've been a great opportunity to promote projects, shoutout some more spotlight to the Mental Health Club and Academic Decathlon, maybe shine some spotlig-"

Elaine immediately interrupts.

"Doesn't matter! We came a long way, right? I can't wait to tour around, connect with some older folks, maybe I might see Steven again?"

The two both beam with excitement.

"OH MY GOD, Lainy! If you see that snarky ass, you better tell him to call me at 1-800-EAT MY A-"

By the time they reach this subject they have stopped by at an intersection that leads to a neighborhood.

"Uh, Anna, I think this is where I go."

"Ooooohhhh, right. Tell your dad I said hi OK?"

".....will do" Elaine halfheartedly states.

The two go their separate ways, as Elaine looks at all the high, two story houses.

A long walk on the flat sidewalk crrkk croakkkk crikk croakkk, straight into nothingness. Except for the occasional chirping of birds and crows.

Elaine finally reached the house, on the left side of a local street circle.

A blue house with many dead plants on the front yard, accompanied by a narrow cracked driveway and a giant splotch on the blue house wall.

Elaine looks down gazing at the cards that she and her team made, a picture of her with a suit titling her as the Vice-President of the Mental Health club is among them. As well as another club advertisement promising to raise the books to donate to the people in Africa. She then looks up, takes a deep breath, and goes in.

Andy's mahogany desk is smudged as a drop of liquid lands on the elegant surface. Coming from a secretion of chewing fluid from Andy's mouth out of boredom. The computer is seen displaying another student also attached in the email to look over, a student named "David Lee". Andy scrolls down very quickly, until a whole set of letters and classes fills the page that reads "Academic History" at the top. Andy shows a sign of dismissal until reading a set of sentences on "Additional information" that seems to lighten his mood.

David's face reflects off a computer, as his glasses show a person speeding on a platform and jumping. David shows a clear exhaustion and some excitement at what he's playing. He has no thoughts, only reflexes and the pops of slight amusement in between his stomach and his chest.

CREAK

David suddenly jumps in shock as the door right to the right suddenly opens up. Instinctively, David puts his head down and is ready yet anxious with what comes next.

"Hoouuuhhhh...David? Are you sure you're done with homework?" rang that familiar feminine voice, David's ears moving up akin to a dog as if this suddenly hearing an owner calling a dog for a treat.

"Uh-yes, I a-"

"I would believe that-" the woman invasively interjects, "if I didn't see you play games all day when I passed by your room. That's all you've been doing isn't it?"

David motions for an answer but of course as he knew from the sudden bump in his heart, he could not answer otherwise. In an attempt to ignore her, he gathers the small nerve in his body unafraid. To put a foot, slide, and the-

"Don't! Close it."

David just stands completely still, the feeling within his chest expanding with anxiety firing all over.

"I said close it!"

David motions to minimization

A hand shake is felt near his head.

/

\

/

\

/

\

David with some resistance finally does, leaving a very incomplete page of some paper. Clearly barely scraping by the first paragraph.

With some relief yet increased caution the woman let out a gasp, air filled with incomprehensible anger, rage, and.....disappointment.

"Why is it so hard for you? Why is it so...." his mother's voice creaks, the son's hand attempting to reach out with empathy until-

BUM BOMP BUM BOMP BUM BOMP

Loud and thumping footsteps can be heard from the outside.

"Hey Mom, how's it goin-"

An older middle aged face emerges only to feel the tense atmosphere crash into his face.

"...what did he do now?"

The mom shakes, "It's OK, it's OK" she speaks, speaking to someone but never facing anyone.

"Why do you do this? This is your future!"

"A future I am ready to make right!" David finally shouts, seemingly letting out every aggression hidden inside to fight back.

"What kind of fu-"

"I already completed the application." David says, which doesn't change his mother's face yet...

"Oh...OK OK OK Ok Ok Ok ok ok ok......

So...do you want to come with us on the beach?"

A deafening silence forms visibility in the air.

Visibly hesitating, his mouth clenching, resisting to say the words, David says,

"No...I can't mom, homework. Also I want to take a break from all that writ-you know."

The two parents are clearly shocked with what has been shown of their boy, but instead of engaging them further look down in solemn and walk away.

GRROOM

Vrrrrhhhhhhhh.....

The car can be heard from the open window pouring air on David's left, as David sits still, his face unmoving and his body popping onto his skin with turmoil. He then stands up and looks at the window with solemn and longing.

Andy jumps from page to page:

Flip flip

Campuses and majors with various schools flash for a brief second in the page.

Cli cli cli cli clic lic lic lic lic lic lic

"Test scores" filled with various numbers of 5s and 4s, 1,748 and 1,287 whitened away, almost trivialized

Images slowly build the physique and silhouette of Elaine, wearing a black suit and blue dress shirt.

Zzt zzt zzzt zzt zz tzz tzzzt zzt zzt ztz

The scroller wheels on, down and up down and up, down and up. The numerous awards, scholarships, and many more being consumed. However, there are quite few

Images constitute a silhouette of David, with messy hair and clearly weathered clothing.

The same noises occur, **but this time accompanied by these two shapes walking to unknown places face to face.**

Tap tap tap tap tap tapt tap tapt atpt tapt at patpa stoms tosmt patp papt papt bum bum buomp bum bomp bum BOMP

"Finally, the meat of all of this." Andy states in relief, as he looks at one of the final sections.

Personal insight questions

The question blots out **Describe an example of your leadership experience in which you have positively influenced others, helped resolve disputes, or contributed to group efforts over time.**

As it fades to Elaine, in a special sanctioned club outfit of a grey cardigan and white and green striped pants.

Vrr vrr vrrr

Her phone purrs increasingly as Elaine frantically takes it out to read a special kind of text: a blue icon indicating a group chat text message from an unknown club. Certainly not the one she is about to walk into right in this moment.

Elaine briskly walks into a door with a room, filled with marble-colored floor tiles and white walls and ceilings. There, she hears a chatter as she steps in; this is the Future Business Leaders of America (FBLA) club within her campus; all wearing tuxes.

"Uh, hi guys." Elaine gestures, "You didn't tell me we were all wearing tuxes."

A boy clearly of mixed race, half-Asian and half-Caucasan steps up.

"Well, you should've gotten the text right?"

"Wha-"

Elaine scrolls over the hundreds of text messages left in her wake, not one of them was from this kid,

"Eli, are you-...huhhh. I'm sorry, I'm just so busy today. I've been overwhelmed by work, this Calculus class, and soon I have to go but I-"

Eli comes up almost to shush her, she notices that it's almost telegraphed.

"Hey hey, it's fine I get it. I don't know though, this is our big announcement and preparation for the speeches we have to give to the State Leadership Conference, you just stay back okay?" he answers calmly to the point of coldness.

Elaine despite feeling more comfortable, could tell something was off as she blurts the words, "But why it's just-"

Eli puts his hand on her shoulder, "Look it's fine, we have everything taken care of, just think of it as a relaxation period, no one's gonna make a big deal alright?"

Elaine notices a slight grin on his face.

"Alright."

Just as she says that word, she notices her peers talking with the board, focusing on Camille - a friend - as she clearly is conversing "normally" but her movement is stiff; as if to hide something.

But Elaine sits by as things proceed normally as several members come into the club.

David is seen as the sun comes down eating with his family, a younger brother, the parents, and two elderly friendly folks who are his mother's parents and by extension, David's grandparents. Eating what looks like spicy noodles among other Thai dishes, everything seems to be calm but David can't go one second without imbuing a limb with motion.

"Stop that!" the dad said sternly,

"Stop what?" David dumbfoundedly asks.

"Your foot."

David is once again dumbfounded by what his father says,

"Your foot is shaking the table."

"Oh!" David gasps aloud, making several heads turn towards him.

David's brother lets out a sigh.

"You know, it's really hard to communicate with you," the mom states.

David could only let out a, "Yeah" with this, as he knew it to be true.

"I guess it comes with not spending too much time together you know, with you focusing on work, but it's all gonna pay off and we can talk to each other again! You two are both finally free."

"Yeah..." David states as he now looks at the floor, changing into a more anguished face.

By the time the club president reaches the announcements on who is going to speak for what subject Elaine finally sees hers...

Completely changed from her original topic of Journalism.

Her eyes become completely wide open from this discovery, fundamentally changing her performance forever in such a short notice. As the claps from these announcements deafened and stopped producing sound, as the chatter afterwards felt trivial, Elaine stepped furiously towards the board room. Step by step did she compose herself however, as the topic was changed to-

"Improv?!"

"Yes, we thought this would be in your best interest." the president stated aloud.

"Best interest?! This is improv! No one makes it in the top 3 with this, this is for the people who barely have any research!"

"Well then it would be **barely** an inconvenience for you" Eli wittingly remarks.

"Wha-but, do you know what this means?! I have to re-write everything!"

"Yeah Lainy, Trent's president of course he would know" Eli stepped up to blurt.

"Shut it." A familiar darker face says, motioning his hand; this is Isaac.

Elaine took this opportunity to proceed, "OK why? Everything has to be rewritten in such a short amount of time! I-I we talked about this, we filled out the form together Eli! I've been working so hard for this club why would you trea-"

"We know what you did" Isaac mutters under his breath.

Elaine, taking a whiff of this, is in complete disbelief at what he's talking about.

"No-"

"Someone you knew told us that you broke and entered into Sharon Quirk Silva's office after hours with fake authorization." Isaac continues, "I'm sorry but someone like that to be presenting in journalism just doesn't seem to fit, not to mention the underperformance and low attendance lately in FBLA-"

Elaine is in shock, "Underperformance?! I scored 3rds and 9ths at worst?! I worked hard! I-

"They weren't documented, I don't know if they were removed or what" Elaine looks at Eli who somewhat smugly shrugs as Isaac speaks.

"-but they don't matter anyway, with this news someone could press charges, so it's beyond our control. We haven't because we're your *friends* but who says he hasn't?", Isaac pointed to the advisor, a grey-haired balding man eating his lunch and typing on a black tinted computer screen.

Elaine just stared as everyone in the board started to leave, as the first bell rang. Isaac quickly broke his stern character and came to her side, dragging her to sit down.

She couldn't process this act of kindness though as every image had started to to become static...become bright....become blurry.

But she did hear one thing...

"I'm so sorry....I'm so sorry, look I'm your *friend* if you ever need me, I'll be there."

"Friend"

"Friend"

"Friend"

"friend"

"friend"

"friend"

"frien."

A high pitched noise is heard, screeching in her mind. As this continues to echo echo *echo echo eccho......*

At this point, everything becomes blurry, as she flashes back to Eli smiling, Camille and the others acting stiff, sitting there laughing.

"HA HA HA HA HA HA HA"

"Man, we had the craziest stories!" a voice was saying...she looked around to no avail, the girl can only spin spin and spin.

Suddenly, a masculine, terrifying voice is heard within her head.

"This is all your fault, you little

twerp! I did all I could in my minimum

wage job, all you had to do was read a

book! I hope you're happy with your

break time now because look where it
got us!"
GOT US!
GOT US!
GOT US!
Her heart starts beating beating beatin beat....*Bum bum bum bum Bum BUm BUm* BUM BOOM BOOM BOOM BOOM BOOM BOOM BOOM
SHE FEELS LIKE SHE WANTS TO EXPLOOOOOOOOOOOOD-DDDDD

Elaine quickly takes off

Elaine walked, huffing with each step, muscles quaking with each movement. It was so hard, she could hear her heart rate so visibly it was a surprise no one else heard her distress as well. THUMP! THUMP! THUMP! THUMP! THUMP! THUMP! THUMP! THUMP!

Booming like a drum wanting to burst out of her chest, Elaine continued forward.

That was when she saw a dreadfully skinny malnourished frame and a noise,
"Hey!"
It was him, it was David.
"Didn't you text on how we would meet and talk about what to do to get people into this book donation thing you're doing?"
Stopping sharper than a light about to turn off, Elaine unhealthily froze.....

Then walked inside Room 230.

"Y-y-yes", Elaine uttered, mustering the strength to talk, "Look, I don't have much right now, you just go on doing that, as you should OK?"

David takes a second to look and nods.

"People haven't been showing up lately, this is our second event in almost half a year you better find a way to do this no-"

David then jumps in the middle of Elaine's sentence, suddenly distressed,

"But how?! What if I mess up again, I.….…I.….."

"How many times do I have to tell you: it's not your fault." Elaine interjects, as if instinctually.

David's face slowly frowns "Not my fault?! I was the one who had planned an event behind your back, forced all of you to try something your heart wasn't set in…if it weren't for me then…"

Tears were slowly breaking through Elaine's eyes,

"Shut up! Just don't mention that! Don-"

"Elaine, I clearly only thought about myself, I wanted the glory and the value of feeling accepted… for the-"

Elaine is now sobbing on the floor, dropping an IGETC to UCLA…

"Our club would've achieved.." David continues,

Moist droplets then drop onto the floor. Tears, sweat, Elaine didn't know just then, a paper was put on to her face. Which, as if it were a custom of some kind made her feel some consolation. However, this paper felt hard, and as she focused on it, she realizes something…

David is also sad and the paper is a copy of insight questions for UCLA.

Describe the most significant challenge you have faced and the steps you have taken to overcome this challenge. How has this challenge affected your academic achievement?

Burns itself on the screen as the ink drops out back to the restaurant the Lee family is eating at.

"Mom, I'm…sorry."

"What kind of person do you think you are?"

"A man with a mission, trying to do better, trying to-"

"Change?! You haven't changed one bit! You're still doing nothing but playing video games and waiting until the last minute! Look at yourself! This isn't right! You talk all pretty and deep but you never changed!"

An awkward air is sent upwards and outwards spreading the scent of malice and pain all over the restaurant as it dilutes from the chatter of the rest of the customers.

"I'm taking you home…no Dad, take him home right now." David's mom commands.

The dad gets up and awkwardly tries to escort David out, as he leaves David takes a last look at his family. His brother trying to ignore it in embarrassment, his mom with that angry face - wrinkled chin and all, and…

His grandfather put his head down in disappointment, muttering a foreign language David could only lament that he couldn't understand as his grandmother spoke to him.

A last deep cut at what he had done.

"It's just the questions right? You have to finish those up?"

"Yeah Dad, just the questions."

David is sitting on his bed, tears on his face. He scrolls on his phone until he sees an email that imbues him with even more emotion inside…

Whoosh

David is now in a camp of sorts, in a cabin, conversing with an older woman but not much older compared to his mom.

"I've let them down, I failed a class last year, I know why but I just can't stop!"

"And now I've made people around me suffer again, because I…I-"

This woman hugged him the moment he was about to cry, he is now trying to hold himself back as she says,

"You have so much love for your parents, I get it. They've given you a lot, but David…you've given them a lot too, when I met them I could tell how much love they have for you. I don't know much yet to describe what exactly but I think that what you give them, based on what you've given us this week; it's a good heart. You're so sweet David, your energy was enough for people to really feel happy and attracted around you. If you knew how to use that to your advantage really control what you feel, you could-"

"But I've tried before."

"I know, and you make mistakes, that's OK. I'm sure your parents, as mad as they are, know that you made missteps; that you're growing. You're right, your future is uncertain David, and you have a lot to correct until those wrongs finally become right. But remember, you have given so many good things out there, You deserve those opportunities to rise above, YOU are going to go do amazing things no matter what. That's what I believe."

I believe

I believe

I believe

BLOOP

David gets up, and finally starts typing. The sounds building up speed, momentum as all the thoughts pour out from his head, the stillness of the night is replaced by the sounds of the fingers stabbing at the keyboard, creating a shockwave, a beat, louder than a drum.

Click clack click clack click clack click clack click clack click clack click clack click clack

Elaine looked outside, looking at the short view of the window. Her mind could clearly see the future could transport itself to the biggest city in the world, filled with its illumination, that warmth,

that love.

But as she looks to her hands, that mind snapped back into her body, and as she look behind her all she could see is darkness, with a purposeless and career ending home, with a dishelveled corpse like father, his artifical blonde hair chipping out like a worn out illusion.

Elaine landed hard on her knees and sobbed, sobbed, sobbed, and sobbed almost tearing the achievements apart and/or dropping several like the trivial pieces of paper they can be.

David's eyes are filled with fear as he gazes at the time.
11:53 PM
10/30/2018
He finally eyes the submit button as he finally moves the mouse as he finally submits it, David is in shock. His body is still, his legs stretched, his back hunched, his face still, his eyes in some sort of trance as he looks at the computer screen.

U
N
A

C
C
E
P
T
A
B
L
E

The computer slowly processes as the clicks of the keyboard bring about in impact. The screen then backs out with a single click as we see the two separate applications in two separate windows.

Elaine is left untouched

David's is besmirched with that dreadful word

A shadow looms over the display, leaning on the top of David's application.

- **Submitted Date: Dec 01, 2018**

Andy slams the desk, quivering the drool and various utensils and snacks upwards. Chunks of these chipped bits fly out in all directions.

"Oh man! Why did I just see that now?! Ugh, what a waste of time."

Andy mutters, as he finally submits these changes on the UCLA website.

JANUARY: AFTERMATH

Winner: Rebecca Leung

FATED BONDS

REBECCA LEUNG

It is not often that Fate thrusts opportunity upon you
It throws good
It throws bad
We learn to make do
But once in a blue moon
Fate tosses opportunity our way
With a wave of the hand and a shrug of the shoulder
And says
'You decide what to do'
Seize it in your fist, do not let it go
Or do
It's up to you

"I didn't know who else to go to."

That was what Evan had said in the doorway of Grant's apartment the second the door had swung open. It was the first time Grant had seen his younger brother face to face in years, decades even. His voice was deep.He towered over Grant. When had he gotten so tall? His shoulders were hunched, and his hair was unkempt. Grant could not guess the last time he had slept.

"What happened?" Grant asked, his expression guarded.

"Carmine is dead."

Grant's heart dropped into his stomach. One of his younger sisters? Evan's *twin?* Dead?

He moved back from his front door, allowing Evan inside. "Come in. Take a seat, tell me what happened."

Evan moved like he was a man possessed, held upright by only a few threads. He sat down hard on Grant's small couch.

Grant sat next to him, a thousand questions pressing against his skull, screaming to get out. How did you find my apartment? What do you mean Carmine is dead? How can I help? What do you *mean* Carmine is *dead?* But Grant pursed his lips tightly, and waited for Evan to speak.

"The doctors said it was quick." Evan licked dry, chapped lips. "Her and her husband were killed almost immediately."

"Can you tell me what *exactly* killed them?" Grant asked, his tone measured, calm. He thanked the stars he could keep the tremor from his voice.

"Their car was t-boned. The whole thing looked like it had been crushed like a soda can."

"How–"

"Drunk driver. Died instantly too."

"So why did you come here?" He knew that Evan wouldn't have gone out of his way just to say that. Grant probably wouldn't even be invited to the funeral, not with all he had endured, and made the family undergo in return.

"The only survivor was Carmine's son."

Grant knew what Evan was going to say next as soon as the word left his mouth.

"You're the only one who can take him."

Evan put his head in his hands, looking so very out of place on Grant's threadbare blue couch. "I don't ask this of you lightly. I know it is a lot. I can do all of the paperwork and figure out all the other crap, I just– we can't take in another child."

Grant worried his lip with his teeth, nodding.

"Does he really have nowhere else to go?"

"Carmine's in-laws live out of state. As far as I know no one's heard from them in a while. His only other option would be the system."

It wasn't much of a choice that Grant had. But, it was more of a choice than the boy was given. And really, Grant didn't have the heart to say no. So he screwed his courage to the sticking place, and shoved the pit of doubt in his chest out the window.

"Of course I'll take him in." Grant put his hand on his brother's knee. "Just tell me when."

"He will be discharged from the hospital in two days. Tomorrow, you can meet him."

Grant's pulse spiked, but he took a steadying breath, "Of course, whenever."

"Thank you," Evan mumbled, his voice shattering as tears began to fall.

Grant pulled him off of the couch and into his arms, letting Evan sob into his shoulder like he had so many times as a child.

Grant rubbed his back in slow circles. He didn't know how long they would need to hug. They had a lot of catching up to do.

"It will be okay," he said, hoping against hope it was true.

It was late when Evan finally collected the strength to leave, and Grant found himself alone. The silence felt suffocating, like the moment before it all came crashing down.

He picked up his phone off of the coffee table, clicking it on. Some default lock screen came to life, darkened by a text message.

Dawn: How was work? Did you finally ask that cute writer out?

Grant sighed, and called his sister. His only remaining sister.

It rang one, two, three times. Grant wondered faintly if she was still at work, despite the fact that it was nearing midnight where she was.

Finally, she picked up.

"Yo, what's up?" she said. Grant could imagine her spinning around in her office chair, phone pressed to ear by her shoulder.

"I have some... news."

"Bad news?" she asked, her tone stiffening. She was sitting up straight now.

"Carmine and her husband have passed away."

A series of impressive swears. Shock, disbelief. Grant waited patiently.

"What happened?!"

"Car accident."

"Who told you?!"

"Evan."

More swearing.

"That's not the only news, Dawn," Grant said calmly, much more calmly than he felt. Crisis would do that to a man.

A sigh, the rush of static temporarily taking over the phone line.

"What else?"

"I'm taking in their son."

"Grant. What do you mean you're taking in their son?"

"His name is Ansel. He's eight years old."

"Grant, you've never had kids before! Are you insane?"

"He has nowhere else to go, Dawn."

"Make Evan take him in!" Her voice grew higher and higher, stress stringing it out.

"Evan has two children of his own, and carries the grief of his *twin dying*. This is the least I can do to lighten his burden."

"You've never raised a fucking *child* before!"

"I raised you," Grant countered calmly.

"Not at eight! I was fifteen when we got the fuck out!"

"I'm not here to argue with you. I just wanted to ask if I have permission to let him sleep in your room," Grant said simply. Dawn went silent on the other side of the line.

"Yeah. Yeah, of course you can." God knew she wouldn't be back to use it anytime soon.

Grant nodded. "Thank you. I promise I won't change anything drastically without asking you first."

"You're really going to go through with this, huh?" Dawn asked, the fight all but evaporating out of her voice.

"Of course."

"Tell me if you need anything. Money, or like groceries delivered to your place. Anything like that. I can send you some now for like... snacks and toys and stuff."

Grant chuckled to himself, knowing it was better not to decline. "Thank you, Dawn, that's very kind of you."

"I can try to ask to go back for a little to help–"

Grant shook his head, and then remembered Dawn could not see him. "Your work is more important, it's okay. I'll be perfectly fine. I can't imagine they'd let you just drop everything like that anyway."

"Yeah, you're right." Dawn was clearly distraught, being stuck playing ambassador with sleazy politicians and slimy lobbyists was one thing, but with this added to the mix? It must be torture.

"I'll keep you in the loop," Grant promised, "hopefully you can come home soon and meet him too."

"I hope so," Dawn sighed, "I hope it all works out."

The next day Grant found himself at the local big-box store, trying to pick out clothing that an eight year old boy would like. He did not really remember being eight years old. He could hardly even remember his younger siblings that small. But he guessed that boys still liked soft pajamas and clean socks, picking a few shirts that may be too small, and a few that may be too big. Just to be safe.

Fruit snacks and granola bars, a box of apple sauce packets. Juice boxes. All went into the basket wheeled alongside him.

Grant flipped through the list on his phone, compiled at three am the morning before from parenting blogs and social media posts about last minute fostering.

A water bottle with a straw that would not leak if pushed over. A plate that kept food separate from one another. Frozen chicken nuggets. A new blanket with starships and planets on it.

The toy aisle was another beast all together. Grant skipped it for now. A box of bandaids with fun colors. Child's shampoo and conditioner. A toothbrush.

All of it was now in a bag balanced on Grant's lap as he took the bus back to his apartment.

He made space for the food amongst the sparkling water and breakfast sandwiches, dug out his sister's old nightlight, and put his straight razor high up in the medicine cabinet.

Clothes were folded and put into empty white drawers, a set of pajamas was laid out on the bed, now fit with the space sheets rather than the lilac sheets Dawn favored.

It was already midday when Grant got the call he had been anticipating and dreading.

"I'm headed to your apartment. I have some of his stuff with me, and then we can head to the hospital."

The box that Evan brought up to his apartment was surprisingly small, his brother carried it with no issue.

"Is that all?" Grant asked, unsure of himself.

"I think they were doing that stupid Montessori thing," Evan said as Grant directed him to the bedroom the boy would be sleeping in.

"...Montessori thing...?" Grant repeated.

"Like, minimal toys and clothes, no bed frame, just a mattress on the floor."

"Oh. Of course."

Evan looked around the room. It was painted lilac and trimmed in white, with a vanity for a desk and gauzy curtains outfitted with fairy lights.

"It used to be Dawn's room," Grant explained.

Evan nodded, taking out a few pairs of folded shirts and pants, and some socks and underwear. It was hardly enough for an extended vacation, nevermind all the contents of a boy's wardrobe.

"Seems a little... spartan for an eight year old."

Evan sighed, nodding. "It doesn't sit right with me."

"I got him some more clothes, just because I didn't know what he had," Grant said, checking the size. At least he had gotten that approximation correct.

"That's good." Evan pulled out a wooden train, and a shoe box labeled 'tracks'.

"If you don't mind me asking..." Grant said hesitantly. A terrible looming dread was rearing its head. "What did the house look like?"

Evan shrugged a little. "It was. It was oddly empty. It felt almost fake."

Grant raised an eyebrow. "What do you mean?"

"There wasn't much food in the fridge. No eggs, no milk. Everything was clean, all the dishes washed and put away. All of the laundry was done."

Grant felt his hands go cold. "That's. Odd."

"I don't think that it was an accident, Grant," Evan whispered, looking out the slats of the window blinds. "I think it was on purpose."

Grant's mouth went dry. "Was there a note?"

"No. But both of their phones are missing."

Doom pressed in from all sides.

Evan turned back to look at him, really look at him, and Grant saw that hollow horror reflected back in his eyes.

"Who was driving, Evan?" Grant asked, his voice barely audible.

"Carmine was," Evan murmured.

"I'm sure the police will figure it out," Grant reasoned. "We have to focus on Ansel right now."

"Right." Evan nodded stiffly. "Right. We should get to the hospital."

It was a short drive to the hospital, but felt so alien to walk into the pediatric wing. Cartoon animals were painted low on the walls, each hallway lined with rows upon rows of identical chairs. The smell of cleaner hung in the air. People moved around them in dizzying patterns, it was all Grant could do to follow Evan.

"Hi, we're here to visit Ansel Finch?" Evan said at the front desk.

"What is your relation to the patient?"

"We're his uncles," Grant replied.

They were brought into a room with a sky blue ceiling.

Ansel was a tiny little thing. The bed was gigantic around his little head of curly hair and the blue cast around his left arm. He was fiddling with a stuffed cat, orange and floppy.

"Hey, Ansel," Evan said, coming to sit next to the bed.

Ansel looked up, a big cotton patch on his face.

"Hi, Uncle Evan," he said in a tiny voice.

"How are you feeling today?"

"Okay. I got jello at lunch today because I'm almost good enough to go back home."

"That's good." Evan smiled, but it was half hearted. "Ansel, I want you to meet someone. This is your Uncle Grant."

Grant waved, standing awkwardly by the foot of the bed.

Ansel waved back.

"I'm your mom's older brother," Grant said, edging ever closer.

"You look like her."

What a peculiar child.

"Uncle Grant is going to take care of you."

"Okay." Ansel held his cat close to his chest.

Just like that? No, that couldn't be right.

"I have a room set up for you in your apartment. Do you like dinosaurs and spaceships?"

Ansel smiled just the tiniest bit. He was missing a tooth, and Grant wondered if he lost it in the crash.

"Brontosaurus is my favorite."

Grant smiled back, "Brontosaurus. Got it."

Grant searched high and low in the toy aisle until he finally found it. Squat and stuffed, a bright teal brontosaurus with a round head and rounder body. He sat it down on the couch, its head peeking out over the armrest. It was the first thing you saw when you walked in the room, if you were child sized.

Evan was back out front of Grant's building the next morning, bright and early. How odd it was to see him so many days in a row.

"Ready to go?" Evan asked, as if Grant hadn't just walked out of his own apartment with his keys in hand.

"We're taking the bus," Grant replied in lew of a proper response.

"I can drive us–"

Grant gave Evan a pointed look, "The child lost both of his parents in a car accident. Do you really think he will want to go back inside a little metal box before the cast is even off?"

"Oh."

"Besides, I don't have a car. Or a car seat for him, for that matter."

"Alright, alright, the bus it is."

There was little fanfare to a hospital discharge. The little boy was standing hand in hand with a nurse, like this was some sort of hostage transfer.

Grant knelt down. "How do you feel, bud?"

"Okay." Ansel shrugged. The cat plushie was jammed between his cast and his side.

Grant nodded, standing back up and offering Ansel his hand. Instead of taking it, Ansel reached up with his free arm.

"Do you want to be carried?"

Ansel nodded, brown curls bobbing.

Grant obliged, finding the child to be lighter than he expected.

Words were being said, words he was supposed to be listening to, but Grant instead found himself pushing stray curls out of Ansel's face and making sure his stuffed animal was properly situated.

Ansel had to come back to get his cast removed, but Grant only partially understood anything that was being said. Sign here. Initial here. A load of paperwork handed to him in a thick envelope. Evan was taking all of the papers from him, nodding his head along and taking notes of exactly what needed to be done. All Grant had to do was carry Ansel.

Being allowed to carry out a child that was not his felt like he was pulling a heist of some sort. But there the three of them were, waiting at the bus stop. Ansel had not wanted to come down, and Grant's arms had not tired.

Ansel put his head on Grant's chest when they got onto the bus, squeezing his eyes shut.

"Are you okay?" Evan asked Ansel softly.

Ansel shook his head, hiding his face in Grant's sweater.

Grant held him tighter, putting a large arm around the boy's shoulders.

"It's okay, I've got you," Grant murmured. It was an achingly slow ride back to the apartment. But it was a straight shot, and the bus was relatively empty at this time of day.

They made it home without incident, getting up to Grant's apartment via the stairs. At this point, Grant's arms were starting to ache from holding him for so long.

"I gotta put you down now, okay?" Grant said in front of his (no, their) door.

Ansel groaned in protest, but Grant put him down anyway.

Ansel resisted going inside the door, but Evan gently pushed on his shoulders, coaxing him inside.

The boy zeroed in on exactly what Grant had intended. Instead of seeing the sagging couch cushions or chipping paint on the dining room table, Ansel had eyes only for the stuffed dinosaur.

"You have a brontosaurus?" Ansel ran up to it, but stopped short of grabbing it, seeming to remember his manners.

"He's yours, I got him for you," Grant reassured him.

Ansel gasped, little hands holding the plushie to his body like it was the only thing that mattered.

"I love him." Ansel grinned up at Grant and Evan.

"What are you going to name him?" Evan asked, settling himself down at the dining room table to sort through the paperwork from the hospital.

Ansel looked at the plushie for a long moment, his face pinched in deep thought.

"Barry," he decided, as solemnly as a child could.

Grant nodded in approval, "A very good choice. Would you like some water?"

Ansel nodded.

Grant pulled the child sized water bottle from the fridge, offering it to Ansel.

Ansel had many things in his arms now, not willing to put anything down. So the cat went under his cast, Barry under the other arm, his bottle held in both hands in front of his chest.

"You can play with your toys out here, Uncle Grant and I have to get some work done, okay?" Evan said, drawing the attention back to him.

"Okay." Ansel sat himself down right on the floor, setting his bottle next to him and holding both animals, one in each hand.

Grant sat down opposite Evan, and they set to work filling out every form and collecting every document.

The brothers were so engrossed in paperwork that time slipped right past them, until a timer went off on Grant's phone, startling all three of them.

"Oops." Grant looked down at his phone. Five pm already?

"I'm going to make some dinner, Ansel," he said, standing from the table.

Ansel, who had made a rather elaborate fort for his plushies out of pillows, looked up from the couch. "What is it?"

"How do chicken nuggets sound?" Grant pulled out the pack of frozen nuggets, pouring some out onto a toaster oven tray.

"I love chicken nuggets." Ansel smiled.

Grant chuckled to himself. "Me too, kiddo."

Ansel was content at the dining room table with his chicken nuggets as Grant and Evan worked.

Finally, the last paper was signed, and Evan had collected everything he needed.

He stood, a full binder of papers under his arm.

"Thank you, for everything," Evan said.

"Any time." Grant stood to face him, almost holding his breath.

They both stood there for a long moment before Grant gave in, pulling Evan in for a hug.

"Don't be a stranger anymore, okay?" Grant mumbled.

"Of course. I'll try to visit often, with the kids so they can play together."

"Sounds like a plan."

Ansel had gotten up from his place, wrapping his arms around Evan's leg.

Evan ruffled his hair. "Bye, Ansel."

"Bye, Uncle Evan…" It took a long time for Ansel to let go, but Evan was patient.

"I'll see you again soon, okay?"

"When?"

"I'll call tomorrow, okay?"

Ansel frowned, but he finally let go, holding up his pinky finger to Evan. "You have to promise."

Evan knelt down to hook his pinky in Ansel's, shaking it. "Promise."

Ansel finally let Evan leave, before turning to go back to play. Grant stayed at the door for much longer than he did, before finally turning around to go get himself something to eat.

"I'm tired," Ansel announced, rubbing his eyes. He had his toy train out, laying tracks over the coffee table, letting it crash onto the floor.

"Time to go to sleep?" Grant glanced at the clock. Seven pm. Sure, that sounded reasonable enough.

"Mhm."

"Alright, let's get your teeth brushed."

Hugging Barry to his chest, Ansel padded over to the bathroom. He looked up at Grant expectantly.

Grant filled up the plastic toothbrush cup, wetting his brush and putting a dollop of toothpaste on it before handing it to Ansel.

"Start a timer?" Ansel asked.

"What?"

"A timer. For two minutes. We should brush together."

Grant looked at him for a long moment before shrugging, getting out his phone and his own toothbrush. He hadn't intended on completing part of his nighttime routine at seven thirty, but it couldn't hurt.

The rest of the nighttime routine felt almost like they had done it a hundred times before. A quick bath and new pajamas, combing and drying wet hair. Ansel scuttled into his new room, almost disappearing into the too big bed.

Grant set about tucking him in, his plushies on either side of him.

"There's a nightlight for you," Grant said as he swept the hair away from Ansel's face.

"Can you keep the door open?" Ansel asked in a tiny voice.

"Of course, kiddo." Grant smiled kindly. "I'll be right outside if you need me."

Grant settled down at his desk, a rickety old thing that had served him well over the years. Lacking a proper office, it was shoved in one corner of the living room, accompanied by a few squat shelves of books and journals.

Booting up his laptop, Grant pulled out his newest journal, flipping open to the next blank page.

It was a notebook of grids, each page full of precise little images of everything from birds and beetles to the human brain and skeleton. Grant spent dozens of hours on each page, making sure his illustrations were perfect.

People paid good money nowadays for diagrams of bark beetles and spider webs to put in their textbooks and scientific journals, carefully annotated with all of the notes and figures that were given to him.

Grant could take a hastily sketched hand and a grainy photograph and turn it into art, scanning it onto his computer for the final touches.

Scratched between the butterflies and bees were grocery lists and appointments penciled in the margins, little bits of quotes from the television or social media.

Grant had a long list of anatomical drawings that he needed to get through, smoothing out the blank pages and putting his pencil to paper to make articulated joints and skeletal structures come to life.

He was so engrossed in his work that he didn't notice the bedroom door slowly opening until a little hand poked his thigh.

Grant jumped, but managed to play it off as he put down his pencil.

"Hey, kiddo, what's up?" he asked.

"Can't sleep." Ansel had both of his stuffed animals, one under each arm.

"I can warm you up some milk?" Grant offered.

Ansel shook his head. "Can I stay with you?"

"Uh…" Grant looked over at his work. "Sure, give me a moment."

He scooped up his notebook and pencil case, collecting his things to settle on the couch.

Ansel put both of his plushies in Grant's lap before climbing up onto the cushions.

He settled down into Grant's lap with little preamble, heedless of Grant's grunts of confusion.

"Well– alright then." Grant had his hands up in surrender.

Ansel was a little bit like a big cat, his knees pulled up to his chest and using Barry as a pillow.

Grant strained to reach the blanket that lay on the back of the couch (it usually covered a coffee stain on the head of the couch), draping it over Ansel.

"Is that alright?" Grant asked. Ansel nodded, smushing his hair against Barry.

"Did you draw that?" Ansel asked, pointing to Grant's open notebook.

"Yes, I did."

"It looks good."

"Why, thank you. I do it for work."

"That sounds like fun," Ansel mumbled. Grant was fairly certain his eyes were closed now.

Grant very gently rocked forward to pick up the notebook and his pencil, so that he could continue his work.

"It is lots of fun. They're published in books for people to learn from, and the people who write the books give me money."

"Do you like it?"

"Yes, it's a very fun job," Grant replied automatically.

"That's nice." Ansel yawned loudly. "Do you have a favorite thing to draw?"

"I like drawing insects, they're all very unique, but fairly simple. Do you have a favorite bug?"

"I like bees," Ansel said after a moment of deliberation. "They all work together."

"A very good choice. In the morning I can show you some pictures I've drawn of bees."

"Cool," Ansel murmured, before letting silence lapse. The only sound was Grant's pencil scratching against the paper.

"Where did Mom and Dad go?" Ansel asked when Grant was beginning to suspect the boy had fallen asleep. No such luck, it seemed.

Grant's heart pinched. He had expected this, had not been able to stop thinking about it, and yet still had no idea how to answer.

"I don't really know, Ansel, I'm sorry."

"Are they coming back?"

Grant couldn't lie to him.

"No, they aren't."

Ansel scrunched himself even tighter. Grant balanced his pencil behind his own ear, reaching down to card his fingers through Ansel's hair.

"I miss them."

"I know, bud." But no, Grant really didn't know. He could hardly even imagine.

"Why did they die?"

"I don't know, Ansel. I'm sorry. There's a lot of things I don't know."

"I don't know a lot of things too."

"We'll figure it out together, okay?"

"Okay."

NOTHING ENDS THE OCEAN

SOPHIA BREEZE

The father had a funny way he'd eat his bread. Making a show of how confidently he could crack into his piece's outer crust, he'd use nimble fingers to pull apart the soft meal of the middle until the warm, oven-cooked scent stained his hands and his plate was a dissection of loaf separating fluff from its golden brown surface. His daughter would laugh, because wasn't her father so funny? He'd press his string of crust above her upper lip as a bread loaf mustache so he could hear her squeal and giggle before she grabbed it, did it herself, and took a bite. The father would only eat the innards at dinner. In the morning, he took the overnight-stale outsides and dunked them into his coffee. He swore it tasted great that way.

Now the daughter crashes a plate upon the wooden table and haphazardly saws into a loaf on the counter, creating crude pieces she'll stack in an almost embarrassing offertory manner. The bread is three days uneaten, but there is nothing else the daughter can care to eat.

Squeaking an old oak chair across the floor, the daughter took her seat at the table and, with food served, finally gave her attention to the young boy she now sat across. Her small and frail brother, the father's youngest child, who picked at his bread and carried a heavy head that bent towards the floor. His weak frame was swallowed up by a bulky sweater and his shaggy hair matched the unkempt, uncombed look of his sister's. One of them sniffs at the quiet and stale air. Outside, the paling dusk crawls through their windows and bathes their home in bluish-gray.

"He kept money in a false book in the bookshelf," the daughter said. "There's more for you. If you're smart, you'll know how to spend it."

"Okay."

The drumming of a ticking clock filled the space neither child wanted to occupy. One tick for one second, then another, and then the daughter took a single bite of her bread.

"How do you feel?" the son asked. His words were closer to a squeak than they were a sentence. He watched with a sudden full-body wince as his sister let her food fall from her hands and onto her plate with an audibly obvious anger in its *thunk*. She was glowering, teeth clenched and the son heard the bitter way they scraped around in her mouth.

The daughter knew she should be kind to her brother, her young and suffering family, her next of kin. Her hands should be making a palm, placed calmly on the shoulder of the son and soothing in the way the daughter knew a tender touch would feel; but her hands cannot move from their fists. They clenched and bit the insides of her skin with their digging nails and she relished in the sting. It was a stupid question to ask. Clear in the roundness of his dark eyes the son had solely wanted his sister to bite back the bile of her vitriol in a way that he could handle when she'd rather rip out her hair.

Inside her was a concavity, a heart lost of its blood. The pulse that now pumped the daughter's body was bitter and burning and she welcomed the drumbeat: the urge to spit and scream and slap her brother's pinched-up babyish face just to feel the breathless feeling of utter guilt. In anger, the daughter wanted to remember and savor the truth that the world is terrible. She wanted to hate until hatred felt hollow. The daughter does not answer the son's question.

Besides, the house had already known full-body sobs and gouging howls into the floorboards from both children. Was there any reason for the daughter to recount the details? Her glare on her brother broke away and returned to the food.

"What?" the son said, and soon he felt his own spark of something angry flicker in his chest. "I can't ask? I'm the one who found him! You've never asked me how *I* feel!"

"I did," the daughter spat with enough strength to see the son shrink down again. "I did! When I told you what I was going to do about it, I was asking. Did your answer change?"

The son was silent.

"Then don't act like there's much else for me to do."

The daughter stood up from the table and screeched her chair back into it, bread still sitting on her plate.

"Tomorrow morning," she said, and the son knew. His sister was going to leave.

Yesterday the father was on the beach, facedown in sand. His gentle eyes gazed at nothing, blind and clouded over, as the rest of his body sank farther into the shore with every wave that reached his neck. One arm reached outwards—to what?—and his graying beard was tangled with beady little rocks; all sticky ocean mess. There was a strand of seaweed wrapped around a soaking pant leg.

The son replays the memory in his mind. The father had drowned, his lips blue. His figure became something of beached wood laying plainly on the island shore, as if something natural to skim over when walking the sand; a cobalt jacket darkened with water made into a black mass that the white and translucent skin of the dead hid beneath, waiting, wanting to be unwrapped. He could feel the touch of the father's wet shoulders at the tips of his fingertips, cold and heavy. Where was his boat? Why had this happened, and why has it happened now?

The son made sure to rub the memory in deep, deeper, hoping the taste of frigid morning air and sound of his pitiful effort dragging his father to grass branded something gaping within his skin: something noticeable and pure. He wanted to make sure he could recall the blistering tears to his eyes. Sitting at an empty dining table with untouched bread, he wanted to remember that he never said "goodbye."

Dawn bled weakly into the sky, both children having spent the night sleepless. The son gazed out his grime-speckled window at first light and watched as the daughter hauled a net full of fish off into the yard. She tossed clumsily the less-than-fresh corpses of the father's last catch onto the grass and when it spilled birds dove down to feast and tangle in the uncut fishnet. She stood off and watched, unmoving against a buffet of wind.

The son stared at his sister's billowing hair, listened to the squawk of fighting birds that broke through the walls and rang around in his bedroom, and stood silently in the moment of a long minute where neither of them blinked.

Though the son emerged from his room much later, his sister was found standing at the doorway, waiting. Her eyes that once glared now stared back at him quietly numb. They could both feel it in the air: the change that rose with the sun.

"It doesn't have to go like this," the son said, a morning-weak voice barely warbling past his lips.

In equal stillness the daughter merely said, "You are a child," and then reached to creak open the door.

Allowing the son to lead, the two winded down the hilltop from where their home sat and walked towards the black planks of the beach dock. The daughter's things were well and packed, neatly stacked by the side of a tiny sailboat since before the sunrise, patient and watching for the children's approach. The son gripped the insides of his sleeves with his fist, feeling the cotton close to his palm as he led his sister, unblinking.

They walked past long grass and paved stones pressed into muddy ground, the distance between them an arm's reach away from a sudden reaching-out and embrace. Both of them were aching from the cold of frames that hung comfortless; bodies screaming for a hug from someone that could never touch them. Even to a waterlogged body the father's children would think, hold me tight, tight, tighter. Hold me and never let me go.

Where had they left the father's body? Too weak for either to carry elsewhere and no real place to put him, the father's children thought it better to forget he was out there. Drenched, decaying, left in the dirt: the father was gone, truly gone. But where was he? The son felt a tug to gaze back behind him, towards the grass and stone, but he pulled his eyes forward and strained them to stay.

The ocean regarded them casually. It was almost gentle: the serenade of waves softly brushing its fingers along the sand without any notion of how the same song might sound in the lungs of something human. The son even enjoyed the cool breeze, the ocean's bubbles and calm rocking of the boat. For a moment, in a splice of sunlight warming his cheeks, the son felt as though everything was going to be okay.

The daughter began to herd her luggage onto the ship without a single sound of effort. The son bit his lip and watched, rubbing mutely his sleeves in a newfound habit. The little sailboat was a sun-baked blue, tired from the long years of sitting stagnant at the dock and tightly packed with the daughter's things until it was clear the ship was built for shorter travels.

"Did you take your quilt?" the son asked.

"Yes."

His sister pitched her sail the same way they saw the father do. They both saw the way the father aged, too. With every year and every day they could see it in his paling hair and tired face. A hitch of his breath here, a stumble on his own feet there. When it was the three of them together, the father's children noticed that the house would sigh with him, the air of the home sucked away entirely into a pair of aching lungs every time he took a breath. I'm old, he said. People get old.

The son started to focus on the waves; their cymbals against the dock's legs and the gradual way they grew louder. The daughter was reaching for the cleat with the blankest of eyes, the dullest of faces. Was this look the way the son would have to remember his sister?

"Um," the son said. "Do you have all your books?"

"Yes."

"Is this goodbye?"

Unbidden thoughts of the father returned to stab the bodies of both, heavy and hanging thick in the breaths of one another until they almost gasped for air. The family, together, walking down the same shore, by the same dock and with the son's hand clasped in the father's own. The father's gray-green eyes, his gentle hands. The way he'd still try to carry his daughter in his arms, the scent of salt pressed into his clothes. The funny way the father ate his bread.

"I can't be the next one on this shore," the daughter said, and suddenly her numbness broke apart into something tense and twisted. "I can't."

"You won't," the son pressed his desperate hands together, squeezing fingers that made his arms shake. "Neither of us will be."

The daughter simply shook her head.

Alone on the dock, the son stayed until his sister's boat was a blurry dot on the horizon, her body swallowed by the mouth of a blue sky.

Turning back, the son dragged his shoes across the wood of the pier until his feet met dark sand. He pressed his heels in deep, making sure to mar the footprints from when they arrived and make the beach a mess of untrackable steps. The roar of a wave bid the son to look behind him, the ocean enticing and infinite in its sun-lit sparkling mass that blanketed the rest of the world beyond. It was singing. The daughter was long gone, onto an island the son couldn't see. He stepped closer to where the sand grew muddy, the tips of his shoes growing dense with water and soaking bits of his socks.

The son pressed his palm into the black muck of the sand and let it sink between his fingers. The ocean came to lap at his hand with its cold and salty tongue, sticking the sleeve of his sweater to his arm in a way that made his skin itch. He was freezing. Something began to burn at the insides of the son's cheeks and nose. Had his father died freezing too? Had he simply walked out into the ocean, head high and stride unbroken, or had he been wretched and grasping for help with the names of his children screamed out into the night without answer; thundering heart and struggling body, the saddest instance of confusion?

With a jolt the son withdrew his hand and held it like it had been burned. In the growing anger of the tide the son turned away and went home.

Outside the ocean was crashing, throwing itself against the island's rocks and vomiting its white foam across the sand. In the echoing house the son lay alone, cocooned in blankets that wrapped at him tightly like a struggling attempt at a hug. He risked a glance down at his hand, still wrinkled with salt water and cold to the bone, and in the effort he took to clumsily form a fist the son suddenly felt the shock of his youth with the ache of a full-body bruise.

Old tears wet his cheeks, the blankets were pulled in tighter. Dark and scary things came from the recesses of night to grope the son's tiring mind: soggy shapes of seaweed choking on his small body, thick darkness, a terrible pain in his ears threatening to burst his head, his sister's sinking ship.

He sniffled and cried without making a sound. In quiet the misery soon shook hands with his exhaustion, blurring away the world and drifting the son into the blackness of his abandoned home.

Maybe someday, he thought through teary-eyed sleep, *I'll forget this is something that happens to everyone.*

WAITING FOR THE SUN TO RISE

ISAAC GARCIA

I should let you know that this story has a lot of important names, a lot of laughing people, and a lot of small, important moments...

Dexter sat on a chair, watching the waves wash over the packed sand. The moon started to set and the city to his back challenged its fading light. He was alone on the beach and his thoughts overpowered the soft seaside ambiance around him. He thought about Junior and all he thought about was how he was one week too late.

"Dexter watch out!" Junior shouted carelessly. He jumped off the roof of his house into the above ground pool.

Even with all his thoughts, his face was still. It sat indifferently with him, keeping the growing ache in his eyes at bay. He wished it was dark. He wished there wasn't a single light around him and he didn't know why, but he knew he wanted it all to be dark. He took a long sip of his bitter beer; today it wasn't so bad. The water washed forward like it did yesterday and like it did a week ago. People slept in their houses like they did a week ago. They stayed out until the early morning, drinking and laughing, like they did a week ago. They drank their coffee and went to work like they did a week ago. They thought about calling their friends, like they did a week ago. Everything was just like it was a week ago for everyone else.

Dexter told himself it didn't bother him that he heard laughter further down the beach; a campfire with friends dancing around it. Under the brim of his hat, he watched, sipping the tangy-bitter beer and nodding along to his thoughts. He thought about kicking sand over their fire and throwing beer in their faces. The smell of salt wandered in with the wind and he thought about how Junior would've felt if a stranger did that to them. Memories wafted in and out like waves.

"Bro, we should do this shot and like suck each other's dicks or something," Junior said, giving Dexter and Lucas a 'what if we did' kind of look.

It was something their group always did: Say something sexual or down right insidious and give a look like it was jokingly on the table. It was a good bit and they all laughed whenever someone did the bit. Dexter laughed like a kid who was supposed to be asleep, shaking his head like Junior was sitting with him saying the bit. He wanted to cry, but he couldn't bring himself to do it.

"Bitch, don't cry."

Dexter grabbed another tall can. His eyes glistened and he remembered another fun moment. *Tsk-click*

Junior, Dexter, and Eddie found a shitty, green rowboat on the side of a small lake. They rowed with an old snow shovel they found and steered with long branches that fell from the pines surrounding the cabin. Dexter was captain, Junior was first mate, and Eddie was the help. Without a thought, Junior took his shirt off, wrapped it around his head, and held a long branch over him like the wild kid he was.

"We're folkin' pirates, mate! Cum of the sea," Junior exclaimed with a stick high above his head with water dripping down onto his bare chest.

Dexter remembered how cold it was and when they explored the woods, snow packed itself in large mounds. They climbed those mounds earlier, sliding down on broken sleds.

Dexter shivered and when he looked at Junior he saw that he didn't give a shit though so Dexter didn't give a shit. He took his shirt off and made it their flag. He waved against the cold wind and his hands calloused with each swing. The S. S. Junior was born.

Junior looked over at the murky water. "How much would you guys give me to jump?"

"Twenty bucks," Eddie said.

"Twenty dollars?" Junior exclaimed.

Eddie shook his head, laughing nervously. "No—fuck. I change my mind."

Junior smacked his lips. "Bitch, why?"

"Cause, you'll do it."

Their friends ran on the green shore, following with a wild cheer in their lungs. The three on their mighty vessel made howling noises like wild bears. The air around them was open and crisp. Dexter thought if he jumped, he would fly. He stood on the edge and next to him, Junior stood like a great war chief. Dexter saw it, the glistening freedom of the vast ocean just beyond the thick woods.

There was a tickle in his heart and he smiled too. He put his hands up with their flag waving it in the sun's face From deep in his chest, he howled.

"FUCK YEAH! We're pirates!" Junior exclaimed in a scalliwags voice. "Give us your shit!"

Everyone laughed and the surrounding forest laughed with them. Birds fluttered.

Junior tossed the stick into the boat and took his shoes and socks off.

"Junior—Dude don't. You're gonna get fucking AIDs or something," Eddie said.

"I'll do it if you do it," Dexter said.

Junior's face rivaled the high sun. "Deadass?"

Dexter smiled and stuck his stick in Eddie's hands. "On three?"

"Nah. Now!"

"WoOaAH!" Dustin exclaimed.

In the air, he saw Junior with his arms reaching for the sky and his legs kicking him closer to it.

A hand startled Dexter and he jumped a little. Jerked back to the beach, the night sky seemed darker and the waves didn't have the energy of the woods. It all dragged across his eyes.

Eddie stood over him, already laughing. "Shit, what's good," he said, putting his hand out.

"Chilling, you?"

They dabbed each other up.

"Shit, I'm tired as fuck."

Eddie set up a chair next to him. He watched the waves with Dexter.

"What time did you get here?" he asked.

"I don't know," Dexter said. He checked his phone. "Maybe thirty minutes."

"What?" Eddie said with a confused laugh.

"What?"

"Thirty minutes ago?"

"Yeah."

"Oh, I'm fucking stupid. I thought you said like you've been here thirty minutes," Eddie said.

Dexter was confused. He looked at Eddie who's eyes were already louder than his smile.

"Wait, that's the same thing," Dexter said, with his hands up confused and a wide grin.

Eddie leaned back, laughing. "Dude, I'm fucking stupid."

"Don't say that," Dexter said. "You're not stupid."

"Fucking idiot," Junior joked to Eddie.

"It's crazy, man. It doesn't feel real," Eddie said.

Everything sounded quieter and the words settled in Dexter's head. He nodded. He sipped his beer. "Yeah, it's fucking weird. Like—I feel like I could call him right now and he'd be like *'What bitch? I'm kidding. I love you'.*"

Eddie laughed. His laugh was like a pig on the plains. It was bright and screechy. They all laughed differently. "On some real shit, same," he said but there was something on the tip of his voice. He wanted to say something, but he just watched the waves with Dexter.

"Is everyone else on the way?"

"Yeah, Everyone should be here soon. I think Leonard was behind me."

"Sup fuckers," shouted a loud voice.

They both turned back and saw Leonard walking up with his button up shirt over another shirt. He had a loose grin and his hands were out for a quick hug.

They both got up and gave him a quick hug.

"You didn't bring a chair?" Eddie asked.

"Nah, I thought I'd just stand and chill—Ya know, just take in the view," Leonard said.

"Okay, but I'm not giving you my chair."

"I'm not gonna want your fucking chair."

Eddie laughed. He knew Leonard was bullshiting. "Bitch your legs are gonna get tired and you're gonna try to sit in my chair."

"No, I'll just sit on the ground."

"Bro, no you're not."

The three laughed. Leonard's laugh was a kid's laugh. It was like it never grew up, as if he was the same kid they new from middle-school.

"It's so fucking dark," Leonard said.

"You think we'll do this every year?" Eddie asked.

"Honestly, that would be dope," Leonard said. "Plus like once we all got more money we can rent a hotel and spend a day together and stay up to watch the sunrise."

"*Fuck*, Junior would'a hella loved doing some shit like that," Eddie said.

"For real—Fuck man," Dexter stood. He needed to stand. "We should've done something like this more often. Junior would've been so down."

Leonard pulled a vape pen and took a long hit. Smoke withered in the wind. "I remember one time, when me and him tried to see who could get the most fucked up fastest, and that motherfucker grabbed a *whole* bottle of Fireball and said 'okay-ready-set-go'—And threw his head back, and drank that shit like it was water."

He laughed at his story and had another hit of his vape. He choked and wiped his eyes. "Fuck, man."

Edgar put his hand on Leonard's back. "He's in a better place."

Leonard took another hit and he felt nirvana creeping in. He blew it out and quickly took another. His body felt light, everything was slower. He smiled through the tears. "I know, man. I just miss him."

Dexter kicked sand. "Hey, you think everyone's gonna get here in time. The Sun's gonna rise in like an hour."

"I'm fucking dead. What the fuck else do these motherfuckers gotta do?"

Eddie looked back at the parking lot on the hill above them. A car pulled in, but it wasn't any of their cars. "You want me to call them?"

"I'll call Lucas. You call Carlo, and Leonard, can you call Isaias? And I'll call Jerry."

They all listened to a ringer.

Isaias answered first. "What? What do you want?"

"How far are you guys?"

"I'd say about ten minutes."

"Why, you miss us, pookie?" Emanuel asked.

"Shut the fuck up," Leonard said, chuckling.

"Come on, you know you miss us," Emanuel said with a grinning voice.

"Fuck you."

"We'll see you in a bit, Leonard," Isaias said; he hung up.

Carlo answered next.

"Sup bitch." he said.

"Hey, how far are you 'cause Dexter said the sun is gonna rise in like an hour?"

"How does Dexter know when the sun is gonna rise?"

"Cause I know," Dexter put his face to the phone, "bitch."

"Alright alright, I see you. I'm on my way, man. I'll be there in like ten minutes."

"Wait, do you see Isaias? He said he was ten minutes away too?" Leonard asked.

A pause. "Wait, is that Isaias in front of me?" Carlo asked.

A car honk blared from the phone.

"He's driving a blue rental right now," Leonard said.

Dexter and Eddie busted up laughing. "Dude, why'd you wait to tell him that," Eddie said.

"What the fuck do you mean? He didn't let me finish," Leonard said.

"Nah, you like hella waited," Dexter said.

Edgar laughed. "Dude, you made no fucking effort to—" he laughed to hard to speak.

"Aw, my bad man," Leonard said.

"Welp, that's not Isaias," Carlo said. He hung up.

Lucas didn't answer. Jerry answered.

"Hey buddy, what's going on?" Jerry asked over the phone.

"How far are you?" Dexter asked.

Jerry smacked his lips and audibly licked his gums. "Mmmm, I don't know."

"The fuck you mean, you don't know?" Eddie asked.

"I mean I don't know."

"What does your GPS say?" Dexter asked.

"Mmmmm, ten minutes."

"You're such a bitch," Leonard said between his soft laugh.

"Oh yeah? Well. . . . You're half a homo. Bye," Jerry hung up.

The three watched the waves. The silence echoed in their ears and their thoughts washed up to the shore. Dexter sipped his beer. Leonard took one last hit of his pen, and Eddie poked the sand with his shoes.

Eddie pulled up his phone and looked through his photos. He scrolled through dozens of photos before he found one of Junior and him; Junior had just got a tattoo of his shitty Honda Accord on the back of his arm. They both were smiling. Junior was shirtless for some reason Eddie couldn't remember, and his arm was wrapped in plastic wrap.

Eddie smiled and a pit in his stomach hardened. He showed Dexter who smiled. "Fuck, I remember I told him that he should'a got a tattoo of his dream car."

"Lowkey, that was his dream car," Leonard said.

"Honestly, yeah," Eddie said.

"Honestly, you're sexy as fuck," a funny voice said behind them.

Lucas strode to them with a folding chair flung over his shoulder. They all stood and gave him a good hug.

"What's good, Dex," he said. "Still putting out fires with your *massive* cock?"

Dexter smiled with a little pride in his eyes. "Dude, I'm fucking drained."

He winked and gave Eddie a hug. "Hey cutie, how are you doing?"

"Dude stop. You're gonna make me blush."

They both laughed.

Leonard walked up and hugged Lucas. "I missed you man," he said in a dazed voice.

"Uh-oh, someone started the party without me," Lucas said.

"Nah, I got it right here," he pulled his pen out. "Want a hit?"

"Nah man, I'm chilling."

"Oh that's right. I forgot you were clean."

Lucas kissed his hand and pointed to the sky. "Thanks to sky daddy. All love."

He set up his chair and they shifted to make a circle.

"So what's been happening, guys?" Lucas asked.

"Fucking working," Dexter said. "Dude, there's been like hella fires over in fucking North-Cal."

"It's all that dead shit. It's fucking bad in The Valley too," Eddie said. "Me and Vanessa went on a hike over at Millerton and there was hella dead grass and shit."

"*Fuck* man, I was driving up to Shaver with Jerry and you could see all the burnt trees and shit where they stopped the fires," Dexter said.

Lucas sat back on his chair with his legs stretched out, his eyes watched nothing as he listened. "Yeah, it's all kinda fucked."

"For real. I'm out there just digging trenches and shit," Dexter said, pretending to dig a hole. "Doing my best to save the trees."

"Yeah? That's honestly badass, man. Like, good for you. I'm happy for you, buddy," Lucas said. "What about you, Leonard?"

"Ya know, focusing on school. I'm almost done with my Bachelor's."

"Oh word?" Lucas said. "That's dope. You still working at—uh," he snapped his fingers a couple of times. "Whatcha-ma-call it?"

"Susie's Groceries?"

"Is that what it's called?"

"Yeah, what'd you think it was?" Leonard asked.

Lucas shrugged. "I don't know, like Lucy's Crack House or something."

Lucas' laugh was like a high hiss, gasping for breath and curling over his stomach. After a bit of laughter, and more banter, they passed a couple beers, and told more stories about Junior. Eddie listened and he remembered the last time he saw Junior.

Eddie listened to rap while he drove down the road to Junior's house. They planned on chilling and working on Junior's car.

Eddie was an hour late, but he was always an hour late. If he wasn't, it was because Junior was driving him.

He turned down a shitty road with cracks and bad fillings of asphalt that rose above the cracks. His car jerked as he turned and saw Junior's street on the corner. It was a nice house on the corner with dead grass, a short iron gate, and a few palm trees. The garage was closed.

Eddie looked around. Everything seemed normal. He thought he heard a car start, but the neighborhood was quiet and all the cars were still. He parked across the street, slammed his door, and walked up to the gate.

He reached for the gate's handle and it opened. It wasn't supposed to be unlocked.

He walked in, closing the gate behind him with a loud rattle. He looked around the side of the house, the fence was closed. He banged on the garage door. "Hey Junior!"

He listened.

He banged again. "Junior!" he said, pulling out his phone.

He waited and each ring sunk his stomach. **"You have reached—"**

He hung up and walked to the front door. He slammed his fist, rang the doorbell. His heart started to pace his chest. Scared, he tried opening—The door opened and he stepped back.

He walked around and took looks at the door. He scrolled through his contacts, constantly looking back at the cracked open door. Dexter was still away. Jerry and Carlo were at work. He scrolled. Leonard was usually asleep. Isaias was in LA right now. He called Lucas. The phone rang.

Eddie marched around, looking for any thugs or cars out of place. He didn't know what cars were supposed to be in the neighborhood. He didn't know who lived in the house next door or across the street. He didn't know what thugs would look like. He looked at everything as if it wasn't supposed to be there. He checked the fence again. He pressed his head against the garage door. He walked back to the front door. He stood with the phone by his ear and each ring was like the end of the call.

Lucas didn't answer.

"Shit," he called Emmanuel.

"Yo?"

"Hey man, what are you doing?" Eddie's voice shook.

"Chilling at home. Why? Everything okay?"

"Nah, something's up with Junior. Can you come over?"

"Yeah, I'll be there in five."

Eddie hung up. He walked out the gate and sat in his car. He watched the door. He imagined Junior on the floor, covered in blood. He imagined the last look in his eyes. His imagination scared him and his eyes hurt. His leg shook.

He kept looking in the rearview mirror and reached behind his seats. He heard police sirens in the distance.

A car drove by slowly. He watched a black Corvette lift over a speed bump and cruise by Junior's house. It was parked on the side of the house. Eddie slunk in his chair. It flipped a U and turned onto Junior's street. It drove down to another house and parked between Junior's and the other house.

Eddie looked at the time; it'd been seven minutes.

Two men stepped out of the car. Tattoos littered their body. They wore basketball shorts and baggy football jerseys. They looked around in Eddie's direction. He thought they locked eyes. He adjusted himself with his hand reaching to the passenger seat as if he had a gun.

They walked into the neighbor's house.

Listening to the ambiance of his car, Eddie waited.

He looked in the rearview and side mirrors. Emmanuel pulled up and parked in front of Junior's house. He stepped out, sweating like he was working under the sun.

Eddie stepped out. "You good?"

"Fucker, are you good?"

Eddie pointed at the gate.

Emmanuel touched the handle. He looked at Eddie. "He never leaves it unlocked."

They walked to the door and opened it to a dark living room. Junior wasn't around. They both step in, peeking around corners before they walk in. They walked to Junior's room. The door was closed and underneath they saw a familiar purple glow.

They opened the door. Junior's room was a mess. Clothes were stuffed in the closet. A few beer bottles littered his gaming setup. His bed wasn't made.

"Where the fuck is he?" Eddie asked.

They walked out to the living room. They looked at the kitchen. They both looked at each other and slowly walked to the kitchen's open door frame.

On the floor was a pool of scarlet blood. Junior's bare skin was soaked and his tattoos were ripped. In his hand was a kitchen knife. Eddie walked closer. His white shoes soaked in red. He saw an indifferent gaze looking back at him.

Carlo, Isaias, Jerry, and Emmanuel walked down the beach with beach chairs slung over their shoulders.

Everyone heard the laughter before they looked back to see the four idiots.

Carlo put his hand out and did a dab in the opposite order. Isaias hugged his friends with both arms. Emmanuel dabbed them up, and Jerry gave quick hugs.

They put their chairs down and they all watched the water.

"Hey Dexter, how much longer until the sun rises?" Carlo asked.

"Shit, I don't know," he said in a dumbfounded voice, a voice they all knew when he really didn't know.

Carlo laughed, gasping, and shook his head. "You motherfucker."

"Hey, so what happened with the guy you honked at?" Leonard asked.

"Yeah, he said something about killing me in my sleep and fucking my corpse? I don't know. He seemed like a cool dude," he said. He looked back and shrugged.

"Fuck, where's Junior when you need him," Eddie said.

"Fucking speeding down a highway in heaven," Leonard said.

"There isn't a cop that could catch him," Isaias said. He sipped his glass bottle of Coke.

"Yo Isaias, did you bring the Fireball?" Dexter asked.

"Yeah, it's in the car."

"Did you bring shot glasses?" Carlo asked.

Isaias grinned, grinned like he had been caught stealing. "No one told me to bring shot glasses."

"How the fuck are we supposed to take shots with no shot glasses?" Carlo exclaimed with his hands out.

"I don't know. I thought we were all bringing our own."

"Well did you bring one?" Leonard asked.

"No, I was just gonna borrow one."

Eddie laughed. "Dude, you're a fucking idiot."

"Where's your shot glass?"

"Up your butt."

"Yeah yeah, what are we gonna do?" Isaias asked.

"I don't know, maybe all take shots one at a time," Dexter said.

"Then what's the fucking point of all doing it when the sun rises?" Jerry asked.

Dexter put his hands up to his shoulders. "I don't know. I wasn't the one who was supposed to bring the shot glasses."

"Well no shit," Jerry said. "Who the fuck was?"

Everyone looked between one another.

Eddie pointed at Leonard. "Bro, it was you, wasn't it?"

Leonard smiled. "Fuck you. It wasn't me."

"Ladies ladies. Hear me out," Emmanuel said, smacking his lips like he was a connoisseur of words. "We all have money. We buy the shot glasses."

"When the fuck do you ever have money, you broke ass bitch?"

Emmanuel leaned forward. "Hey hey," he whispered to Jerry. He licked his lips. "Shut the fuck up."

"No."

Isaias stood up. "I'll go get them. E-man, you coming?"

"Fuck it."

Kicking the dirt with their feet, Isaias and Emmanuel walked back to the car.

"How long until the sun rises?" Isaias asked.

"About half an hour."

"Alright. . . How you feeling?"

"Tired as fuck."

Isaias nodded. "Yeah. It's crazy. I had a dream last night that Junior was still with us."

"Yeah?"

They stepped in the car. "Yeah. We were all in my grandma's living room and he was laying on the couch with a baby on his chest. I remember Dexter was sitting in the chair next to him with a beer. We were all sitting for a picture. I don't know who's baby it was, but I'd like to think that it was his, and he was happy."

"Yeah, if only. Ya know, I like to think that he was happy before he died."

Isaias smiled. "I think he was. I know he had his moments, but I know he wanted to live. We'd talked about it once."

The engine started and the wheels turned as he reversed out of his spot.

Junior, Emmanuel, and Isaias sat outside a local burger joint, eating with the smell of greasy meat on the grill.

"Dude, I'm literally gonna cum in this burger," Junior said.

Isaias laughed like he always had the hiccups. Emmanuel's was like a lumberjack in the distant woods.

"We should make this a tradition," Isaias said as he licked the ketchup and mayo off his fingers.

"For real, this can be our spot," Emmanuel said as he opened his big mouth for another bite. Grease and sauce oozed from the burger and the savory flavor washed his mouth. A bit of lettuce clung to his beard. He took a sip of his milkshake and the burger's flavor made it even sweeter. He moaned into his bite.

*Junior laughed. "Are you eating or are you **eating**?"*

"Brother, I am fucking this burger."

They made more jokes, each playing off the other until the burgers were gone. It fell quiet and they ate the last of their fries. They listened to the cars speeding by and watched cats wander the sidewalk.

"We should do this more often," Isaias said.

"Motherfucker, you're always busy," Junior said, smiling like the answer was obvious.

"I know. I don't know why I work so much."

Junior gave Isaias a pat on the back. "Cause you're gonna do great things man. When do you leave?"

"I got a month before I head out."

"We should do something before then," Emmanuel said.

"For real, we should have a poker game or just chill, ya know," Junior said.

Isaias nodded, thinking about it. "Yeah, I'll let you guys know when we get closer."

"For sure man. And hey, you know we all got your back," Junior said.

"Aye, I know. And if you guys are ever in LA, don't be afraid to call or ask to stay over," Isaias said.

"For sure. For sure."

"How have you been doing?" Isaias asked. "It's been a minute."

"I've been alright, ya know. Shit happens, but I keep on driving. It's kinda fucked," Junior began.

They heard the subtle sorrow that he didn't want them to hear. Junior started talking and they listened to his struggles, pings of guilt rubbed their hearts. They kept thinking they should've been there. They nodded and tried to assure him things would get better and how they always had his back. He knew they would and he knew they meant it. They said it before but they felt they needed to say it anyway. They listened and quietly thought how they could help him. He rambled and he forgot what he was first talking about. He said sorry, and they shook their heads, told him sometimes you gotta let that shit out.

"What are you guys up to after this?" Isaias asked.

Emmanuel shrugged. "I got some homework I gotta get done."

"I'm probably gonna go to the beach after I drop off Manuel."

"I got work in a couple hours," Isaias said.

"Fuck, I was gonna say, pull up."

"Yeah, maybe next time."

Junior nodded and his eyes dipped away from his friends.

Isaias and Emmanuel squinted as they stepped into the bright convenience store. Aisles of bright bags of snacks were highlighted by the pale light. They wandered through the aisles before looking for the shot glasses. "You wanna talk about how you saw him last?" Isaias asked.

"Not really."

"Have you talked to anyone?"

"Me and Jerry talked about it for a bit."

Isaias nodded and started looking for the shot glasses.

Carlos sipped his coffee while waiting for the sun to rise. He hadn't cried since middle school, and it was fine with him. He didn't want to cry now. *Get that shit outta here,* Junior said in a funny voice when he saw tears.

He heard the waves and listened to his friends' trade stories.

He felt not nothing, but empty as if he was alone on the beach. He saw and knew he wasn't, but the feeling nagged at him. His stomach ached and he set his coffee on the ground. He listened.

"I remember one time—Fucking, we were gonna head to Shaver. It was me, Junior, Jerry, Leonard—Dex, I *think* you were there. Not too sure, but we were heading up and Junior was fucking hella ahead of us. Like, *miles* ahead—"

"Dude, I always tell that motherfucker to slow down," Eddie said. "I remember he told me how he turned a two hour drive into an hour one time."

Leonard told a similar story about how he got a call from Junior after work, and how Junior wanted to brag about how fast he was going down the freeway.

Dude, there's no fucking police in this bitch, Junior said into a choked chuckle like scuttling crabs. *"I'm fucking wildin'."*

They all laughed and remembered similar stories of their own. Lucas' laugh was a gasp for air before silence while he slapped his chair or jumped back. Carlos was a dying chuckle that ended in silence like Lucas'. They remembered Lucas was telling a story.

"Dude, we were going up the mountain and fucking—something happened with Junior's battery or something and he had to like pull off to the side of the road," he laughed a little. "Dude, had hella fucking shit on his battery. Like homie poured straight battery acid on it or someshit"

"Oh, the fucking corrosion was hella bad?" Eddie asked.

"Yeah. And I was like—'Dude, what have you been doing?' Junior just goes, 'ah you know, sucking toes.' And I start laughing like 'Junior you're a fucking idiot.' Like, how are you gonna drive your shitty car knowing the battery's fucked?"

Carlos sat back, laughing with his hand over his eyes. He saw Junior's dumb smile and he laughed harder. His eyes hurt and he lost the real laughter in his stomach. He wiped his eyes, pretending they weren't tears. He took another sip of coffee.

Isaias and Emmanuel took their seats in the circle with a bag next to Isaias' chair.

"Oye," Isaias called.

Carlos snapped to the beach. He looked at Jerry.

Jerry had three empty bottles around him and a numb gaze that sagged on his skin.

Carlos looked Jerry in the eyes and saw his splintered stare. He watched.

Isaias' chest turned into a pound of lead. He stood and put his arms out. Jerry took a long, shakened breath, but he didn't stand.

"Jerry," Isaias said.

"I know," he said as he leaned back.

Lucas had Jerry's beer in his hand and put it where Jerry couldn't reach.

"I remember," Jerry began.

Jerry and Junior sat in their cars, revving their engines. Cold air blasted through Jerry's vents and the sun turned the dusty, beat up track into a wavering horizon. With his hand on his clutch, they watched the man in the middle raise his arm. Jerry's face was red and his muscles were stiff.

Go!

Jerry's cheeks were wet and his laugh was confused. It was a mixture of sadness, and happy nostalgia. "I never gotta race that motherfucker," he said with a fake growl. "He went out undefeated."

They each wiped their own tears away with similar smiles.

"Eddie," Lucas said. "You saw the body."

Eddie pressed himself against his chair.

"Eddie," Lucas said.

Eddie nodded and the tears pushed against his eyes.

"Let it out, man."

He shook his head and looked up, praying that the tears would fall back into him.

Everyone waited for Eddie.

He wiped his tears and looked at the waves. "Dude, I miss the fuck outta him. Like, that motherfucker was my homie for real," his voice cracked. "I know he hated us fucking complimenting him and all that shit, but fuck—I saw him. Me and fucking Emmanuel saw him. My shoes still got his blood on them. He. . . He was ride or die. If you called him at two in the morning, he answered. He always tried killing motherfuckers for us. *For no reason!* That motherfucker was on some shit with killing fools."

He saw the waves almost touch his shoes. "I was an hour late. I could've saved his life or got him to the doctor."

Eddie fell back and his sad laugh turned into a whimper in the palms of his hands.

Lucas pulled Eddie to his feet and wrapped his long arms around him. He cried with him and Jerry cried.

"Fuck, man," Dexter said on the verge of tears. "I was a week—I just needed one more week and I would've been there. I could've said goodbye. I could've protected him."

Isaias wiped tears from under his glasses and he rose to hug his brother. Leonard hid behind his vape pen and smoke, but they heard the soft whimpers in his breath between each puff. He wandered closer for a hug. Emmanuel wasn't ready. He watched and racked his brain for a way to comfort his brothers. He stood with his arm around them.

Carlos watched. He had already buried it. He stood and hugged his brothers. He didn't know what else to call them but brothers. He never called them that though. It was a weird thing that existed between them. He knew them longer than he knew some of his family. He knew who they used to be back in the day. He knew what kind of drinks they liked and what their laughs sounded like. He knew a lot of stories and was a part of a lot of their stories. He knew a lot of things, but he never knew how hard it was to watch the sunrise without one of them.

He didn't know how to lose a brother.

"Y'all are like brothers to me," he said and his voice cracked.

Eddie wiped his face and wiped his tears. His chest, like all of their chests, was free and he felt like the world wasn't as heavy.It was like Junior was next to them and his smile made them feel like they could fly. Eddie could tell his story a million more times. "Honestly. It sounds like corny and shit, but you guys are like brothers to me."

Carlos watched the sky turn into a purple and told them the sun was gonna rise.

The sky simmered with dark color. They passed shot glasses with Fireball and waited. Slowly, dark purples faded into dark blues and the sky bloomed into reddish orange like heated metal. The sun rose above the dark ocean. Their eyes were slowly set ablaze and glimmering streaks made trail down the faces. Their chests stretched like long unused muscles, gasping with the sudden freeness thrust upon them. They all stood with their glasses raised, light dancing off onto the sand.

"For Junior," echoed eight voices.

And as the sun began to break from the horizon, Junior watched, sitting in front of his friends, with his knees tucked to his chest, and his arms wrapped around his legs. He looked up at all his brothers who couldn't take their eyes off the sunrise. He smiled and was excited for the next time he'd see them together.

When they got in their cars, he stayed to give them a head start and watched the waves wash against the packed sand. The sky was bright blue and the wind was salty. He never stopped smiling. He imagined the next adventures they'd have, doing crazy, childish things that kept their hearts beating. He thought about more jokes and comebacks to jabs at each other, and he sifted through all his memories with them, their tears, their laughter, it all molded a shimmering face for each of them.

He stayed until his eyes were heavy and the sun was at her peak. Humming an old song, he stretched and walked to the car as he dug through his pocket. His car, an old soul of metal, rumbled to life and he revved the engine just to feel the old thrills he had with her. He started out the parking lot, slow and steady at first, knowing he'd beat them all back home.

THE EARTH, LOSS AND EVERYTHING IN BETWEEN

SURAJ RAJENDRA GANIGER

It was the younger one who found it, as younger ones typically do.

Younger Brother had decided to spend the rest of the day Outside. He was especially fond of the scant trees, and how in the mornings, the sun shone through them, its crepuscular rays illuminating all in its glorious gaze.

Though, sadly, there weren't many trees left anymore, nor could he remain Outside in the Sun for too long. The Burning was indeed scary, but one just had to make sure they had plenty of water and Preservation. No, the Burning was not the source of his fear. It was the *Harvesters*, roving groups of people, if that was what you could call them, who did unspeakable things to whatever poor soul they came across. Of course, most adults knew that, though it had happened before, there was little possibility that the Harvesters would get into The City, where Younger Brother lived.

But children are not without fear.

For right now, though, these terrors were absent from his mind. At this very moment, this little boy was digging holes. As little boys typically do.

As the Sun steadily began its ascent, and the winds picked up, he stood up for a moment, enjoying the cool relief on his face. A newspaper with the title "Seven Seconds to Midnight" fluttered past. The rusty swings creaked. Distantly, a TV blared, probably with the evening newscast.

Panting, he leaned against his shovel and uncapped a bottle of water (synthetic, of course, only the well-to-do could afford such expenses) and began drinking it in refreshing, greedy gulps. Wiping the sweat beading his brow, he surveyed his kingdom with a small smile of satisfaction. Holes of various sizes and shapes dotted the cracked, dry Earth. Among them, there was a trampoline with a large hole in the middle, a few scraggly trees, an unused bike, and, crammed against the wall, various pieces of refuse. His eyes finally rested on a derelict planter box, and with a pang of guilt, he remembered his broken promise.

He traced his hand along the edges. It was his mother's idea, of course, who else would think to plant beauty in this wasteland? But they built it, all of them, and when they had finished, it stood bright and vibrant, full of blossoming plants, a stark contrast against the dying grey world. Though, now, years later, it was faded, and held nothing but dead plant matter. He mumbled an apology and went back to his digging.

Some time passed, and as the day began drawing to a close, and Burning Hour approached, he wondered where his father was. He should have returned home by now.

"DAD!" He yelled as loud as his little lungs would allow. "DAD!"

However, the rotund and bespeckled man that the little boy knew to be his father, did not appear. Rather, a lanky teenager appeared on the verandah. This was Older Brother. He rarely came out ever since The Incident happened, and only really stuck to himself.

He called out. "Where's Dad? Where did he go?"

Older Brother flinched and slowly turned around, evidently surprised to see his younger brother outside.

"He's working another shift tonight." His eyes momentarily flit to his younger brother's as he shifted his feet.

The younger boy narrowed his eyes. There was no issue in his statement. Their family of, now three, had fallen upon hard times. But why did he have a full backpack? What's more, why was he wearing multiple clothes on each other?

Almost traitorously, his older brother's keys chimed against one another.

He bristled as his eyes filled with tears. His older brother was running away. Running away despite promising his father that he would not do so, until, in his words, they were all back on their feet and had healed enough to sit down and talk about the Incident, and to see if that was what he *really* wanted. But he must never, ever, even think of going now, because he would leave his younger brother alone, and *she* wouldn't have liked that one bit.

"You're running again," he noted quietly, in a tight voice.

Older Brother said nothing.

"But you promised you wouldn't leave me!" He choked out, fear and desperation creeping into his voice. "You promised. *You promised!*"

Older Brother still said nothing.

"It's like you don't *care* anymore!"

"You're right." He said finally. "I don't. I don't care. About anything. Not anymore."

The younger one was too fraught to notice what his brother said. He continued his onslaught ('you promised!') until Older Brother had quite enough.

"SHUT UP!" he roared.

A pause.

"YOU shut up! I know what you do," the little one snapped, "with those people you started hanging around with, all of a sudden."

The older one blanched. His face went slack with shock.

"Maybe I should tell-"

He grabbed his collar. "Shut up!" He hissed. "Do you want Dad to hear?"

His breath smelt foul and stale.

"You forget," the younger brother said, voice quivering, "he's not home."

Older Brother scoffed and released his collar. They both eyed one another, warily.

"They're not your friends," the little boy said quietly after some time. "And you know that."

The older boy said nothing.

"You haven't been the same since-"

"Y'know what? I'm leaving."

"NO!" He pleaded grabbing his older brother's sleeve with his frail hands. "The Harvesters-"

Older Brother snatched his hand away. "They usually don't come this far in. There's even a lesser chance of them choosing you of all people to harvest from. Are you daft?" He growled in frustration.

"Are YOU?" He howled. "Don't you remember what happened to m-"

And then he clamped his hands over his mouth and glued his tongue to the roof of his mouth, for he spoke of The Incident, and you were never ever, ever supposed to speak of The Incident. Tears pooled in his eyes and gently dripped through his clenched hands.

"When are you going to start acting your age?" The older brother said, disgusted. "This isn't what men do— sniffle and sob and act all sad," he said (with a lump in his throat). "When will you grow up?"

Another loud, almost palpable, silence grew between the two brothers.

Older Brother fiddled with his coat strings.

"Looks like you're on your own." He said at last. Turning around, he trailed his backpack behind him and headed to the car.

And that was it.

The blood boiled under the young one's skin, and the heat rose to his face. *So what?* Thought he. *It doesn't matter. I don't need him.* He began furiously digging into the ground.

So great was his rage, that he didn't notice that his shovel had, several times, glanced off a large black, glossy metallic plate.

He glimpsed downwards and gave a great shout of surprise. The brother, wheezing, ran back.

All semblance of speech was lost as they stared at the large metallic plate protruding from the dry, cracked Earth.

Without exchanging a word, both brothers grabbed a shovel and began fervently unearthing the plate, curiosity gradually mounting. They worked through the evening, only taking a break during Burning Hour, as suggested by Older Brother. He slathered Preservation on them both, paying special attention to the back of Younger Brother's neck and ears, lightly admonishing him ('I bet you forgot to put it on earlier,' he murmured). The Sun beat against their dark skin, but they persevered, ignoring the sweat beading on their lips and foreheads and the dull stinging from their blistered hands.

After many hours of labor, the result lay before them: A large metallic black box. Hardly any taller than an adult, it stood in front of them, inviting.

Both brothers stared at this strange structure, transfixed.

"Well…?" Inquired the Older Brother. He motioned to the box in front of them.

"Well… what?" Gasped the younger brother, clutching the stitch in his side.

The older one, with some difficulty, bit back his scathing retort, and instead rolled his eyes. "WELL, are you going to open it?"

Younger Brother panicked. "I'm not opening it! What if it's a bomb laid by the Harvesters? It'll blow up, and they'll swoop in with their weird scary knives and start harvesting our or-"

The older brother sighed, defeated. "It's not. See the handle, the hinges? It's a… Cabinet? A box of sorts?" He glanced at the box again, and it seemed to… change? *Was it really just a cabinet?* He rubbed the dirt out of his eyes and squinted. *No, it was a cabinet… Right?*

He bit his lip. "I'm going to open it."

"Be careful…" The younger brother hid behind him.

He approached the box carefully, one foot in front of the other. Breath trembling slightly, he touched the handle and swallowed hard to steady his nerves. In one forceful motion, he yanked open the door with one arm, and, in another, wrapped his arm around his younger brother, protectively.

No explosion occurred.

But now it was open. Mouths agape, they stared at the metal box, who finally revealed all of her trinkets and secrets.

Caught in the wind, a note fluttered out.

The older brother grabbed it. He smoothed out the paper and lay it on the ground. The brothers saw their last name on it, and then the words 'Family Chest.'

Heads bent together, both of them, young and old, began to read.

Hello there! Stranger! Stranger in the future! Weird to think about, isn't it? The future, which I am writing a message to, here in the past. The future which I, that is to say, we, are trying to save.

It's fascinating, isn't it? Time, that elusive concept, stymies even the brightest of minds! Communication and time travel have been long dispersed by many scientists (dare I say scientists smarter than I?) Leaving a tangible message to the future, and passing things, quite literally and metaphorically, would be an impossible feat to accomplish even after so many of our breakthroughs.

As a Chronologist (a time professor, if you will), the act of creating a time capsule feels like a poor attempt to achieve exactly that– to rebel against time itself.

Can you imagine the beauty?

The beauty in this bridge between eras—a chance to connect with people we'll never meet, exchange words we'll never hear, share smiles we cannot see!

The reason I wanted to do this is to pass on lessons to you, my dear family member, lessons, and of course, things of value. Immense value, yes, yes, because you see, well, the real reason I did this, is for... you see... The truth is sad. Humans have continued to exist, but only just that. Not live, but exist. They've lost their heart. The altruism once exhibited by humans (humanity!) no longer exists, and so we call it 'ity'. No 'human' in 'humanity.' Just 'ity,' or 'its' for better pronunciation. We cannot sit by and let this continue.

*All of us chose a single thing that represented who we were and also taught us something valuable. This project, undertaken by all of your family members, past and present, is a preservation of our family, yes, but also a preservation of humanity and what makes being human **beautiful**.*

The younger one laughed. "A time capsule!"

They rummaged through the things inside, the dust billowing around them, until finally, they uncovered their first treasure.

A multilayered cloth with loops on the end. A mask. A mask that had big scary letters that made no sense to either brother:

"SARS/COVID-19 FACE COVERING"

They read the note that came with it.

Respiratory Pandemic. People died. I chose this for its symbolism (and if my studies are correct, many people will need these later on). This mask is a reminder of the world's resiliency and adaptability in the face of desperation and death. It is the simple power of science, and how, for the very first, and only, time in our history, we were united as one people.

It was not signed, but an image conjured in the Older Brother's mind of a young, fidgety man with glasses.
Younger Brother laughed. You couldn't blame him, the mask looked quite funny.

"How do you wear it?" He asked. He put it on his face, pinching the mask to his nose, but neglecting to fully wear it.

"It goes around your ears," the older brother said impatiently. He took it from his hand and looped the threads around his younger brother's ears. As he was doing so, he was hit with a memory. A happier time only a few years before. He had helped looped... what was it? A hat? Yes, a birthday hat over his brother's ears for his birthday. He had needed help then, and he had needed help now. Younger Brother must have also had the same realization because his eyes began to pool up again. Older Brother quickly pulled out the next item and handed it to him, who immediately forgot his woes.

He held it up against the flaming sky, a strange fabric with vibrant colors. It took a bit for both of them to realize that it was a flag.

The description read: FROM (not with) LOVE, ISTHIA. poet by day. sleeper by night.

I chose this as a reminder to act with our benevolence and kindness to all other humans. To treat them as we would treat our own. Evil sometimes triumphs. It will always be there, a little pull at the back of our minds. We must never let it win.

It feels impossible, no? How can you be kind to someone you hate?

Simple. In the quest of life, remember this– you are every person that has lived. You are every person who is living. And you are every person who will live.

Therefore-

Each person you injure, you injure yourself. Each person you love, you love yourself.

So why not try some

Love?

This is a flag of a nation that exists no more, except in the minds of its people.

The younger one was downhearted. "That's... really, really sad."

"Yeah. That's history for you, I guess. Love the message though." The older brother pulled out the next artifact from its seal. It was a computer chip, signed "A burly man in a hard hat."

It must be because of my age, but as time goes by, I fear we may approach the point where all knowledge will be gatekept behind money. Where multi-billion-dollar corporations decide who gets the right to education and who doesn't. It isn't fair. Education and knowledge saved me from my abyss, so I must try and do the same.

That's why I present to you the entire database of human knowledge! This chip here is a 100GB download of everything known to man (if you do not know what a gigabyte is, or the terminology is outdated, think about it as enough 'room' or 'storage' to furnish an entire library floor with books!) Take it with a grain of salt, though, some things are inaccurate. But it's the best thing we can do.

"Isn't that… technically already a thing? Like school and college?" He asked his older brother.
"Yeah. I bet he's European. Lucky dog."

They carefully sealed the chip back into the seal and set it aside.
The younger brother grabbed a thin rectangular sort of brick from the box.
"What the heck is this?" He asked nobody in particular. His older brother surprised him by answering.
"A phone. A very, very old model. I recognize it from mo-" he stopped suddenly. The sentence hung in the air until Younger Brother broke the silence.
"Well, whatever it is, it looks funny." He fiddled around with it. "It doesn't work," he said, disappointed.
"Of course it doesn't," The older brother sneered. "It's been, what, a hundred years? Read the note that came with it."

This is my favorite! Let this be your reminder to be in a state of moderation. The instrument you hold before you helped mankind greatly. It was supposed to help us, humans, become more interconnected, boost our technological progress, increase information, and make our lives easier. But it didn't. It hurt us in ways we could never imagine. Many people just dedicated their lives to the little boxes on their screen, 'till they grew ill, 'till they grew weak. I could, I would, say more, but paper and pencil nowadays are expensive…

Life is a balance. Strive for balance.

– Someone close to your heart

After extracting a promise from the older brother that he would do everything in his power to fix the phone, they moved on to the next bit, which was a movie. This person had chosen not to sign her name, leaving only three words: A young immigrant.

Both could only make out part of the title, which read 'Ever…' the rest was too faded away with time.

i watched this movie on a whim, i think. so many people said it was good, so, why not? and plus, i didn't care how i spent the rest of my life, y'know?

my generation had multiple crises. as someone who lives (or lived, i guess, depending on how far off you open this) i can say that what has resulted from all these crises is a sense of nihilism. a sense of hopelessness and cynicism. that nothing matters in this life.

i'll be the first to admit that i felt this way. it was horrible.

but there was the beauty that the movie taught me: since nothing matters, then by default, everything matters. for, there is only life and what you do with it. be absurd, be silly. there is life and the people you love. there is life and the people you cherish. there is life and the people you share it with. be kind especially when everything is hurting. i hope this heals you, as it did for me.

Touched, both brothers moved on to the next item. There were several metal cylinders. When the older brother went to pick it up, he snatched his hand, cursing, as it had given him a cold burn. It wasn't signed, but both had a feeling it was from the time professor.

These are plant seeds. I'm sorry. We tried everything.

Now, at this moment in time, when we are well past the warming threshold, there is little doubt of the decline of the biological future of this world.

Our planet fell victim to humans, her own creation.

These seeds are a new start. These are some seeds that we have predicted will no longer exist, that have already gone extinct. I want you to take these seeds, and plant them, yes of course, but also take them as a reminder to strive for what you believe in. I want you to never compromise your dreams or ideals, even in the face of overwhelming defeat. When you are at odds with life, preserve what is important and push towards the best outcome. Never let your burning soul extinguish. We hope these seeds find a good home.

(Password to deactivate the Cryo-Freeze is 1.5degreesC)

They stared at the seeds with heavy hearts.

"We have a job to finish." The older brother lightly gripped Younger Brother's shoulders and gently pulled him away.

They rummaged for a bit and found a hammer, chisel, and a piece of wood crudely wrapped by a blueprint. A photograph was included, of a young, balding man with eyebags, a crooked nose, and a beautiful smile.

These...things, admittedly, will probably have little to no use for you, whenever in the future you open it. But I chose it for its symbolism. You do not get what you dream of. You get what you work for. Sometimes that work is hell. But it is only through these trials of hard work that you can progress. And I promise you the fruit of being closer to your goals, monumental or gradual, tastes all the more wonderful.

They both touched the collection of tools, feeling them in their hands and gently put them aside.

They delved further into the cabinet and found a notebook with a mirror on the first page. The writing was elegant and loopy, immediately making Younger Brother think of a fussy old woman.

STOP COMPARING YOURSELF.

This is something, personally, that everyone struggles with, regardless of time. Simply put, it is foolish to compare yourself to someone else.

As for the items, I hope you are not so imprudent as to think of them as useless. A notebook and a mirror– Their importance and use never falters through time! So I encourage you, dear family member, to take a hard look at yourself. Listen to your heart. What does it whisper to you? Your meaning in this beautiful life? How do you measure your progress and your own pace? Only you know your own capabilities, and it is up to you to do so.

Comparison brings unwanted change. I am close to the end of my time and wish I had dared to live a life true to myself. But maybe, just maybe, it's not over for me yet.

The younger one giggled. He flipped to the first page and began making funny faces in the mirror. The older one smiled and turned to a rather tall parcel, with a strange sort of wrapping around it.

As they peeled the wrapping from the frame, the older brother gasped, for it was a painting, and he recognized it. It was of an elegant black woman. She sat up straight on a high chair, her dress flowing around the portrait. Her stern, yet kind gaze offered a simple challenge: *Bring it on.*

This painting is of the former First Lady of the United States of America. How do you think the painter managed such a feat? Patience is needed. It is a powerful portrait, designed to inspire. Both of these women, painter, and subject, did much good in their life. Through their actions, many other people spread good. Upon seeing the contrast I am struck with so many different emotions. I am struck by the powerful tale of identity and art.

Never forget patience with your artistic tone. I always do.
– Ms Fehuaj

They stared at the portrait and basked in its warm glow before pulling out the next item, which was another box, titled 'LITTLE CULTURAL COLLECTIONS'

They opened it. There was an X-ray of 2 people kissing. There was a notebook with samples of every single color known to man. There was a photo book of people laughing, photos of people dancing, crying, and mourning, and photos of babies and adults of all races, clad in all clothes of religion. Photos of people, of living.

While flipping the pages, a strange structure tumbled out, which they would later recognize as a coral reef, a gift from a certain Kuria Viuyt.
The label said something about man's short-term desire over future security, but it too, like the movie, was damaged beyond comprehension.

Underneath it was a blank thank you card. No signatory. No information.

The secret to happiness is gratitude. Gratuity in others, in yourself, in small things, small joys. No explanation needed.

Older and Younger Brother both tucked the cards into their pockets. Older Brother felt around the edges of the metallic cabinet to see if there were any more things they had missed. His hand hit something, and he grabbed it. It was a docket titled 'Antibiotics and Phage Therapy by Farhe Lexin'

This was an interesting case. To sum it up, we created revolutionary medicines that made it so a human would not die from a bacterial infection from something such as a simple cut. We called them antibodies. But they don't work anymore, and people are dying young again. I blame doctors for over-prescribing these. I blame patients for pressuring doctors. I blame companies for overmanufacturing. I blame farmers for giving them to their animals. There's enough blame to go around, but that's not what I'm trying to teach you. Blaming people doesn't do anything anyway.

So we came together. We created something new. They're called phages, and they're essentially 'hacked viruses' that target specific bacteria. It's an absolutely engrossing, enthralling field of science. And by god, I'll defend it, even here years after my death.

I bring this up to make two points.

Point One. Our ancestors dealt with essentially the same thing, the same problem. They turned to the natural world for it, and we took inspiration from them. I say this because, to change the world, one must look not only to the future and modern world, but also glance at the past, for the past is littered with answers. They used the divine art of science and found a solution. And so did we.

Point Two. They came together! They united as one to achieve a common goal of good. When people see the good in you, they will be with you. They will grow and learn, you will grow and learn.

"That's awesome!" The younger one shrieked. The older brothers' eyes were wide in agreement.

But now, both their eyes fell upon the last, the final item.

Both siblings, almost sadly, touched it. It was two pieces of paper, a letter, titled 'Sorrow Passes and We Remain,' and a note.

"Together?" The younger brother asked.

"Together." The older brother affirmed.

Now this is my final gift to you, dear reader.

Much has changed, and will have changed, by the time you have opened this. Truth be told, I doubt you will be able to tell what some of this stuff is.

But one thing is constant, in light of all of these changes in people and in society. One thing that does not change, and will never change with the passage of time (especially concerning humans) is grief. Grief will never go by another word, another feeling.

Sadness and desolation will always be with us, like the dust that settles on the photo of a deceased loved one. But it is what makes us human. I leave you with a copy of this letter from an author, Henry James. He wrote this to his longtime friend, Grace Norton, after receiving worrying letters from her regarding her recent familial losses.

It is widely claimed to be the most moving and human testament to compassion and advice-giving, since its conception, back in 1883. Also widely believed is that none have passed its grace. At least in our time. I've been stalling too long now. Good luck, my dear friend. Happy reading.

Heads bent together, both of them, young and old, began to read.

The younger one was dismayed. He wasn't able to understand the fancy jargon of the letter. He could not touch the words for they dangled, tauntingly, above his reach. And the few that he could reach, he could not understand what they meant, for they slipped from his grasp, like grains of sand in an hourglass.

But the older one did. You could tell by the way his eyes streamed and the way he gave little gasps here and there, and how his breath was stifled.

The words on the page eventually came to an end. They sat there, considering everything until the sun came up.

A few stars peeked out from the dark canopy of the night sky and twinkled, amused at the happenings of the world below them.

They then faced one another, in a comfortable, yet, vulnerable, silence.

"Can you tell me more about mom?"

The older one's eyes softened.

"Of course."

Almost as if rehearsed, they rose in unison and headed indoors. The younger one jumped and bounced and slammed the door open, peals of laughter bouncing off the walls.

The older one paused and turned around. He looked at what they unearthed, together. Making up his mind, he walks inside with his brother, a small smile on his face.

.

.

.

in the ruins of the planter box, a seed begins to germinate.

ECHOES THROUGH THE MOUNTAIN

SAMANTHA PACINI-CARLIN

Blood caked the roof of Cerallia's mouth. Rivulets had also dried in her throat, and pressed dust against it. She coughed. Knives slashed at her windpipe from within, then sent a shockwave of pain through her body. Gods, it felt like an army took hammers to her flesh. She reflexively curled her hands, splayed across a pile of pebbles, into fists. Tears streamed down her cheeks. It stung, yet freed her eyes from the dust that glued them shut.

Stone bricks carved with birds in flight – most gashed into oblivion – blurred into view. Rubble spilled out below it like a person's guts. Dust leeched the plush red from the carpets, leaving a blanket of gray in its wake. Crystal fragments crawled over it. Their dim light, similar to a candle's without the flicker, darkened the shadows beneath the rubble.

Where was Sir Hendralvia?

She crawled to her feet, though winced from another shock of pain in one leg. Well, it could've been worse. Her arcane shield, long since shattered, had taken blows that would otherwise take her to greet Death themself.

Idle thoughts such as those did her no good. Cerallia spun around the hallway of stone, scanning the area for any signs of Hendralvia. Dust twirled off her long blonde hair. Most of its strands had been torn loose from the half bun, and stuck out at odd angles. Tears disgraced her silk shawl. Scratches dug into the leather cord belt that held it in place. She cared little for its condition, but the dust and blood stains on her Anointed dress would be unacceptable to the Midnight Court. They'd scoff at the portions of her violet skirt – cut for easy movement – nibbled away.

Gods, the Court. She paused to check the state of her arms. Unlike her ghostly pallor, a thin layer of midnight violet speckled with stars clung to the bone like the skin of a starving man and consumed it up to the sockets. The left one's essence, however, reached her heart. She grimaced. If her arms were worn out to this degree already...

Blood stuck to the pile of rubble further ahead. Cerallia ignored her own pain and raced to it, memories flashing in her mind: Hendralvia, who rushed ahead to charge the green-coated Thyme Witches. Chunks falling from the ceiling as the stone itself roared. The stars swirling to the fingertips of her outstretched hand, and-

She swept the rubble off a body. His body. The stone pinned him into a kneel reminiscent of the First Blades' portraits in the training hall, but his head slumped rather than gazed into a greater destiny. Dents ruined his sleek silver armor. Blood seeped out from under his copper hair and dribbled down his face. Two irises, once an intense blue, stared downwards – dull and sightless.

Cerallia froze, helpless against the waves that crashed against her mind with the fury of a sea god's wrath. Sir Hendralvia was dead. The one whose safety the Court swore her life to nights prior died while within her reach.

Oh, gods. She had failed them both.

The gravity of her negligence pressed down on her – choked her lungs, and squeezed the walls of her dust-scraped throat tightly. It sapped what little strength she had mustered. Her knees slammed against the carpet, which sent a cloud of dust into the air. She had expected tears to clean the threads below her. None came. Exhaustion hit her instead, and bid her to curl into a ball at Hendralvia's feet. Darkness came thereafter.

...

Yet some part of Cerallia persisted, flickering against the rest of her that wished to end her story there. It wrenched her eyes open. Nothing new awaited her in these halls, save for the little flame of life within her.

Wait. Something had changed since she lost consciousness again – a rhythmic scraping against stone past the corner of the hall.

Cerallia reluctantly pulled herself to her feet. She limped towards the corner, but paused at its cusp, drawn back to Sir Hendralvia's body. It seemed foolish to take him with her. She couldn't lug him all the way back to Passings for the proper funeral rites, and gods know how the mages would react to her failure. Could she simply leave him here, though?

No. She dragged herself back to him, then sat and crossed her legs at his feet. Those hollow eyes twisted her stomach into knots. She tore her gaze away from it, digging into her mind to recall their conversation from the night before. He mentioned he loved saltglade trees, a rare subterranean tree found in coastal caves. Well, the mountain that buried him overlooked the sea; perhaps such a tree could thrive on magic until the salt-scented breeze could break through the stone of his tomb.

She placed her hands over his heart. The stars flecked throughout her arms swirled to her fingers and vibrated with potential. Light tethered them together like constellations. It grew brighter, until it drowned the midnight hue in its white-hot flare.

Cerallia forced an exhale between her clenched teeth. The light burned worse when the essence drew closer to her bones, but she kept her focus on a quiet hum. She summoned an image of the tree: gray bark twisted into cords, its grains rough yet smooth when one traced their finger over it, and soft where the moss hung. Its branches splintered into leaves that drooped down to veil the wood. Those felt more like feathers than plants. Hendralvia had chuckled at the mention of it, and remarked that he wanted a pillow made of them as a child. His attempt to make one went poorly, though. And now, thanks to witches' forces, he would never have a chance to try it again. But she could offer something akin to it for his eternal rest.

Hendralvia's skin faded to bark, melding with the saltglade tree that blossomed from his back. Roots burrowed into the stone. Vines slithered from the points of its branches, then burst into a bright blue glow. It outshone the light on her own arms – already dimmer from the magic drained by her spell.

Once the burn faded, she inspected them. Gods, she could see the gap in her forearms' bones through the midnight stretched across it. She hoped the day wouldn't call for more powerful spells.

Cerallia picked herself up. She lingered on his wooden face, eyes open yet peaceful, before parting the leafy veil. They did feel like feathers. Hopefully he could feel them, too, on his trek to Death's palace.

She stepped out of the canopy with some of the burden off her shoulders. The mere thought of reporting back to the Court, however, made the rest weigh more than the building they resided in. They wouldn't hold an Anointed who couldn't protect their knight in high regards. Would they strip her of her position? Even if they did not, what knight would want someone who failed to protect the last one in their charge? Nobody rational, certainly. Perhaps she should plan to spend the rest of her days in exile, then, and make preparations to train for a life without arms. Perhaps she should lay herself to rest before they learn of her shame.

She approached the corner. Dread skittered down her spine a few steps towards it, though, and froze her in place. The scraping from earlier had stopped.

A shadow cast onto the floor from around the corner ducked out of sight.

"Wait! Please!" Cerallia tried to call. Her voice grated against her throat, which reduced her word into an incomprehensible coughing fit. It was a miracle her lungs stayed in her body.

The shadow didn't respond. Its footsteps grew quieter as they traveled further into the hall.

Cerallia cursed her limp. It caused her to lag behind the shadow, turning the corners it passed moments after it. And when she forced herself to pick up the pace, she stumbled over rubble. The strain soon left her gasping for breath. Still, she pressed on. Whatever cast this shadow offered something besides the thoughts of death and shame. She *needed* its tangibility.

She turned another corner. Stones toppled over busts tucked into small alcoves, bright colors mixed with the raw gray pulled from the inside of the walls. More had surged through a large iron door and suffocated it. Where did the shadow go?

Something tackled her from behind. She slammed face-down onto the carpet, but managed to twist herself around.

Another woman with dust-smeared dark skin loomed over her. The ties of her bloodied white blouse fluttered inches away from Cerallia's nose – soft in comparison to her snarl. Her violet-black hair also hung loose. She clearly hadn't been prepared for any fights, but she still managed to clamp a hand around her wrist and smother it in the carpet with unusual strength. The other, wrapped in bandages emblazoned with ink, held a dagger. Portions of the wrappings leaked smoke.

Cerallia used her free hand to grab the dagger hand. Her strength was a mouse's compared to a cat's jaws, however, and proved futile as the blade sank closer to her neck. The blade glimmered, hungry for her blood.

"Any last words, shit-hands?" the woman growled.

Her blade grazed her skin as the last of Cerallia's strength waned, yet it did not cut her. She stared at her attacker, mind racing. She didn't wear green, though she must be allied with them if she wanted to slay her. Why offer her, an Anointed, last words, though?

"Well?" The dagger drew a bead of blood from her neck.

She looked past the battle-wrought anger and snarl to gaze into the woman's eyes. Fear? No, hesitation flickered within them – the kind a knight felt when they faced their first opponent in the field. It tangled itself with the necessity of delivering death. It stayed their hand when it should've thrust their blade through flesh without hesitation. It was something they forgot with time.

"I can help," Cerallia croaked.

The woman studied her, though kept the dagger trained on her throat. "What was that? Mutter any sort of magic, and you'll kiss Death on the lips."

"I-" She coughed. Her hand fell away from the woman's, and brushed her neck. A warm pulse washed through it. When she spoke again, the knives within were dulled. "I can't imagine you want to wander here until you starve to death. Let me go. If you don't kill me, we might be able to find a way out." Yes, she could focus on that – sunlight, not the end promised in these dim confinements.

Her brow raised. "And how do I know you won't blast me while I turn my back?"

"Because I'm stuck down here, too."

Their eyes locked together, each searching the other for any deceit. Cerallia sensed none from the woman. She did not seem to sense any from her either, and relaxed her snarl into a contemplative frown. The dagger retracted a smidgen from her neck.

"Fine." She slipped off of her, then stood up. Her dagger was pointedly still trained on her – a warning to not misbehave.

Cerallia did not intend to for the moment. She pushed herself onto her feet and backed away from the woman, rubbing her wrist. Gods, she felt like a chicken trapped in a cage with a fox. The beast's belly was full for now, but if its allegiance lay with the witches, it would strike soon. She doubted she'd wait for her powers to return if that happened.

The woman jerked her thumb to the rubble-choked door, which left a smoky afterimage behind it. "Way's out that way. I tried clearing a tunnel with my hands, but it's tedious work. Were you made to blast things?"

She ignored her question, too fixated on her bandages to bother answering. "Strength wards," she hissed.

"Pardon?"

A sneer spread across Cerallia's lips. "You are aligned with the witches, if you so readily use such unclean magic. How primitive. I assume some turn-back wards are mixed in as well?"

"Shut it." She stomped forward, and leveled the dagger at her throat again. "Do you want to escape, or should I just slit your throat?"

She shuffled towards the rubble. Once the woman lowered the blade, she turned her attention to the rocks. Ideas began to bubble in the back of her mind in regards to her, though she tucked them away for the moment. She laid a hand on the stones instead. If she could find its weakest point, the whole thing would collapse with one strike. "I will aid you."

"You'd better."

She pressed into a pile of smaller pebbles, and burned a little essence to send her senses through it. Her awareness bounced off the rocks within. One giant piece, submerged in the shallows of the surrounding wreck, held everything together.

"Well, are you the blasting type?" the woman asked. "It seems to me like you're just petting them like they're dogs."

Cerallia rolled her eyes. "I am not an Anointed Striker, but I have the capacity to attack when shields do not work. But what we do is not 'blasting'; it is far more refined."

"I don't give a damn about what it's called, just carve us a path."

She limped a foot away from the rubble, then trained a hand in the giant one's direction. Light devoured her arms again. The burn swept down them to focus on the palms like she gripped a burning piece of charcoal. It took a small layer of essence with it. Compared to the funeral rites, though, it consumed drops rather than a pond.

Cerallia thrust her hand back. The light tore off of it, and exploded out towards the rocks. It singed through the rubble with the ease of a mole tunneling through dirt. The pile groaned in response. Its pieces tumbled over one another in a tiny avalanche, dismantled with the giant piece's destruction. A wave of dust followed. Once everything settled, a path cut through the mountain that previously blocked the doors.

The woman stepped to her side. She twirled the dagger between her fingers, but fumbled it because of their slight quiver. "So you *are* useful."

"I am far more effective than your dirty magic," Cerallia retorted.

She shrugged. "Maybe. At least my 'dirty magic' protected me from a limp and sore throat. But say what you will." She swept her hand towards the path. "After you."

"I do not particularly feel like turning my back to you." Cerallia folded her arms.

The woman barked out a laugh. "Neither do I, shit-hands, but stabbing each other doesn't seem wise while we're still buried here. Not if you intend to strike first, that is."

"Refer to me as *Cerallia*, the Anointed Shield." Well, that assumed the Midnight Court would allow her to keep that title when she returned to them. It held true for the moment, though. "I could think of an insulting title for you, should you not refer to me as such. My tongue isn't gold enough to be above such things."

She smirked like a jackal baring its fangs. "Mine isn't gold enough to say that full title, Cerallia, though you can call me Lilt."

"Lilt." In spite of its pleasant connotations, the name rolled on her tongue with a sour aftertaste.

She slipped her dagger into a sheath at her hip, then wandered over to a statue. From behind it, she withdrew a bag. She tossed it over her shoulder, and secured it to her belt to hide her weapon. "Well, why don't we walk side-by side to better keep an eye on each other? We won't go anywhere if we just stare in suspicion."

"If I must."

Lilt joined her side. The two climbed over the stones, gripping onto larger pieces to keep their balance. Part of Cerallia was inclined to blast her down at its peak, but she restrained herself.

A large chamber more silent than dead in their coffins stretched out before them. Chunks of the ceiling smashed into wooden tables. Splinters mingled with spilled ale, porcelain fragments, and food mashed beyond recognition. Other puddles, crimson, seeped across the tiles. Cerallia prayed it was spilled wine from goblets under the rocks, not...the kind she'd prefer not to think about.

She let her thoughts distract her. The sooner she could leave Lilt's side, the better, given her plans to return to the court; she doubted they'd be pleased with her company. Then again, this woman presented her with an opportunity. Lilt used those foul wards. Her involvement with the witches also meant she aided in Sir Hendralvia's demise. What if she turned in the sinner to them? Surely they'd see how, despite her failure, she redeemed herself through delivering justice to his killer. Through that, she may yet retain her Anointed status.

"How did you get those wards?" Cerallia asked.

Lilt eyed her. "Funny question coming from your type. Are you trying to weigh my soul before Arcanai gets a chance to?"

"It is simply a question."

A wry smile cracked across her lips. "It's a question from an Anointed. Whatever I say isn't going to matter, since your mind is already made up. Using, making – it's all equal to your folks. You'll end it the same way, won't you?"

"I do not fault us for doing so." Cerallia swept her arm across the chamber, slowing to emphasize the blood under the rocks. "This is what you wreak without our justice."

Lilt crawled over a smaller mound. "And you're certain your little interruption didn't cause the ritual to malfunction, hm?"

"You should not have attempted it at all." She glared up at her, blood boiling at the woman's audacity to smirk. "I pray we were able to slay whatever horrid thing you summoned, else the common folk pay the price for the corruption you spread. We are not the ones who deserve such mockery. We are all that stand between the tidal wave of spirits you usher in, and all that is *good* in this world."

Lilt strode ahead, and kicked another set of doors open. "Are we, now? Tell that to the old woman your people burned for the sake of it."

"What?"

She whirled to face Cerallia, dropping the smirk. "The Thyme Witches passed through my home, and arcane inquisitors 'happened to show up' days later. They also 'just so happened' to suspect the elder of witchcraft. Why? Because they 'found evidence' – nevermind what it was, or how they came to that conclusion." Lilt snarled. "How convenient: a sinner to make an example of in a village witches brushed by. Gods, I can still see the bloodstain and ash scattered on dirt when I close my eyes."

Cerallia bristled. She opened her mouth to reply, but Lilt didn't give her a chance.

"Don't give me that 'deserved' shit, either. I know what she was, and she wasn't someone like *me*. But they don't treat their orphans any better, do they? Tell me, did it hurt when they decided to Anoint you?"

Warmth under the blankets robbed by the cold night air. Chanting. Screams reverberating through the little room. Light. A hand far larger than hers clamped on her arms like shackles, dragging her to the light. Blindness. The pain of flesh and bone burned to cinders. Her own screams added to the chorus. "No."

Lilt shook her head, anger fizzled into a burden. "Sure. All you do is deny the pain your Court causes, then condemn us for trying to cauterize the wounds you inflict with the scraps that remain."

"And with those scraps, you demand more," she hissed. "The divine made their judgment when magic graced the world. It remains with *us* and *us* alone – not those who use pale imitations to deny them. To deny *us*."

She glared at her. "Better to deny 'em and die than to sink into complacency under your thumb."

A pebble tumbled in front of them, kicked by something unseen. The dagger flashed into Lilt's hand. Cerallia herself whipped towards the noise, hands raised in anticipation of a spell. Did someone else survive the collapse?

A hand flopped on top of a rock mound – limp, as though pulled into place by strings. Its fingers gripped nothing.

"What in the godsdamn?" Lilt whispered.

The body shuffled up after it. Blood consumed the green of the man's coat, and his arms were bent at the wrong angles. His neck cracked as he raised his head to look at them. Gods, she wished he hadn't. Skin sagged over the hollow spaces of his eyes, which opened to two red abysses. His jaw, mirroring his skin, swung loose. Before the taste of vomit could well in Cerallia's mouth, the thing pounced at Lilt.

Her grunt cut off her cry. It knocked her to the ground – satisfying, danger notwithstanding – and bent its arms to throttle her. Vines sprouted from under its skin to aid it.

More things scrambled over the rubble behind Cerallia. She spun around to face two more not-people, one of whom's skull was caved in to reveal a tangle of vines for a brain. The other's legs had been battered to a pulp. Something similar to a vacant expression hung on their faces, though the lack of eyes communicated very little. Their gurgles, however, sent shivers up her spine. A vile mixture of blood and spit dribbled down their jaws, falling on the rocks below.

Both pounced. Cerallia leapt out of the first's way, but the second caught her bad leg as it crashed to the ground.

Vines burrowed into the flesh like worms. She yelped, though its grip was too strong for her to pull away. In fact, it pulled her to the ground with ease. The other used this opportunity to claw towards her with broken fingers, its gurgle now a roar of spittle.

"Enough!" Cerallia growled. She threw her arms forward and slapped her palm onto the thing's temple. How *dare* this lowly creature attack her!

The stars shot towards the inside of her hand, blazing with her fury. It singed the cold skin off the thing's head, though the smell of burnt flesh mixed with grass almost made her retract it. But now was not a time for weakness; she forced her nausea back into her stomach, then pressed it deeper in.

Its insides evaporated. One last gurgle emitted from the thing before it doubled over, then lay still.

Cerallia kicked its vines – now shriveled up – off her leg, and rolled away from the second one's claws. She grabbed the vines that surged out of it. They wriggled in her hands in an attempt to find skin, but she scorched them to ash. Simultaneously, her other hand curled into a fist, which punched through the thing's ruined body. Ribs crackled from the heat. It, too, collapsed within moments of her strike.

She scrambled to her feet, searching for Lilt. The woman wrestled three creatures at the top of a rubble pile, limbs in a blur of kicks and slashes. She held most at bay, save for the one clamped on her side.

Cerallia stumbled over the rubble, hands outstretched. She grabbed the necks of two of the creatures and reduced them to cinders. Lilt, still fending off the third, flashed her a smile. Her dagger sank into one of its empty sockets while a burn ate through its chest. What little intact pieces of it remained fell limp at her side, its jaw stuck in a rictus of pain.

"This is what you summoned?!" Cerallia demanded. "An army of corpse-defiling nightmares to plague all of Ralva?"

Lilt raised a finger to her lips and surveyed the rubble.

She bit her tongue. If their shouts had drawn those things towards them, gods know how many more might be lured in by the fight. She bounced her senses through the room. Fortunately, the rest of the bodies under the rubble lay still, resting in Death's embrace.

"This is probably a byproduct," Lilt whispered. "What they meant to summon was more…pleasant. I wouldn't be surprised if your interference twisted it into something worse."

She wiped her hands on the rubble to rid them of ash. "We should get moving."

"Agreed." She slipped the dagger back into its sheath, then slid to her feet. Her shaky footsteps betrayed how much it affected her in spite of the casual gait she projected. "This way."

The next set of doors led to a wider hallway punctured by alcoves fitted with plush sofas. It might have been cozy before the collapse. Now, the warmth it possessed was dampened by the scent of iron. An occasional limb emerged from under the rocks. Bent spears and swords, some still clasped in hands, spoke of the chokehold the soldiers fought in. Cerallia longed to uncover her people. Her escape took precedence, though, and carried her past the faceless dead.

"For how 'up it' you are, I'm thankful," Lilt said suddenly.

Cerallia raised a brow at her. "A strange thing to feel, but think nothing of it. I was made to protect others. You should be more thankful that we are not currently on opposite sides of the battlefield."

"I am in a sense, I suppose. It would've been easy for you to abandon me, however, and I wasn't raised to take that for granted."

"Hm." Well, she had other reasons to keep Lilt alive – ones she didn't need to know about. Still, her words oddly warmed her. Such duties were simply expected of the Anointed, who needed no encouragement or incentive to carry them out, yet that warmth…

Lilt slowed her pace, and patted at an empty space by one of her dagger sheaths. Upon finding nothing there, she frowned.

"Is something wrong?" Cerallia asked.

She sighed. "I forgot to grab some things from my room. Give me a moment." She swerved towards the wall, and stopped in front of a wooden door.

"I had assumed you already possessed everything you needed."

Lilt grappled the knob and shoved it, but the door refused to budge. "Damn. This is just extra supplies I had from before you stormed in here." She nodded her head towards the bodies under the rubble. "Bit hard to run in here when everyone's stabbing each other, and harder when rocks block the way."

She kept her focus on the door – not the broken limbs. Not on the swords. "Do you-"

Lilt backed away from it. She then charged forward, slamming her shoulder against the wood. It let out a squeal shiller than a pig's, and swung open.

"Rusty hinges," she said with a shrug. "They never bothered to fix them while I was gone."

Cerallia followed her in, but lingered at the entrance. She almost anticipated the woman to leap at her again from a shadowy corner with daggers drawn. Thankfully, a trunk captivated her attention. She had swept the fallen rocks off of it, which left dents in the curved wooden top. The bed did not fare as well; its frame collapsed under the fallen ceiling, while dust slobbered over the sheets. Next to it, rocks smashed

an armoire to splinters. Bits of clothes spilled from the wreckage –
fineness reduced to tatters fit for the streets – though one color caught
her eye: green. It belonged to a sleeve that crawled over the others
like a bug.

"You don't wear your witch's coat," she mused.

Lilt cracked the trunk open, and dug through its contents. Jars
clinked within. She set them to the side to continue her search. "That
would give me away. If I wanted to wear it out, I may as well scream
that I use wards while I strut through the cities, too." She examined a
roll of bandages. "It's not like they're considerate of who they slaughter,
though."

Realization struck Cerallia like a lightning bolt. "You're a spy! Gods,
we thought we cleansed or drove them all out of the Court."

"The Court, yes." The corner of her lip twitched into a sneer. "But
I'm one of many eyes scattered through your precious little territory.
Well, I am for now."

She eyed the ward-bandages. "'For now' – does that imply you plan
on turning against them?"

Lilt paused. "Not quite 'turn against'. I'm just volunteering myself
until I get what I need. Isn't that why we put a stake into some cause or
another? The witches give me mine. Gods know how much you enjoy
yours for the price of murder."

"Whatever benefits I receive are meager compared to the importance of our work."

She rolled her eyes. "Sure. I suppose that helps you sleep soundly."

Cerallia's thoughts wandered to the Court. She did miss her bedroom nestled in the sleek obsidian halls. Her back twinged from laying
on the stone floor, which left her with a longing for the embrace of her
mattress. Gods, nothing had gone right today. She should already be
back there, sitting with Sir Hendralvia at the dining table with a plate
of honey glazed pork and cooked vegetables, not buried in a mountain.
She should walk through its halls, exchanging smiles with the fellow
Anointed, not subjected to Lilt's bitterness. Still, those were small benefits. They mattered little in comparison to the entrustment of Ralva's

peace and justice, didn't they? Yes, she could acknowledge the awards while pursuing her sacred tasks.

"There you are," Lilt purred.

She snapped back to the present. Lilt now held a strange dagger in her hand while she fastened its sheath to her hip. Clear crystal jutted from the hilt. A sprig of lavender was trapped inside, easily mistaken to be floating if not for the crystal's sheen. Its scent, underscored by burnt incense, wafted throughout the room.

Lilt waggled it at Cerallia. "Dust hasn't clogged your nose enough to block out its scent, yeah? Lavender's a nice contrast to all the blood. But what do you think?"

She didn't like the jackal's grin that stretched across her lips again. "You wish to hear my thoughts?"

"Sure."

She took a cautious whiff of it, though detected nothing harmful. There was something different about the lavender, however – a note of something fresher than any she smelled before. "It has a lovely scent. I have never quite smelled a lavender like it, but it is one without a doubt."

"It's the loveliest you'll ever smell." The grin collapsed into a frown, and her eyes grew unfocused. "The last of it you can smell, too. They burned my grandmother's fields when they killed her, claiming it was some kinda component to her spells. Every single one." Her voice dropped to a hiss. "Well, it'll be the last thing they smell when I'm through with them, too."

Cerallia took a reflexive step back. "Your grandmother was the elder you spoke of?"

"Of course. Why else would I try to get closer to you shithands?" She sheathed the dagger and used the trunk as leverage to pull herself up. "Damn witches thought I was better suited for civilian work – not the deeper stuff."

"Pure revenge is hardly a way to live," she scoffed, "especially given our defenses and your hesitation in killing."

Lilt growled. "Shut it. I'll be able to do it when they're an inch from the blade. And you're one to talk; gods know how many of your lives are wasted in petty battles and wars."

"*Justice and protection* is worthwhile. Your narrow minded chase after death is not."

She snorted. "Whose justice? The people – those you let starve in the streets? The wealthy? Your *cult?*"

Her knight. She stiffened at the thought. Had her notions of "good" been that embedded in one she met in recent times, or did she simply assign it to him?

Lilt cocked her head. "Did I break you too much with that? Well, try to pull yourself together before those things decide to crawl around the corner. There's much more we need to cover, too."

Cerallia nodded, grateful for the escape out of the conversation. She let her take the lead, then trailed at the woman's side.

They fell back into silence while the ambient lavender faded. Cerallia cast her senses out every so often, and thankfully found no trace of the plant-things. She silently thanked the gods for their luck; the last fight drained the translucent layer over her bones, leaving her with less essence than she would've preferred. Hopefully she wouldn't need to clear more rubble.

After a few turns, Lilt gestured her over to a smaller set of doors. "This is the quickest way to the entrance. Normally that shouldn't be an issue, but it leads to the garden."

"Oh."

She opened a small latch on it and peered through, though little could be seen through the darkness past it. "Well, we have your fire hands. Care to burn more of those freaks, or should we find another way? Either way, I'm sure you'll be effective."

"Step to the side." Once Lilt obliged, she went up to the hatch and echoed her senses through it. Nothing moved inside. Actually, it felt like very little lay inside, save for patches of the ground. She squinted, but couldn't make anything else out. "I sense nothing beyond it. That includes the land itself and those things."

Lilt stepped away, then scooped a crystal fragment off the ground. "Wonder what is."

"You are free to check, but I am certainly not stepping through."

She nudged Cerallia back. "Well, let's see." She cracked the door open and held the fragment inside. "Damn, you weren't kidding when you said there was nothing."

Cerallia wrenched the door open. Had Lilt not told her its purpose, she wouldn't think of what remained as a "garden". Dirt spilled from stone basins. Smashed glass mingled with soil and stone tiles with patterns torn to shreds. Chasms pocked the floor. Another set of doors were embedded in the opposite wall where pillars of the ground jutted out from the abyss below.

"I don't feel like throwing myself into Death arm's," Lilt said, "but you're free to do whatever you want."

She grimaced. "There must be another way around this. Find one."

"You're not in much of a position to demand things. Still, there are a few other ways I know of."

Lilt crept through the witches' lair, silent as the fallen soldiers they passed. She stopped at the corners to peek around them. Few other monsters haunted the path ahead, though their vine-laced throats were slit or burned long before they spotted them. Their surprised gurgles rang in Cerallia's ears. Gods, they almost sounded human.

Their path led to a door suffocated in fallen rocks, at which point Lilt turned to her expectantly. "Well?"

Cerallia sighed, but sent her senses through the pile. It seemed to stretch beyond the doorway, and obscured anything that could lay past it. She'd collapse sooner than she could clear it all away.

"It is far too thick."

Lilt glanced at Cerallia's arms – a thin layer of essence that clung to the bones. "Hmph. Guess we can try a few others, then. It's a damn shame you spent so much of it on that tree."

"On proper rites," she corrected her, ignoring the punch to her gut. "He deserved nothing less."

She directed Cerallia on another path, speaking in a hushed tone as she kept her eyes forward. "He? That person must be important if you couldn't ignore his body." She set her jaw. "Gods, a lot of people I talked to here are probably dead, too. Huh..."

"He was my assigned knight."

Lilt glanced at her, eyebrows raised halfway up her forehead. "*Really?* Aren't you supposed to be his shield? Gods, I thought your type was supposed to die long before them."

"The battle separated us," she replied bitterly. "You then brought the ceiling down before I could reach him again."

She bit her lip and looked away. "My companions are dead too, you know; turnback wards are only so effective against an onslaught of blades and a rockfall. Your side isn't the only one to suffer casualties. I'm sure that makes you feel better, though."

"No. I just wish for this day to never have happened." Cerallia blinked, surprised to hear herself speak those words aloud.

Lilt turned the corner. "I hate to say it, but I- *godsdammit!*"

She skidded around the corner to find more rubble with no door to be seen.

"Of course I wouldn't get out easily," she laughed. "The only other way is through the garden, and gods know if the ground is stable. We may as well throw ourselves in! Shit!"

Cerallia's face grew cold as the blood drained from it. She had little essence left to spend; one slip, and the world would vanish into the darkness. But darkness awaited her anyway if she did not escape this place. If the path to redemption forced her to leap over the void, so be it. Nothing else mattered. "The broken garden is the only way out, then."

Lilt let out a long sigh, shoulders slumped into acceptance. "I suppose so."

They trekked back to the garden, though anxiety tied her stomach back into knots. Lilt kept her mouth shut in reflection of her own fears. Each glance around the corner took longer, like she wanted to delay the time it took to reach the door.

The inevitable could not be delayed forever, though. Cerallia found herself in front of the door again, darkness spilling out of the open hatch. Its iron felt colder in her grip. The door itself groaned as she opened it, like it dreaded what lay ahead. Well, the ear-splitting noise did little to dissuade her. She already felt the clutch of dread on her heart and the recklessness of this path without a deafening reminder.

Cerallia stepped into the garden. She kept a hand locked on the doorframe, then applied pressure to the next tile with her foot. To her relief, it held her weight. The same might not apply to the area closer to the chasm, but this bit seemed safe enough.

"I'm surprised you didn't tumble in," Lilt remarked.

She stifled the urge to pull her into a pit, and ventured deeper in. Her voice bounced off the walls. "You would be pleased with that, wouldn't you? Regardless, the ground seems stable enough to traverse at the moment. I would hurry before it changes its mind."

"Fine." The light of the woman's shard grew brighter behind her, followed by the echoes of her footsteps.

Cerallia kept a wide berth around the first pit. She swore something moved within the darkness – something that slithered like the tentacles of an octopus. Was it the source of those faint scrapes? Perhaps they came from her feet grinding against the dust coated ground, misattributed to her imagination.

She slowed her pace to let Lilt draw closer. "Do you hear that?" she whispered. "The pits – I believe something might lurk within it."

Lilt glanced into one. Her face paled, and she nodded.

Gods. Cerallia crept further away from it, terrified that whatever lurked underneath them could hear the thunder of her heartbeat. It seemed content to lurk underneath for the moment, though. Would that change when she had to leap across the chasms? She mouthed prayers to every god she could think of for the amount of essence to defend herself against it, if not luck to sneak past it.

None answered her, but the crack of a tile under her foot did.

The slithers hissed like a forest shaken by a storm. Vines raced out of the darkness below – a vibrant green with blossoms larger than a person. The bouquet of skewered victims, however, dampened the beauty of its flowers. Their limp bodies flopped around with broken bones. Around her, more vines exploded out from the ground, which shredded flesh and skin off the people attached to it. What little scraps of their clothes remained carried traces of green and violet. It hadn't spared either of their people.

A sickly sweet fragrance flooded her lungs. She ignored the urge to hack it out until it bloodied her throat, and forced herself to sprint forward. Behind her, Lilt's light bobbed away from her side.

Cerallia couldn't glance back at her. The vines lashed out at her with their too-sharp tips, while others tried to bludgeon her with their bodies. Her training kicked in, though. She leapt over its low sweeps, then rolled under the swipes overhead without hesitation, driven by the drum of her heart. Damn this thing. Damn it for attacking her at her weakest point!

Lilt swerved into view ahead of her, chased by a vine. She sprinted to the edge of the floor, where the pillars emerged from the pits. This woman had hesitated to kill her before. She expected the same fears to stop her at its edge, but she threw herself across without hesitation.

Time froze. A vine whipped out of the chasm below, decorated with a woman's body, and snapped towards her.

It missed her foot by an inch. Lilt tumbled onto the first pillar, then used her momentum to spring to the next. The moment she leapt off the ground, vines crushed the one she had landed on.

Cerallia didn't dare think; to think about what she needed to do or the agony in her leg was to hesitate, and she'd be skewered if she hesitated. If it skewered her...no. She kept her eyes trained to the edge, in which Lilt soared over the chasm with vines at her tail. If a ward-witch could do it, she could, too. Once she reached the edge, she flung herself off with an unrefined screech.

The air roared in her ears. Her abrupt skid onto a pillar cut it off like a conductor of an orchestra. She sprung out of it, and cleared the second gap.

The skittering of vines chased her, and its tendrils clawed at the pillars she left behind. Bodies sloughed off them in their rampage. They fell into the darkness below, hollow expression meeting hers as the chasms claimed them. Cerallia shredded their faces from her memory. She couldn't let them distract her, especially if they belonged to the Court.

Lilt crashed through the door. Relief washed through her, but annoyance overtook it. Now that one prey left the thing's range of sense, it turned all of its attention to the other. Vines shot after her faster than before. She danced away from them, though some sliced across her face and dress. Blood now flew in the air behind her with each jump. In the brief moments that she stayed on one platform, red beads dripped down her cheek. Gods, they stung. She gritted her teeth and blocked out the pain, eyes focused on the door.

Four pillars away. Three. Two to salvation, then one. Cerallia grinned, leaping from all fours towards the door, where Lilt turned to look back at her.

In midair, a vine slammed into her side. The door turned sideways as though cocked in confusion, and terror robbed the breath from her lungs. Everything fell into darkness before she could scream.

Cerallia squeezed her eyes shut, though tears welled out from under them. She had failed yet again. Perhaps this was the destiny Arcani intended for her: to be forgotten, name lost along with the knights that fell, and thereby proven to be unfit for Midnight's blessings. Food for a monster. Already, vines began to wrap around her body to hasten her fall. Hopefully Death would make it swift.

Fingers wrapped around her wrist, then yanked her to a halt. She pried her eyes open. Where she expected to see a vine ready to skewer her instead swung Lilt. A long piece of ward-bandage stuck to the ground far above them, on which the ink curled into rivers of smoke.

"Not yet," Lilt growled.

Cerallia, numbed by her acceptance of death, could only stare back up at her. But this reprieve was finite; the vines pulled down on her, while more lashed up to catch Lilt.

The woman kicked at them. It held off the thing for a time, though her resistance amounted to little. Once one caught her foot, a swarm followed. The tendrils shed the bodies stuck onto them in their eagerness to devour them. Her grip on her arm quivered. Between the vines that tugged Cerallia below and her own fight, she would drop her in mere moments.

Her senses jolted her out of the numbness. Cerallia ignited the thin layer of essence left on her arms, and screamed as she pushed it into a fiery bubble around her.

The vines fizzled into ash. Those who had escaped it reeled back, trailed with fire. Lilt flashed her a grin. While the thing was distracted by its pain, she tugged on the ward, which shot them up to the ground in the blink of an eye.

Both fled through the doorway. More darkness lurked within it, forcing Cerallia to stumble blindly through it. Gods, her lungs wanted to collapse. She heaved air through them as her footsteps thundered with Lilt's in a panicked rhythm. Their sprint lasted an eternity. It was only when the hisses faded into silence that her legs buckled.

Lilt groaned. "This is why I'm not on the front lines."

"Better this exhaustion than a limp sack of bones possessed by a plant." She stared up in the void around her, and willed it to be illuminated with light. Sparks sputtered on her arms. Dizziness crashed through her mind like a wave, which swept her feeble attempt away. "Where is the crystal?"

"Shit." Her clothes rustled. "I shoved it in a pocket when you slipped, but I guess it fell into the chasm. You're welcome, by the way."

Cerallia wrinkled her nose. "I acknowledge that things may have gone worse if you were not there, and nothing more."

"Should've just left," she muttered. The scent of smoke wafted around them – likely a byproduct of the wards that fizzled out. "We should move before it decides to chase us again."

She rolled to her feet. Her muscles wailed in torment, but she plowed through the darkness anyway. It did not make the walk easy, however. She kicked rocks more often than she took a normal step forward, and holes caught her foot when the path seemed clear. With considerable restraint, she bit back many swears. She hoped that meant Lilt couldn't sense her struggles, much less the quiver in her hands.

"Are you having trouble, Cerallia?" she chuckled.

She glared in the direction of the smoke, but stopped once the implication struck her. "You can see me?"

"Wards. I always have a night vision script on hand, though I never thought I'd use it today." The smoke grew stronger at her approach. "As funny as it is to see you so graceless, it'd be better if we can pick up the pace. Take my hand."

The Anointed within her recoiled, hissing at the mere idea of willingly offering a hand to a witch. She should have smacked her dirty wrist the moment it closed around her in the chasm. But she was tired. The day weighed heavily on her, and nothing could ignite her essence until they rested. To withhold assistance for her pride was ridiculous. She sighed, then stretched her hand towards the smoke.

Lilt laced her fingers between her skeletal ones, the gentleness a profound contrast from their earlier struggle. It should not have stirred something within Cerallia. This was a simple gesture meant to hurry her forwards, yet it moved her heart in spite of her mind's disgust.

How long had it been since anyone touched her with such softness?

"Let's go," she said, and pulled her through the darkness.

Cerallia did not know when she spoke over their footsteps – only that it echoed through the tunnel around them in a garbled mess, much like her inner turmoil. "It did hurt. Nobody knew what was happening, but we all heard the screams before they dragged us to the light."

"Figures. If a little pinprick for my wards makes me clench my teeth, I can't imagine what sacrificing your arms feels like."

Cerallia hesitated. "Not pleasant, and more agonizing in the week that followed." What was she doing? She could almost hear her superiors gasp in horror at such an admission – to a witch, no less! But it felt...good. A lightness settled in her chest, like a burden she did not know she carried lifted ever so slightly. Could she admit more?

A bead of light twinkled through the dark, distant as the stars. Lilt gasped, and towed her towards it. Cerallia's own heart fluttered at the gleam, which grew with their approach. It was not a star; it was their escape from this stone tomb heralded by the daylight beyond it.

The star burst into the sun, which blinded her. Fresh air rushed to fill her lungs, made sweeter by the dust choked breaths she'd taken in the mountain. Nothing else seemed to matter compared to this bliss.

The world that faded into view, however, evaporated any peace her escape provided. Clouds smothered the sky. Sunlight limped to the ground in tiny rays, some of which faded the moment they appeared. Gray stretched where trees should've swayed. Foam churned on the shore, and nibbled on the sand until little remained in sight. The sea itself reflected the bleakness of the sky above, tossing about uneasily.

"Arcanai help us," Cerallia whispered.

Lilt was fixed to the spot. She stared at the barren landscape, hand raised to her dropped jaw and eyes wider than the full moon. Her other, still intertwined with Cerallia's, trembled. "This wasn't supposed to happen."

"Yet it did. It is likely to have devoured nearby villages in the time it took for us to escape."

"The villages," she mumbled, words barely cohesive on her still lips.

"Lilt? Are you well?" She snapped her fingers in front of the woman's face.

Lilt shook her head, and pulled her hand out of Cerallia's grasp. "We didn't plan on releasing another monstrosity onto Ralva. Not to aid in the terrors your Court has already wrought. Gods, it needs to be stopped." She slid down a nearby gravelly patch.

"Do you have a plan?" Cerallia called. She swept an arm across the grimness with a pit in her stomach. "It seems to me like you are rushing into something certain to kill you."

Lilt paused. "Maybe, but there's going to be a lot of people left as corpses if I let it be."

"So you are going to fight it alone?"

She licked her lips, and spoke slowly, forming a plan as her words tumbled out. "Not if I get help. Maybe the Court can do something, too, if you get back to them. It was created by witches, after all." She laughed bitterly. "Gods know you prioritize that over everything else."

Right, the Midnight Court. Cerallia slid down to join Lilt, though avoided meeting her gaze. "I might find myself...discharged if I return to them now, regardless of the news I bring, and they will likely find out about it in time. They might also work against you, given your practices."

"Isn't that always the case?" she retorted. "But someone needs to do something instead of waiting or cowering."

An image flooded into her mind: Cerallia the Anointed Shield, who valiantly captured the killer of her knight and witch of the scourge she'd eventually lead a company to victory against. They'd lay a Midnight cloak over her shoulders. Pupils would stop to whisper to one another in awe as she passed through the obsidian carved halls. Knights would vy to be under her protection. If she could just steer the witch into the court's hands, she could dream no longer of such respect. Yet some part of her drew her eyes back to Lilt. She had little to gain from confronting the summoned monster, save for the endangerment of any she involved and the court's attention. She must know that, but still wanted to expose herself to fight it. Why?

In her reluctance to pursue the plan, another idea blossomed within her – one not reliant on a backstab. "What if I were to accompany you?"

"An *Anointed*? You, help a witch willingly while not at knifepoint?" Lilt's eyes narrowed. "Are you sure you won't just sell me out?"

Cerallia held up her hands – more skeletal in the daylight without the dimness to obscure them. "I have little to return to with my knight dead. Killing that which aided in his death seems like a far better option." Perhaps it could exonerate her, too, if her name returned to the court as its slayer.

She studied her. "Fine, but you'll regret it if you cross me."

"Thank you."

Lilt blinked. "Did I just hear what I thought I heard? Now?" She shook her head. "Damn, maybe you are sincere."

"I can assure you I am." She pulled her mouth into what she hoped was a genuine smile. It had been too long since she wore one without mockery or bitterness.

With that, the two started down the mountain.

HOLD

INAAM ZAFAR

At the end of the world,
we pushed each other off the velvets
      we live on to reach ourselves
First.

We fought
under no clouds, no shade
but i can still feel it rain
      in my room—
with no good-byes but *Alvidas,* knowing well
      there was no stopping the blood Sun

before we could hold the moment in our mind long enough
to remember any more of the prayers where
we used to think the words meant more than the
confession we held behind them, the confessions we
could have told through them, if only we had
held the moment long enough
to realize what it means to be us now.

To confess we had once known, but now couldn't remember
      what the blood Sun meant, was
to confess we had lost too soon.

& now my words stink
of a butcher shops because at the end of the world,
          after all we've done
                    been through,
we put on the glossy reds on our

even though all we knew was that
the world will see us clearest
                    when the city burns.

THE LOST CAUSE

JASON NGUYEN

Twizzles of the summertime, the nortern lights of yore.
I memba the time, the cuckoo up 'nor!
Dull greens and dark browns is now all that can be seen
Such clowns and the world around just makes one wanna lean

I 'road around, around town to see the quin 'neath the rough.
But to break it to you 'der lad seeing the good is tough.
Not an 'ordin, so believe me when I say no nution' can be changed.
But maybe seeing and telling you, 'der lad give me hope to be re-
arranged.

Not jus' teh wurld of curse, but of meself, this wreck.
I gave now with clearer eyes, what of world, to keep in check.
The viscous liquid, tiny things beaming with life within
The one when I used to look down, see beyond the clear skin.

The water...cleaning the water...

OH MY! WHAT THE?! DID YOU HEAR THAT?!
THAT BOOM! THAT AIR! OH NO, NOT YOU LAD?!
I-I CULD 'ELP YA TRIP TEH AI-HER TO MAKE IT EASY
FUYR ME TO GIVE YA POWA!

BUT THE….but the feelin' teh feelin' of blud
hunger….I……can't…..

Lad, Lad, Lad, Lad!
Miss it will you?
That movin' lifet, that make you move.
As that heat leave yer bluudy, make you cooled
If only I culd…culd…**BLOOD….RED…BLOO-ED**

RARRRGH ARMPH ARGG AWRGH MMMM

Walkin' through lyfe, once again.
Teh purpose to fight, ceases any gain.
Teh end of this brown and red soaked wurld, is it in sight?
Can we can take a step, drag our long pile of flesh into the light?

That wulrld now for me is forever gone, as I go back into the lorry,
where I only know black and white.

FEBRUARY: DYNAMIC

WINNER: ACHILLES VALIANOS

WORKPLACE PROFESSIONALISM

ACHILLES VALIANOS

Smoke clouds the city streets of Caliapolis, pillars of gray holding up the endless blue of the sky. With a sort of playfulness, they curl themselves around skyscrapers and each other, leaping from the destruction of collapsed parking structures and abandoned apartment buildings. A symphony of car alarms, shouts, and explosions fill the air with its melody. In particular, one unlucky red vehicle sits in the middle of it all, wailing happily away—

Before being crushed into silence by a falling chunk of concrete.

"You!" A voice shouts from above the poor car. It comes from a blonde man, dressed in gold and white, a Colombina-style mask covering the top half of his face. He hovers a great way above the ground, light emanating from his ankles, somehow keeping him in the air. "Get *out* of the city, Cryptosonic!"

Across from him, also in the air, a woman with tight, light pink curls glares at him. Technology covers her form, further seen with the modified jet shoes she wears that also keep her in a constant state of flight. Her chin juts out in a defiant gesture. "Make me, Helios."

Really, by now, the whole thing is just protocol. He narrows his eyes, tackles her as they fly up in the air, she inevitably fights back. They both hear the whistle of wind rushing past their ears as they careen back down, and, as per protocol, they'll smash into something. Create a scene.

Crypto looks to the ground as she feels them turn upside down. The sight of an old apartment building greets her, rapidly approaching, closer, closer, closer—

—She breaks free, but not far enough to escape him, and in a last-second decision he goes in for the punch—

The force of their combined bodies manage to break through two floors, at *least.* Thank hell for super-strength— Crypto is alive enough to sit up through the rubble, and it looks like Helios was able to stick the landing better than she did. Her face fucking *stings,* though.

"Ow!" She presses her palm to her jaw, moving the bone down and up, feeling it click as it sets into place again. "Jesus!"

Helios himself leans forward, hands resting on his knees. "Whew!" he shouts, staring at the concrete floor. He blinks, urging the stars to fade and leave his vision. "You okay?"

"Yeah, I'm good," Crypto replies, blinking away the vertigo. "But God *damn.* You've gotten way stronger, man. Have you been lifting?"

Helios looks up from the ground, eyes bright and toothy grin showing off his bleeding gums. "Yeah, actually! You can tell?"

"Sure can," she says in a dry tone, a friendly sarcasm embedding itself into her words. Helios's smile grows on his face, but before he can reply, the small crackle of a machine coming to life makes itself known.

"*That looked rough, Helios,*" a tinny voice sounds from Helios's earpiece. "*You alive down there?*"

Helios gives a dry chuckle, pressing his finger on the sensor behind his ear. "Sure am," he reports back. He looks to his temporary companion with a mischievous glint. "Crypto was kind enough to break my fall."

Crypto glares right back, raising her enhanced brass knuckles towards him, and pushes a blast of energy towards his head. It intentionally misses, just barely two inches to the left, leaving a frankly impressive crater deep in the stone.

"You're lucky she hasn't broken anything else of yours yet," the voice obliviously continues. *"Hey, that implosion was pretty big, by the way. You guys could totally swing a few minutes, if you want. Nobody's gonna question it."*

"Roger that, Kelvin. How much time do we have?"

A different voice chimes in this time— lighter, more feminine. Seryph's voice. *"Looks like the top few floors caved in. I'm guessing three minutes or so. No more than five, unless you guys wanna shake the room a little. Oh, and tell Crypto I like what she did with her outfit, will you? She's got these new stun-rings—"*

"Heard. Thanks, guys." Helios says, before releasing the sensor and heaving himself up. He strolls to where Crypto still sits, his demeanor a far cry from what it was not even a minute ago, and she lets him: leaning back on her hands, not at all concerned with anticipating a fight or the general approach of an enemy. The tension in both of their shoulders has released, if only momentarily.

"We've got about five minutes before the press starts looking, and Seryph likes your rings," he reports to Crypto. His hand reaches out and she doesn't hesitate to take it, nodding in agreement once she's on her feet again. Their hands fall apart before Helios points to the blaster on her wrist— the very same one that had been shooting at him not minutes before. "Is that new?"

With practiced ease, Crypto flicks her wrist to turn the weapon on. The lights from inside the machine glow with a pale pink light that pulses with eagerness to be put to use. "Brand spankin' new," she confirms with pride. "I just finished her up a few days ago. Concentrated sound, made into a pitch that will explode on impact. It's a whole new tech system, it can't be deactivated by electricity or power surges or anything like that."

"Woah," Helios quietly marvels, leaning closer to admire the sleek build and design. "So that's why my surge didn't work this time. Guess my side's gonna have to find another way." He leans back, looking up to Crypto again. "Really living up to your name! Man, you'd be so cool if you weren't a villain."

"I have no idea what you're talking about. I'm already cool." After a moment of thought, she opens the latch keeping the thing on her arm. It falls open with a soft *click.*

Crypto holds the bracer gun out in offering. "Wanna try?"

The stars Helios was seeing earlier come back to fill his eyes. *"Stop,"* he says, green eyes wide behind the mask. "For real?"

"Why not?" Crypto passes the blaster and watches him attach it onto his own wrist. "Your friends said we had to shake things up, right?"

Helios laughs, pointing his arm towards an empty wall fifty feet away. His stance looks clumsy to her, but it must be stable enough to withstand a recoil; they have similar fighting styles, after all. "I *knew* you tapped our wire!"

"It's my job, Helios. Here, the trigger's on the bottom of your palm."

"Got it." With another breath, Helios closes one eye and aims— and shoots— and **boom.**

The blast explodes the wall, sending pieces of debris and dust into the air. The floor of the building shakes and trembles with the sound, no doubt heard for miles and miles around.

After the ground stops shaking, there's no noise but the sounds of battle outside and the ringing in their ears; that is, until Helios whoops, loud and celebratory.

"Dude!" he gushes, taking the bracer off and handing it back.

Crypto gives him a grin, herself. "I know."

"That's sick as *fuck!"*

"I *know,* right?"

He sighs as he looks at the carnage he made. "It would be *so* much cooler if you didn't kill people with it, though."

"Yeah, well." Crypto shrugs. "Priorities. The nine to five. What can you do?"

Helios gives her a side eye, that insufferable nobility heroes have falling into his body language. "You could not be evil, for one," he says with a hint of distaste. Despite the condescension, he reaches into his belt for a flask.

"I'm not evil," Crypto disagrees with a scowl. "Besides. Without us, *your* side would be out of a job, too."

Helios grumbles and sips out of the water flask, effectively ending the conversation because he knows that she's right. Once he's done he offers it to Crypto, and she gladly drinks her fill as well before handing it back and watching him tuck it back into his uniform.

"Anyway," he says to dispel the silence. He looks back up at the hole they fell from, hands on his hips. "It's probably been long enough, you think?"

"Probably," she echoes, eyeing the edge of the hole as well.

He turns back down to her. "Do I look rough enough?"

Her eyes search his face, jumping from one side to another, looking in every scrape, every abrasion, every smudge of soot on him. He looks a little too similar to when they fell in— a little too untouched. "Could probably use another punch," she says honestly, shrugging her shoulders.

He sighs, looking up to the beam of light shining from outside through the hole, but after a moment his head drops again. He motions to himself.

"Alright. Hit me."

She gladly shakes out her right hand, closing it into a fist. "Where do you want it?"

"Wherever seems best."

"Hmm. Nose?"

"Not the nose, if you please. Skelton gave me a broken nose last time."

Crypto draws her arm back. "Eye it is," she warns, and then punches him right around his left eye socket.

Helios falls back with a grunt, but in true hero fashion, bounces right back up to face Crypto again. "Damn," he mutters. "Better?"

Crypto nods definitively. "Now we're even." She gestures to herself. "How about me?"

Helios looks Crypto down, and then up again. "I think you're good. Rumple your suit a little."

She acquiesces, looking to another patch of stone wall nearby. This one leads outside, if they could break through it. From the corner of her eye, she sees Helios follow her gaze and come to the same conclusion.

"I'll clear us a way out," she offers, feeling her arm blaster pulse preemptively.

"Sweet!" Helios thanks before pressing on the comms sensor again. "Kelvin, Seryph, Puma. Helios and Cryptosonic, coming in hot."

This close, Crypto doesn't need to eavesdrop to hear the following affirmatives. Helios drops the connection and turns back to her.

"Alright, dude," Helios holds up his fist, which Crypto bumps with her own in no time. "Good luck out there."

"You too," she says back, watching Helios take one, two, three, four, five steps back. "I'll tell Skelton you said hi."

She gets one last smile from him before it drops into something more threatening. Something more scornful, more dangerous, more appropriate for a hero fighting a villain. Something the press will like.

She watches him shift his stance, his weight, his demeanor. She waits until the exact moment he takes off running to launch a blast of energy at the cinderblock wall behind them, expecting both the force of the explosion *and* the force of him tackling her—

Boom.

Out of the sky they fall, the pillars of smoke whispering their greetings around them as they rocket toward the ground. It's a fight in itself, to wrestle against each other in midair, to refrain from activating their flight, to not die on impact when the ground reaches up to meet them— but another collision sounds as they make it out alive, somehow, dragging themselves up and facing each other.

The immediate area is evacuated, like it is during every urban battle in Caliapolis. People are watching, though. Through news channels, drones, helicopters, and livestreams. The city has its eyes on them, and by *God,* it's *their* job to give these people a show.

Helios tils his chin up, light flaring between his fingers. His eyes are hard. "You'll regret this," he ominously, heroically announces. His voice is filled with honor and righteousness.

Cryptosonic sneers, letting the expression blossom into something a little more evil and a little more insane. Her guns whine with the charge they hold, just waiting, *waiting* to break free. "Then *make* me regret it, Helios."

A LITTLE BIT OF CHICANERY

REBECCA LEUNG

A Little Bit of Chicanery

What a little angel, talking to the screen
It's just so cute to watch her preen

What a good boy, waving for the crowds
His family will be so proud

She's the best of the best
All her skill put to the test

He's just so talented
Can't take this for granted

Look at her climb so high
It almost looks like she could fly

Look at him run
Oh, won't this be so fun

No one watching at home knows
They won't be happy until up in flames it goes

The letter was hand-delivered to her apartment door.

A man whose uniform was much too crisp to be from her local post office was holding out an envelope expectantly in a gloved hand.

"You're Aeryn Krane, yes?"

"...Yes, that's me," Aeryn said slowly, looking him up and down. She had just come home from work, still in her sparkly purple leotard, sweats over her tights.

"You have a message from the President's Desk."

Aeryn took it hesitantly. The messenger nodded to her, turning on his heel to depart.

She let the door swing closed, holding the heavy cream envelope in both hands. There was an honest-to-god red wax seal on the back, her name printed meticulously on the front. No sender, no return address, not even her own address was printed on the front.

She was oh-so-careful in pulling up the wax seal with her fingernails, lacquered to match her outfit. The seel came free from the paper without so much as a single white fiber clinging to the back of the drop of crimson.

Piercing gray eyes scanned over the letter.

Dear Aeryn Krane,

You have been chosen to participate in the Capitol's 50th annual Showcase of Ages to perform for the people of the Republic. You will be contacted by your sponsors for information about compensation, travel, and housing. Expect one month away from current responsibilities.

President Rex

A grin split Aeryn's face, and she took off running across her cramped studio apartment with grace. She flicked the letter on her kitchenette table, careful not to wrinkle it as she tore open her junk drawer.

A minute of scrambling and she was flipping open a phone with only one purpose.

She hit the speed dial, buzzing with barely contained excitement as she rocked back and forth from her heels to her toes.

"I did it," she said in lieu of a greeting.

"You did it?" the other end said, their voice garbled to the point of anonymity.

"I did it," she repeated, "Just got the letter from President Rex delivered by one of his messengers."

"Good job, Krane. We will be in contact."

The line went dead, and Aeryn grinned down at the phone before tossing it back into her junk drawer.

Aeryn had her 'work outfit' on under a brightly colored windbreaker and sweats as she boarded the bus the next day.

The bright lights of hotels and casinos flew by as she turned up the music on her headphones, careful not to lean her head against the back of the seat. Twenty-seven minutes on the dot and Aeryn stepped off the bus, her boots silent on the pavement as she picked her way past tourists and valets.

The *Cirque de Folie* was a microcosm of what people imagined Versailles looked like. Every window was a cramped hotel room with sheets that hadn't been changed in decades, and all of the gold paint on the gates and doorways had been heavily lacquered so people didn't scrape it off with their stubby fingernails.

But Aeryn did not enter from the double-wide doors in the front of the hotel. Instead, she slipped in the back entrance of the rightmost wing of the building, where the full-sized theatre was.

Down the stairs into the basement Aeryn went, taking them two at a time.

Other acrobats and performers were already running around, everyone in various stages of glitter and glamour. She had been looking for her manager, but it looked like he had the same idea, standing with arms crossed in front of her changing room door. He was deep in thought, his bald head dipped forward.

"So you got the news, Puck?" Aeryn asked with a grin.

He looked up sharply, his stern face breaking out in a grin, pushing the edges of his handlebar mustache skyward.

"I'm proud of you, little bird." He pulled her into a crushing hug, and Aeryn patted his bicep with a wheeze.

"Thanks, big guy."

"Take as much time as you need, I doubt you'll even need to come back here." Puck chuckled, "One of our performers, in the Showcase of Ages! I can't believe it!"

"I'll make you all proud."

She was on the aerial silks today, wrapped in soft golds over twenty feet high. She hooked her foot against the silk, climbing higher and higher, hearing the gasps of the crowd beneath her.

She reached the apex of her climb, pivoting her body so that she was parallel with the floor. Looking up at the kaleidoscope of lights above, Aeryn took a deep breath and closed her eyes.

She let herself spin down the silks, going round and round until the hard stage came into stark relief.

A microsecond before her brains would have painted the stage all shades of crimson, Aeryn splayed her arms and hooked her leg in the silks, perfectly halting her descent like a four-pointed star hung from a wire. The screams of the crowd never failed to thrill her.

This time, the letter Aeryn received was not hand delivered by a man all in white, but rather sat atop her dressing room table when the show had concluded.

Aeryn was already pulling off her costume before she spied it, sitting down to take off her heavy stage makeup.

Her blonde hair was pulled out of its bun with one hand, the other ripping open the letter with the back end of a makeup brush.

She skimmed through all of the fluff and filler, using an eyebrow pencil to circle the places she had to go and people she would have to meet. A few names stood out to Aeryn immediately.

It looked like some beauty company wanted to be the first in line to shower Aeryn in money to be their walking, talking advertisement.

The next man on the list was a name Aeryn recognized. Hank Crawford, the kind of man who was rich simply because he had the fortune of being born into the right family. She had a meeting with him scheduled already.

It was an excruciatingly long trip to the Corporate District, where all of the skyscrapers held not tourists drunk on cheap whiskey but businessmen high on coke. It took a metro trip, a bus ride, and a half mile walk to the building yawning into the sky.

The main lobby was as big as the theatre Aeryn performed in. Her boots made no noise against the marble floor as she crossed to the front desk, a circular fortress in the center of the room.

"Hello," the woman said without looking up from her computer screen. "What brings you in today?"

"I'm here for my meeting with Hank Crawford," Aeryn replied.

The woman glanced at her, a single well-groomed eyebrow raising as she looked at Aeryn.

"You?"

"Yes."

The receptionist's face clearly said *I doubt that very much.*

Aeryn forced herself not to roll her eyes. "Aeryn Krane. Krane with a K and Aeryn with an A-E-R-Y-N."

The woman shook her head as she typed out the name.

A look of brief bewilderment passed over the woman's face, before she regained her composure.

"You're early. Take a seat and I'll buzz you up when Mr. Crawford is available."

Aeryn made a self satisfied smirk, turning on her heel and crossing over to the plush waiting room chairs. She sat down triumphantly, crossing her legs.

There was a large flatscreen television bolted to the ceiling for all of those who could not bear to be apart from the harsh realities of life.

Congress deadlocked on vote to pass emergency aid funding to help victims after record breaking wildfires... insulin prices to hit record highs as pharmacy companies stocks skyrocket... President Rex declined to comment on allegations of campaign finance violation during his history making fifth bid for presidency...

Fifteen minutes later and the receptionist looked up from her screen.

"Left elevator, it will take you up to Mr. Crawford's office."

The elevator was big enough to fit thirty men, but it was just Aeryn in the middle of the silver and ivory box. It looked like Hank's office was on the top floor. Of course.

With hands folded behind her back, Aeryn hummed along to the soft elevator music as she rose higher and higher.

It was a full minute (and two loops of the elevator song) before Aeryn finally reached the top floor, the pleasant ding announcing her arrival.

Hank Crawford's office had an honest to god *parlor* leading into it, a waiting room of sorts furnished with a few armchairs and a carved coffee table sitting atop a large rug. Bookshelves full of books that had certainly never been read lined three of the walls, punctuated with exotic plants and tiffany lamps on matching tables. A set of double doors that reached the ceiling led to what Aeryn assumed was Hank's actual office.

The one thing that seemed to be missing was the man himself. Aeryn stepped out of the elevator, sizing up the room. Surprisingly there were only a few thin windows, vaulted and arching like a cathedral. The view outside was nothing but blue sky, this was the tallest building around.

Aeryn moved across the sapphire rug, sitting down in one of the indigo chairs and folding her hands in her lap.

Her eyes swept the room, seeing the blinking red light of security cameras in each corner of the room and then some. She was fairly certain she even caught one nestled in the leaves of a plant that was more hole than leaf.

It was a good five minutes longer before the doors opened, just a crack.

An older man slipped out, letting the door slide closed before Aeryn could see the other room.

He had longer, shaggy gray hair and a scruffy beard, dressed in a deep navy suit that was tailored to an exactness that Aeryn didn't even think was possible.

"Ah, Miss Krane." He broke out into a smile that crinkled the corners of his eyes, crossing the room to shake her hand enthusiastically. His grip was warm. There was strength in those rough hands. "It's lovely to meet you."

"Likewise," Aeryn replied politely, even more aware of all of the cameras pointing at them. "It's an honor to meet you, Mr. Crawford."

"Oh, the honor is all mine!" he laughed, a gruff, genuine noise. "I've read up about you, it feels like we already know each other."

"Who doesn't know Hank Crawford?" Aeryn joked with a soft chuckle. She stood. She was on the taller side, and he was on the shorter side. They were almost perfectly eye to eye.

"Soon, you'll be just as well known as I am." Hank clapped his hands, his golden signet ring flashing. "We have a lot of work ahead of us! Why not step into my office?"

Aeryn unfolded herself from her seat, smiling sweetly. "Lead the way."

Hank pushed open the doors with ease, exposing his inner office.

This, in stark contrast to the parlor, was almost all glass, with deep red carpet and a large desk with a leather high backed chair facing a wooden chair with a velvet seat cushion.

The doors stayed open this time. Hank pulled out the wooden chair for her, gesturing for her to sit.

Aeryn sat as Hank eased himself into the leather chair behind the desk, leaning back. There was very little on it, a slim monitor and some writing instruments, but not much else.

He picked up a fountain pen of gold and red, with a ruby on the cap like a drop of blood. He spun it casually in his fingers.

"We have a month to prepare you for the Showcase, Miss Krane. That's not a lot of time."

"Am I going to get a crash course?"

"Oh, for sure. The second we go public with your preparation for the Showcase, it's going to be interviews on every network, for every paper, all the social media shit too."

"I feel like I'm going to be thrown into the deep end."

"Hey, best way to learn to swim, right?" Hank chuckled, pulling the cap off of his pen and pointing the sharp nib towards the door. "Let's get down to the real brass tacks, ey? Close the doors for me, Miss Krane."

Aeryn got up without a hint of hesitation, spinning on her toes and spreading her arms wide to grab the handles of the door, drawing them closed. She watched as the cameras that had been staring at the entire exchange were obfuscated behind thick doors.

Hank sighed, running a hand through his hair. "Sorry 'bout all of the showboating, kiddo."

Aeryn laughed, sliding back into her chair. "I know we have to keep up appearances. I gotta say, this is way better than having to talk on that old flip phone."

"That it is. You're always one step ahead of the game."

"That's the kind of determination that gets me one of the top performer slots in the country in only a year," Aeryn said smugly. "And it worked too."

"Damn straight it did." Hank shook his head. "I was skeptical at first when you said you could do it in time for the Showcase."

"When have I ever let you down?" Aeryn gave a false pout.

Hank held up his hands in surrender. "You got me there, kid."

"Did everything else get sorted?" Aeryn asked. She bit her lip, reassured herself it was safe to utter his name. "Is Leon going to be there?"

"Leon got his invitation just this morning. I'll be sending him the same sponsorship letter in a few days." Hank gave her a reassuring smile, and Aeryn felt the weight lift from her shoulders, just a bit. She couldn't wait to see him again.

"Do you want to know what the game plan is?"

"Don't tell me what the game plan is right now. I don't need to know anything but when we're planning to light this pop stand."

Hank grinned wide. "True professional to the end. We're shooting for opening night. Everyone will be there and watching."

"Who else is on the list? I know you got the information before they were told."

Hank nodded, pulling out a manilla envelope from his desk drawers. He pulled out a few sheets of paper, complete with headshots.

"Read these at your leisure." Hank slid them to her.

"And I assume you'll be shipping out to the capitol for the time being?"

"Mhm," Hank nodded. "Have a nice little place picked out. I'm going to sweep it clean soon so we can talk business there. You will be shipped out too, there's a villa where they have everyone live and train."

"As for my official duties as your main sponsor, I'll mostly be scheduling for you. Media, training, that sort of stuff. I'll be sure to make sure to keep people off your back as much as possible," Hank continued.

"Anything else I need to know?"

"I'll be ready to get you into the villa in a few days. I'll call you on your normal phone. Send anyone who tries to talk to you my way."

"I won't let y'all down."

Aeryn's phone was plugged in on the kitchenette, just where she had left it. She swiped across the screen, her far too-long passcode typed in with nimble fingers. A flurry of messages greeted her from a number that wasn't saved to her contacts.

UNSAVED NUMBER: *Hey, heard that you're my competition in the Showcase. Name's Leon. I'd love to get to know you before our little performance at the Capitol. Off the books, of course.*

Aeryn grinned, quickly saving his number simple as 'L'.

Aeryn: *ur bold*
L: *Boldness won the Bear*
Aeryn: *im pretty sure thats not a saying*
L: *Do you want dinner or not? I'll pay with my pretty sponsorship pennies.*
Aeryn: *where were u thinking*

In lieu of a response, Leon sent her a location. Italian, of course.

Aeryn: *does lunch tmrrw work i work nights*
L: *One pm?*
Aeryn: *its a deal*

The restaurant was in the next city over, suited more for the family-friendly crowd. It was outfitted like an old Italian vineyard, complete with trellises bursting with artificial grape vines and frescoes painted on alabaster walls.

It didn't take Aeryn long to spot him. Black curly hair, slouched posture, and long legs stretched out in front of him, flipping through his phone without a care in the world.

A smile stretched across her face as she quickened her steps across the fake marbled floor.

She tapped the tip of her boot against his, and he looked up from whatever video he was watching.

His face lit up like a thousand spotlights, grinning as he bounced to his feet.

"It's been too fucking long," he said, shoving both of his hands in his pockets. Aeryn was sure it was to restrain himself from throwing his arms around her.

Aeryn had to tilt up her chin to look into those beautiful blue eyes. "I agree. You sure this is safe?"

"Of course it's safe," Leon's grin turned lopsided. "These faces aren't public yet. I love the blonde, it's a good look."

Aeryn felt her stomach do a perfect backspring as she played with a loose strand of gold. Ten points on the landing. "I gotta admit, it's a lot to upkeep. You didn't change much."

Last time she had seen him, he was all slacks and pressed button-downs, but now he was skinny jeans and a beat-up leather jacket. Aeryn didn't mind the look.

"Nah, just grew out the hair a little." Leon ruffled the back of his curls. "I miss the undercut."

"Ever thought about a beard?"

Leon laughed, making his way up to the hostess desk. "I can't grow one to save my life. I look like I'm banned from living 200 yards from a school when I try."

Aeryn couldn't help but laugh as well, shaking her head.

"Did you get us a reservation?"

"Of course, I had to."

"How did you get here so fast?"

Leon looked at her for a moment, squinting. "I… drove?"

"Oh. I didn't get a car. I just take the bus."

Leon laughed. "I'll drive you home."

They were led to a little booth in the corner, a bit away from the buzz of the lunch crowd. The menus were large, with an entire page dedicated to just red wine.

Aeryn was spoiled for choice, folding her menu almost immediately.

"Order for me," she decided.

Leon raised both of his eyebrows. "What were you in the mood for?"

"Mm, pasta, maybe something that pairs well with red wine."

"Pasta and red wine sounds like a fantastic idea to me. We'll share the bottle, hm?"

Aeryn folded her hands, placing her chin atop laced fingers. "Sounds delicious."

Leon nodded along as she babbled on about the Folie and her acrobatics, only pausing to order for them. Mushroom risotto and some ravioli in red sauce, along with a wine Aeryn could only guess was expensive.

"Looks like we've both been busy." Leon laughed to himself. Aeryn could hear him go on and on about the videos he made of all the tricks and challenges he did.

"It's been fun." They were both used to this little tango. A mission could take months or years. Time spent integrating into new neighborhoods, settling into new jobs, wearing a new face, and being called by a new name. It was these brief intersections of their lives that Aeryn cherished most. What had once been a convenient excuse for why a young man and woman moved into a college apartment together became so much more, a force unstoppable even when they were apart.

They chatted about nothing in particular, jobs and the day-to-day flowing by like so much after in the vast river of their lives.

"Here, do you want to try some of my risotto?" Leon picked up one of the small spoons that was probably supposed to be used for an appetizer, scooping up a bit and offering it to Aeryn.

She grinned to herself, leaning forward and opening her mouth so that he could feed her.

"Good?" Leon asked, his eyes looking at her oh-so softly. It was almost too much for Aeryn's heart to bear.

"It is," she admitted after a moment, "would you like some of mine?"

"Of course." Leon let Aeryn feed him in turn.

They didn't speak for a moment too long, stretching the silence out across an eternity of things that they could not say.

"Are you worried about what's going to happen?" Aeryn asked.

Leon looked up, as if her voice had startled him."Of course I am. I think it'd be a little weird if we weren't worried. It's nothing new. We've lived our whole lives for this, it's like. Destiny or something."

"I guess," Aeryn conceded, spearing a ravioli. "Have you thought about what happens if we don't do it?"

"We die," Leon replied automatically.

"We might die anyway."

"Yeah, I know. I think I'm okay with that." Leon smiled at her.

Aeryn smiled back, small and sad. "I guess we're in agreement then. Do you want to come back to my place after this?"

Leon grinned, that goofy grin of his looking just a tad more sincere. "I'd love that."

Aeryn was awoken from downy dreams of spiced cologne and cigarette smoke by her phone alarm.

She groaned, slapping her phone screen. Bleary eyes squinted to read the time, swearing softly.

That woke up Leon, who flopped over onto his side to wrap his arms around her, broad chest to bare back.

"What is it?" he asked sleepily, burying his face in her hair.

"I have work," she grumbled.

"Mm, can't you skip?"

"It's, like, one of my last shows." Aeryn untangled his arms from her.

"Can I come with?" he asked, letting her go.

Aeryn sighed, sitting up to look at him.

"We both know it's too risky."

He pouted, but sat up as well, looking around for his discarded clothes. "Yeah, I know. Have a good show, yeah?"

"Yeah," Aeryn replied. She looked at him for a long, long moment, trying her best to stop her heart from squeezing all of the rationality out of her mind. "Yeah, I will."

All of Aeryn's personal possessions fit in a single duffle bag and a small backpack.

She cast her eyes over the now sparse studio apartment. Most of her things had been sold or given away, the clutter cleared out. She only kept those few things that she truly loved: a small mint tin full of jewelry, a few pictures, handwritten notes jammed in a spare wallet, favorite windbreaker and her only spare pair of boots.

It was yet another bus ride for her, but this time she had to walk a full mile deep into the luxury district. Sleek black cars that cost more than a house sped by her, the occupants inside creasing their brows at her presence in their bubble of perfection.

Aeryn paid them no mind, walking with her head held high as she made her way to the train station. A ticket cost as much as a week's worth of groceries in Aeryn's former life, but all it took was a swipe of a credit card with Hank's name on the signing line.

Train was a bit of a stretch, since there were only a few chambers on this boxcar sized vehicle, and she was the only passenger. She would be shot across the country on a series of monorails, arriving at her destination exactly when she was supposed to.

What would have been a full day trip by car was reduced to just an hour on the bullet train.

Hank would be there waiting for her. When she stepped off that train, she would no longer be Aeryn Krane, circus performer. She was Aeryn Krane, Showcase of Ages competitor, now. Whatever her next name would be, whatever her next job would be, nothing would be the same. She would forever carry the brand of insurrectionist on her back.

After an excruciatingly short time, a train station of gold and marble came into view. Behind a set of velvet ropes men and women were dressed to the nines, barely held at bay with all of their microphones and cameras.

Hank was in front of them, dressed in a gray linen suit with his hair slicked back.

Aeryn knew what to do, picking up her bags and standing up so she would be revealed by the sliding train door.

Aeryn felt herself slipping into the role like a second skin, smiling in a way that she knew made her look cute. Naive. Here to make everyone proud and do her best. It was almost too easy.

Reporters instantly started shouting at her as she stepped out of the train car.

"One at a time, one at a time!" Hank shouted over them all, hands up placatingly. "Give her a chance to breathe in the Capitol air!"

She waved to all of them, her smile not slipping an inch.

"How are you feeling, Aeryn?" Hank asked, putting his arm around her like a father would. She knew it was so that fewer cameras could take unobstructed pictures of her face.

Aeryn laughed. "A little overwhelmed, if I'm honest."

"Do you think you have what it takes to be able to win the showcase?"

"I sure hope I do!" Aeryn put down her duffle bag.

"Any significant others watching you from home? Boyfriend? Girlfriend? Both?"

Hank's expression darkened for just a moment, cowing the reporter into silence.

"Let's not ask unsavory questions," he said. It left no room for argument.

Hank flicked his wrist to check his watch, holding up one hand as he reached down to grab her bag.

"No more questions now, guys! We have to get Miss Krane to the Villa."

The reporters and cameras parted like the Red Sea as Hank led her away.

A Crawford Classic car was waiting on the curb with its chrome bumper and hubcaps, deep black with tinted windows. Hank clicked a key fob, and the car purred to life, the trunk opening so Hank could put her duffle bag away.

Hank opened the door for Aeryn, ushering her in before climbing into the driver's seat.

"You don't have a chauffeur?" Aeryn teased as they pulled out of the train station lot. The interior was all black leather with silver stitching and accents on all of the buttons, levers, and dials.

Hank rolled his eyes, laughing. "Nah, I like to be behind the wheel when I can be."

"That wasn't too bad," Aeryn murmured. She was hugging her backpack to her chest, however, betraying her anxiety.

"You did well," Hank replied approvingly. "I'll keep 'em at bay as much as I can. Only contracted media appearances for you. I'm basically your agent now."

Aery let out a sigh, uncurling herself and straightening her posture. "Okay. I can do that."

With her mind put at ease, Aeryn was able to look out of the windows. It turned out that they were transparent from the inside, and nearly opaque from the outside.

Each building was unique, stretching up hundreds of stories higher than the buildings Aeryn was used to. Spires of silver and glass twisting in dizzying geometries reached for the sky, an orb balanced upon a thousand-foot tall needle in spite of gravity.

It wasn't long until they were in the heart of the Capitol, where even the skyscrapers were replaced with every sort of entertainment a rich man's heart could want. Opera houses and theatres, golf courses of perfect green grass.

"We're headed to the stadium, the villa is just off to the side of it," Hank explained.

Aeryn took a deep breath. "Do I have to do anything for security?"

"No, I got it all sorted out. They already have your ID card ready and everything."

Aeryn laughed slightly. "Yeah, yeah, okay."

The small series of squat buildings looked like a Greek pavilion, even if it was difficult to see it through the twenty-foot tall fence. There was a gate in the fencing where a guard house sat, and Aeryn felt her stomach do a low somersault.

Hank rolled down the window as a man with a perfectly pressed dark blue security uniform and glasses came out of the guard house.

He lowered his sunglasses.

"Sir. Miss. Nice to meet you." The guard produced a freshly pressed ID card. Her name was on one side, and *Showcase of Ages 2065* on the other.

"You're all set." the guard grinned at her. "Knock 'em dead."

The villa had a small parking lot in the center of the U-shaped collection of buildings but only two cars. Hank was able to pull right up to the front.

"Men on the left, women on the right. You each get a building to yourself."

"How generous," Aeryn commented flatly. This place, as big as a housing complex, stood empty for three hundred and thirty-five days out of the year, but for the best of the best, oh, they could experience the true luxury of living in their own home for a full month.

Hank chuckled to himself as he grabbed her bag from the trunk. "You'll get a chance to meet with some of the contestants that showed up before you."

"Who's here?" Aeryn asked as they walked to one of the buildings on the right. Aeryn's housing was right in the middle of the row.

"Leah Wilson and Nick Kisinger."

Aeryn knew them off of the dossier she had memorized and promptly burned to ash. Leah Wilson was a track and field star, breaking the 400-meter dash in under 48 seconds at only 22. Nick Kisinger was a world-champion figure skater, known for his outstanding choreography and winning personality off the rink.

A golden name plaque was stamped on her door. She swiped her card and the door popped open.

Aeryn looked around at the mudroom, stepping into the kitchen, and made a small circle to look at the living room like a model home. It was as open concept as open concept could get, with only a slim curtain dividing the master bedroom from the rest of the house and curtainless glass sliding doors that led to a small back porch.

Hank and Aeryn worked in tandem to sweep through every inch of the rooms, setting down her bags and looking for any cameras (hidden and not so hidden). One trained on her front door, one hidden in one of the paintings on the living room wall. None directly trained on her bed in the bedroom, but one near the large window. None in the bathroom.

"Okay. We know that the bathroom is the safest spot," Aeryn said as they both stood inside the small room. "I can make that work."

Hank nodded. "Ready to meet the others?"

"I hope so."

The training center was open-concept as well, the size of a large gymnasium with every sort of machine and set of weights possible, impeccable lighting, and some esoteric designs for each contestant. A full indoor track, a small simulated ice rink. A set of aerial silks and a hoop. A set of boxes and railings. A shooting range even though, to her knowledge, none of them were professional sharpshooters.

Leah was tall, all lean muscle and dark tanned skin, wearing casual running shorts and a tank top. Her hair was pulled into many braids down to her waist, pulled back with a thick wrap. She paused as she saw them approach, offering her hand to Aeryn.

"You're Aeryn, right?"

Aeryn nodded, taking her hand. "Leah Wilson, yes? I've seen you compete on TV."

"Well, it looks like you two are getting along peachy," Hank said. He checked his phone, brows knitting together for just a moment before clearing his throat. "I have to head out now. Talk to you both soon, alright?"

"I know that Nick is excited to meet you," Leah said in a conspiratorial whisper as Hank departed.

"Is he? Is that good?" Aeryn asked, feigning ignorance.

"Between you and me I think he's a bit of a showboater, but he has the skills to back it up," Leah replied. "I have to get my cooldown in. Why don't you talk to him for a bit?"

Aeryn nodded, taking off with a crisp salute that made Leah laugh.

The ice rink radiated cold, with Nick already leaning expectantly on the ledge, waving to her.

He had blonde hair, mussed from so much exercise that his bangs fell in his face. He wore a tight white athleisure pullover and black tights that highlighted his signature bright blue skates.

"Aeryn Krane," he said with a million-dollar smile, "you're the woman of the hour!"

Aeryn reached out to shake his hand, but he instead took her hand up to his lips and kissed the back of her hand.

Internally, Aeryn cringed. Externally, she giggled. She tried not to think of the way Leon gently kissed her ring finger in her bed, an invisible promise that they could never make to one another.

"It's a pleasure to meet you," Aeryn said, knowing it was what Nick wanted to hear.

"The pleasure is all mine," Nick laughed. "I saw one of your last shows. Had to see what the competition looked like, you understand."

Aeryn's eyebrows shot up, but she quickly smothered it with a smile. "Did you like what you saw?"

"Oh, definitely. The silks were put in at your sponsor's behest, yes?"

"Oh, yes." Aeryn laughed, doing her best to soften it so that it sounded sincere, not incredulous. This guy really was laying it on thick.

Nick leaned forward, and Aeryn could feel his expensive cologne claw at the back of her throat.

"A little birdy told me they're planning a little action game for opening night."

Aeryn played dumb. Maybe a little too dumb. "What's that?"

Nick laughed. "Oh, you're a riot. Have you ever played laser tag as a kid?"

Aeryn shook her head. Her training had skipped over frivolous approximations of real firepower.

Nick's grin was just as plastic as the rest of him. "Just stick with me, we can help each other out against the competition."

Aeryn couldn't help but laugh. "Alright."

"Any plans for tonight?" Nick was tracing little patterns in the ice rink wall.

"Just settling in," Aeryn said vaguely.

"Well, you know where to find me if you need any help."

Aeryn awoke the next day surrounded not by the comforting, cramped apartment she had gotten accustomed to, but the cold, wide bed that was more hotel room than home.

She groaned, rolling over twice to grab her phone.

Crawford: *Meet me at 10 after training*

An address was attached, within walking distance.

The house Hank had picked was on a lot of land that stood out like a sore thumb amongst the endless concrete and steel. It had a tall wall surrounding it, a multistory mansion sitting amid a thick garden with fruit trees and a gazebo.

Aeryn walked up to the gate, hitting the button to be buzzed in.

It only took a moment of being scrutinized by the camera before the gate slid open.

She went up to the house, the door swinging open as she stepped up to it.

"Nice to see you're settling in, kiddo," Hank said as she was led through the house, sterile and swept clean. He led her to an office, closing the door.

"Shouldn't we wait until Leon gets here?" Aeryn asked, trying not to sound too eager.

"I'm going to be telling Leon the same things separately, so don't worry, he'll be up to speed. We just need you two to not be seen... together too much. You're close competitors, nothing more." Hank gave her a sympathetic look. "I know it's hard."

"It's part of the job," Aeryn sighed through her teeth. Stolen time in the dead of night, reminding them of fond memories in the months apart.

"And we're forever grateful for it."

Aery laughed at that, but it was dry at best. "So what's our opening?"

"The opening night of the Showcase has the most members of the Council in attendance, including President Rex. Good for PR, and it gets the big wigs out in the sun for a little. Makes them look human, you know?"

Aeryn nodded slowly. She had seen the nigh impenetrable viewing box that the Council all sat in, too great to even breathe the same air as the riff-raff around them, separated by heavy steel and blast-proof polycarbonate. "So this is an infiltration and assassination?"

"Sort of. We're pulling out all the stops for this one. There's a no fly zone over the stadium, except for the three plane salute overhead. We're loading a targeted weapon on one of the planes and blowing up that whole Council's box."

Aeryn was nothing short of a picture perfect example of incredulity. "You're fucking kidding me."

Aeryn blinked, shaking her head. "What the hell do you need me for then if you're just going to nuke them?"

"I may have been a little overzealous when I said we're blowing up the box. I'm good, but I ain't that good. We're using an electro-bolo, two small projectiles that will charge the air directly between them. The metal on either side of the Council's viewing box will conduct the current beautifully. It's like getting struck by lightning. Instant death."

Aeryn crossed her arms, her expression dark.

"It's very hard to aim a weapon of that type, especially from ten stories up. Leon and you are going to have to launch trackers on either side of the box. The first event is a kind of capture the flag, with modified airsoft guns to simulate the old style of war games."

Aeryn grinned to herself. Looks like Nick was right on the money.

"Each of you is going to get a special cartridge that has extra propellants in it and the tracker. Other than that, they shoot exactly the same. You only get one shot."

"How will we know when to shoot?" Aeryn couldn't imagine they would be able to get away with holding a gun, even one perceived as useless, at the Council's box.

"We're going to have an inner ear comm link I'll pass to you with the cartridge. I'll tell you to find your best place when the plane is inbound, then give you a three second countdown to line up and make your shots."

"Will we get time to practice with the guns?"

Hank nodded. "They'll give you time to practice with them on the training ground as soon as all the contestants arrive."

"Plenty of time." Aeryn smiled lopsidedly.

"Precisely."

Aeryn could hardly wait for Leon to arrive. The woman's side of the wing had been filled out soon after Aeryn had settled in, with Charlotte Schuyler arriving to much hubbub, giving Nick someone else to turn his affections on.

Charlotte was kind enough, and they chatted when practicing in the same area. There was no doubt to Aeryn that Charlotte was a better performer and athlete than she was, but only barely.

"Have you considered bringing any equipment into the arena?" Charlotte asked, up on the Lyra as Aeryn stretched below.

"Are we allowed to do that?"

"If your sponsor can get it for you, yes. I was tempted to ask for a Cyr wheel. I doubt they've thought of putting one in the arena already."

Aeryn shrugged. "Maybe, yeah."

A thought struck her and she grinned, abandoning her warm-up to grab her phone.

Krane: *Hank, do u think u can do a favor for me?*
Crawford: *Depends what it is*

__Krane:__ i know we get special stuff for the games can u get me a silk and a harness?

__Crawford:__ What are you planning

__Krane:__ climbing ;)

__Crawford:__ I'll see what I can do

Roger Moore stuck to himself, quiet even when he was training with a barbell twice Aeryn's weight.

Finally, *finally,* there was a little bit of news.

"I heard that the last of us is finally arriving today," Nick mentioned offhandedly, using the treadmill right next to Aeryn despite the four other unoccupied ones.

"Leon, was it?" Aeryn asked, forcing herself to sound entirely neutral.

"Mhm. The parkour artist, yes. I wonder what took him so long?"

Aeryn shrugged. "Hopefully they'll finally be able to tell us about the actual games we're going to be playing." They only had a few weeks left, after all.

"I'm sure they will. Have you heard anything else about them?" Nick asked, running his hand through perfect blond hair.

"No, not really. I've been busy doing those little over the phone interviews and stuff."

Nick laughed. "And how have you been liking that?"

"It's fine. They always ask the same questions, though." And she always had the same answers. She had her story straight from day one.

"That they do."

She saw Leon's face on her phone screen the minute he stepped foot in the Capitol. On the front page of every news site was his familiar face, grinning with his arm slung jovially around Hank's shoulders on the same train platform she had been on.

Who is Leon De'Amico?

Aeryn smiled as she clicked her phone off, shoving it in her pocket.

She definitely wasn't waiting from her front door, peeking through the windows every three seconds for Hank's car to pull into the lot.

She definitely wasn't watching as Leon unfolded himself from the car, slinging a duffel bag over his shoulder as Hank led him to his temporary residence.

She *definitely* wasn't ready at the front door with her gym bag over her shoulder to just happen to run into him as they exited his front door.

To both men's immense credit, they only looked mildly surprised to greet her. She stopped just short of being too close for comfort, bouncing on her heels.

"You're Aeryn, right?" Leon said first, breaking out into a bright grin.

"Mhm." Aeryn had to bite her lip to stop herself from tackling him in a hug.

"I'm Leon," he said, putting out his hand, "It's great to meet you."

She shook his hand, finally letting herself smile. It lasted far too long, and not long enough. All she wanted to do was wrap her arms around him and never, *ever* let him go. "The pleasure is all mine."

Aeryn didn't get a chance to see Leon until after she had taken many a picture of herself holding vitamin bottles and pretending to eat gummy bears that were supposed to make her hair grow stronger and brighter for her sponsors. As if the money even mattered. She was pretty sure that, in one afternoon, she had tripled the amount of pictures she had of herself, but they would be edited to anonymity anyway.

Even though she felt exhaustion raising its hackles at her, Aeryn got herself together to at least pretend to exercise.

Leon was there. She had to see him.

He was by the weights. By himself. It was evening, no one was in anymore. Aeryn knew Nick was going to be on late night television, and Leah and Charlotte were at some fancy banquet.

Aeryn slid up to him casually, hyper aware of the security cameras in every corner of the room. She tapped him on the shoulder twice. *Love you* it meant.

"Hey," she said.

"Hey yourself," he replied with a grin, his tongue pressed to his teeth. *Love you too.* He was wearing a low cut tank top and basketball shorts. He would've blended in in any gym.

"How have you been settling in?" She sat down on one of the benches as he did his curls.

"Pretty well. The place is ridiculously fancy, it took me like an hour to figure out how the shower even worked." Leon gave her a lopsided smile.

Aeryn laughed. "Yeah, it's… it's definitely different from what I'm used to too."

"What have you been up to?" Leon asked, a touch of breathiness to his voice as he set down the weights for a rest.

"One of my sponsors wanted me to shoot some promotional stuff for them." Aeryn shrugged. "It was fine. Maybe a little tiring. I haven't had to suck it in and smile so hard in my life."

Leon laughed, but it was a touch sad. "I met up with Crawford today. I know he's your sponsor too. He got me up to speed with everything."

Aeryn blinked. "Everything?"

Leon caught her eye in the mirror, his gaze serious. "Everything."

Aeryn sighed, looking down at her shoes for a moment. "Do you think it's doable?"

"I think so, yeah. You wanna start training on the range tomorrow? I hear they're going to teach us how to use it."

Aeryn perked up at that, smiling. "Yeah, that'd be fun."

The problem at the range was not trying to figure out how to put the finicky cartridges in the airsoft guns, or that every target had to be manually taken down and put up. It was trying not to look *too good* at reloading, aiming, and filling the target with holes.

She had to choose little places to aim for. Just left of the third ring. In each corner. A bullseye now and again. Leon was doing the same, Aeryn could tell. He was a better shot than she was, and with barely any recoil and at such a short distance (only fifty feet!) It was a piece of cake.

Nick was utterly abysmal at shooting. Charlotte, as expected, was by far the best, and had no problem showing off a perfect set of ten bullseyes. Leah and Roger clearly found it a bit tedious, departing quickly.

Eventually, it dwindled down to just the two of them, ramping up their speed and accuracy carefully.

Leon emptied his last cartridge (he had grabbed the rest from the others after they left) before turning to Aeryn. "You're a good shot."

"Think we're good enough?" Aeryn asked, examining the paper targets peppered with holes.

"Oh, of course. We're the best of the best for a reason. Same time tomorrow?"

"Are you sure that's a good idea?" Aeryn asked.

"Hey, practice can't hurt, right?"

Aeryn rolled her eyes at his goofy grin. "Yeah, okay."

"Are you ready for showtime?" Leon asked, Aeryn crouched over him with arms extended in case he failed his bench press (which he definitely hadn't done on purpose the week before).

"Very nearly. My outfit for opening night was just delivered to my doorstep."

"Did you get the stuff you wanted?"

"Yeah, Hank really pulled through," Aeryn replied, only half listening.

Leon paused, hands gripping the bar. "Nervous?"

"Of course I'm nervous. It'd be insane if I wasn't." Aeryn squinted down at him. "Are you nervous?"

"I decided to be insane instead."

Aeryn chuckled to herself. "Keep telling yourself that."

If there was anything that the Capitol was good at, it was fanfare. An honest-to-god red carpet was rolled out between the villa and the stadium, already filled to the brim with screaming spectators.

A thousand cameras, everything from a phone to a contraption that strapped onto a man's chest, to capture everything in glorious detail.

Aeryn was wearing her outfit, a deep purple sparkling leotard with a loose navy blue blouse on top that fit seamlessly with the half body harness around her waist and thighs. She had a long coil of navy blue silk at her hip. Hank had really pulled through.

Leon was dressed in what rich men thought streetwear was, with baggy pants and strong boots, a tight fitting tank top in blacks and grays with far too many straps and buckles.

The others had clearly had a hand in designs as well, with Nick's open shirt and Charlotte covered in sequins and rhinestones.

The arena was familiar now. They had all been shown pictures beforehand, with its trees of thick branches and tall canopies. But the seats were full now, not just media men and reporters in the front rows, but full to the brim with *people*.

Aeryn tried not to squint in the bright light, scanning the crowd. It wasn't hard to see the Council's Box right in the front of the stadium, metal and glass holding eight old men in their black tuxedos and expensive jewelry like a mobster's funeral procession. Behind them stood a dozen guards in all black, each dressed like marines ready to storm the beaches.

Aeryn could barely hear any of the introductions or announcements over the pounding of her own heart. Leon was standing at her side, one hand shoved in his pocket as the other waved to the crowd, as they all did. They both knew how this was going to go. The national anthem played, the competitors and their sponsors were introduced. The game would be announced, they would be able to galavant around for everyone's entertainment. Simple.

Aeryn was shaken out of her thoughts by a strong hand on the top of her head, ruffling her hair and sliding the comm link over her ear.

Hank grinned at both of them in turn. He was wearing a tuxedo and smelled faintly of citrus.

"Are you two ready to roll?" he asked.

Aeryn laughed lightly, brushing her hair behind her ear to make sure the comm was hidden. "I sure hope so."

"Oh, don't worry about it. You'll both kill it."

Aeryn was vaguely aware of the rules that were being explained. Targets lined the arena, it was each contestant's objective to shoot as many of them as possible with their respective color paintball. Accuracy and the number of targets would determine points. It didn't matter to Aeryn.

"We only got a couple of minutes until the show begins," Hank continued. They both knew he didn't mean the competition.

"We'll make you proud," Leon laughed gently.

"Knock 'em dead, kiddos." Hank patted them both on the hips before stepping back.

Leon and Aeryn both slipped their tracker cartridges into their pockets as one.

They were all sent to their respective corners, six places outside of the ring of the arena. Leon and Aeryn were opposite one another, they couldn't see each other through the thick artificial trees. But they knew where they had to be as soon as possible. One tree in the very center of the arena was taller than the rest. It was perfect.

A horn blew, and they all jumped off of their platforms and took off running.

Aeryn tore through the underbrush, feeling the squishy, synthetic dirt under her boots. She had her gun in hand, casually shooting whatever targets she happened by. She wasn't the main attraction, she wouldn't be until it was too late.

It didn't take long until she heard those four, fateful words in her ear.

The package is inbound.

On his end of the arena, Leon took a running start, catching the bottommost tree limb and easily scaling his way up. He heard the oo's and ah's of the crowd as he jumped from branch to branch. There weren't enough cameras to cover all of them all at once, and they had gotten plenty of footage of him jumping around. He could climb in peace.

Aeryn clipped herself into her harness, throwing the leading rope of her personal silk as high as it would go, about halfway up the tallest tree right in the center of the arena. She tied it off close to the ground, testing it with all of her weight. It wasn't going anywhere.

She climbed, quick as a whip, stopping only to tie off the silk at the halfway point, scaling the rest of the tree without the use of the rope. It would be vital to a speedy escape.

Aeryn looked over the tops of the trees at Leon, both grinning like maniacs as they stood tall over the arena below.

The crowd screamed, countless faces clapping and cheering for their personas.

A single nod between them contained a thousand words and even more promises.

They ran towards one another, fleet of foot and assured in step. They met right in the middle. Close enough to touch, but not just yet.

Three

Aeryn slipped the cartridge off of her belt, clicking it into place like she had envisioned a thousand times.

Two

Leon cocked his gun, the tracker sliding home.

One

Moving as one, they raised their pistols, took aim, and pulled the trigger.

The scream of the jet overhead drowned out the sound of gunshots, but all Aeryn could see was Leon, finally, *finally,* wrapping his arm around her hips and pulling her close.

The sound of a million amps cracked through the air in a burst of white light.

Aeryn threw her hand around his neck, the other holding tight to the silk harness she was still hooked to.

They both leaned backwards as the sound of screaming and the smell of ozone filled the arena.

Everything would be different when they landed, but it didn't matter. They were finally together as one.

THE PEACH PIT GHOST

SOPHIA BREEZE

Maggie loved her lighter like a friend, its slick and palm-perfect red frame that could click its flame open in an instant, a precious thing that always stayed by her as something that could never be successfully stolen away, never dissuaded. Though, of course, there was also much to love about the romantic strike and spark of match against matchbox: it's almost earthy and instinctive feel that sent sparkles down her fingertips each time she heard its sound—a perfect swipe. But the matches did not last long. They crumbled apart into black crumbs after a few seconds and they would stain with ash. The lighter, however, was loyal. It loved her back.

Maggie tied a fat worm to a string and then to a small branch before the lighter was lit. Its yellow flame stood under the worm as she watched it wriggle and writhe, flesh hardening, blackening to the heat, shriveling away. People didn't like Maggie much, but that was okay, because she already didn't like anyone to begin with.

"We're just worried," Mama said. "About her."

In the gray walls of her school counselor's office, large windows hopefully one-sided and speckled with students walking past it, Maggie had sat in a cushioned burgundy chair staring absentmindedly at the room's only pop of color: an oversaturated poster of a cat and dog cuddling in a flower field. *Who is we?* she thought, because it couldn't have been Dad.

"She'll talk to me, sometimes. But I keep being told she just won't talk at all. Then, last Tuesday, when she went and cut that boy's shirt with a pair of scissors."

"Hm," Mr. McIntosh hummed. He was an old-fashioned looking man in tweed and thick glasses with a tendency to stare. "For bothering her."

"Yes."

"And the main concern," Mr. McIntosh folded his hands under his chin, a pose too practiced, too purposeful in trying to look like someone smart, someone Maggie should be listening to. The poster dog was a golden retriever and the cat a gray tabby, snug in the warm crook of sunshiney fur. "Well, you know, I don't really like to use the term 'firebug'."

"Yes."

"But there is something to be said about it."

"Yes."

"What I really think Margaret needs is to socialize. Something after school, to distract her. To really engage with and grow that young brain." Mr. McIntosh turned to face Maggie, a small smile and a moment of silence for steady eye contact. "Margaret, have you ever thought about soccer?"

Maggie stared back. In the deep pits of her pocket she was thumbing her red lighter, fingers always dragging back to the spark wheel.

The worm was dead now, both sides scorched. The twine she used to tie it had lit up too, though Maggie had expected the same. Through damp grass she crunched closer towards it and studied the thing in her palm closely. Leached from its wet life, reduced to whatever was left behind: a flat husk.

"What's that?"

Maggie looked up and out of the woody ditch she stood in and saw silhouetted against weak sunlight a girl peeking down from the sidewalk, her shabby yellow dress waving softly in the wind. Her black hair was close to the shade of Maggie's and shone slightly with grease.

"Worm," Maggie said.

"Oh," The girl said, and stepped down closer. "What are you doing with it?"

Maggie presented her lighter and brought its flame to life, its mesmerizing dance at her beck and call.

"Wow," The girl got closer still. "Your parents let you play with lighters?"

"No."

The girl then placed a hand to her neck and glanced around, other palm brushing at her dress like a nervous tic. "Sometimes my Mom lets me play with gardening tools. Like, the shears and stuff. I cut up plants, sometimes bugs."

"I used to burn plants," Maggie said. "But it's boring. I'm meant to be at soccer right now, but that's boring too."

"I don't like sports either. Running makes my chest hurt and the wind gets my hair thrown in my face," the girl said. Then, unprompted, almost unwelcome, a sudden opening of doors. "People call me Lemon Pepper, by the way."

Maggie didn't really know what to say until sluggishly, spilling from her mouth like a slow-turning faucet, her own name dripped from her tongue.

"Maggie."

Lemon Pepper smiled, a single tooth slightly chipped. "Um," she said. "Have you ever tried to burn a butterfly?"

Lemon Pepper did not go to her school, Maggie was quick to realize. On the walks back from hours of forgetting what was said as soon as a teacher had said it, she would not see Lemon Pepper and her litany of yellow dresses until a certain crosswalk saw them on the same path.

She was a subdued girl, but not always quiet: more so patient and willing to follow rather than lead. Lemon Pepper buzzed with a brightness that made Maggie almost annoyed to be around, but what was forgiving was her utter lack of questions, of want for reason. When Maggie found dead sidewalk birds Lemon Pepper would bring the sticks to poke it with, and, certainly most importantly, no sparks or bursts of flame ever found Lemon Pepper disgusted with what they ended up lighting.

They walked under afternoon skies into lamp-lit streets, aimless and always random in returning home. Maggie did not want Dad to see Lemon Pepper, or even Mama, for that matter. She wanted the secret of seeming normal to stay unseen, locked behind her teeth and non-descript answers, no further exploration, no explanation and no weight-off-the-shoulders sigh from her parents. *Thank God,* they'd think. *She'll start loving soccer in no time.* What next? The sudden dis-appearance of her first friend, the lighter. Mr. McIntosh's glowing review.

But the ruse could not last. In the moonlit scene of her shoddy back-yard of unmowed grass and stumps of dirt did Lemon Pepper sneak to-and-fro a flimsy fencepost and in full sight of Dad, standing quietly in the kitchen, peering into night from the blanket of dark.

When Maggie opened the back door she saw him there, a shadow with a mug of indeterminate drink in hand.

"Friend?" he asked.

Maggie shrugged. Dad placed a single palm on her shoulder, shook her, and let his fingers slide off as quickly as they rolled on.

Lemon Pepper was holding out the daisy as Maggie singed the petals—one at a time, careful not to catch the whole flower at once—when she asked a question; her first question.

"Why do you only burn things that are alive?"

"Because," Maggie said simply. "this is what happens when a living thing dies."

Strangely, Lemon Pepper seemed puzzled. "No," was all she man-aged to say. "No?"

"When people die, they get burned up." Maggie moved her flame to the egg-yolk middle of the daisy and watched it burst. "My Dad said that. They're going to burn me up, too. All of my heart and brains. It'll be ashes somewhere, like dirt. Dirt you step on."

"You sound really sure," Lemon Pepper blinked. Another daisy was presented.

"I am sure," Maggie said. "When you die you go away and when *I* die I'll go away, too. I'll be set on fire and then my ashes will get thrown out and nobody'll remember me 'cause nobody even likes me."

Lemon Pepper thought for a moment.

"I'm not so sure about that," she said. "Have you ever heard of a peach pit ghost?"

Maggie lowered her lighter, lid swung over and snapped shut as she stared back at Lemon Pepper; her way of saying "no" without the record of admitting it.

"Whenever you eat a peach, you leave its pit," Lemon Pepper started. "And in that pit the peach still lives. When you throw it aside or bury it in dirt, at night, the peach pit ghosts rise from the ground, mist-like, making fog every morning and evening.

"They haunt themselves—their seeds. In the ground or trash. They rise up and bring up their sprouts until they grow into big peach trees with many fingers and flowers, and then, in their flowers, the ghosts return to them."

Lemon Pepper was staring deeply into Maggie, unburnt daisy pressed close to her chest, delicate white petals weak and waxy from where she now reached to pinch them.

"Even if you burned up a peach and its fruit, you can't burn its pit, not really," she said. "It keeps on living, forever."

Maggie didn't know what to say, but her thoughts had now been formally drifted to fat peaches and sugary, sweet juices. She took Lemon Pepper to the nearest corner store with the few dollars she always found crumpled in one of her pockets to have them: pink and orange, round and fuzzy. A little underripe, but still full of flesh, and the two returned to Maggie's backyard to eat the fruit now warmed by their hands and high noon sun. Though Maggie flicked her pit away Lemon Pepper kept hers close and, eventually, pawned it softly into the palm of Maggie's with a knowing smile and cock of her head. *Forever,* Maggie heard her, the sound echoing wordlessly within her skull.

Dad stood from the window and stared.

"There's something I need to tell you."

Dad blocked the door. He spoke flat, the exact same stern and serious he'd been back when Maggie had taken a pair of his too-few tube socks and openly burnt them atop a trash can lid on the lawn. Maggie looked through him. Nothing of his had been burned lately, so where could this waste of time be going? He motioned for her to sit down.

"This is pretty important, you know," Dad said. "What I'll tell you."

Maggie blinked back.

"And you're pretty difficult when it comes to changes."

The sentence was punctuated by another beat of dead air, a begging for reaction.

"Like, we know you skip practices. We know you skip a lot of things and act like we don't know, but we notice, you know. So I'm kind of hoping you'll work with me here, Margaret, and take what I'll say like a normal kid and listen because, you know, you should respect your parents. And I don't see a lot of respect from you. I really don't, so…"

Maggie had already stood from her spot, deeply disinterested. Dad was a mumbler, deceptively shy in his tendency to ramble rather than get to the heart of his thoughts: deeply boring, too.

"Margaret?"

Under her bed Maggie hid a long, beautiful feather plume she'd found stuck to the sidewalk when walking to school the other day. Would something so soft and sleek catch fire like dry kindling, or, deceitfully, did it hide itself behind easy-to-catch down to keep the truth of its slippery body being nonflammable?

"Margaret!"

He grabbed Maggie by the shoulders, throwing her back down into her seat with a bounce of her body and her hand rapidly reached to grip tighter to her jacket pocket lighter. Her eyes, bugged, returned to her father's as they shared a moment of empty air staring.

Dad drew back and sighed, the known sigh his replacement of "sorry"; one that said, *I can't believe I did that,* and, *yes, I wouldn't do that. I'd never do that to you, not anyone.* He rubbed his temples, aired out his lungs again and slumped back, sad. *That wouldn't happen, and, also, it didn't.*

"I know I haven't really been at home," Dad started. "Or at your games."

"You haven't."

Dad sighed again, cadence of misery lost and seemingly more annoyed that Maggie had now been bothered to talk back.

"There's a reason for that."

Maggie had seen Lemon Pepper's mom before, close in facial structure to her daughter, youthful body and light hair that was cut shoulder length and curled into golden ringlets.

"I know this might be difficult to understand," Dad said. Lemon Pepper's mom, from her emergence of the hallway's open mouth, slunk into Dad's arms, linking them like something stuck together with a misplaced splatter of gross and oozing glue.

Then, the implosion: the divorce. Maggie knew it was coming, it had to, but the absurdity of finding herself dragged through the fracture, the legal formalities and household furniture divided neatly into boxes and hauled away was altogether sharp and strange, like needle shots, like swallowing sticky cough medicine. Mama and her quiet tongue, her calm recession into shadow, Dad and Not-Mama close together, pressed in places that felt kind and comfortable, and at the very end of it all, in her ratty yellow dresses and big-teeth smile, Lemon Pepper.

Her world had not imploded, it had simply gotten bigger.

How delightful, she must've thought, that Maggie would be here all the time. As per arrangement Maggie sat cross legged in Lemon Pepper's little apartment living room, Not-Mama cooking in the nearby white and dirty-tiled kitchen. Lemon Pepper beamed, hands clenching fistfuls of shag carpet and body leaning forward, excited, relaying rapidly to Maggie her stacks of favorite DVDs, her collection of bottle caps she kept in an empty bear-shaped honey bottle on the shelf nearby, the room she'd made in her bedroom so both of them could sleep there. It was like a sleepover but only better, only more: a fixture.

Maggie listened, but kept her eyes to the kitchen entrance, ears tuned to Not-Mama's pots and pans.

"It'll take some getting used to, I'm sure," Not-Mama had said while setting the table, her plate beside Dad's. "But it'll be okay in the end, right Maggie? We can all get along."

Maggie stepped deeply onto Not-Mama's foot and she jumped back with a yipe. When Dad asked about the sound she simply wagged a hand and said she stubbed her toe.

Time grew thick, and like sweat-sticky humid air it hung heavy and dizzied the mind. From Mama's, her home, to Dad and Not-Mama's and school then back again while all the while pervaded by Lemon Pepper at her side like a stain. She had invaded, Maggie realized, and inserted herself so close she'd stabbed hooks with the newfound formality of something inane: sister. *Sister.* Even the once gentle way Lemon Pepper would bring her slugs to burn and blueberries stuffed in pockets to split now made Maggie want to scream. The paths they walked they walked together, footsteps in sync, all known: nowhere to hide. Nowhere for Maggie to shut her eyes, clasp her lighter, and pretend it wasn't real.

Sister. She hadn't said it, but Maggie knew that's what she thought. *Sister.*

Was she now meant to hold her hand, stand together and bring their hearts close enough to beat in sync? Share clothes? Braid hair? The pitiful act of pretending to be cut from the same cloth was wilting her away, reducing her in height, returning her to the seat of her school counselor and his long stares, chilly room. What's wrong with you, Maggie? Let's talk it out.

In the white early hours of morning Maggie made sure to always rise from her sleeping bag bed in Lemon Pepper's room as soon as possible, disappearing to the living room or outside the apartment entirely as to make sure she'd never wake with her face to greet her, the imprint of Maggie's sleep the only sight of her. The smell of match smoke Maggie's ghost floating in the hallway.

What did Mr. McIntosh know, anyway? What did Dad, or Mama, or anybody besides Maggie even know to have the confidence to tell her that what she'd seen was wrong; that how she felt honestly meant feeling harmfully? The world ended like this: red giant, scorched earth, no mourners, everyone and everything a flat husk of ash. And yet, Lemon Pepper had disagreed—she'd invited herself as Maggie's shadow and followed, yes, but then stepped aside and started to point themselves to different paths and points in the sky where clouds broke apart to ask, "What about what's over there? What about wherever else?" She held out her hands, told her stories, smiled with a brightness Maggie had never seen or been shown.

It's okay, Maggie. I like you.

Other times, in the dense hours of pitch black night, Maggie climbed from the sleeping bag atop Lemon Pepper's covers and stared at her sleeping. She'd crawl closer until she sat atop her stomach, to which Lemon Pepper would stifle, look up and unbiddenly giggle in blind bewilderment at the shadow that now perched on her: *what's going on? Is this some kind of dream?* Then the lighter's flame would wake a centimeter from her nose and the sharp heat forced the heavy, sleep-bound body of Lemon Pepper's to jolt as much as her thawing brain could, shoving Maggie away and back to the floor, eyes wild and wide with panic. Sometimes, instead, Lemon Pepper would wake to her hair carelessly tugged and cut off in chunks, littering her pillow and bedroom room floor in ugly, messy masses.

"Stop that! Stop! What did I do Maggie? Maggie, what did I do?"

Her new brand of question, the one she would ask over and over and over again.

The strained anger of parents (and not-parents) voices as they fought their fights, both contained ones and embarrassingly bitter ones, was expected and so close to ordinary they might as well have been a heartbeat, the sun setting every night, a bee dying once its stinger is stung. At Mama's home, Maggie's home, the place was left vacant: the conversation had moved elsewhere, with Dad, with new kindling. On the days Lemon Pepper would speak to her she'd screw up her face, eyes tired and red, and wonder aloud, "Why do they have to be so loud? What's wrong?" and Maggie would have no answer other than a shrug.

Dad and Not-Mama shared a shoe with a pebble in its toe. Maggie sat from the kitchen table and watched them as they'd burst, Dad in lead, towering, pointing as Not-Mama kept to her quieter, colder anger until both would fizzle and return to cuddling in places on the couch, bodies clasped and faces cupped. There was something youthful in the air: they could scream and shout and stomp away and yet Not-Mama returned to him, and him to Not-Mama, and both could embrace without a breath of apology or promise to stop. Sometimes Not-Mama would look up and catch Maggie staring, seeing in her eyes the question of when everything might crumble before their wobbly, half-second of eye contact broke apart and melted away.

Harsh tones, groans, heads in hands were a routine, a symphony both could conduct for their respective daughters to hear until Dad took the acidity of his actions to another step: he shoved Not-Mama down the bottom of the apartment steps where she found herself tangled into a twisted ankle.

Something foundational crashed and splintered onto the sidewalk alongside her. Dad, frantic, came to Maggie and snapped his fingers. "Car keys! Car keys?" And soon he'd piled Not-Mama into the passenger seat and sped to a doctor like she'd been shot. Maggie found Lemon Pepper, sitting with tears in her eyes and hands combing her hair obsessively, body curled into a fetal pose until she got up, shambled off, and locked Maggie out from her bedroom with a quiet shut of the door.

There was no cast needed, just a small cane. And yet, despite its presence as a black stick to hold, it blemished the whole of everything just for Not-Mama to carry it around: a reminder alongside the invisible ache of injury that something faulty stuck out of every couch-laden kiss and giggling honeymoon fluff. Dad seemed horrified. Ashamed, even, and so much so that Maggie was shocked to see he had pulled out all the stops to save him from that shame: he said "sorry." He said sorry again and again, begging with his naked heart and desperately waiting outside her window, outside restaurants and parks. I'm sorry, I'm sorry. I promise I'm sorry. I love you, really.

It didn't matter. In his persistence came the severance: the restraining order. Court-declared, quick, and cold. The last Maggie saw of Not-Mama she seemed hardened yet sad, sadder than Mama had been, tightened upwards by strong posture and messy curls of her hair curtaining steady eyes that stared with the dejected ache of a whole-soul sigh, an ash-tasting acceptance of the parting. There was no need for Maggie to step inside Lemon Pepper's apartment home anymore, no more sleeping bag bed or echo of once had excitement over the thought of being twin flames intertwined, forever friends and forever meant to be. *Sisters.*

In two weeks' time the contents of the tiny place were sucked away into boxes, packed with Not-Mama and Lemon Pepper, picked clean and cavernous, the sound of squeaking shoes marching away heard on the pavement, the slamming of car doors and suddenly—goodbye.

Maggie studied Dad for a reaction, but he had folded over into something dull and gray. The only time she'd seen him cry was when Gramma died, and even then she'd heard him spit sternly into his phone, "I'm not going to take the urn. I don't want that in my house."

"Are you feeling alright?"

Mama sat with a book on her lap, unopened, and inclined her head to Maggie in her floaty way of overtly conveying her concern.

"Why?" Maggie had been staring out the window. Her red lighter sat quietly in her fingers.

"I don't know," Mama sighed. "So much happened so fast. Like tugging you back and forth. It's not really fair."

"OK."

"I'm sorry I signed you up for soccer, by the way. I know you didn't like it."

"OK."

"You could've made friends your own way, I see that," Mama said and heavily furrowed her thin, brown brows. "It's just...you two seemed so close. It was nice to see you happy, Maggie. I know you must miss her and I'm sorry about that, too."

"No," Maggie said and pressed her forehead hard against the glass. "She ruined everything. Lemon Pepper ruined everything and if she didn't show up then none of this would have ever happened. She isn't my friend. I don't care where she is or where she went. She's not my sister."

Mama's face pinched up and deepened her frown, wincing like she'd just heard the most miserable joke in the world. "Oh, Maggie…"

"What?"

"Lemon Pepper…" she trailed off.

Lemon Pepper's face returned to Maggie, looking as she did the day they met: a girl haloed by sunlight while she stood killing worms in a muddy ditch. Her hands ever moving, her chipped front tooth she'd told Maggie happened when, at five, she'd excitedly bit down on a rock painted to look like a big red strawberry, her many moles dotting her forehead and arms. Yellow dresses always because yellow was her favorite color, of course, though green was the second, and black slip-on shoes because Lemon Pepper's shoelaces always managed to come apart and trip her. Her long and wavy hair a shade of black close to Maggie's, her eyes the same tint and set as Dad's.

"Men are never happy with what they've got, are they?" Mama said, though it was clear she now spoke to no one. "They always want more, more, more. Younger, younger, younger."

Maggie stopped listening.

Groping under her bed Maggie reached for an old tupperware container she'd stolen from the kitchen and stashed away an age ago. With a drag onto rug and pop open of the foggy blue lid she unearthed a fruit pit, peach, old and dried, and pressed its indents into her fingertips. In silence she laid to rest her lighter in its place—it had finally run out of fuel a few days before—and slid the tupperware back under the bed.

In the deep blue of night Maggie crawled atop her covers and laid flat on her back, head propped up by pillows aimed at her bedroom window. She held the pit against her chest and thumbed it, brushing against the sharp tip and wrinkled ridges over and over in soft circular patterns. Outside her window stood a tree, itself a dark silhouette backlit by a warm street lamp, clusters of leaves fluttering gently in the nighttime air. Its bark is gnarled and jutting, grown like tectonic plates cracking outwards from its skin, and growing too, unseen, below the trunk, hands of roots reaching to hold each other between strong fingers. A loving grasp of arms.

She thought of the peach pit ghosts and the ghost of her own clutched pit, risen now in fog bodies, searching for their sprouts. Mist-like forms floating through the streets and mingling together from late hours to the early sun, woven with each other like bracelets. The blood of peach juice dribbled down chins and staining hands, sticking fingers together as they clasped into pinky promises. The blood of Maggie's heart, of Lemon Pepper's. The rise and return; the true meaning of forever.

Maggie's ever-standing bedroom tree was leaning closer towards her, guided by a push of wind, its branches of children stretching to tap at her window a message.

Goodnight, it was saying. I'll see you in the morning.

WILL WE BE SISTERS?

NINA SIMPSON

It was another fight between mom and dad. Kira hoped that it was one of the fights that would end with her parents leaving the house and coming home hours later a lot happier, maybe with McDonalds. But it didn't seem like one of those fights.

Kira sat on the stairs while they kept shouting at each other about whatever it was this time. Money? Feelings? Whatever, it didn't matter. But Kira still sat on the stairs.

If she went into the living room she'd be pulled into the fight, and if she went into her room then her parents might barge in and demand she pick sides. She figured out a while ago that the stairs was a good middle ground. She'd be ignored on the stairs.

The front door opened and both of them stopped shouting for a second.

It was Isa! Isa! Isa!

She tossed her newly dyed purple hair over her shoulder and just glared at their parents.

"You guys are seriously fighting again, aren't you." Isa said with barely concealed rage. Not asked, because Isa never asked. She always said.

"Isabella, please, this is important." Their dad said.

"Oh, sure it is." Isa said, rolling her eyes. "Whatever this week's fight is, *has* to be so important." She said, sarcasm dripping off her voice.

"It is." Their mom said. "Apparently, your father didn't tell me that he spent a thousand dollars on the truck. Can you believe him?"

"It wasn't a thousand dollars, and it's my truck. I don't need your permission to spend my own money!"

"You need to tell me everything. I'm your wife!"

Kira slid a few steps down the stairs and waved to Isa who saw her and crossed the living room, getting to the stairs.

"Let's go to the balcony." Isa whispered leaning closer to Kira.

Kira bit her lip. "What if they get angry and start yelling at us again?" It had only happened a few times, but it happened enough that kept her on the stairs.

"I don't think they're that focused on what we think, this time." Isa said and glared at their parents.

"If you hate me spending my money, why don't you just leave? You've done that before, haven't you!" Their dad shouted. Well, technically Isa's dad.

It was technically Isa's dad and Kira's mom, but Kira had never remembered a time when Isa wasn't her sister.

"And split up this family now?" their mom gasped.

"Hell no! Not now. I'm not having my daughter deal with a divorce while she's still living under my roof!" Next to her, Isa clenched her fists.

"What about Kira? She's your daughter too!"

"No, she's not! She just came with you."

Oh.

Kira felt herself move up the stairs, down the hallway, and onto the balcony in the blink of an eye. She sat on one of the rickety old chairs and curled up into a ball with her face in her hands.

Maybe if she was even smaller. Maybe if she even more quiet. Maybe if she didn't say anything, just stayed out here, she'd be forgotten about. Maybe it'd be okay.

Why was she even upset? It wasn't like that was a new thing. He never seemed to like her. He never talked to her when the rest of the family wasn't around, never tried to reach out to her, never treated her like he treated Isa.

Although that might be a good thing. He and Isa argued a lot. Maybe not as much as her mom and him, but often.

The balcony door opened, then closed and Kira felt a blanket wrap around her.

"Here's some soda." Isa said and handed her a coke can. Kira just moved it to the table next to her and whipped her tears away.

They both sat on the balcony in a not really quiet. Kira's mom and Isa's dad were still arguing downstairs, and the neighborhood was also a little loud tonight. There was a party at one of their neighbor's houses, and the music was just barely decipherable.

But at least the view was nice. There were some rooftops of the neighborhood, but past that, the well set sun made the sky a pretty dark orange, with a few stars dotting the sky and a cloud or two floating by.

"Are they actually going to split up this time?" Kira asked in a quiet voice.

"Probably." Isa said solemnly. "My dad's been talking about moving once I'm in college, and my graduation is in two days soo. . ." she trailed off.

"So, you're going to be leaving soon?" Kira asked.

"I'd be leaving no matter what-" Kira's heart sank "-but I'll also be coming here to see *you* no matter what." Isa said.

Kira finally looked at Isa, her sort of sister. Not by blood, maybe not legally anymore.

"Will we still be sisters?" Kira asked.

Isa's face softened and she leaned next to Kira. "Of course. Our parents don't get to decide that, right?"

Kira rushed Isa and gave her a hug.

"Of course." Kira said.

MARCH: THE CLOCK AND THE GUN

Winners: Rebecca Leung & Quentin Gutierrez

AN UNGUENT FOR YOUR LOVE

REBECCA LEUNG

The Ship of Theseus
Built with love
Worn by age
Put back together
And loved all the same

Mankind loved their festivals.

It wasn't as though the elven didn't, it was just... man did it so differently.

Cedar was used to bonfires in the dead of night, praying to their ancestors for a mild winter, mourning those they had lost, or celebrating a good hunt with the entire settlement getting together to butcher the largest of the deer.

But man, man was not like that.

They cleared out their cobblestone squares, put on their most colorful clothes and sang, danced, and drank until the barrels of mead ran dry.

It was on one of these festival days that Cedar Ironheart found himself in Ambrodian, the largest human settlement within traveling distance.

He was carrying a rack of antlers on his back, lashed together with rope to make the heavy load a little easier. It had been as successful an expedition as anyone could expect in the cold of winter.

His herbalist's kit hung at his hip, bouncing as he readjusted the antlers. He just had to sell these and buy some pickling salts from the apothecary. Maybe something to eat.

Hopefully the apothecary would be open. The streets were full of people, and Cedar had to move quickly through alleyways to avoid the crowds.

Cedar's footfalls were soft, moving quickly despite his heavy load before he rounded the corner to where the apothecary's stood.

And when he tried the door, it was locked. Great.

The soft sound of music that had been the backdrop to this entire adventure was growing louder, and Cedar looked back to see a honest-to-gods parade approaching him.

They were led by a tall woman with an intricate set of braids and ribbon in her brown hair, a lyre propped up in the crook of her arm. She was leading the crowd, moving them ever forward in a beautiful, mesmerizing march.

Cedar attempted to hide, but not even he could blend into the background with a rack of antlers on his back.

She locked eyes on him, and Cedar froze as her face broke out in a bright grin. It was like being caught in a bonfire.

Before he could make a plan to flee, the parade was upon him.

"Who are you, my dear?" the woman said, her voice gentle and strong.

Cedar felt the tips of his ears heat up.

"Em, I'm Cedar Ironheart."

"Aurum Ardove, a pleasure to meet you." she grinned up at him.

Cedar was fairly sure he was supposed to reply with something witty, but his mind and mouth could not decide on what that would be.

"What are you doing in town? I haven't seen your face around here, and I never forget a handsome face." She managed to say all of this while still strumming on her lyre, leading them to gods know where.

"I just needed to sell some… stuff…? But the apothecary doesn't seem to be in right now-" Cedar was stuttering, knew he was only making half sense.

"Oh, of course! Last I saw the apothecary, she was drinking every sailor worth their salt under the table."

"Lovely," Cedar mumbled. "You don't happen to know anyone sober who would be interested in antlers?"

Aurum looked up at him, squinting a little bit. Her eyes were striking, deep brown and utterly captivating.

"-How much?"

Cedar blinked, realizing a half second too late that he had not heard anything she had just said.

Aurum laughed. "I need some new pegs for my lyre. How much for the antlers?"

"Um," Cedar floundered. "Seven gold?"

"Sold." Aurum grinned. "Do you mind carrying them for me for a little longer? Normally I'd carry it myself, but my hands are a little full."

She had been strumming along to the parade's song the entire time, seamless even as she continued to speak.

"Sure," Cedar replied lamely. "Where are we going?"

"Back to the inn of course! I'm the guest of honor there"

"Oh."

The procession to the inn was thankfully short, with everyone spilling inside for more drinks and merriment. Another bard was already sitting by the hearth, tuning his lute. Aurum and he exchanged a nod of approval, and he started up his own rousing song.

Aurum finally slung her lyre against her back, gesturing for Cedar to follow her to the bar.

She fished a silver piece and a few pieces of copper on the bar table. "A raspberry mead and..."

She looked at Cedar. "What do you want?"

"What?"

"To drink."

"You don't have to buy me a drink."

"But I am. What do you want?" Aurum repeated, her voice leaving no room for argument.

"Um. Ale?"

"And an ale," Aurum added.

The bartender swiped the money off of the counter and bustled away to get them their drinks.

"You're a very odd sort of person," Cedar said before he could think better of it.

Aurum laughed. "Why thank you, I try to be."

"Are you sure you want the whole set of antlers?" Cedar asked.

"Oh, sure, sure. I could use a new set of combs and buttons and hairpins and things," Aurum shrugged.

"Do you want me to pay you back for the drink?"

"Nah, just tell me a little bit about yourself. I am always looking for the newest story."

Oh, right, yes, she was a bard.

"Well. I do my best to live off of the land. It supplies me with everything I need, I draw my magics from the earth, I eat what I can get from nature or barter for with what I can scavenge."

"Ah, so you're a druid! Do you have a tribe you travel with?"

"Not usually. I go back to my homeland for celebrations, but I prefer to keep to myself."

"Oh, a man of mystery! A bit of a lone wolf?" Aurum was leaning against the bar, sipping her mead.

Cedar shrugged, "I don't get along with most."

"I think we get along just fine."

Cedar felt his face redden, and he took a long draught of ale to hide his face. "I guess we do."

"Where are you headed to next?" Aurum asked after a moment of almost too tense silence after polishing off half of her mead.

"I need to go see the local druids in the next town over. They supply the best purified water for potions of restoration."

"How lucky!" Aurum broke out into a grin. "I'm headed that way too. Do you want to come with me?"

He looked up at her, not sure if he heard her right. "You want me to come with you?"

"I mean… only if you're not doing anything else important." Was Aurum blushing, or was it the lamplight on her cheeks? "I'd love to travel with, uh, partner."

Cedar smiled a little, trying to contain all his excitement where it would not show on his face. "I'd love to accompany you."

~~~

"You really were a little clueless, love," Aurum giggled, running her fingers through Cedar's hair as they lay in bed together. It was over five years of travel, countless festivals, and one refurbished cottage on the edge of the forest later. Cedar almost couldn't believe it.

"Yes, I know, I know. Thank the gods you had enough and finally told me to my face." Cedar played with the edge of Aurum's nightgown absentmindedly.

"I couldn't wait a second longer! I'm not getting any younger, better get it while it lasts," Aurum grinned a crooked grin at Cedar. It wasn't the perfect smile she showed her audiences, it was a smile just for him.

Cedar buried his face in her side. "Don't remind me."

"I know, I'm sorry love," Aurum murmured. A small silence stretched between them.

"I don't want you to be tied down to just my little life," Aurum said finally. "You have so much time ahead of you."

"I'm not tied down," Cedar protested, propping himself up on his elbows to look at her, "It's all I could ever want. I want that life to be with *you*."

"Oh, hun." Aurum cupped his face in her hands, running her thumb over his stubbly cheek. "I'm going to spend the rest of my life with you."

"I can't stand the thought of living a second without you in my life," Cedar mumbled. "You have given me everything I have ever wanted. The least I can do is do the same for you."

"I've always heard the tales of the wizards and druids that lived forever, heroes of old granted long, magnificent lives. I never understood
~~~

why someone would want to live forever until I met *you*," Aurum smiled.

"Maybe there's some truth to those stories. Maybe we can do it."

Aurum laughed gently. "I'm good, hun, but I don't think I'm good enough for a god to bless me like that. I'm already a little past my prime as far as female bards are concerned."

"Don't say that," Cedar frowned. "There's lots of druid stories of regeneration, of rebirth. Something we can do together."

"Yeah," Aurum said, pushing the hair out of his face. "Yeah, maybe we can."

"I won't rest until I find a way to promise you forever." Cedar decided, making Aurum laugh, light and beautiful.

"I love you, you silly little sapling."

"Love you too, my songbird."

~~~

The sorcerer's home was not much to look at. She had been living at the edge of town for as long as Cedar could remember.

Aurum had said she had been an adventurer back in the day, many of her tales immortalized in song.

He was doing this for Aurum, he reminded himself when the curl of anxiety started to pinch his gut.

Cedar knocked on the door.

It was almost too long before the door opened a crack.

"Hello," Cedar said to the single eye visible through the door. "I'm Cedar."

"What do you want?" the woman said, her voice tinged with annoyance.

"I wanted to talk to you about your studies," Cedar replied.

The woman sighed, opening the door fully to allow him inside. She was wearing the deep purple robes one would imagine a sorcerer would wear, but they hung loose on her aged body, her back hunched slightly from years of work.
~~~

Every available surface in the small cottage was covered in papers, potions, books, and scribe's materials. Not wanting to touch anything, Cedar moved as carefully as possible.

"Name's Vida," she said, easing herself into a chair next to what Cedar assumed was her main workbench. "Come here. What did you want to know about?"

Cedar came to stand before her, since the chair opposite her had a stack of books in the seat.

"I-I wanted to know what you knew about resurrection-"

Vida frowned at that, and Cedar worried he had already said the wrong thing.

"Why do you wish to extend the span of your life?" Vida asked, poking a bony finger in Cedar's chest. "Are the years given to you by your blood not good enough?"

"No- that's not what I meant-" Cedar stammered. "I don't want it for me-"

"I've looked for immortality my entire life," Vida said bitterly, sweeping her hand over the counter and the workbench, the shelves crammed with potions and tinctures. "And look where it got me. I'm withering away as we speak."

Cedar opened his mouth, but Vida barrelled on.

"The fountain of youth isn't real. So you need to think real, *real* hard if this is what you really want."

Cedar closed his mouth, looking down at his hands for a long moment.

"I have married a human woman. She is- she is the love of my life, she is my everything. We built a home together with our own hands, we are with child. It has already been years but I am just as happy now as I was when I first saw her face, heard her voice. But time is much less kind to humans than it is to elves."

Vida's mouth was pressed into a thin line. "How old is she?"

"She has three dozen winters to her name."

"Have you discussed it with her? You lot mate for life, but not all humans are like that."

"She told me not to worry about time, to enjoy what we have when we have it- but we've both been looking for ways to help- help her fight against her fate. She's been working to procure a potion of longevity, but we don't want to risk it more than once-"

Vida sighed heavily, almost in defeat. "I can't hand it to you on a silver platter, but this may be what you're looking for."

She shuffled around the many papers and books on her desk, procuring a slim journal bound in leather.

"Reincarnation is a tricky game." She put the book in his hands, folding her gnarled fingers over the book. "It's hard to learn, hard to find the ingredients. Even harder when you only have one shot. Only a few can learn it, all this research ended up being useless to me."

Cedar gulped. He had heard of reincarnation, of course, but he had thought it was simply a fanciful spell meant for only the truly powerful. Or the exceptionally foolhardy.

"The first half of the book is the ingredients you'll need. The second is the procedure."

"Th-thank you." Cedar held the book in both hands.

"It only works on the already passed. Do you understand what that means?"

Cedar's heart dropped into his stomach just at the thought. "I do."

"Are you sure you'll be able to do this? I ain't in the business of giving out false hope."

"I have to try."

Vida smiled a yellow toothed smile, full of sadness and hope in equal measure. "Good enough. Get out of here and make the best of it."

Cedar tucked the journal into the pocket of his cloak right over his heart, hurrying home. Aurum would be coming home from the market soon. The small trip into the very edge of the woods towards their modest home always helped to clear Cedar's mind. The small curl of smoke rising from the chimney meant that Aurum had beat him home.

He pushed open the door gently, finding her strumming her lyre at their dining room table, the hearth already crackling and the smell of something delicious.

"Ah, love!" she bounced up from her chair, pecking him on the cheek."I got a stewing hen from the market in exchange for helping the farmer fix his wife's favorite pot. A hole rusted right through the bottom, but nothing a little prestidigitation can't fix!"

Cedar laughed gently, leaning down to kiss the top of her head. "Your skills of trade will never cease to amaze me."

Aurum grinned, but quickly had to sit down, rubbing her pregnant belly. "I think being a few trimesters along helps. How was your visit?"

Cedar sighed, sitting down across from her and setting the book on the table, sliding it to Aurum.

She cocked her head to one side as she spun it towards herself.

"Resurrection?" she whistled appreciatively, "I'll be honest with you, I thought it was a one in a million sort of spell. Like a wish."

"I think it is. The woman was… very clear that it was difficult. I've heard of it through the older druids but… no one ever said they could do it."

Aurum looked down at the book, then up at her husband. "Have you looked at the spell yet?"

He shook his head. "I wanted to do it with you."

Aurum nodded as they opened the book together.

The list of ingredients was long. And expensive. Agar hartwood oil heralding from the southern isles. Black petal rosewater. An unguent of healing made from rendered gelatinous cube fat. Other various oils that came from slightly more reasonable sources, rosemary, eucalyptus, some other herbs and various ointments.

Cedar rubbed his face, the prospect of even *getting* these ingredients feeling like nothing more than a far off dream.

"Well." Aurum said after a moment of reading. "Resurrection doesn't come cheap, unsurprisingly."

"We can do it-" Cedar couldn't keep the desperation out of his voice.

Aurum looked at him with a bright little smile. "I know we can. Best to get started now, hm?"

Cedar nodded, sliding off his chair to sit on the floor and put his arms around her waist.

"I promise to you it will be forever-" Cedar murmured into the folds of her deep blue dress."

Aurum ran her hand through his hair. "I know you do."

~~~

"Momma! Momma! Look at all of the things we got!" Amaryla burst through the cottage door, her face and frock spattered with dirt. She had a fistful of carrots in one hand, a bundle of rosemary in the crook of her arm.

Aurum smiled, wrinkling the corners of her eyes. "Do come show me."

Cedar came through the door a moment later, carrying a basket of the rest of the foraged goods.

"Amaryla also tried her hand at target practice," Cedar said proudly, slinging the crossbow safely on the shelf too high for the young girl to reach.

"Oh, and how did that go?" Aurum asked, a wet dishcloth in hand to clean the dirt off of Amaryla's face.

"I hit the target twice!" Amaryla said proudly.

"You'll be a marksman in no time!" Aurum laughed.

Cedar kissed the top of Aurum's salt-and-pepper hair as he plucked the rosemary from Amaryla's arms. He crossed over to the small work-bench next to the hearth, uncapping a glass flask of pure water to rinse the herbs carefully in a shallow basin.

"Papa found a bunch of mushrooms too." Amaryla smiled up at Aurum. "We left some behind to make sure that they can still grow too."

"That's very good," Aurum said approvingly.

Cedar dried off the rosemary with a fresh cloth, placing the bundle carefully in a jar of argan oil, placing it on the windowsill. He always preferred making his own spell ingredients when he could.

"We don't want to take too much from Mother Earth." Cedar rejoined them at the table, sitting down at his seat and swooping Amaryla into his lap.
~~~

"Because it has to last us a super long time!" Amaryla added.

"Exactly," Aurum couldn't help the sadness that slipped into her voice, but Amaryla was blissfully unaware.

~~~

The woods around the cottage were filled with music. Lyre and lute, trading off chords as mother taught daughter her craft.

Cedar watched from where he sat plucking the leaves off of a long branch of eucalyptus he had bartered five gold and a wolf pelt for from a traveling merchant. The leaves were still green and supple. Full of oil for him to harvest, made into a salve with exotic ingredients squirreled away all year.

. He couldn't help the smile on his face as he caught Aurum's eye. She winked at him and he laughed.

"Dad, do you want to sing too?" Amaryla asked.

"Oh, no, I leave the singing to the experts." Cedar shook his head.

"Aw, please?" Amaryla smiled up at him. Who was Cedar to say no to a face like that? He carefully wrapped up the leaves he had collected, putting away all of his ingredients in their proper place before wandering over to their side.

"Okay, okay, just this once."

~~~

The years went by all too quickly. Amaryla grew into a talented young woman right in front of Cedar and Aurum's eyes. She was just as skilled with song and word as the greatest of the bards thanks to Aurum, and was already carving her name out in the content, one ballad at a time. First came the trips to the next town by herself, then she stayed the weekend in the next city, then she only visited for holidays.

Cedar did not worry when she was gone, they had taught her well, and armed with her lute bearing her bard's mark and her crossbow

Cedar crafted for her, she could go anywhere. The entire continent would know her name, he was sure of it.

The small collection of tinctures and oils in the box under Cedar and Aurum's bed was slowly growing more complete. Every bottle and tin was carefully labeled, a checklist more than half complete by the time Amaryla had seen two dozen winters.

She had even contributed to the ingredients, proudly presenting a waterskin full of the sticky green goo of a gelatinous cube she had encountered eating through a mining town's meager food supply. Cedar had spent a full week rendering it carefully, mixing in ground emerald dust and eucalyptus oil from far off lands to make the proper salve.

Every day, Aurum got a little older. Every day, Cedar fell a little more in love with her. Every day, he became even more aware that his time was running thin.

~~~

"What if I'm different when I come back?" Aurum murmured, her face tilted towards the soft spring light filtering in through her bedside window. Age had softened her face, carrying the lines of her life like the lyrics of a song. She was no less beautiful to him now than she had been in her youth, even if her voice had thinned and her body slowed. They had spent almost seventy winters together. It still didn't feel like enough.

He squeezed her withered hand gently, his own still strong and smooth. Years of strumming a lyre had rendered her arthritic, unable to grip back with knobbled, sore fingers. He cursed his longevity, looking at the small jar of vitality ointment that he had finally gotten not a month prior. The last on the list he had to find. He had not left her bedside since, not wanting to miss a precious moment with her. The backboard of their bed was lined with ointments and oils, a scroll of the incantation that Cedar had memorized all of those years ago.

"I will love you all the same."
~~~

"I love you, Cedar," Aurum murmured as she closed her eyes. One last gift to her husband: he wouldn't have to see her lifeless eyes look where he could not follow.

"I love you too, Aurum," Cedar forced down the tears closing his throat.

He felt the awful lurch in his entire universe as it fractured in half, feeling a numbness entering his bones as trembling hands spread salve on quickly cooling skin, over her forehead and temples, rubbed into pulse points as he recited the chants, the *prayers* that would bring his love back.

Please. *Please.* **Please**. He could not live without her. Please, to the gods and goddesses above and the powers that be, please don't make him live without her.

He pulled on all of the energy he possibly could summon from the woods that they had grown with, from the soil under the floorboards, from deep within himself and his forefathers.

The change was miniscule at first, like all changes are. The stiffening fibers of tissue started to glow softly, light weaving throughout her skin as energy overtook flesh, molding it, *changing* it. But it still felt so very Aurum.

Cedar forced himself to watch, his chanting punctuated by silent sobs as her body began to dissolve away, an insubstantial mass of energy writhing like its own pulsing star.

It grew, power and light too intense for Cedar to keep his eyes open any longer. But still, he chanted, arms raised to the heavens. The words were seared into his mind, almost in a trance as he jumped from line to line. It was like music in its own way. Music for his songbird.

The ballad came to a close, the grand gestures slowing as his hands dropped into his lap. The glow behind his eyelids faded, but he was still too scared to open them.

A nimble hand found his and squeezed, accompanied with a bright laugh.

"You can open your eyes, my little sapling," Aurum said, her voice light and strong. Cedar knew everything would be alright.

2 4

QUENTIN GUTIERREZ

Alma Robledo gazed at the omniscient digital timer on her left forearm. It read 00:00:01:00:00:24 Alma normally wakes up at 5:30 sharp, but tonight she refused. Normally,Finality is something to be celebrated. You invite your friends, have a little party, drink a little too much alcohol, numb yourself to the point where the increasing vibrations become too painful to ignore. Alma received her first one now. A surging pain shocked all throughout her limbs, and veins. "Like being shot" was what she told the men of her precinct. What good that descriptor was to a bunch of rookies, let alone cops. Alma hated them. They made her work so much harder. Alma is in the Advanced Proto-col Division. APD for short. They are only dispatched to help people, completely separate from the supposed "protectors of the community" in the Phalanx Division. They're a completely separate company, and yet, they have to share the same building. 'Murderers, all of them'. she thought. Especially egregious to Cadavers. That's what everyone called them anyway, disrespectful. Silbons was what Alma preferred to call them. Now she preferred to call herself that. She believed the worst part about the Phalanx Division was their requirements. High Finality numbers was one of them. What she hated the most was the way they got those numbers, Leeching, was what Alma called it. "Sharing" was what the PD called it. Most of the members just Leeched a few years off of their parents once they were off the force, a little loan that they would have to pay back later. Paid directly from any Silbons they could leech from while on duty. Speeding? That'll be an hour. Stealing? 10 days. Caught with drugs and money? Well you better hope the money was all they take, realistically the courts will give you Finality, give all your spare time to the precinct. The negatives had become overwhelming at times, especially at night. She decided to think of the good they do at the APD. They help people, anyone who needs it on their day of Finality. Loners who have no one else, people afraid of being Leeched, or afraid they might Leech out of desperation. Alma did the best she could for Silbons, too much, more often than not. There had been more than a few times where Alma would give them a few more minutes, hours... days. She wanted to continue to help people, even in her Finality. Alma decided she would need sleep in order to be at her most effective. She slept immediately, and awoke once again at 5:30 AM, like clockwork.

00:00:00:17:28:56

Alma arrived at her office at about 6:32 AM, 2 hours earlier than her usual schedule. The doors were locked, which was odd. She began to reach for her master key when the heavy glass door slowly creaked open. She stepped into nothingness, fumbling for any source of light. She approached the main breaker and switched every light to the on position. "SURPRISE," Alma's entire being left her for a second. She thought she would have died on the spot if it weren't for her countdown reminding her that it wasn't time yet. Her coworkers all stood under a banner that read 'FINALLY, FINALITY!' an inside joke between Alma and her favorite gremlin, Keke, who was at the center, holding a goopy pan of uncooked cake batter. Alma couldn't help letting out a snort from the ridiculousness of it. Keke awkwardly fumbled with the cake batter pan, setting it down on a nearby table.

"Thank you all so much, honestly!"

Exclaimed Alma, giving her best corporate smile. As the group dispersed back to their decorated cubicles, Keke approached with a gruff expression.

"What the hell, Alma! I knew you were gonna be early, but two hours? You know how long it took to set up that banner?"

Alma let out a giggle, then replied

"I don't know, how many Kekes does it take to set up a banner?"

Keke playfully smacked her friend on the arm, then said

"Man, whatever, you're lucky I set up anything at all. I know you don't like parties and all, but you still deserve one." She looked down at her pan of uncooked cake batter.

"And you better eat all of this too! Took me way too long to make a good vegan version!"

Alma laughed again. *Maybe sometimes parties are okay*, she thought to herself.

"I'm gonna miss you, Flaquita," said Keke before embracing Alma in a powerful hug.

Keke only gave hugs to people in Finality; Alma had seen it on the job whenever they went out on duo missions together. Something felt so odd about this hug to her; she had seen it a thousand times before, but now she was experiencing it. It was like a child saying one last goodbye to their dog before euthanasia. One last hug before the lights go out.

00:00:00:16:16:32

Alma savored the final bite of her slice of strawberry shortcake, ecstatic that Keke had remembered such a small detail about her favorite treat. The silence was palpable now. Alma gazed at the beige file on her desk, her final job. Technically those near Finality weren't allowed to take any jobs, it was too risky. People with low numbers tended to act out. Luckily Keke had pulled some strings with the boss. She agreed to it as long as Alma was only a chaperone, legally it was still Keke's job. She would also need to cater for the boss's daughter. Which Keke agreed to at a discounted price to sweeten the deal. It was times like these where Alma really understood her dedication. Not just for Alma either, but for Finality as a whole. The thing was, Keke had lost her wife, Taniya, 5 years ago. Her numbers were high, nowhere near even saying the word Finality. She was killed by an officer of the Phalanx. Leeched. Her name was Taniya. Taniya was trying to help a Silbon, give him a little more time. Unfortunately, he was an agent of the Phalanx, a piece of bait left out for an unsuspecting victim, someone with too good of a heart. Taniya was found by one of the members of the APD with only 10 seconds left on her clock. Her last words were "My light". A reference to her and Keke's wedding vows. "My light will guide my love, and my love will guide my light, we'll glisten on forever, like the bright white stars of night." After Keke found out what happened she cut off contact with pretty much everyone she held close. Extra concerned one night, Alma made the trek to Keke's apartment and found her huddled up in a blanket, with a book beside her titled *101 Recipes for Love.* The two were supposed to finish it together. Around the apartment there were clumps of noodles stuck to the walls, burnt pieces of toast tucked away under the sofa, and 3 pans which contained chocolate cake batter, vodka sauce, and a turkey respectively. Alma took a seat next to her on the loveseat,

"I love what you've done with the place," she spoke softly as if it were a genuine compliment, carefully trying to ease Keke out of her chrysalis.

Keke only sniffled. They sat in silence for at least 10 minutes, until Alma spoke again.

"Let's get you cleaned up, stinky." She then wrapped up and stored any salvageable meals, washed every pot and pan, and then began a shower for Keke.

"Now are you gonna walk there, or am I going to have to carry you?" asked Alma. Keke simply looked at her with her puffy eyes; she absolutely hated being carried, and she knew Alma had the ability to do it too. She stood up, still a wrapped sushi roll, and waddled to the restroom. A few weeks later, Keke called Alma to let her know that she had finished the book. Now, it was Alma's turn to finish a book of her own, the final chapter of *Life* by Alma Robledo.

The drive was awful; Alma preferred two wheels; no one ever gets bike-sick. There was also something about watching the time on the GPS go down that made it extra painful. Each minute was one she could have spent ensuring the safety of the Silbon who was waiting for them, let alone a minute less of her own being. Still, they arrived on time. The place was a long strip of dock, gazing directly toward the sun. At its edge sat an old woman with exactly 5 hours left. Interestingly, her death clock sat on the back of her neck. This was a rarity, even among rarities; the most common area was your forearm, but there was the occasional Silbon with it on their legs or their upper chest, but the back was much more odd. The mystique of death might feel intact if you couldn't constantly see it; one might forget about Finality for once, blinded by the happiness that life can bring without the constant looming of darkness. The two sat at the edge with her, allowing their feet to hang and swing.

"Oh, hello, dears, are you the ones I rang on the telephone?" She spoke with a very gentle English accent, another rarity, in the U.S. at least.

"Yes, we are, ma'am. My name is Keke, and this is my friend Alma."

"Oh, how lucky for me to be with two beautiful caretakers. My name is Jacaranda."

This woman was so unique, Alma wondered what kind of life she must have lived. Someone like her should have hundreds of connections to call, yet she had chosen the APD, how odd.

"It is lovely to meet you, Jacaranda. Is there any way we can help you through your journey in Finality?" Alma said with a smile.

"Oh heavens no, I want to sit here on this dock and talk to some strangers. My family wanted to make some extravagant dinner for me, much too posh for my tastes. I don't need any of that; I'm a simple gal with simple tastes." Jacaranda giggled.

"Oh, come on now, that was a joke; one look at me and you know I'm not, ladies, please."

Keke laughed and then began to look off into the distance.

"Look, when you get to my age, you learn that regretting never does anything. We live our whole lives wondering what we could have done in the past, but what about the now? Don't regret, do. Do something about it. The second you start taking action for what's been done, that's when you start to feel true bliss. I don't want a party with my family; I could've sat there and taken it to my grave, but instead I told them exactly what I wanted, and now I'm gonna get it. I really do just wish to sit here. I don't want to know how much time I've got left, and I don't need any more. I've had a wonderful life. All I ask is for someone to listen." The three women stared at each other, then at the big ball of light in the distance, not a cloud in sight.

00:00:00:10:10:55

Jacaranda was gone. Her final request was to be buried in the flowers of her namesake. Keke and Alma had never mentioned anything in relation to Jacaranda's final hours, but the ever-present buzzing kept reminding her anyway. Still, she always played it off like nothing had happened, a constant that surrounded many of her life stories. Eventually, her family arrived to pick her up, and thanked them for their support and love in her Finality. Keke and Alma recounted her final requests, got in the car and drove away.

00:00:00:10:00:10

Alma braced herself for another shock; they would be at the top of every hour now. As it coursed through her veins again, Keke held her close. Her screams were muffled into her friend's arms and eventually dissipated into nothingness.

"Okay, Flaquita, you had your last job. Now it's your turn; what's the plan?"

Alma pretended to think for a moment, but the conversations with Jacaranda echoed in her mind. She took a deep breath and then spoke confidently,

"We're gonna find the bastard who killed Taniya."

00:00:00:9:34:17

The remaining car ride was silent. When they finally reached the stairs of the APD offices, Keke decided to speak.

"Listen, I'm not one to deny your 'final wish' or whatever, but I just wanna make sure you're actually doing this because you want to. Don't do this just because you think I'm gonna be happy with the result. Are you sure this is what you want?"

Keke stared down Alma, never blinking.

"Keeks, I've never been more sure of anything in my life."

Alma turned away, jogged up the stairs, and opened the door for Keke.

"After you?" Alma said as she gestured in a fanciful manner.

Keke allowed herself to smile.

"Just desserts, comin' right up."

The two walked in unison to the Phalanx Division file room; normally, there were strict parameters to be followed when entering it. Luckily, the PD had loosened their restrictions in regards to paper-work. Many of their busywork tended to get sent to the Advanced Protocol Division anyway, claiming that they knew much more when it came to Cadavers. Many members of the APD tended to go straight to work as soon as their field jobs were done, which made it easier not to get flooded.

"Hey! Where do you think you're going?"

Alma and Keke stopped in their tracks, they slowly turned around to the hefty security guard at the window. Their hearts boomed like the bass of a speaker.

"Wait right there, and don't move!"

Said the security guard. He unlocked the entrance to the tiny cubicle and walked out. He paced closer and closer before giving Alma a massive bear hug. Tears began to well up in his eyes. Keke turned around to see their favorite clerk, Boden Boyle, who preferred to be called Bobo.

"Bobo… you're… choking me."

He quickly let go of Alma and apologized profusely. Bobo loved hugs, but he would often forget that some people didn't.

"Shoot, Alma, I'm so sorry, I just... Today is your Finality and, well, I'm gonna miss you so much. Can I please give you a hug?"

Alma often reserved hugs for final moments; they were extremely special to her and were not often normal in her household. She understood that this could be the last time Bobo would ever see her alive again. She carefully opened her arms and said,

"Yes, Bobo, you know we love you," she said, gesturing to Keke.

"Oh yes! Keke, you wanna join too?" He asked like an excited puppy.

"I don't think your numbers are down enough for that, Bobo, but you two have fun." Keke stared at Bobo's arm as he lovingly embraced Alma for what would be the last time. His clock had over 80 years left. Bobo had never once leeched. He was just lucky, born that way, and since the Phalanx Division members are issued by birth, there was nothing he could do to get out of it. Alma always thought he would be a perfect member of their team. A loving soul for those who needed it, and in this moment, Alma really needed it.

"Hold on, I got you a present!"

He quickly zoomed in and out of his office, carrying a small black and silver photo locket. Its outside was decorated with an hourglass. Upon opening it, there was a picture inside of Alma, Keke, and Bobo. It was taken several years ago, when Alma first started at the APD.

"I thought you'd need it for once you go to the great beyond, you know? Something to remember us when we finally get up there." Bobo gave a toothy grin, and then ran back into his cubicle, locking the door behind him.

"I'd never forget you, Bobo." Alma said no more as they swam into the sea of paperwork.

00:00:00:6:10:17

After hours of finishing their work and searching every detail for connections, they had found him. The PD hardly bothered trying to cover it up. Here it was in writing, clear as day.

"On March 14th, 2065, a woman by the name of Taniya Naser and a man by the name of Jordan Dawson were found in Finality. Field Officer Joseph Aubrey discovered the two and approached cautiously in order to question them, investigating reports of illicit drug deals in the area. Immediately, Mr. Dawson withdrew a firearm and began running towards Officer Aubrey. Officer Aubrey responded by using a taser to incapacitate Mr. Dawson. After which, Mrs. Naser attempted to physically assault Officer Aubrey. Officer Aubrey reacted by pinning Mrs. Naser down and handcuffing her to a nearby pole. Officer Aubrey then handcuffed Mr. Dawson and properly followed protocol by contacting the Advanced Protocol Division in order to grant Mrs. Naser and Mr. Dawson peace in their finality."

"What a bunch of bullshit!" Keke threw the file back into the stack of useless papers. She put her head down into her arms, and could not stop herself from letting the tears pour out.

Alma apologized and set her arm on Keke's shoulder as she stayed silently sobbing.

00:00:00:6:00:00

Alma was once again overwhelmed with a scorching surge. It was incredibly difficult this time, and she tried her best to hide her squeals of anguish as they left the building. Officer Aubrey had been sent on another "drug-related" mission; they had gotten the tip from one of the Phalanx members before they left in exchange for some of Alma's birthday cake. This time, the area of investigation was a massive nearby slaughterhouse that was very familiar to her. Not exactly a beautiful location, but fitting they supposed. They drove Keke's Remodel of the '62 Mustang prototype towards the front of the building where an electric fence opened for them to enter. A woman with a yellow and white security outfit sat in a booth with a screen of buttons. She began to speak loudly through what looked to be a CB radio.

"State your name and business," she blared through a loudspeaker. Keke decided to speak for the group.

"Yeah, hi. My name is Keke Naser; this is my partner, Alma Robledo; we're from the APD responding to a call about a few Silbons whose last location was here." She looked toward Alma and winked playfully.

"Please place your IDs on the screen, ma'am."

Keke did so with their badges and received a green light.

"Thank you; please offer them my condolences," she said with an empty, monotonous voice. The dual-layered metal gates then swung open with the screech and scratch of the hard concrete floor.

They drove around the building until they spotted Officer Aubrey's Phalanx vehicle decorated with an ancient warrior helmet near the Greek letters Rho and Delta. They moved toward the marked entrance and walked in. The room was a large warehouse, and it smelled similar to the carnicerias of Alma and Keke's youth. A sour, meaty scent that permeated the entire area. They walked up a nearby steel spiral staircase that led to the storage areas. It was better to have a vantage point so they could plan their attack before confronting Joseph Aubrey. As the two moved further along the guard rail, they began to hear distant, sharp squeals. As they slowly approached, the yelps became screams. Eventually Alma and Keke could see the animals voicing their terror—a group of a dozen live pigs with their hands and legs clasped together. Hogtied with metal shackles, a laser light made careful incisions into their abdomens. Two men carefully directed the lasers and took notes based on their reactions. Alma could only look away in horror. Keke forced herself to look carefully, and noticed something on each of their stubby pink legs. Etched on the left sides of all but one was a digital clock.

Keke moved back to the corner where Alma sat, shutting her eyes.

"Alma, they've got numbers," she whispered.

"What? Th-That's impossible; animals don't have numbers." Alma's voice accidentally echoed throughout the warehouse, she was fully aware of her mistake when the two men standing below gazed up toward them. They grabbed gas masks, equipped them, and flipped a switch. The walls all around began to shut with large metal doors, and smoke began to fill the entire room. Keke and Alma stared into each other's eyes as the entire world went black.

00:00:00:1:00:01

Alma finally awoke with the most painful buzz she would ever experience. It shocked her entire core, then extended itself straight into her skull. Her body felt like it was being stretched too thin as it extended into her legs and feet. Her eyes were wide open now, awake to see the torturous conditions in front of her. Keke stood with her arms and legs shackled together, still asleep. Alma stared at her arm as it counted down slowly, it was either now or never. She tried her best to force herself not to stare at the nearby pigs, but the numbers on their appendages were too difficult not to gaze at.

"Ah, you're awake, perfect." Said the first man.

"Just in time to witness the next step in our evolution." The second man remained silent as they both removed their masks. The first man was Officer Joseph Aubrey; his eyes glinted with wonder and excitement at the new potential subject in front of him. The second man removed his mask to reveal the sweet, kindhearted face of Bobo. He simply looked away and allowed Officer Aubrey to speak.

"Isn't it wonderful? Humanity will live among the gods, free to do as we please with all the time in the world. Observe. " Aubrey grabbed one of the terrified animals as he leeched its life force away, the numbers on its clock began to dwindle into nothingness, the poor pig collapsed onto the floor with a loud thump. A tear rolled down Alma's cheek as she witnessed the death unfolding in front of her. He culled the herd, until all that remained was a single piglet.

"Relax, they're just stupid pigs." yelled Aubrey

"Takes one to know one," said Keke in a drowsy slur as she spat at the ground next to him.

"You know what? I think you're right, because one of them is standing right in front of me." Aubrey walked right up to Keke, grabbing her arm with malice.

"Happy Finality!" he shouted as he began to leech Keke's life away, just as he had done to Taniya.

Alma watched with horror as her friend was slowly being drained of her entire humanity. She screamed in anguish until Bobo slammed Aubrey into the ground. Aubrey was powerless under the weight of his former partner. A heavy fist connected into Aubrey's face, and then another, and then another. Bobo quickly grabbed the keys to the shackles and unlocked Alma's left arm. He handed them to her and ran back to the officer to strip him of any weapons and secure him in handcuffs. Alma unlocked her right arm next, then her right leg, and finally her left leg. She tripped slightly with the last lock, but caught herself in time. She ran toward Keke, who looked faint. Alma unlocked her arms and legs, careful not to let her fall. She sat her down and propped her up against a nearby table. She then walked over to Bobo, who was now equipped with multiple weapons.

"I was supposed to be undercover," he said awkwardly.

"I'm a special agent. They told me to get evidence of all of this and then report back. I'm sorry, I didn't mean to scare you. Or for either of you to get hurt." He looked away.

Alma's eyes moved toward the deceased, innocent pigs. The final remaining pig had no number and looked more like a piglet. It stared up at her with a fearful expression. It was shaking a little, and the hair of its fuzzy black spots stood up. She picked it up carefully, gave it a soft pet, and placed it in Keke's lap. She was awake now; she stared up at Alma as if to ask 'what now?'

Alma looked at her two friends, their lives now changed forever, and said

"We're gonna burn this whole fucking place to the ground"

Keke let out a shocked scoff and began to laugh

"Hell yeah, flaquita!"

A short groan came from Officer Aubrey, the three watched as he came back to consciousness.

He slurred his words heavily like a toddler with food in its mouth.

"Y-y-you idyuts, when ph-ph-phalanxth finds out, you'll all be DEAD."

"I got news for you buddy, I'm already dead"
Said Alma

"You guys head out, I'll take care of the cargo".

Keke embraced Alma for her final hug.

"Te amo, flaquita. Tell Taniya I miss her, ok?"

"Love you too. I'll tell her all about the inches you've grown"

Keke gave her best friend a rough punch to the arm. The piglet let out an angry little squeal.

"You better keep that little guy too." Alma said

"I will… I'll see you in hell, babe" Keke said

Bobo and Keke opened the large metal doors using the nearby control panel. Their footsteps began to trail away slowly into nothingness.

Alma spent the remainder of her time spilling any flammable liquid she could find. Big tubs of grease, and oil cans, mainly. She used the control panel to direct the laser onto the mixed concoction in front of her.

"You know I won't die here, you dumb bitch. I've still got years on my clock, there's NOTHING YOU CAN DO" Officer Aubrey yelled to nobody

Alma knew what she wanted, she didn't care if Aubrey wouldn't die, he'd be doomed to a torturous life of burns, lost limbs, and suffering. It was what he deserved. After all, sometimes death is a mercy. Alma took a seat on the cold concrete floor of the warehouse. She took a deep breath, and smiled as the world went up in flames.

00:00:00:00:00:10

Alma gazed at the omniscient digital timer on her left forearm, she had always lived life according to the needs of others, but today she refused. Normally Finality is something to be celebrated. Well, tonight, Alma would go off with her own fireworks. As her time began to tick tick tick away. Each shock was a short burst of memory,

9

She remembered Keke's wedding, and the way the light shone onto her beautiful, brown, skin. The way her lavender dress meshed with the mint glow of Taniya's.

8

She remembered her Mother excusing herself from the dinner table in her Finality, silently sobbing in her room as the void took her.

7

She remembered her father's unwavering strength as he faced the music. And the way he swore that in his final hours he could hear Death's siren song.

6

She pictured her younger brother in a hospital bed. His bright smile knowing that his organs would go to people who needed them.

5

She pictured her first Silbon, her beautiful eyes that were individually blue and green. The refusal she had at the offer of a little more time.

4

She pictured Jacaranda, and her contentment of her final hours of bliss.

3

She gazed at the picture of herself, Keke, and Bobo, remembering how it felt to finally be a part of making the world a better place. Helping those she loved.

2

She remembered the final bite of her Strawberry Shortcake.

1

"See you in hell"

TEARS ON PHANTOM SKIN

SAMANTHA PACINI-CARLIN

Avery stared out the bars on the window – one of the few indications that he was in a cell. Well, the bars in place of a wall also gave it away. But other than those ominous metal pipes, he found the room rather cozy. The bed, complete with pillows and sheets, creaked as he perched on the edge of it. A pale blue coated the brick walls. Its color reminded him of clear skies, which the night's brewing storm robbed him of. Even then, the view was nice. Valmishra's city lights twinkled in the dark canvas like stars, creating the illusion of the sky reflected in a lake. A shame that the one in the hall outside his cell couldn't join them; its light, created by a tiny teal-ish crystal set in iron, had been dimmed by the last guards.

He sighed. Stoirm, he wished they gave him something to do besides pace around, look outside, or twiddle his thumbs. Even someone to chat with would be nice. Sure, his cellmate Hubert filled a corner of the room when they wanted to and let him monologue without interruption, though that entertained him to a certain point. The guards weren't a better option, either. They were a skittish sort, and ducked past the bars with the speed of wary mice moving through the space between shadows. It smarted every time they cringed at him. He supposed he could understand why to some degree, but he always chided them on their biases. It wasn't every day a person saw someone with charcoal bones and purple veins pressed against a patch of pale skin on their cheek. Oh, he *had* warned them about that patch. They insisted on pulling the hood of his tunic down, removing his red scarf, and brushing aside his long black hair to get a look at his face, though. Maybe he should've smudged some dirt on it. At least they didn't roll up the gloved sleeves or make him strip down. If the sight of his face almost made them faint, seeing the rest of his body might've killed them.

Footsteps pattered down the hallway. Avery leaned forward, snapped out of his musings.

"-have to?" a lad's voice asked.

A gruffer voice grunted, exasperated by his partner. "Neither of us'll die from touching him. 'Sides, I've seen far worse than a little bone."

Two guards came into view. Both wore pieces of leather armor over teal coats with clubs at their sides. The long cloth secured on their waists bore Lord Ferrow's crest: a raven with a brilliant blue gem for an eye. One wore his armor with less confidence than the other, though. He futzed with the sleeve and clamped onto his club for intimidation. The other, older, regarded him calmly. Avery gave that one a grateful smile, though that offset the man's tranquility.

"You are to come with us," the older man commanded. "Cooperate, or we'll drag you there in shackles."

Avery rolled his shoulders and stood up. "Did the lord ask for me? I'm flattered. Half thought he'd leave me to rot for a few years, not see me hours after the crime."

The lad slotted the key into the lock, then nudged the door open. He looked to the older one for guidance.

He muttered something under his breath – probably a complaint about the other's cowardice – but stepped into the cell. Avery let him place a hand on his shoulder. Though the older man projected confidence, he could feel the hand settle awkwardly on him. Would he be more hesitant if he knew about the "cursed" spot there? Probably. But good on him for trying not to let his prejudice overwhelm his fear.

"Come along, now," the old one said, pulling him towards the door.

Avery complied. He was halfway to the door, however, when he suddenly remembered Hubert. The lad (lassie, perhaps?), in spite of their silence, had been a good roommate; it didn't feel right to leave without a proper farewell. Not again.

He glanced back at the cell, then Blinked. A second set of eyelids fluttered down under his normal ones, which bathed his lashes in frost. They gave him sight into the Spirit Realm. Here, a less kind world overlapped the Seen one – its slate gray bricks coated with centuries of grime and slick with water that dripped through the cracks. Rust devoured the bars. A plain bench was fastened where his bed stood, sagging from the weight of a hundred bodies. Lightning crackled in the storm outside. Its flashes illuminated the dim interior, but never drew detail onto Hubert in the corner. The rope their shadow hung from creaked with each sway. Ferrow had enough sense to remodel the prison, yet a little makeup could not undo the damage done to the deceased. Perhaps that could change with time. This world was, after all, created by the memories souls brought to the afterlife. Could enough people die in these walls to make its reflection a happier place, or would it forever remain soiled?

These thoughts didn't matter. He Blinked to restore his normal vision, waved at Hubert, who rudely refused to return the gesture, and walked into the hall.

Avery couldn't figure out the architecture of the prison. If he had a blueprint, he might be able to trace his path through it, but the endless twists made his head spin. Ferrow probably kept that aspect of the old prison. Disorienting a prisoner for a moment could be the difference between recapture and escape. Fortunately, they led him to an area he recognized: a wider set of halls sealed from the entrance itself by massive doors. Gods, he wished they would've escorted him there. Instead, the younger one buried the club into his back, prodding him into a side door. A glimpse revealed the table and chair within.

"Careful with-" Avery began.

A voice like stones grinding together cut him off. "Thank you. Stay outside to guard the door, but do not disturb us for any reason."

They both saluted, then exited. He didn't bother to watch them leave, and instead focused on the man seated before him. Gods, he looked…wrong. The Ferrow he knew was supposed to wear battered leather armor, not a buttoned vest. He had replaced his open dust coat for a fine one of green and silver — spotless, untouched by the roads they once walked together. Still, he recognized other elements of his old friend. The Lineal Pendant, made from unpolished aquamarine, swung on its leather cord like a metronome. His fine clothes stretched across the muscles underneath. Time only deepened the creases around his brow, and he hadn't unclenched his jaw since the last time they were in a room together. The blue veins that fanned out across the side of his face were still vibrant, too, which glowed with magic that stung his dark skin. He had earned that from a particularly powerful spell. It drained him far beyond the Pendant's reserves, and feasted upon his innate magic. The strain then burned itself into his face, never to be healed.

Good.

Ferrow sighed. Ah, his constant exasperation still clung to his breath, which was oddly soothing in the moment. "I don't even know where to begin with you, Avery. Whatever this is stems far beyond the petty pickpocketing you did on our travels. And yes, I did notice your little antics back then. But never mind the past; what in Volm's name happened?"

"To me, or to the building, Row?" Avery swung into the chair and folded his legs, flashing Ferrow his best grin. "Guess your ogling of my face answers that question. I want to hear you ask it yourself, though – put it into your pretty words."

His eyes flickered to his cheek. He tore his gaze away quicker than he settled on it to meet his eyes. Stoirm, it strained him to be cordial, didn't it? "I admit that your new…additions are of some concern to me, Avery, though I'm one to speak about how offputting magical scars are. It certainly unnerves some of the ambassadors."

"D'aw. But don't worry – it's not like what happened to your face. Just experiments gone wrong." He kicked his feet up onto the table. "Honestly, I would've preferred for it to be from the Last Stand, not from my own stupidity. Yours is cooler, too. Never got to say that before I left."

Ferrow set his elbow down and massaged his brow. "And the arson?"

"Don't know why the guards got all wound up about that; I made sure nobody was in there. Reoth above, I don't think anyone wanted to touch that hunk of brick and wood before I found it. Besides, how else was I going to get your attention?"

"Did the thought of sending a simple letter ever cross your mind?" he snapped. "Leaving a note at the gate? For Volm's sake, have you *ever* thought about doing something the simple way, Avery?"

"Tried to."

Ferrow paused his massage, and looked at him between his fingers. "Did you? I certainly remember nothing of your sloppy handwriting."

"I sent you loads of 'em over the years. There were more after…well, after we 'doffed the black', but I never got a response." He pushed his feet against the table. The leg chairs reared up like a leopard about to pounce, though wobbled with his shifts. "Guess you never cracked them open."

Ferrow froze.

"Oh, I'm not mad about that. I just figured I needed to do something more dramatic to talk to you again."

He turned his head away, lip fighting its twitch into a frown. "My apologies. I have much on my plate, and some things slip away from me. I sincerely hope the building is worth this talk, however."

"I figured it out, Row."

"Figured out what?" Ferrow cocked his head back at him – expression on the border of snideness and genuine surprise.

Avery swept his legs off the table, then leaned forward. "I know how to bring Vale back."

Silence. Once his words processed in Ferrow's mind, though, his jaw dropped like its muscles were severed. "What? How? *When?* Have you told anyone else about this?"

He grinned. "Too much time cooped up in dusty books and many, many more failed experiments. But no, I haven't told anyone else. Wouldn't dream of it."

"You're talking around a question, Avery. *How?*"

Avery rolled his eyes. Snow-in-sky, Ferrow liked his details a little too much sometimes. Could he never be content with simpler explanations for things, like how the gods painted the sky blue with their blood? "It's a ritual and some components I already gathered. Thought you would've been happy about this, but you're not thrilled by it, are you? Do you want her to still be gone?"

Ferrow sighed again. "I wish for her return more than anything, but the byproduct of your research gives me pause." He gestured at the patch on his cheek. "It's necromancy, isn't it? Forbidden crafts?"

"She'd do the same for either of us."

He glared at him. "Don't use her against me – not when she isn't here to speak for herself."

"If you're that worried, then you can sit to the side for the ritual," Avery hissed. He bit back the rest of his annoyance. "Actually, you don't even need to do anything. I just need to borrow your Sanctum tonight, and she'll be back with us in the blink of an eye. But it has to be tonight."

Ferrow shielded the Pendant from him, then glared back. "You'd insist on touching my life – my *city,* full of innocents who rely on it – with corrupted magic? No!"

"Oh, what's a little blackout going to do?"

He growled. "Haven't you looked around, Avery? *Everything!* Street lights, shields, medical equipment, my very *existence-*"

"For her return!" he snarled. "Stoirm, you just needed to say 'yes' to make things much simpler for me. To redeem yourself. But I suppose I shouldn't have expected anything better from you. You always dig in your heels at the worst times, Row, and never when it's wise. Wish you did that for our last mission. But you don't need to bother yourself with her death anymore, do you? Everything is about you, until it's *your fault.* Then you just run away."

Ferrow flinched like he'd been slapped across his face. Avery didn't have time to wait for his response, though – not that it would've done anything to change his mind. He had spent far too long pacing in that cell; the hour would be upon him soon, and he couldn't wait a millenia for it to return.

Avery rapped his fingers against the table. Sparks of energy burst to life in his flesh, twitching his arms in anticipation. "Well, go hide away from the sunlight, little boy. I'll do what you never had the courage to."

"What?"

He leapt up from the chair, then clawed his fingers through the air. They dragged through something cold – almost gelatinous in its texture, but with more air than liquid. Few could feel the Spirit Realm's presence. He had been amongst those blind folk, once, though his research opened his eyes to it. He could not close them again. He *would not* close them again. The ability to grasp onto and part the curtain that separated it from this world was as natural as walking now. Wielding his sparks came easily, too. He focused them into his fingertips, and ripped the world's fabric open.

Ferrow lunged forward. "AVER-"

The bastard disappeared, folded away in the rearrangement of the Seen World's texture. The little room stretched into a larger hall. Its paint darkened, and molded into pebbled walls. Chains slithered down like snakes amongst tree branches, from which hung ash-covered lanterns. Blue flames flickered in their iron maws. They reverberated with the screeches of tortured souls, whose insanity garbled the words they spewed.

Avery's muscles seized up. The Spirit Realm pressed against his body in an attempt to freeze him with horror. His kind didn't belong here, he supposed. It could sense the stink of the living on him, and despised it.

He'd roll his eyes if he could. There were humans far more terrifying than a world filled with ghosts, and its cold easily gave way to warmth. He just needed memories to ignite it. Simply imagining fire, however, kept his body locked in place. To regain control over himself, he'd need to dig deeper – reach out to memories that warmed his heart.

Halevale. Avery reached out to her, and walked with her through his mind. A different sort of chill washed over him: one of a pine-speckled winter in his home mountains, where she pelted Ferrow's face with a snowball. She laughed as he coughed out snowflakes. Her own shorn blond hair, woolen cloak, and suit of armor were coated in white, but she cackled like she'd been untouched. Avery cut her laughter short with his own snowball, though. After she swept it off, she spent the next hour chasing him across the snowscape with a vow to bury him in the field. Ferrow, happy to not be her target, helped her. They ended the fight with him stuck under a tower of snowballs from their combined wrath – a fight he'd been happy to lose.

His fingers twitched. He dove into the next memory, following her thread. It led him to a true prison built from wet darkness that pinned his arms down so teeth could scrape against his skin. Beads of acid dripped down his face. It left a stinging pain behind it, and filled his nostrils with the scent of burning flesh. He didn't dare gag; more could drip down his throat, destroying his vocal cords. Thankfully, a light broke through it. Halevale, gritting her teeth, tossed her sword aside to pull him out of his confinement. She didn't care about the discolored splotches on her armor. He had stammered out a hundred apologies for it, berating himself for his overconfidence making him waltz into the plant's mouth, yet her embrace shut him up instantly. Nothing had made him feel safer since then.

Nothing ever would again, unless she returned to the world. He had felt numb during her funeral – a quiet display funded by Ferrow, who held it in the castle's garden – but the loneliness hit him when he returned to Galfethrm. There, in the quiet apartment, life faded from his world.

Meals were silent without petty arguments or drunken retellings of fights to accompany it, and he found nothing to occupy himself with now that the call to adventure was extinguished. The roads did nothing for him either. The vast landscapes reinforced his loneliness, and every battle he threw himself into nearly killed him. Sure, they tried to kill him before, though he could laugh it off with companions who had his back. Yet nobody was there to laugh anymore. It was just him, his cuts, and his bruises illuminated by the campfire deep in the darkness. His grief whispered to him in those moments. It choked his own voice, and told him that he deserved whatever pain he earned because he helped put her in the dirt. He deserved to be alone. Only hints of resurrection, scattered in the tomes he salvaged, quieted that voice. If he brought her back, he'd make things right, wouldn't he? The mere idea reignited passion within him, and gave shape to something he could dedicate himself to, regardless of the other sorts of pain it inflicted on him.

But what did Ferrow do while he toiled to save her? He just buried her amongst the flowers, brushed his hands off, and pretended like his own actions hadn't led to her death. Stoirm, he ignored all of Avery's letters, too. He had to set a goddamn building on fire just to force him to talk for the first time since the funeral, for Reoth's sake! Did he truly "forget" to read those letters because of lordly duties? No. No, the bastard just wanted to forget that he ever knew them, didn't he?

The Spirit Realm's pressure dissipated. He stumbled, trying to re-gain his footing on the uneven ground. This world still worked against him, unfortunately. His foot caught on a raised brick, which knocked him to the floor. A sharp turn mid-air forced his shoulder to take the brunt of it.

He rolled to his feet, face alight from embarrassment. Snow-in-sky, he had spent far too long bent over those damned tomes, and not enough on his dexterity. He picked himself up, then continued on.

The Spirit Realm either disliked or couldn't understand how things moved in relation to people. Its environment blurred and warped with each step. Avery kept his mind trained on Halevale, though, and unfocused his eyes. Staring at the taffy-like stretches would make him barf – another aspect he doubted the realm appreciated about living folks. How did spirits navigate this damn landscape? Perhaps it was be-cause they, like the realm, were composed of pure memory. The latter were rarely linear, too. They swirled to the forefront of one's mind when they least expected it, or faded from neglect. Some flowed right to the next. Others popped up like bubbles, disjointed from whatever came before. And collective memory? Well, not even death could paint a thousand perspectives into one sensical portrait.

Headache-inducing landscape aside, he navigated it fairly well. The spirits' deaths amongst the brick twisted it into a labyrinth, but the memories of the entrance should've wormed its way into its construction. And the fire, though ominous, cast the shadows of spirits he preferred to avoid. Those precious seconds let him hide around the corners. Where Halevale might've charged through every spirit in the way with her sword swinging, he preferred quieter methods.

Unfortunately, that did not save him from the two spirits that bumped into him at a shadowy corner. They whirled around to face him before he could duck away. Musty breath strangled into a quiet hiss escaped from their throats. If they were trying to threaten him, they didn't need to say anything; the shine of their skulls through thin skin, rags connected by threads, and jaws that swung about like wood on a rope did everything for them. And were those maggots crawling around in the right one's eye? Whatever they were, more crawled around in the other's soiled shirt like worms seeking dirt to wriggle into.

Reoth above.

Avery dashed the other way, chased by their screeches. *Stoirm, stoirm, stoirm!* Other screeches joined theirs in a horrid choir – all alerted to his presence, and equally eager to tear his soul from his body. Their collective ire stirred the Spirit Realm itself, too. He clung to his memories of Halevale, refusing to acknowledge its cold even as it lapped at his ankles. He couldn't pay mind to the screams that grew louder, either. Avery had to keep moving. He found himself in chases like these a thousand times, and whoever hesitated first lost. The key to victory was in an obstacle. If he could just find something to block them around this corner, then-

The doors! They loomed over him in a silent challenge to any who wished to wrench their iron jaws open, but, judging by the dust, hadn't been opened in a century. Well, he didn't need to break them open. Having a foot in each world was a gift with endless benefits, one of which would save his ass now.

Cold creeped over his neck – its shape skeletal, and swathed in limp skin. It shot through his flesh. Did it know about the sparks, seeking them out to stop him from leaving?

Avery gritted his teeth. A stupid, nameless spirit wouldn't foil his efforts now, nor would the Spirit Realm claim him yet. He flung his arms up. Numbness slowed the muscles in his fingers, yet he managed to bury them in the curtain. With a growl, he tore a hole in the world once again. Crystal light claimed his vision.

Reoth above. His head swam, and his mouth was drier than a desert. He leapt to his feet before his vision could clear, terrified that he'd be met with a squadron of guards. Fortunately, the room seemed to be safe. It was larger than the interrogation room he'd been shoved into, though still small compared to the rows of cells. Shelves had been hammered into the walls. Tables lined the spaces underneath like people huddled under canopies when it rained. Knickknacks rested on all of them. He picked out his twin daggers from the piles – both of which he sheathed on his hips – and, after shoving some things aside, found his bag.

It was innocuous at first glance. Who would think to give a plain leather bag anything more than a passing glance? The subtle shimmer of magic, however, betrayed the enchantment Ferrow blessed it with: the ability to hold far more than its little body could normally carry. But did they take anything from it? He rifled through it, checking its contents against his mental list of components. Thank Reoth; those idiots kept everything in there rather than sort them out. Ferrow needed better guards. The era of peace they forged together must've made the people soft, he supposed. Still, they could kill him if he let too many surround him. Better not to taunt the people with pointy things, though. The universe had a way of listening in on people's thoughts, and would react to them appropriately. Good wishes or humble thoughts granted good fortune. Overconfidence or vile thoughts…well, he preferred for things to go smoothly.

Avery slung it over his shoulder, then jogged towards the doorway. He grabbed the doorknob, eager to continue onwards, but someone else flung it open. Stoirm.

"Hey!" the guard shouted. Her auburn locks spilled out from her helmet, strands of which fluttered over her wide eyes. 'He's here! The prisoner is-"

No, not now! Damn the universe for exacting its toll! His magic flared in his body, spurred by the panic that overtook his thoughts. He moved before he could restrain himself. One hand grabbed the front of her armor, and forced the sparks to rush into it. The iron crumpled in his hand like paper. He then yanked her into the room and flung her across it with a flick of his wrist.

She slammed into a wall. The items on the table beneath her skittered away, afraid of her intrusion on their space. A sword, however, toppled into her hand. He expected her to grab it and leap up, ready to swing it at his head. Would she unsheathe it, or try to bludgeon him with it?

But she did not stir.

Dread crashed down on Avery – its weight more paralyzing than the Spirit Realm. He should use this opportunity to move. To run. To get away, and continue on to the Sanctum. Halevale needed him. Every second spent stuck in place meant another wasted, yet he couldn't move towards the door. Instead, he sprinted towards the woman.

Stoirm, the way she slumped over reminded him too much of *her*. He could see her form overlap the guard's, with blood dripping out of her mouth and her back too hunched for a normal spine. She wouldn't be dead if he had been faster. She wouldn't have thrown him aside to take the brunt of the scaled horror's blast instead, which then crushed her into the mountain. Why did she do it? Why did she do it with a smile, as if that could reassure his horror? Why did Ferrow force them to march on his goddamn conquest for personal revenge?

Why was he the only one that cared about her?

He reached the guard's side and grabbed her wrist. Thank Reoth; a pulse, though faint, beat within it. Her chest also rose with shallow breaths, which drifted out from her slightly open mouth.

Voices rose somewhere outside of the room. Avery wanted to drag her to them, but he couldn't slow himself down. Ferrow would probably find her, anyway. Hopefully he'd stop to heal her before resuming his chase, or order someone else with powers to aid her. Then again, he hadn't done that last time. The killing blow on the monster was far more important to him than a friend on the brink of death, even when the other screamed for him to help. It had, after all, helped him take his inherited city back. Would he make the same mistake here? Avery hoped not. A "benevolent" lord needed to uphold a certain reputation once he shed all the blood needed to rule – a caring and merciful persona, not one who nonchalantly tossed employees at dangers that killed them. The colored lens of a savior could only cover his ass for so long.

He slipped out the door. A wooden chair and desk sat on the opposite side, likely where the guard had been stationed before she found him. Stairs spiraled up in front of it. Muffled voices echoed through the large doors behind him, distant yet closing the gap.

Avery ran up the stairs. His heart pounded like his feet on the bricks below, urging him to move faster. Snow-in-sky, it took far too long to get to the top.

The two guards stationed there whirled to face him, taken aback by an escaped prisoner. He pounced on them. Rationality broke through his adrenaline, thankfully, and stopped his daggers from slitting their throats. Instead, he Blinked. Their faint shapes appeared in the other world – souls, but not departed from the Seen World. Still, he could access them from this side. He summoned dust into his palms, imbued them with the shreds of happiness he had left, then flung them at the guards.

They both collapsed. Their shock melted into dazed smiles as the dust Lulled their souls into slumber. Whatever they saw in their sleep would be tailored to their pleasure; he knew it firsthand. They'd be groggy once someone awoke them, but otherwise unharmed.

He sprinted on. Through the blur of the creamy white hallways, he could pinpoint the damage from the Last Stand: a section of bricks that didn't quite match the rest here, missing vases there, and paintings with fresher coats than the rest. Ferrow had made plaques for the fallen soldiers, too. Did he also put one on Penumbra's Crest, where Halevale met her doom for a stupid cause? No, he couldn't think about that now. All wrongs would be righted soon, and everything would go back to normal. Everything hinged on his success. Everything hinged on the Sanctum in the castle's heart.

Guards shouted behind him. Ah, so their incompetent behinds from the prison finally caught sight of him, did they? He growled at them. How dare they try to stop his noble quest and think themselves to be better people.

He Lulled the thinner ranks to sleep. When crowds blocked his way, he switched paths and leapt into the Spirit Realm. There, another battle waged through the castle: one of fiery blasts from phantom lizards's jaws, bricks shattered by cannonballs, throngs of skirmishes between soldiers, and the pungent scent of blood. The spirits here paid him no mind; they fought wars stained into the castle stone itself — for Valmishra or whoever attacked her fair visage. He had to cover his ears, though. The screeches of men trapped in the moments before death's release was worse than those who screamed for his insides.

He skidded into the final hallway. Suits of armor stood guard between pillars, each polished to perfection. Light from the crystalline veins above reflected off of them. Some had fused their tendrils into the doorway ahead, which encapsulated a silver door. Beyond that would be the Sanctum.

"By order of Lord Ferrow, halt!"

Avery sighed. He dashed ahead, and threw his body against the doors. They groaned open, protesting the interloper. Well, they wouldn't have to tolerate him for very long if things worked as they should.

"Halt!" A throng of guards raced around the corner – all with swords and spears pointed at him.

He grinned at them. Unfortunately, he didn't have time to give them a quip, but he did send a shockwave of magic into the pillars.

The stones buckled. Dust rained from the ceiling, and a cascade of stone washed over the room. Avery slammed the door shut before it could reach him. Rocks pounded on it from the outside, yet they held strong against the avalanche. Hopefully those guards didn't have any shovels handy.

He spun to face his hard-earned prize: the Sanctum's Lineal Gem – a tear-shaped aquamarine the size of an oak tree, the bottom of which shimmered in the puddle it floated over. A crystal ring circled the gem's point. Its veins fanned out like eyelashes, casting a glow throughout the room.

Avery's hands quivered with excitement. He set the bag down, then raked his fingers through the odds and ends within it. After an excruciating moment, he withdrew the white chalk. Many of those damn street mages and shopkeeps had tried to sell him something more "potent" to draw ritual circles with. They'd wave midnight sticks speckled with stars in his face, or waft the dust of ground-up dragon scales under his nose. Didn't he want it to work? Weren't things with more flair better for magical rituals? Those price tags, however, led him back to the regular kind. It never failed him before; why would it fail him now?

He hummed to himself as he dragged it across the floor, tuning out the muffled shouts of the guards. First came the circle. Then came a dozen stars, squares, and triangles that forced him to pivot after every line. Stoirm, this bit made him dizzy. How did Ferrow never barf when he drew his own ritual circles?

After he completed the final star, he scurried back to his bag. He pulled out components by the armfuls, driven by the buzz of his magic – a reaction to the thinning veil between the worlds. Indeed, the whispers of spirits from the beyond tickled his ears. He ignored the temptation to fling everything into place, but hurried to set everything in the right spots. A crow's skull went on one point. Across from it was a bundle of candles melted together like a mushroom colony. Oh, and here was the dried manticore eye. He practically hurled that onto a cross of lines, off-put by its squishy, sandpapery texture.

More and more spilled onto the floor. Soon, he could barely see the chalk marks under the clutter, save for the center. Avery danced over them, grinning. Once he reached the center, he dropped into a kneeling position and laid his hands on two points of intersection.

Now to reap the rewards of years of study.

Avery flared his magic, then bellowed out the chant. Truthfully, he understood fragments of what he spoke – its language second to his Gathish, smattered with sounds he could connect to simple terms. But understanding it was a fraction of magic; proper inflection and force of will mattered far more than comprehension. He just needed to speak the universe's language to get its attention. It, in turn, would bend to him, shaped by concepts communicated in raw emotion wielded by his dreams. That surprised him when he first delved into rituals. Mages spoke of the frustratingly hard-to-obtain components and proper terms, not their own stake in their spells. Maybe their knowledge made up for their weak drive to cast them successfully. But where his own knowledge faltered, pure determination carried his words to the cosmic things that needed to listen.

And listen it did. The air around him warped as the Spirit Realm seeped into the Seen World. It pressed down on him. Avery pushed against the chalk-covered ground to keep himself upright, and continued to chant in spite of the strain. He would not be so easily cowed – not for Halevale's sake.

Something pulsed through the pressure. Light filled the Lineal Gem, which beat like a heart stirred from stillness. Each wave cut through the force that filled the room. Snow-in-sky, it reached out to him. *Called* to him. Did the ancestors within recognize him from the days when he stood by Ferrow's side? Did they just see someone in need? Regardless, he never anticipated the gem to offer a hand in kindness. This made things far easier for him.

He grabbed onto the next wave. Something thrummed through his body, powered by a chorus of angelic voices that filled his mind. Was

Ferrow's late father amongst them? Perhaps he had encouraged them to reach out to him. He tried to sift through the voices to find it, but the voices blended together too well to hear any singular person. Even the mere attempt to grasp onto anything gave him a headache. Their notes wandered around to the beautiful melody of chaos, untouched by the restraints of traditional music. In less dire circumstances, he'd lose himself amongst the voices. Instead, he-

A doorway carved itself into the wall on his left. The stone there shimmered away, replaced with dozens of guards in its mouth. At their head was Ferrow. Magic swirled from his Pendant to his hand, forming his rapier – a blade of glass he called Te'thror. He had wielded it in defense of Avery countless times. Now, he turned it against his old friend. Stoirm, he barely hesitated before he charged forward and gave the same command to his people: "STOP HIM!"

Could he afford to waste a drop of power on this distraction? He could use it to throw up a shield. But he doubted the guards or Ferrow would give up their onslaught, which meant he'd spend more to replace it every few seconds.

A drop, then. Avery bent his index finger at the mass that charged at him. Dust erupted from it. It devoured the interlopers in this world, and breached the curtain to suffocate their souls in the other realm. One by one, they dropped. One by one, they slipped into the sweetest dreams he could muster – ones they'd never experience again. They'd thank him when they awoke. Ferrow, though, refused to comply. He dropped to his knees, yet forced his eyes to stay open and stare at him.

"Avery, please, just wait!" he hissed.

With the incantation complete, he began to funnel the power from his body into the ritual circle. He should've put his full concentration into maintaining the spell, but something in Ferrow's voice irked him. "*Wait?* I've waited for this moment for *years*, Row. *YEARS!*" he snarled at the bastard. "While you tried to forget about it all, I've poured *everything* into righting our wrongs! Why should I listen to a coward like you?!"

The hairs on his arms spiked up, raised by the crackle of magic in the air. One of its flashes summoned a figure before him. She was translucent and flickered between realms, yet the glimpses he caught of her made his heart swell.

For the first time in years, he beheld Halevale.

Glass shattered. Avery whipped back to the Lineal Gem, which bore a crack on one of its faces. Would it survive the ritual? He didn't dare think about the consequences of the loss of power; planar timing aside, where else would he get power like this? Nowhere.

Ferrow's rapier clattered to the ground. He collapsed to the floor, hand clutching his chest. The Pendant spilled out in front of him, now with a black streak swirling through it like a leech in water. *Stoirm!* He wanted to break away from the ritual now and help him, but Halevale was *right there.* Couldn't he survive this a little longer? Snow-in-sky, his castle should be stuffed with more Regeneration scrolls than a healer's ward. Surely a guard would come running with one under their arm. They wouldn't let their lord die.

Another crack shot across the Lineal Gem, causing Ferrow to writhe in pain. Halevale, however, became more stable. Bones grew under her translucent skin like frost on glass, and veins flowed into existence. The sight of her evaporated all of Avery's concern. She was almost real. This had to be enough to convince him to weather through the pain, right?

Of course not. He twisted his head to Avery, and spoke through clenched teeth. "Avery. Please, the cost isn't worth it!"

"Do you not see what it'll grant me?!" he shouted. "Look up, for Reoth's sake! It's *her!* Did you forget about her so quickly, Row? Don't you miss her?"

"Every goddamn day, but look at what it's doing to you!"

The ground softened under him. Avery glanced down, surprised to see the Spirit Realm bleed through this part of the curtain. Well, he had thinned it to the point of nonexistence. What did it matter, though?

Hands whipped out from it – all skeletal, with flesh melting into a puddle. Something had twisted their bones into spirals. What little skin remained on their palms were more gnarled than an old man's. He'd be terrified of them months ago. But the shock of these rotted forms quickly wore off after multiple confrontations. Even when they grabbed onto him to drain the warmth from his skin, he merely hunkered down and kept his magic flowing through the circle.

Ferrow reached out to him. "Please, end this madness before it kills you."

The hands pulled him down, consuming his legs in the cold of the flesh puddle. "I don't care. Reoth above, you were the one who marched her to her death! Even then, I should've *died* then! Vale didn't need to sacrifice herself for me, but I'm fixing that tonight. She won't be buried and forgotten in the dirt any longer. I will pay the price for the future that should've been, *not the one you twisted into fruition.*"

Shards of the crystal ring dimmed. They broke off the ceiling, then smashed down around them. Splinters flew past Avery, some of which brushed against his skin and left red streaks in their wake. The hands, in the meantime, had submerged his waist in their mass. He fared better than Ferrow, though; the bastard collapsed, finally silenced by his spell.

Maybe Avery should be screaming. He had faced death with Ferrow many, many, many times, but now it seemed as though it would actually claim him. At least his end contributed to a noble cause. But how would she fare, restored but alone in the Seen World? Would her lungs remember how to breathe on their own, or would it take time for them to adjust to her renewed life? He wished he could help with that. She was strong, though – far stronger than either of them, and would find a way. He just needed to accept the universe's toll.

Avery closed his eyes, awaiting the darkness.

"AVERY!"

Something slammed into his side, and flung him out of the ritual circle. *Ferrow.* Goddamn Ferrow, who could barely keep his eyes open, pinned him to the ground with the weight of his body.

"GET OFF!" he yelled. He tried to pry himself out, but Ferrow grabbed onto his wrists and restrained him there.

The choir was severed from his mind. Power fled his body like a mouse out of its burrow, and left the world as a hollow shell compared to what he had held. Only horror kept him from slipping into unconsciousness – horror at Halevale, who unraveled into shimmers of light. She floated there one moment, serene as the two words held her in suspension. In the next, she vanished.

He had let her die once again.

Ferrow stumbled to his feet, massaging his temples like he had a headache. "I'm sorry, Avery, but you would've sacrificed far too much. You must-"

"Row, you BASTARD!" He threw himself at him with daggers drawn. Snow-in-sky, he'd gouge his throat out until nothing but bones remained between his head and body.

Te'thror flashed into Ferrow's hand. He twisted it up, which knocked the daggers off course – away from his throat, though it still cut his scar. "You would've thrown away everything we fought for! That nasty little ritual was corrupting the Gem, and Volm knows what would have happened to everything attached to it! Did you truly wish to waste our efforts? To waste your life?"

"I DON'T HAVE A LIFE TO RETURN TO!"

Ferrow backed away, rapier still raised defensively. He sidestepped the bodies of his sleeping guards without looking – a showoff in even the most tense of moments. "That cannot be true. What of your home city, or the other sights you wanted to see?"

"I wanted to see those with Vale." Stoirm, he was tired. He didn't notice he dropped his daggers until they clattered onto the floor. "And what do I have left in Galfethrm, Row? A snowed in, single-room apartment cluttered with research that amounted to *nothing?* My work gave me meaning. If it killed me, at least I would've gone out doing something good. Something that mattered."

Ferrow lowered his rapier, expression softening. "Your life has meaning by simply existing, however difficult it is to find it in darker times."

"Oh, like you'd know." He laughed, and sank to the cold floor. "Your entire life was handed to you on a silver tray, no questions about where your future was headed, except for when you'd retire. Stoirm, it ended up killing her, too."

"Avery-"

Avery laughed even harder, overtaken by a mixture of mania and exhaustion. "Don't. I don't need you to lecture me or try to shove a purpose onto me, Ferrow. Not after you injected yourself into our duo to impose yours on us. Not after you reaped all the rewards from it."

"Is that truly how you felt about me?" Ferrow hushed his voice. "If so, why did you keep trying to reach out if you blamed me for everything?"

He spoke before he could stop himself. "Because you're all that's left of the group, whether I like it or not."

Te'thror shimmered into dust. Ferrow let his hand fall to his side, then hesitantly closed the gap between him and Avery. "I-" He cleared his throat. "I thought the same after Halevale's passing. Truthfully, it is why I never opened your letters, though I deeply regret ignoring you. I had a city to run. People needed me to be strong, and I believed the best course of action was to close myself off from anything that would hurt. That included you, unfortunately. I cannot ever be sorry enough for pushing you to the side."

"Always about you, never other people," Avery muttered.

He grimaced. "It was, and continued to be. But I promise you, Avery, I am here for you now. I will...what was the phrase you told me? 'Get my head out of my ass'?"

"Too late, unless you can give me other means to bring Vale back." He stared numbly at the ritual circle. Remnants of power sparked off of the chalk lines – useless now that the perfect time had passed.

Ferrow sighed. "Power source aside, I believe those means will always demand a great sacrifice. What will you use without people or spirits forced to die for your cause? Other innocent souls you personally harvest?"

"I'll find another way," he snapped. "I just need to…" To what? What did he need to do, anyway? Everything he studied led him to this ritual, and provided him with no other routes to follow. The few he did taunted him with dead ends. So where did that leave him? Where could he go with this broken hope, save for the conclusion he resented?

Nowhere.

Ferrow said nothing, but kneeled next to him and brought him into an embrace. Avery was too tired to fight it. Reoth above, he could've used this chance to bury a blade in his throat – avenge Halevale, even if that wouldn't bring her back. Instead, he collapsed into his arms. Tears blurred his vision, then slipped down his cheeks. Had he suppressed these over the years? Sure, plenty were shed in grief and frustration, yet those were drizzles compared to the storm that hit him now. He couldn't fight this, either. All he could do was try and fail to hold back his sobs while Ferrow brought him in tighter.

Once the worst of the storm passed, Ferrow spoke again. "It might be good for you to rest a bit, Avery. I'd have to smooth things out with the warden, but the castle has plenty of guest rooms."

"Think that'd be nice."

He smiled, then pulled Avery to his feet. "Thank you." The smile cracked somewhat as he glanced at the fallen guards, though. "Quite a bit to smooth out, indeed. You did not kill any of them, did you? I know Marla was injured, but-"

"They're just dreaming," he croaked. "I made sure they'd have good dreams, too."

Ferrow nodded in appreciation, and guided Avery around their bodies. "I'll send a healer to wake them. For now, though, let me ensure that you will have a room to stay in. I think one close to the rising sun will do nicely."

"Thanks." How long had it been since he woke up to sunlight rather than a dark room stuffed with paper? "Actually, I wouldn't mind some-thing to eat first. Magic makes me starve." He laughed – the sound choked by his renewed grief. "Maybe talk a little bit, too. I don't want to be left alone with my thoughts yet.

"Would biscuits and tea do?"

Avery smiled. "Better than the road rations. Probably better than Vale's cooking, too."

Ferrow led him to the hidden door. Before they walked through it, however, Avery Blinked. She wasn't there, of course. He swore for a moment that he saw her sword buried in the ground, but he must've imagined it. Stoirm, he'd spent too long living amongst the spirits. Perhaps, for at least one night, he could try to remember how to talk with the living instead.

APRIL: HEAD-TO-HEAD

Winner: Andre Ochoa

PENANCE

ANDRE OCHOA

Cries rang out as armies clashed. The legions of Heaven descended upon the abyssal hosts in their millions. The host of the abyss met these heavenly hosts in their billions fueled by hatred. Crags in the rocky landscape began to fill with blood. Soon rivers had formed where no rivers once were. And yet while the armies clashed and met in slaughter and carnage two combatants could be heard over all decimation.

One born of fiends and the other born of celestials. One of the heavens. The other of the abyss. Both artisans of the blade. One a dancer of twin swords the other an armor-clad juggernaut armed with blessed steel and holy shield. And yet the fight rang of two songs. Two dances.

One of sorrow, regret, guilt, and remorse. The other of hatred, contempt, and relish. Grace met force. Cruelty met guilt marred mercy. Contempt met resignation marred hope. As blades clashed with equal precision. Concordia weaved an intricate web of feints and strikes struggling to find an opening in Conquista's defense. The shield always led the offense. The truly violent and aggressive use of an otherwise defensive tool proved harder to combat than Concordia anticipated. Still, she held her tempo. After all, she only wanted a few more moments.

"Why must it come to this? What is the sin you crucify me for? Were you not the one who sang of redemption? Now you know only slaughter."

"Only slaughter? Concordia, surely you jest. You always did have a taste for humor. But no, I should thank you. Really, I should. I have learned much more than slaughter. It is through your council that I rallied Heaven's legions. It is from you that I learned the truth. There is no redemption." Conquista thrust out her blade drawing a crimson line across Concordia's cheek.

"My council? I came to you with hopes of destruction; it is true. But you granted me that peace and that hope. You showed me more than hunter and prey. More than exploitation and expendability. Why now do you turn from your ideals?" Parry and riposte into another parry. Never seeking to draw blood just to delay and so Concordia's dance went.

"I was a fool and that was made clear. No fiend can be redeemed. No evil can hope to change. It simply must be eradicated. You say I turned from my ideals. And now I have found them."

"You have been deceived, Conquista. My kin now they will win and have led you to a slaughterhouse. Why do you fight? For vainglory? For self-righteousness? Conquista! You would throw the lives of your kin away simply to eradicate that which has no end? We had sworn oaths! Oaths to uphold compassion and empathy. Oaths to fight for those who have not strength. Yet now you waste your legions on that which can not truly die."

Conquista answered in turn with a thrust of her blade and the crash of her shield. Concordia parried the blade but was met by the shield. That terrible shield. A cruel and crude weapon that could not be the make of any celestial. No. It was a pilfered treasure from one of the many warlords that patrolled the abyss. It bore sharpened, jagged spikes on its front and secreted potent toxins. Toxins that invited madness and bloodlust. Toxins that invited depraved rituals of mutilation that the holy might be turned to the heretic. Toxins Concordia feared had invaded Conquista's mind and twisted it to madness with torture all too common among her kin.

"You want my answer, Conquorida? This is my answer!" Conquista rammed the shield into the side of Concordia's face. A sickening snap could be heard as unholy steel met horn. It was then that the shield revealed its true nature. The spikes pumped toxins into the many wounds on Concordia's face causing her to stagger. Her horn hit the rock on the ground and was quickly trampled under heavy steel boots. "The breath that evades you Concordia is the breath that was stolen from my kin. It is the breath that I intend to take back. And I'll do it by your own design."

Conquista raised her sword and struck. Despite the toxins, Concordia was not dead yet. She'd not let Conquista ruin herself in her grief.

"You have lost yourself in your grief with only sycophants to console you. They have turned you against me on lies of betrayal. They say I have betrayed you to my kin. I, a prisoner of my own people, sought the ruin of the one I have sworn my soul to. Why do you deny redemption? Simply because of pain? You have been met with treachery from your own kin. Yet you blame me. Why do you turn from me?"

"Turn from you? I am to believe what you say simply because of who you are. You are a fiend Concordia. You turn from the redemption I have given you. You reject my will simply because you disagree and then turn to your kin. You have played me for a fool as was always your goal. But I shall have the last laugh. To the death, Concordia. No more of this dance. TO THE DEATH!"

"Till death do us part." Concordia sighed and drew her blades once more.

"Even your blades and your armor are the make of your kin and your station. Dressed as temptress and deceiver. Just as the rest of your kin!"

"Conquista, please. I beg of you. End this madness. Let us return home. Let us be whole once again. Let wounds heal and not fester. You are hurting. You feel betrayed. But I've returned. Call off the attack. Rid yourself of this needless pride."

"Enough!" Conquista crouched for a moment and then sprung forward. Leaping with her sword resting on her shield. She intended to finish the fight there, but Concordia easily predicted the move. Bringing her own blades up Concordia deflected her sword and hooked her shield. As Conquista drew back she felt Concordia lock her blade round her shield and tear it from her grasp.

The shield crashed into the ground, wedging itself in newly blood carve crags. Pushing her opening Concordia launched into a furious and desperate attack hoping to push Conquista ever further from the shield. Yet despite her best attempts she was losing ground as Conquista could afford to take hits thanks to her armor. Concordia was offered far less protection by her inadequate and almost skimpy armor.

Conquista braced herself letting Concordia land ineffective hits on her holy plate. Her eyes darted from blade to blade watching for an opening. A moment of weakness. A single mistake. And then she could end the wretched harlot. And then there it was. Conquista surged forward with sudden, malign speed and thrust her blade toward Concordia's heart.

In desperation, Concordia parried with both her blades hoping to halt the moment, but she was not strong enough as Conquista ripped the blades from her hands. Conquista pivoted and turned, forced to realign her attack.

"Pick them up!" Conquista waited. "Pick them up!" Still, Concordia made no move. "Pick Them Up!" Finally, Concordia crouched and picked up her blades.

"I know you grieve for you believe me lost. You think I turned back to my kin to bring your ruin. But I did not. I came looking for you, yet it was your kin who sold me back as a slave to my own. I have searched for you and was rejoiced to hear of your arrival. Yet now I see sadness. I see hurt and pain in your eyes." As Concordia rose she turned and faced Conquista allowing the blades to slip from her hands. "Strike me. I will fight you no more. Strike me!"

For a moment Conquista hesitated. For a moment, she saw the woman she had sworn her soul to. But then it was gone as cruel, malign intellect took over. Conquista leveled her sword and charged. The blade impacted with a loud crunch as flesh gave way to bones, which gave way to soft tissues and then ultimately Concordia's lungs.

Yet Concordia did not flinch. Instead, she clasped the blade and pulled herself closer to her lover.

Her lost, pained, tortured love. Willing herself forward, Concordia wrapped her arms and tail around Conquista embracing her. She could feel her breath faltering yet she still had the will to speak and so she whispered to Conquista just as they used to under the witness of stars. She watched as a moment of recognition flashed upon Conquista's face. A sudden recognition as Conquista gazed upon the slave's branding marking her neck.

"You are forgiven. I release you of any guilt just as you did me. I grant you the same mercy you showed me when I was not deserving of such. I offer what second chance I can as you offered to me. The one who showed me a better way. The one who showed me compassion. Who taught me empathy. Who showed me love. Love I had never known. I have lived long enough. I have seen evil. And have known goodness. I have known Compassion."With her final strength, she pulled Conquista into a kiss. And held her there until her strength gave out.

"I absolve you of sin. Be reborn. Receive your earned redemption." She whispered in her dying breath. Concordia clasped the sword as she fell. Willing the holy blade to finish her as it drank in her blood staining itself crimson.

They say the kiss of a succubus is the final act before a mortal is truly damned. And yet for Conquista, it is what saved her. It was as if some curse had been broken. She had been renewed. It was as if her soul had been returned and she was woken from a truly horrid hallucination. She watched as Concordia drew her final breath. Their eyes locked as Concordia willed herself one last smile. And then that was it. Everything was over. And all that was seen was the truly black abyss of guilt and grief.

It is said that Conquista still wanders. That still she travels. Looking for a way that she might resurrect the one she pledged her soul to. It is said that Conquista has cast off her rank of archangel and has instead taken a mortal form as penance. That she may truly learn righteousness and compassion.

LIMINALITY

QUENTIN GUTIERREZ

"Ginger, awaken!"

Ginger's eyes unrolled from the emptiness of their mind. Their pupils, fully dilated; their lungs, no longer filling, but their heart slugged along. They peered around the room with a soft focus. The entire room looked like cotton candy—at first bright pink, then lime green, then a deep space-purple. They carefully felt the thickness of their hair; they tried to inhale the scent of the air, but to no avail. Still, they felt as if there was a sweetness that completely engulfed their body. As they stood up, they noticed the lack of resistance in their bad left knee. They still withheld the scars of their youth that they had come to accept, and their tattoos still remained. Yes, even the tattoo of the Taco Bell logo. They began to giggle, remembering their teenage friends both picking fast food restaurants to get. How were they supposed to know they were joking? As their loud giggles echoed throughout the cotton candy room, a loud humming began to reverberate in the air. It was a noise that sounded like a tuba. But it felt like the bass of a speaker, wailing all throughout Ginger's body. As the reverberations grew stronger, Ginger's room began to shake violently. The tremors built and built until a creature burst through the floor of cotton candy and made itself visible in front of them. It was a massive being surrounded by light, completely made up of rapidly rotating wheels and eyes.

"Be not afraid," it proclaimed.

Ginger simply stared. The whirring of the wheels began to slow, but the humming continued.

"I am here to help you." Its eyes blinked at several different paces.

"It is time for you to move on. Ascend to the next phase of your life." Ginger could feel fear, yet their heart never raced. Any panic that should have surely ensued by now was nonexistent. They looked directly at the creature with confusion and finally spoke.

"What are you talking about?". Ginger continued with confidence.

"This is The Everness. This is permanence, purgatory. We will remain until you are ready." The creature began to hover toward what Ginger understood to be the southern wall of the room.

"You're not making sense; what do you want?" They yelled.

"I want you to remember. Any memory at all. Focus on it, feel it, and then follow it." Ginger's eyebrows furrowed with curiosity.

"Whatever you say, Wheels.".
They began to close their eyes and picture their first pet, a silly little Border Collie named Scruffy. The once again purple room began to shake heftily as before.

"Yes, keep with the memory!" It exclaimed. Ginger continued on, remembering their puppy's black and white fur, the feeling of its muddy paws, and the silly shrieks of their mother as Scruffy jumped at everyone, staining curtains and tablecloths, and zooming at a lightning pace throughout Ginger's childhood home. As soon as Ginger opened their eyes, they were in a brand new room, standing on a shiny, dark brown hardwood floor. They peaked down at their tiny little hands. Instead of the clothes they had on before, they had on adorable little blue overalls and bright white kitty slippers. Ginger quickly looked up, expecting to see Wheels, but It was gone.

"Oh my God! My cat slippers." Ginger had meant to say this with an excited tone, but instead their voice was sorrowful. They once again peered down at the slippers and noticed dark brown blotches of mud from the dog jumping all over them.

"Language! gInGeR". Ginger was suddenly taken aback. Mother would never use their chosen name. The memory suddenly became foggier, but its accuracy prevailed. Mother began to run angrily at Scruffy, carrying a heavy, rolled-up magazine. "Come here, you mutt!" Ginger no longer wanted to remember what happened next, as the scene faded out of existence.

"Why did you stop?" said Wheels.

"I didn't like the ending," Ginger said with a scoff.

"Neither do I," whispered Wheels. The room halted Ginger's crying as it shifted to lime, almost as if the room were sentient. It was silent for a short while. Then, Ginger attempted to take a deep breath with their imaginary lungs and spoke with vitriol.

"Okay, you need to tell me what the HONK is going on here." Ginger was once again taken aback as the sentient room now silenced their swearing.

"No, no, none of this Good Place garbage; why can't I curse?" They began to look up, irritatedly searching for Wheels.

Wheels whirred into the room to speak.

"I don't know; this is your room. You make the rules here, not me. Every piece is a fraction of your formation. I am simply catering to your creation," Ginger began to pace. The eyes followed them closely.

"Then why do you look like a... biblically accurate angel?" they asked

"Well, we are tied to human belief systems; we transform into the closest to what their beliefs were; though, technically, we can be anything."

"Yeah, okay, I get that, but I'm not religious; I don't believe in anything, so what the HONK. AND PLEASE LET ME SWEAR." Ginger's anger began to bottle up to the surface and then dissipate almost immediately, like a bottle of flat soda. They rubbed their face and eyes as Wheels began to speak.

"Well, from the information I received, you grew up Catholic. Your favorite memories from that small amount of belief were reading about the descriptions of the angels in the Bible, though I can take on any form you'd like. Our most popular animals for non-religious folk are animals like dogs." Wheels began to transform into a tiny beagle puppy, yelping with joy.

"Is this more comforting?". Wheels looked up adorably.

"Yeah, sure, I guess so. That still doesn't explain the swearing, though." Ginger really understood why there was no swearing allowed here. They had banned themselves from doing it ever since the death of their father. He had always been extremely supportive of everything but swearing. It even became a running gag on their visits. One of his final requests was to have his urn become a swear jar after his ashes were scattered.

"Maybe you'll remember soon." Wheels slowly began to morph into a small black and white Border Collie.

"I think that one's better." Ginger said with a smile.

"Quite." Wheels began to hover towards the center of the room, which looked especially silly as a dog, though the reverberations continued just as powerfully.

"Now, since you understand how memories work, it is time for your task. In order to move on to the next stage of life, you must first pass our test."

"Oh, HONK not again. Ugh, sorry, Dad." Ginger spoke into the void.

"Oh wonderful! You remember why you do not swear now." Wheels let out a little barking giggle.

"That's good, because this test will involve a great deal of remembering. What you must do is think of your most vivid memory, down to the most excruciating detail. If you succeed in a perfect recreation, then you will continue on toward ascension. However, should you fail, your soul will pass, and there will be nothing left for you." Wheels began to whimper and cover its cute little eyes with its paws. Ginger looked off toward the horizon.

"Did my dad go through this too?" They spoke, their voice breaking slightly. Wheels paused for a short moment and then said,

"All things must end up here. Eventually."

Ginger started with a solemn smile, then shifted toward determination.

"I have one in mind," They were as confident as they'd ever been.

"Good luck," said Wheels.

Ginger began to close their eyes and picture the past. The colors of life began to swirl around them. The heat bared down on their shoulders on the brightest day of the summer season. Not a single cloud dared challenge the sun, yet the wind howled against it. It was the final day of the international kite competition. Ginger was in the finals, versus their rival and best friend. George "Spider" Takahashi. He was wearing his signature dark chocolate brown leather jacket that read "�����" across the back in a blood orange color. They specifically recalled these colors because he was insistent on not being a black widow. He was always saying,

"I'm a brown widow! I look scary, but I'm pretty harmless once you get to know me."

Ginger also definitely recalled the kite runners, especially for what would come next. There were three boys, triplets, all wearing the same matching uniform. The boy's theme was super heroes. They each wore a gorgeous silk red cape that floated behind them as they ran, along with a black headband over their eyes that their mother had cut eye holes into in order to create a mask. They had tennis ball-colored swim shorts that matched with their big, bright rain boots. Which now looked more brown, coated in sand. Ginger also remembered how silly they looked since they were also shirtless. And who wouldn't be? It was truly a perfect day for a swim. The boys weren't planning to swim yet, though; they were ready to grab whoever's kite fell first. According to the rules, any runners are free to grab the loser's kite and keep it, and neither Spider nor Ginger wanted to lose theirs. Ginger remembered working for weeks on their kite. They and their father were determined to make it not only as gorgeous as possible, but as deadly as possible. Ginger's theme was spice, specifically peppers. They figured the reference was inevitable, so they might as well embrace it in the best way possible. Ginger absolutely loved spicy food. Being Mexican and Punjabi only fueled the delicious fire. They gazed at their wonderful creation. The kite was habanero orange, meshed with serrano green. There were also bits of red and white near the bottom of the kite that ran throughout the strings. In order to match the flags of their heritage. They were ready, as ever, to fly.

"Fighters! Positions!"

Spider prepared his creation as well; he had named this one Joro. It was a lovely lemon and lime color combination with thick yellow strings. He had spent every day after school working on it with his grandfather. The two would often be up until midnight, not noticing until they would look out the window of their home and realize it wasn't morning anymore. Spider had won the last two tournaments, and he was looking for a threepeat! Ginger recalled David vs. Goliath; their underdog story would begin here, no matter what. The duelists took their stances, and prepared for a fight. While the runners took their stances, and prepared for a free kite. They released their creations into the air, enjoying the calm before the storm. The small crowd of Spider and Ginger's family members waited in anticipation. A single drop of sweat proudly showed itself off on Ginger's forehead; it gleamed with light, eager to join the sand.

"BEGIN!" Shouted the referee

Ginger and Spider began to engage in a dance of graceful aggression. Ginger preferred to stay on the offensive; it was one of their greatest strengths throughout the tournament. It had also become their greatest downfall in the past. Spider's incredible fearlessness was never easy to overcome. He trusted his workmanship. He was ever vigilant in every battle, waiting for the perfect opportunity to strike. Just like his namesake, he waited until you were stuck, trying desperately to search for an escape that would never come, until it was finally time for the killing blow. Ginger felt like a bird of prey, lunging at every opportunity, then gliding away to safety before another attempt. But birds are also victims of arachnids. Spider stabbed toward the exposed throat of Ginger. To a lesser flier, this would have surely been the killing blow, but to Ginger, it was the perfect bait and switch. They let up on their string, loosening and maneuvering so that their own kite formed a chokehold around Spider's. Joro tried desperately to hold on, but Ginger's heat was a slow burn. There was only so much he could handle before needing water. As Spider's kite snapped away, the triplets literally dove headfirst into the ocean and held their brand new legacy champion reward.

"Everyone! Give it up for your brand, new champion!" announced the referee. Ginger's father was the loudest during the cheers; he picked them up in one swift motion, hoisting them for everyone to see. The cheers slowly began to fade away as the memory of Ginger's victory returned to their mind. The fluffy room of delicious treats returned in pink.

"What a beautiful scene." Said Wheels endearingly.

Ginger stood proudly in their joy of victory, ready for the congratulations from Wheels that would never come.

"That wasn't it, was it?" They said softly. Wheels remained silent. Two opportunities remained. Ginger deeply pondered their next plan of action. They were also deeply confused, though they figured it must have been a mistake in the cheering of the crowd. Maybe the specificity of the grains of sand also had to be remembered. They kicked themselves, furious for picking a beach memory, but then relaxed immediately, as was the nature of the room. It shifted to green once more. Ginger wracked their brain hoping for a truly pixel-perfect memory.

They first thought of childhood, but any memories involving their mother would not be ones they would like to remember. They thought of the distractions of youth; they began to remember video games, the ones they played with their then-best friend Karlos. Though Karlos was less like Spider in the friend sense, it was just easier to explain that way. They were more like the older brother they never had or a cousin they were really close to. Their dads were really close friends growing up and had stayed that way ever since they were kids. Karlos was 3 years older and always made time for Ginger. Whenever there was a household argument or a report card they needed to hide, Karlos was always there for them. Ginger began to grin and close their eyes, ready for a hilarious memory. It was a chilly afternoon after class had ended. Ginger was in 7th grade, and had just begun sprinting home. Karlos had texted them, saying he had just bought the new Nintendo Wii and was itching to play it. When they finally arrived at their friend's door, they yanked it open without knocking and gazed upon the holy grail of video game consoles. Karlos and his dad had just finished plugging everything in. Karlos's dad looked at the crazed child that had just invaded their home and began to laugh his hearty self to tears.

"You're a silly one, Ging," he said, handing them each a single Wii Remote and holding one in his hands himself. They then booted up the console, which gave off a wonderful hum from the disc already inside. As Karlos began to set up the language, nickname of the console, and such, Karlos's dad brought Ginger into the kitchen to fetch them some snacks. They brought out a plethora of chips, mixed nuts, and Chex mix, along with a veggie stick tray, which would likely remain untouched. As Karlos started the game, a beautiful musical tune rang through the house the clockand Karlos's surround sound system. The whimsical piano tune of Wii Sports. The three gamers were hooked in immediately and guided their hands toward the array of sports in front of them. Karlos's dad immediately voted to start with boxing, but the two children had other plans. Baseball. After weeks of broken windows, clumsy strikeouts, and several injuries, they had both been banned from playing it out on the street. It was finally their time to return. They selected America's favorite pastime and got to work. Karlos was first up to bat, with Ginger pitching. They let out a killer fast ball.

"STRIKE!" yelled the announcer. A swing and a miss! Ginger readied themselves again. They threw a shockingly smooth curveball.

"STRIKE!" yelled the game again. Karlos had fear in his eyes; he would never be struck out, and the game would have to be rigged if that were to happen. He held himself with his knees in a slight bend, his right elbow pointing toward the sky, both hands perfectly on the bat. Or so he thought.

As Ginger flew one final fast ball, Karlos's Wii Remote slipped out of his hands completely and struck at light speed against the TV screen. A massive spider web crack completely engulfed the screen as the announcer yelled through the still-powered speakers.

"STRIKE! Batter out!" Karlos's dad tried his hardest to maintain anger and suppress his laughter, but the man could never refuse a hilarious moment. He began to chortle and snort, and the three began to all laugh simultaneously in ecstasy. At that exact moment, Karlos's mom walked in with her mouth completely agape. The laughter suddenly came to a quick halt, and the memory suddenly disappeared shockingly quickly. Ginger did not wish to remember any longer. Wheels began to speak

"Why did this one stop? I've seen it before. Mother laughs too." Wheels whirred closer toward Ginger.

"It's not the memory." A tear rolled down Ginger's cheek before the room cleared it away. They paused for a short moment, then said,

"He was shot and killed three weeks later. Just the wrong place, wrong time, I guess." They looked off into the purple, which now looked more empty than ever.

"Oh… Yes, I remember now." Wheels began to whimper, cuddling up to Ginger, who was now sitting cross-legged.

"I guess that one wasn't enough either, huh?" The silence was palpable. Ginger had one last remaining opportunity. They looked into themselves further, searching for a level of introspection they had not felt in years. Birthday parties, first relationships, even negative emotions. Through them all, one memory still rang true in their minds. The clarion ding of the Taco Bell logo. They laughed and laughed until the laughter brought them into the memory of their high school friends.

"Yo! I'm definitely going with In n Out, funny, and I could play it off as religious to my pops; I might even get a discount!"

"I'm pretty sure literally any restaurant would give us a discount for a tattoo on our body; it's probably, like, illegal not to or something.".

"Ok, I'm definitely getting it then; what about you, Ginger?" Ginger looked at their two friends, unsure of how serious they were being.

"We're dead serious, Ginger; this is going to change our lives!" Ginger remembered a complete and utter lack of sarcasm in their eyes and tone.

"Well, I feel like the best one is Taco Bell." They said sheepishly. The two friends looked on with wonder.

"Yes! That's perfect! Imagine with, like, an Enchirito on the side!"

"No wait! What about LIVE MAS right under it? Then it has some meaning too! Ginger, you HAVE to get it!" Ginger looked on with amusement and then began to laugh at the two goofy 17-year-olds in front of them. Ginger was the only one who could legally get a tattoo, being 18. They agreed, and the hangout continued. The next day, Ginger went to a nearby parlor and asked for an artistic rendition of the Taco Bell logo complete with the signature "Live Más." The artist did it, no questions asked, for only 50 bucks. It looked flawless. Ginger recalled the looks on their friend's faces after the reveal. Complete and utter disbelief. They were indeed being sarcastic, but they were also true friends. They agreed to an oath; as soon as they turned 18, they would both also get the exact same tattoo on the exact same forearm, always vowing to "Live Más." They all hugged as the memory slowly faded into the Everness. Wheels paused for a long, long moment. Ginger looked into nothingness and prepared for the great abyss.

"Ginger," said Wheels.

"Yeah. I know." Their eyes began to close.

"I must confess, I have been hiding something from you." Wheels hovered away from Ginger toward the center of the room once more.

"Each of the memories you have shared with me have been perfect." Ginger looked up, puzzled.

"However, by giving me these memories, you do not move on to the next phase of life. You cannot move on to a next phase that does not exist." The room rotated to pink again.

"I am known as a Watcher. I am all seeing. Therefore, I witnessed the final moments of your life; I saw the pain in your heart, the suffering you were going through, and the ways you wished for it to end."

Ginger began to cry, but this time the room did not stop them.

"If you know how I got here, then why did you make me go through all that?" they yelled angrily. Wheels spoke with nothing but what could be interpreted as love.

"I simply wished for you to remember that your life is still worth living. Each of those memories encapsulates the ones you love. Although some are no longer with us, you are proof that their memories still remain."

"Yeah, I've heard it all before," said Ginger.

"I know. But I need you to remember that people are never truly gone. Normally, this process is reserved for those on their last legs. They come here when there is no life left in them. We offer solace in the end times. The Everness provides peace and unlimited access to your memories until you are ready to go. When your father arrived here, he left me with a message. I brought you here because I believe you needed to hear it. Although you will return here eventually, I do not believe it is your time just yet."

Wheels began to take the shape of Ginger's father and then spoke in his voice.

"I will always love you, Ginger."

The two began to hug each other as the entire room dissipated, leaving Ginger laying alone in their bedroom.

They looked at their father's urn on the right side of their bedside table and picked it up. They began to embrace it before saying

"I fucking love you, Dad."

They placed a dollar in the brand new swear jar, laughing with tears in their eyes.

BECKY BECOMES AN OWL

EVERETT COOKSTON

"Where are you?" the phone rattled.

"I'll be there soon," Becky lifted it up closer to her face "relax, it's an art table."

"Whatever you say. I'm waiting here."

"Okay…you feel alright about this?"

"Absolutely. We're going to have a good time."

"You always do say that," she said.

The phone closed with a terminating slap. She quickened her pace into a jog. *Was this really the right call? Seemed fitting that the club would ask her to step in at the last minute. And to work with him of all people.* The thoughts buzzed around Becky's head, unwilling to relent. Regardless of this mental fog, she made her way to the center of campus.

———

In the courtyard, the easy-ups bloomed towards the sky like an isolated patch of flowers, desperate to make their situation work. The table was nothing less than Becky had imagined, still she couldn't help but sigh. What could pass off as an excuse for a scene was topped off by her club member, Rick, leaning his body against the table. His posture suggested that he had been leaning there for a while, but Becky knew that he was exaggerating. *Makes sense.*

"Morning," Rick said, "how are you?"

"Ready for the day to end," she said as she walked up to the table.

"Oh come on, don't be a grump," he said as stood up and motioned towards the cheap table, "we get to work together."

In front of her sat a work surface with a couple of pens, some pamphlets, and a clipboard: it only had a few papers on it. A sign with far too many colors and emotions laid before it. As pretty as it was, Becky longed to know why she couldn't be satisfied with it. Maybe because he made it, or because she didn't.

"Not the most ideal workstation." she said before she pursed her lips.

Rick drooped his shoulders. "No, I guess not," he pulled out the chair and motioned for her to sit. "But we'll make it work."

"If you insist that it's that simple." She said as she walked over to the chair with her arms tightly folded.

"There's a cooler with water in it, and I got this easy-up out of my Dad's garage while I was home this weekend. It's worn, but it works. At least it will keep us from becoming tomato-heads."

"Thank you, for making this tolerable." She said with a small smirk.

Rick pulled off an imaginary top hat, not forgetting to put it back on before addressing her. "I'm doing what I can."

———

"Does your club talk about Cryptids?" the kid said.

"I don't know if that's a common topic…it's an art club." She pointed down at the loud sign.

"Oh that reminds me, I once saw a sketch of a Cryptid that is rumored to be in the area. It's called the Riverside monster. It was…"

What is he going on about? Does he really think I care about some weird creature? I don't believe in fairytales, myths and especially not miracles.

She rubbed her temples to slow the chaos in her head.

"What are you doing?" the kid asked.

She perked up. "Oh I…"

"Oh, we're both tired, " Rick's voice pierced the stiff chat, "we probably need more water," he laughed.

The kid's smile shifted to a blank stare and then he walked away, searching for other people to lecture with his nonsense knowledge.

The talk of cryptids is an unorthodox conversation, but it was Rick's reaction that had Becky's head spinning. *That was...Strange.*

"Thank you," she said with a smile.

Rick leaned back in his chair. "No problem."

Becky's smile shrunk back to a hyphen before she laid her head down on the table.

"Damn. That kid was annoying."

"What, are you telling me that you don't like Bigfoot?" Rick said as he threw his arms in the air.

"No. He walks and walks, but he never stops to consider the photographer who is trying to get to know him. He's the worst."

"~Oh I see. Well, did you know the bigfoot in that famous footage is thought to be a girl. She sparked the whole thing. So maybe you should be mad at her."

Becky lifted her head. "At least in that film, the female turned and looked back at the camera."

————

A small vapor was forming on the inside of Becky's water bottle. Many areas were condensed into thicker beads of the liquid. Their movement seemed to be the only thing that Becky could captivate herself with. Sliding furthered down the slippery walls of the bottle, doomed to drip back into the void of water beneath.

"What's that!"

Becky flicked her head up in shock.

A young girl had emerged from the crowded walkway, no doubt a younger class student. She focused on Rick with a strong stare. Her smile doing everything it could to show all her teeth, as she twirled her hair around her finger.

"Oh hi," he said.

Why is she talking to him? Becky thought as she fidgeted her thumbs.

"Hello, my name is Stephanie Hassel." She pushed her hand against her chest and showed the twinkle in her eyes.

"Well nice to meet you. Welcome to the art table," he said

"Does this club allow art pieces to be used for other clubs?"

Becky forced her voice in. "We don't allow that!"

"Really?" Stephanie flicked her hand forward, "because I'm a part of several clubs, and I need to find a place that provides art supplies. I'm working as a public relations officer for all of them and I need to make the posters." She smiled and tossed her ponytail behind her head.

Really, you're playing that game. That's the only reason you want to join the club?

Becky scooted in her chair, "Sorry, but we don't allow that."

She pulled the clipboard and pen off of the table.

Stephanie widened her eyes before replacing them with a grimace.

Rick scrunched his face at Becky, before grabbing the clipboard back.

"Nothing like a joke, right," he said as he put the clipboard back on the table, "why don't you put your contact info here."

Stephanie smirked and plucked the pen out of Becky's hand.

"Love to!"

Rick gave a toothless smile. "Thanks, we're looking forward to having you."

"I intend to show up. Bi-bye," she said before turning and walking off.

Bitch!

"What was that about?" he said.

"I don't know. I just didn't understand her."

———

Becky pulled out another bottle of water cooler. She straightened herself in her seat, and cranked the cap up and it made a pop. *Not many have been interested today. I guess that shows how Rick and I do as a team.* The crowds had died down, leaving just a few people walking.

"Whoa, things slowed down a bit," Rick said.

"I guess so."

"Hey, I know," Rick leaned forward in his seat, grabbed a few blank pages and pens, "how about we draw some patterns."

"Uhm…ok." Sarah picked the supplies from Rick's hand.

"Let's make this interesting," He pulled out his and started tickling the screen, "Let's see what we can come up with in 30 seconds!"

"Alright…"

"…And done!" Rick said, "Let's see what we made."

The pattern on Becky's paper was simple in its design. Its complexity was not exceeding that of what could be found in a geometry book. On the other hand, Rick produced a pattern that would make anyone pause and observe. While unfinished, its curves looked like that of a blooming tapestry.

"Well, I guess that you win," Becky said, tossing her pen back down on the table.

"I'm not trying to win, I really just like drawing this pattern."

"Well it doesn't make sense to me!"

Becky turned to meet Rick's reaction, but paused. Instead of any resistance, his face only offered a blank expression. It almost looked like failure.

"I guess that makes sense," he said before standing up, "I'm going to go get a drink.

With that, Rick walked around the table, passing the cooler with a single bottle left in it. His form was slowly getting smaller, fading.

Becky looked down at the table and started rubbing her temples harder, trying to extinguish the headache that bloomed in her mind. *Shit.*

She closed her eyes to rest them, hearing her heartbeat getting louder with no end in sight. At that moment, the sunlight bloomed into a bright aura. One that could not be ignored. She opened her eyes to see a figure in the unrelenting sunlight. Shielding her eyes with her hand, what greeted her was a matured lady. Her stance was strong and intimidating. Despite that, her eyes gave the impression that Becky was no longer invisible.

"Hello."

"Hi…"

"My son was looking for clubs to join, and I figured I'd help him."

"Oh, that's great! Is there something in specific that you want for him?"

"No, I'm not looking for anything particular." She placed her arms in front of her. "Why don't you explain to me what this means to you."

"Oh well the art club-"

"I'm sorry, I don't mean the club." She held her hands out. "You seem to be conflicted. Is everything alright?"

Becky paused before looking back at the table. "Oh nothing...It's just been a long day."

"That's it?" she said with a puzzled look.

Becky contemplated the remark. Something about the lady screams to her. *It's ok!*

"I," She choked on a lump in her throat, "I messed up!"

The lady didn't say anything, her silence leveled the whole area.

"Interesting..." She said, placing her fist under her chin. "Well, have you ever thought of being an owl?"

"What?"

"An owl."

"I'm sorry, I don't follow?"

"You see, owls are great. They get to sit on their perches all day!"

"..."

"That's why owls are great. Their perception is unmatched, because they get to see everyone else's. They have the gift of looking at something from a different perspective."

"..."

"So what does this mean to you?"

"I guess I should try-"

"Interesting, I'll have to tell my son." The lady smiled and started walking away. "Have a good day sweetie!"

"..."

———

Becky twisted her Art club pin between her two fingers, her sight getting lost in Rick's movement. He was picking up any piece of trash that he saw. Becky couldn't tell if he had missed any pieces, but she knew that he was trying his best. With no trash can in sight, he opted to throw the trash into the empty cooler.

"I guess we made it." Rick said as he approached the table.

She smiled. "Yeah, I guess we did."

"Well then, no reason to stay longer. Help me close this thing."

He reached under the table, only leaving his free hand on the table for stability. Becky walked up to the table, and paused. She extended her hand and caressed his arm.

"Actually, I don't mind staying for a little bit longer."

Rick looked up from under the table and met her eyes. The two of them were locked in a gentle gaze. One of familiarity.

"Are you sure," he said.

"Yes. Why don't you show me how you drew that pattern."

LOVE AT FIRST SLIGHT

NINA SIMPSON

Miriam fiddled with her new wedding ring and looked for her girl-friend- fiancee. She was her fiancee now! Because they were going to get married!

It shouldn't have been this hard to find her. After all, the two of them didn't have a big apartment, but they did invite a lot of people to their engagement party. Maybe too many people.

Every room was filled to the brim. All taking and dancing and prob-ably gossiping about Miriam and Valory, her fiancee, *fiancee*. People kept trying to take a moment to congratulate Miriam, and it was lovely to be the center of attention, but she had to find her fiancee.

Miriam took a moment to think. If she was Valory, where would she be? Not around too many people, probably taking a quiet moment for herself. She snapped her fingers and walked across the apartment and found her fiancee, on their balcony, taking a breather.

"Hello my lovely fiancee." Miriam said and wrapped her arms around Valory and kissed her bare shoulder. Because only Valory would be crazy enough to wear a sleeveless dress in the almost winter.

Valory half turned and smiled. "Hello there. Sorry for ditching the party."

"It's fine. We probably invited too many people. I can go and kick them all out if you wanna." Miriam said.

"No, no it's fine. I just wanted a break. I'll go back in, in five." Valory said and kissed Miriam on her forehead.

"All right. Do you want me to stay, or do you wanna be alone?" Miriam asked.

"I've told you, I like being with you more than being alone." Valory said with a sweet smile.

Miriam's cheeks went pink, and not from the cold. "T-thanks."

"Aww, are you blushing?"

"No! You're just . . . it's whatever. You're silly." Miriam nestled into Valory more.

Valory laughed. "You sound like when we met."

Miriam groaned. "No, no, don't start with that. I've had enough teasing from everyone about when we were kids."

"But it's so funny."

"It's not!"

"How is it not?"

"Because I was terrible to you as a kid! We were terrible to each other. We were bitter rivals."

Valory fully turned to her and raised an eyebrow. "What? Bitter rivals? We were in kindergarten."

"Exactly! We were so mean to each other, or maybe it was just me, but it was really bad." Miriam groaned and buried her face in her hands.

There was a long pause before Valory started giggling. "I-I'm sorry, but, did you not like me when we were kids? Because I thought we were friends."

Miriam gave her fiancee a look. "No?? What the- I hated you with all the fury a five year old could. I stole your jacket during winter."

"I didn't care about that. It wasn't even cold. And I thought you needed it more."

"Wha- well I went out of my way to be your partner in the plant project so I could try and sabotage you."

"I thought you wanted to be my friend. You were very enthusiastic about spending time with me."

"Ugh, well, I-I-"

"Miri, why are you trying so hard to find a reason for me to be mad at you?" Valory asked.

Miriam looked away. "I-I just want you to know that I'm sorry for all that." she mumbled.

Valory wrapped her arm around Miri and kissed her cheek. "You don't have to apologize for something that happened when we were five. Okay?"

"Okay." Miri mumbled.

They both stood together on the balcony. Inside, there was a party, and outside there was a busy city. But on the balcony, it was just the two of them.

"Although. I am a bit curious about why you hated me."

Miriam went even more red at that. "Ugh. That's probably the stupidest thing ever."

"If you don't want to tell me, it's alright."

"No, no, it's fine." Miriam cleared her throat and looked at her fiancee. "Remember Kevin Dolt?" Valory nodded.

"Well, on valentines day, he gave you a big candy heart, or something, and I got really jealous. I remember thinking that I was jealous of you, because I thought I liked him. But really . . .."

Valory chuckled. "But really you were five and you didn't know what a lesbian was."

"Well obviously. So I just thought that I was competing against you *for* Kevin Dolt, not that I was competing *against* him."

Valory laughed and laughed and looked like an angel in the moonlight.

"Miri, you were never competing against him."

Miriam rolled her eyes. "Obviously. One, we're lesbians, two we're engaged, three he moved in like third grade and we don't know where he is."

"Of course. But, I was talking about how I'll always choose you."

Miriam looked at Valory with stars in her eyes, and kissed her deeply and genuinely.

"And I'll always choose you."

They kissed again. Then both just held each other.

After a few minutes Valory sighed. "We should probably start heading back in."

"Or we can kick everyone out and watch TV until 3 am together."

Valory laughed again. "That sounds perfect."